AMARILLO MARIPOSA

Yellow Butterfly

TALES OF JESS E. HANES CONTINUE

By

D. RUDD WISE

II CHRONICLES 7:14

If my people, which are called by my name, shall humble themselves, and pray, and seek my face, and turn from their wicked ways: then will I hear from heaven, and will forgive their sin, and will heal their land.

(KJV)

Bookman L.L.C.
Publishing & Marketing

Martinsville, Indiana
www.BookmanMarketing.com

AMARILLO MARIPOSA

Copyright © 2003 by D. Rudd Wise

Library of Congress Number:

ISBN#: 1-59453-137-4

This book was printed in the United States of America.

Note: Quoted scripture is taken from the Authorized King James Version (KJV)

To order additional copies of AMARILLO MARIPOSA, contact:

drrmwise@npcc.net
www.novelsbydrwise.com
www.bookmanpublishing.com

Another novel by D. Rudd Wise

Operation: Eyewitness

ISBN: 1-4010-209902, trade paperback

ISBN: 1-4010-2098-4, hardback

ACKNOWLEDGEMENTS

- I appreciate everyone who had a part in editing and guiding me with the research on this second in a series of Jess E. Hanes adventure stories.

- Thanks to Zenda Douglas of the Durham Convention and Visitor's Bureau, and Dale Coats, Site Manager of the Duke Homestead State Historic Site and Tobacco Museum, for feedback about Bull Durham Tobacco.

- Another special thanks to Gayland Corbin, Melleta R. Bell, Becky Hart and others at the Archives of the Big Bend, Bryan Wildenthal Memorial Library of Sul Ross University, Alpine, Texas.

- Correspondence with Joseph Green at the Barton Warnock Environmental Education Center, Terlingua, Texas, produced valuable information about the Lajitas area, mining and the permission to use the name of his cinnabar/quicksilver/mercury Mariposa Mine.

- Jan Bolton of Mobile, Alabama, sent various research papers on the early settling of the Terlingua area and the mining of the Big Bend's mineral deposits. Another entire novel could be written based on Jan's historical information of Southwest Texas.

- Information from my Grandfather C.J. Wise, Senior's book, *Here It Is*, was especially important with history of the cinnabar mining in the Terlinga area.

- I appreciate Chuck Hornley's days and evenings of professional editing.

- Thanks to my nephew and his wife, Mike and Heather Pierce, for his technical expertise on aircraft as an Indianapolis charter pilot, CFI and her suggestions from knowledge and experience teaching in the Ben Davis school district.

- Thanks to Victor Mojica for assistance with my Spanish.

- Thanks to my cousin, Catherine Ann (Wise) Dean, for information on the Texas Rangers and Border Patrol.

- Foremost, special appreciation to my wife, Rachel Marie, for the many hours of patient suggestions, readings and editing of the manuscript– thank you Love.

The aeronautical map on the outside cover of this novel is reprinted with the permission of the National Imagery and Mapping Agency. Publication of this novel has not been endorsed or otherwise approved by the National Imagery Mapping Agency, or the United States Department of Defense (10 U.S.C. 445)

CONTENTS

THE END

PREVIEW – SEPTEMBER 11, 2001

Following Jess E. Hanes' return from Morocco three years prior, he and his wife, Marie Ann, had been placed under the U.S. Government's witness protection program. Threats from the terrorists he had opposed in Morocco had now decreased to a point that tight security for their safety was about to end. They had settled into their new ranch home and were enjoying the quietness of the Texas Hill Country, south of Austin.

On this particular clear, bright and sunshiny, September morning, Jess and Marie Ann had packed to fly to a reunion in Virginia. Breakfast, devotions and prayer were finished. Jess, walked toward the front living room, carrying a note pad. He scratched off another line on their list of things to do or take.

"Hey, Love!" Jess called out to Marie Ann from the front hallway of their ranch home, "I'll be watching the morning news up front."

She was in the spacious high ceiling kitchen with their cook, Lolita Jordan, packing a cooler for their trip from central Texas to Virginia Beach, Virginia. They were scheduled to leave in an hour in their new, twin-engine, Beech King Air 200. Marie Ann walked over to the telephone. Using the kitchen intercom, she said, "Don't forget to put your new sandals in the backpack."

Jess turned toward the intercom on a small table at the end of the couch where he sat, "I'm wearing them!"

"Okay!"

He had the television tuned to the local station to watch the weather to the east of them. Then, he selected the satellite channel for national weather. He slid over to the telephone and dialed the number for 'NOTICES TO AIRMAN' (NOTAM).

"Hmm, that looks good! Nothing special along our flight path," he spoke quietly to himself. Scrutinizing his aeronautical charts, he made a few notes and put them in his flight bag. Looking back at the large screen TV, he selected the local station again for the last part of the local 8:30 morning news. The news program was showing a tall skyscraper on fire.

"Looks like another made-for-TV disaster movie," he said, glancing away as the telephone rang.

"Good morning," he said.

"Do you have your TV on?" asked the familiar voice.

"Sure do. Why?"

"Do you see that one of the Twin Towers in New York is burning?"

"Yes! Looks like another burning building movie, so?"

"No, Jess! It's real! A passenger plane crashed into it about five minutes ago . . . about 8:45!" the excited female voice stated.

Realizing that this was no movie, Jess took a careful look at the screen. "The way it's burning, the plane must have been full of fuel!" Jess replied.

He stood up and yelled back toward the kitchen, "Marie Ann! Turn on the TV back there!"

She yelled back over the intercom, asking, "What station?"

"Any station!" Jess answered.

"We have it on satellite news! We heard that an aircraft hit a tower in New York!"

"You watch that channel, and I'll stay on this one." He quickly moved over to the entertainment cabinet and turned on the tape recorder, shoving in a new tape. Stepping back, he selected 'record'. "Do you have an empty tape back there?"

"Yes! It's recording!"

"Jess!" the voice on the telephone yelled.

"Yes, Madilene?"

Madilene Ash was a U.S. Marshal in charge of the safety and security of Jess and Marie Ann, and the ranch.

"Hold off going to Virginia Beach until I check with our offices in Washington." She hesitated, "I don't have a good feeling about this. I'll also call your nephews at the Texas Rangers headquarters."

"Why? Don't you think it was an accident?"

"No! I have the feeling this is another terrorist attack on the Trade Center!"

"We will stand down and make other arrangements to attend that ship's reunion . . . if necessary!" Jess' voice was uneasy.

As he laid the remote control on the coffee table, he could not believe what he was watching. Another airliner was banking straight for the south tower of the World Trade Center. It was only ten or fifteen minutes since the first aircraft had crashed into the north tower.

"What! No!" Jess threw up his hands in disbelief. "This can't be happening! What in the world is going on?" He ran to the kitchen where Marie Ann and Lolita were staring at the TV.

Marie Ann covered her mouth with her hand. She faced Lolita and the two women hugged, comforting each other. They both turned to Jess with bewildering expressions. Marie Ann grabbed Jess around the neck; her tears soaked into the shoulder of his tan sweater.

Lolita's husband, Juan Jordan, came through the kitchen's outside door from the horse stables. She ran to him and hurriedly told him in Spanish what had happened. The four grouped together in the center of the kitchen. They sat on stools at the island serving bar, still staring at the TV in unbelief.

The FAA closed the New York airports, and the city closed all bridges and tunnels to Manhattan. In Florida, President Bush called the crashes ". . . an apparent terrorist attack on our country."

Lolita stood and walked to the refrigerator. She quietly moved around the kitchen preparing homemade iced tea and set a large glass of it in front of the others. They kept their eyes on the TV while sipping the cold tea. Every so often, as replays showed the aircraft crashes and the towers collapsing, moans from everyone could be heard, and tears continued to flow.

Suddenly, the network switched to Washington D.C., showing where another airliner had crashed the Pentagon. Jess jumped as if, he had been shot. Marie Ann grabbed his hand and held it tightly. His face turned red, and his eyes were wide with deep wrinkles in his forehead; his anger grew.

"Who do those people think they are? We've got to stop them, but what can I do?" Jess said, throwing up his loose hand in frustration, still watching the TV. "We better alert security here at the ranch."

He nodded, "Juan! Go tell them to continue their routine, but double the guards. If this is terrorists attacking, we could be in trouble here!" Pausing, he took a deep breath, "Yes! Do it, while I make a phone call." Marie Ann did not want to turn loose of Jess' hand.

"What are you up to, Jess?" she questioned with sternness in her voice.

"That was Madilene on the phone, awhile ago," Jess replied with tightness in his throat. "She is supposed to call back about this situation. I'm going to get the hand-held transceiver from my pilot's handbag to listen to Austin's Airport Advisory. Be right back."

Before leaving the kitchen, Jess turned toward the women, "Ladies, pray for those people in New York and Washington! Especially the people trapped alive in those buildings and aircraft!"

"Jess, come back! Oh, Lord Jesus!" Marie Ann yelled, pointing to the TV.

The television was showing that the south tower of the World Trade Center was collapsing. Jess looked just in time to see the tower disappear in a huge cloud of dust and debris. The north tower was burning at the top floors with black bellows of smoke moving across Manhattan and Brooklyn. The television network audio broke in with information that another highjacked airliner had crashed, this time in Pennsylvania. As they watched in horror, the north tower collapsed.

Both of the women began praying as Jess slowly moved down the hall to the front room. He could not believe what he had witnessed. He retrieved the transceiver and walked back to the kitchen. Terror had struck the United States and the hearts of its people. Jess knew in his own heart that someway he must assist, but how?

He remembered what the Holy Bible said, "God's love casts out fear!" and claimed the victory for them at the ranch and for the people involved in the crashes. "Lord, continue to help President Bush and his advisors!"

For the remainder of the day, everyone at the ranch was on high alert, listening to the radios and TVs, waiting for telephone calls from law enforcement officials, and their families, especially from their two Texas Ranger nephews.

The kitchen intercom announced, "Visitor at front gate. Madilene Ash, U.S. Deputy Marshal."

Jess moved quickly to respond, "Let her inside! You guys stay undercover out there. I don't want anyone shot!"

He was now remembering the confrontation he had with terrorists in Morocco a few years back and how it had affected his whole life's activities, endangering his family. The Moslem terrorist groups were at it again, and he prayed it would not spread.

Madilene came to the kitchen's back door, knocked and entered. Two other marshals followed her. They too, looked toward the TV and watched a replay of the morning's attacks.

Then she turned to Jess, "I'm sorry to have to do this to you, but I have to release all our marshals from their assignment here and send them to Austin." She smiled at Marie Ann; "I have made arrangements with a security firm in San Antonio to send a couple of people to be permanent. They are trained in terrorist resistance, plus they are cowboys. So, I'm not leaving you stranded! Sorry!"

"When will they arrive?" Jess asked.

"Within the hour. They left thirty minutes ago." She handed Jess a folder on the security firm and names, "Their photos, background, and here's a photo of their aircraft. I'm sure you'll like it! It's a new, beefed-up Pilatus PC-12 . . . 2002 issue! Although it's a single engine turboprop, your King Air will not keep up with it!"

She was trying to ease some tensions, but was not successfully doing it. She hugged Marie Ann, neither of them wanted to let go, and their tears rolled. Finally, she stepped at arms length, "Marie Ann, I will miss my weekly trips out here visiting with you. I don't know where my next assignment will be. God bless you!"

"He has, and He will!" replied Marie Ann.

Madilene walked over and gave Jess a big hug and kiss, "Take care of yourself and Marie Ann, Jess E. Hanes! I don't want to come back here and find any messes to clean up!"

"I won't make any promises! Might make some noise anyway, just to get you hanging around again," Jess said, not looking her straight in the eye, and then turned away.

She grabbed him by the arm, "Look me in the eyes, Jess!"

He turned toward her as she pointed a long finger at him, "Promise to behave? I'll be checking with your boss!"

He threw up both hands, "Yes! Yes! But that takes all the fun out of it!"

She hit him with a glancing blow on the arm. "You'd better!" She turned and motioned the other marshals to go. "Let's get out of here, before I start crying again!"

They all followed them out to the government aircraft that was stationed at the ranch. The security aircraft had just taxied and shut down when the marshals waved from the windows a 'goodbye.' It did not take long for their King Air to disappear toward Austin.

Marie Ann and Lolita walked back to the house, hand in hand. Jess and Juan chocked the Pilatus tires and waited for the security crew to get outside. Jess had not opened the folder Madilene had given him. Otherwise, he would not have been surprised to know another woman was involved. When the door opened and a long-legged blonde walked down the steps to the tarmac in her tight blue jeans and western shirt, Jess knew right away that Marie Ann would not take to this tall, shapely cowgirl. She looked like no 'cowboy' Jess had ever seen!

Juan looked at Jess and grunted, "*Señor*, this may be trouble! *Si*?"

"*Si!*" Jess replied. He walked over and extended his hand, "Jess Hanes. Welcome to the Circle MJ Ranch."

Ignoring his extended hand, she smiled, acknowledging his welcome, turned back toward the aircraft and motioned for the others to get out of the aircraft. "This is the place. Remove all the equipment not needed for the aircraft!" Turning to Jess, "Mr. Hanes, where's the bunkhouse?"

"Hold on!" Jess said, holding up one long finger, "Just one minute! Come in here with me," he demanded, while opening the folder. "Let me look through this folder that was just given to me." He walked into the hangar for shade. She followed him.

Juan stayed next to the aircraft watching the parade into the hangar. He shook his head, "*Señor* Jess, big problems!"

"Nice hangar! Is that the bunkhouse in there?"

"Nope! That's for the pilots," Jess replied. "Bunkhouse is between here and the ranch house . . . uh, Miss Aleta Brittle?"

"Yes, Sir. In name only! I'm far from being brittle! I can fly or ride anything you have! I'm a Marine and ex-Texas Ranger. I'm fluent in six languages. I'm originally from Spain, but now I'm an American citizen with a master's degree from Harvard. Spent six years with security in the Marines and rode with the Texas Rangers for ten years, before I started my own business in San Antonio."

She sidled up to Jess, shoulder to shoulder with him, "And, I can lick most any man in a gun or a judo fight! I don't make trouble for my bosses . . . just solve them and keep problems to the minimum! I'm good at what I do, Mr. Hanes!"

He stepped back away from her, "Now, that's quite a statement you've made. Pretty bold!" Pushing his old Stetson straw hat up on his forehead and squaring his shoulders, he looked her straight in the eyes. He was a good five foot ten when he straightened. She was a smidgen taller. Jess had his back toward the others who had followed them into the hangar.

"Folder states six persons in your crew are here to run security?"

She nodded, "Yes," and waved her hand toward the aircraft. Jess turned to see five more females standing at attention, all in blue jeans, chambray shirts and military style boots.

"Hold everything!" Jess gritted his teeth. He turned toward Aleta with a red face, "I am not equipped here for six additional females in the bunkhouse. Plus, I don't like the idea! Period!" Shaking his head, "Whose idea was this anyway? Madi's?"

"Certainly was!" Aleta replied with a broad grin, "We are the best you have available at this time – men or women!"

"Who has your records? All of your people's records?"

She snapped her fingers toward one of the other five, "Brandy has them!"

The shorter of the five hurried over to Jess with the five's folders. She smiled at him and returned to her position with the others. He motioned Aleta to follow him into the hangar office just as Marie Ann came through the outside door.

"Hey, Love! We may have a big problem here. Madi threw me a curve or two!" Motioning toward Aleta, "Aleta, this is my wife, Marie Ann. If I agree to you and your group staying as security, you will answer directly to her. If she isn't around, then me."

He turned and walked away from them, "Give me a few minutes!" he said, and then went into the hanger office, closing the door.

Marie Ann knew by the tone of Jess' voice that he was definitely agitated about something. She had not yet seen the other women in the hangar, but she knew this one was enough to set him on edge. Just her stance in front of Marie Ann was plenty to set off both of them.

Aleta was a head taller than Marie Ann and stood feet apart like a judo expert, ready for any advances by an aggressor. Then, she relaxed her stance. Walking over to Marie Ann, asked, "Did I intimidate you?" And with a smile, Aleta extended her hand, "Nice to meet you, Mrs. Hanes. I will do everything possible to keep your ranch secure." She nodded toward the inner office door, "Mr Hanes seems to have misjudged my initial statement. Sometimes I forget that I'm no longer in the military. I'm told I'm rude with my status and rank. I will apologize when he returns."

"Aleta, your observation is correct!" Marie Ann smiled, and then carefully accepted the handshake. "He does not like foreword and boisterous women." She tightly held onto Aleta's hand and slowly released it, "This also, is from his military background. Have a seat!"

Marie Ann sat down on a cedar bench offering a place at the other end for Aleta. For a split second, their eyes met, and Aleta turned toward the open door to the hangar. She turned toward Marie Ann, their eyes locked. Marie Ann held her stare then said, "I, also, do not like pushy people! Especially women!"

Aleta finally broke the eye contact. Looking away, Marie Ann firmly made her point, "Now, so that we do understand each other, I, too, am well trained in the Asian art of Judo, Karate, and other special arts of self-defense. You can work here with us as a team, but by now, you know who's boss at this ranch."

"Yes, Ma'am!" Aleta said, as she turned her eyes back to Marie Ann. She had no glaring in her eyes this time. She had softened somewhat.

There could be heard the shuffling of boots on the concrete hangar floor, echoing in the empty space for aircraft. Marie Ann stood with her arms folded, as the five other women moved into the front office. They all snapped to attention when Aleta stood.

"This is Mrs. Hanes! You will always address her as such and show her respect. We will work as a team and have success as a team," she said, barking orders like a drill sergeant.

They all grunted, "Yes, Sarge!"

Jess had opened the office door behind the five and slammed it shut. None of them jumped from the bang. He turned his head and grinned, then turned back toward Marie Ann and Aleta. Shaking his head, he walked in front of the nearest woman and snapped around facing her with a hard stare looking her over for a moment. He then, sidestepped, to the next and the next, until he had inspected them all. Turning toward Marie Ann, who had a gleam in her eyes, he winked and sidestepped in front of Aleta.

With a straight face, grim and as stern as he could muster without laughing, he turned back toward the women, "Ladies, I do not want to hear or see a grouping like this again! Not on this ranch! This is not an extension of the military. I run a tight organization here and I do it without what I just witnessed." Turning away from the five, "Did you hear what I said?"

All six security women replied in unison, "Yes, Sir! Mr. Hanes!"

"Alright then! Let's cut some slack here!" He slowly walked past them toward Aleta, "We are now, all of us . . .," gesturing with his hands, "involved with terrorist in our country, whether we like it or not!"

Jess stopped, turned around to them with his hands on his western pants belt, "At ease, Ladies!" They did and had their eyes directly on him. "How many of you have seen the murders that took place in New York, Washington and Pennsylvania this morning on TV?"

No one raised a hand or spoke.

He turned to Marie Ann and motioned to the TV mounted in the wall over the counter along the outside wall. She turned it on, and then with the remote control, she started a tape of the morning disasters. All the women were in tears before the tape ended. Jess turned off the television.

"Ladies, take a seat wherever it is comfortable for you," Jess said, standing next to Marie Ann in her chair.

He began to relax and spoke as a man to his family of friends. "It is our custom here, when faced with uncertainties, and/or unknown foes, . . . " he paused, causing each one to take notice of what he was about to say, then continued, "We pray to our Heavenly Father for guidance. I am not going to preach to you, but I am asking our God in Heaven to protect and lead us. When the time comes, you will not be leaving here by aircraft, perhaps by cars or trucks."

Jess walked over to each woman and shook her hand, softly praying for each one. When he finished, "After our little meeting in my office, you are free to leave if you are not staying as our security. Transportation will be made to where you need to go. Some of you may have loved ones you need to get to or to telephone. The phones are available at no charge. Do not call collect or charge it on your accounts."

He turned to Marie Ann, "Love, you have anything to add?"

She shook her head, "Not now!"

"Ladies, please introduce yourselves to my wife and then, come into my office, one at a time. No more inspections! No more calling the troops to order!"

He received a round of applause as he opened the back office door. Then, he turned facing them, "Thank you! Please, leave the door open when you come inside." Nodding to Marie Ann, he instructed them, "You and Aleta come in here when they are ready for an interview. Everyone else can lounge in there or inside of the hangar. There is free water and free soda in a machine out in the hangar. Help yourselves."

It took Jess less than thirty minutes for the interviews. All that time, Aleta was wide-eyed at Jess' actions, as if she was at a loss for words. After the interview, Jess called for them to gather their equipment and belongings in the hangar.

"Okay ladies! We will consider you a lady until you prove otherwise!" Then motioning to the hangar, "As I said in the office, I will treat you as a lady, as long as you are under my supervision here on the Circle MJ. When we show respect for each other . . . the same will come back to us."

He walked over to Marie Ann and put his arm around her shoulders, "Don't forget who's the boss around here! Report to her first, then to me! Like I said before, Aleta will handle personal problems among you, and if she needs assistance, then Mrs. Hanes will assist. Ranch problems, the two of us will handle. The government's witness protection security was going to end here this month, after three years of use. But now, with problems in New York, I'm not so sure!"

Jess moved over to Aleta, extending his hand to her, "You and I got off on the wrong foot. Please accept my apology?"

"Yes! Accepted with pleasure, Mr. Hanes," she said, with a big smile. "We'll make you proud to have us!"

"That's great! Keep alert! Supper will be at 6:00 p.m. at the big house. Starting tomorrow, you all will have chow at the bunkhouse dining room." Jess continued, "We have one fantastic cook and his wife, who will take care of us all. You will meet them at suppertime."

Marie Ann held up her hands for attention, "As you know, Mr. Hanes and I haven't talked about how we will handle you ladies as a security unit. He has the files on your specialties. We will try to get together, with you as a group, in the morning after breakfast. See you at supper."

As they all moved from the hangar, to the bunkhouse, and then toward the big house, a slow flying, C130 aircraft flew dangerously close over the ranch house. Men pushed out two objects from the open cargo ramp. One of the objects hit in the middle of the corral and exploded into white powder. The powder blew over the yard and up the side of the big house. The second object hit the aircraft flown in by the security team. It exploded into the fuselage behind the wings and cut the aircraft into two pieces. White powder was all over the aircraft and the tarmac in front of the hangar.

It took only a few seconds for everyone to realize what was happening. Then they ran or dove for safety.

Jess yelled, "Stay under cover! They may come back! He disappeared over that mesa to the southwest."

Leaving Marie Ann near the ground door, to an underground basement complex, he ran to the hangar office and retrieved an M15 rifle and binoculars. "Anyone I.D. any markings on that aircraft?" He ran back to Marie Ann, where Aleta and her crew had formed.

"No!" Marie Ann excitedly replied.

"Ladies, get your weapons and radios!" Aleta hollered. "Find your stations around the big house as you have been assigned."

She pointed to the basement complex, "Any radios down there?"

"Yes!" Jess replied, and then turned to Marie Ann, "Emergency Plan - A. Call the military, Texas Rangers and County Sheriff. They may have a satellite or AWAC fix on that aircraft." He motioned them into the shelter, "Our three years of quietness is over! Stay down there until this settles. Take out your weapons. I'll be back!"

Aleta followed Marie Ann down into the underground complex and closed the outer door behind them. Marie Ann turned the lights on at the head of the stairs that descended deeper and opened into one large room with several rooms along the two sides. She motioned to the first room on the right for Aleta and followed her into the radio room. They had all of the communications equipment necessary for contacting law enforcement agencies. She showed Aleta the monitor console that remotely tied twelve locations by video cameras to their own separate monitors. Turning it on, she waited for the monitors to warm. They were marked for the area that they viewed.

Then, Marie Ann moved to another location in the complex and opened a hidden door in the wall. A light turned on exposing an assortment of firearms. She selected an Israeli Desert Eagle .357 automatic pistol, and placed its loaded magazine in the handle, then racked a round of ammo into the breach. After applying its safety, she placed the weapon in a holster with its ammo belt. Strapping it around her waist, she returned to the room where Aleta had been watching her.

Marie Ann closed the door behind her and approached Aleta, "Did you bring your own weapons?"

"Yes, if they were not damaged by that drop that hit our aircraft." She said, with a question in her tone.

"If they are, there should be enough for all of us down here," Marie Ann said, confidently.

Aleta smiled, "Looks like you're very comfortable with firearms! That fantastic!"

"Yes, I was raised with them on a farm in Indiana." She walked back over to the monitors. "These have audio and proximity alarm panels below each monitor," Marie Ann said.

"Mrs. Hanes, this is very impressive," Aleta said, as she examined the surveillance equipment.

"This is all automatically taped when a system alarms," Marie Ann said, while checking all the systems' monitors, "Look at this! Two of the southwest cameras locked on that C130 with good focus. Fantastic!"

"Why hasn't that aircraft been grounded anyway? Nothing is supposed to be in the air!" Aleta questioned as she sat next to Marie Ann at the monitors' console.

Their traveling plans for the remainder of 2001 were placed on hold until the terrorists were held somewhat at a distance.

#

America's reactions calmed down except for the all-out war against terrorism worldwide. It is now two years following that September 11th day of disasters in New York, Washington DC and Pennsylvania, and then at the Circle MJ ranch. The United States declared war against the al Qaida Moslem terrorists in Afghanistan, Pakistan, Iraq and Iran, who planned and carried out the attacks on the United States of America.

President Bush was threatening to send our troops into Iraq to search out the terrorists who were being trained and supported by Saddam Hussein. The President said in reference to intensifying contacts with Iraqi opposition leaders, that he had no timetable for deciding on a military strike against Iraq and may not decide this year. He stated, "And if I did, I wouldn't tell you or the enemy!"

The United States' borders, foreign incoming airline flights and vessels had tightened security with immigrants and tourists. All Americans felt the death delivered by the Moslem extremist of the al Qaida band pledged to Osama bin Laden from the Middle East.

Jess was a strong supporter of President Bush and prayed daily for God's wisdom and direction for him. Although he had retired from the Air Force, Jess would have reenlisted if he had not been too old.

He and Marie Ann had finally restored peace at the ranch and had not witnessed any more low fly-overs by aircraft. The female security team had settled into a tight, well-organized unit. They both were well pleased with how the group turned out. Now, the two of them were on separate trips, which was very uncommon for them. Marie Ann was in Indiana visiting her side of the family, and Jess had left for Odessa to continue the research of his grandfather's history living in southwest Texas. His research was taking him to the rugged Big Bend country on the Rio Grande River.

Santa Elena Canyon

Carved by the Rio Grande River, this spectacular gorge is more than 15
miles long. Perpendicular walls tower 1,600 feet above the river separating
Mexico on the left, and the United States on the right.
(Ross A. Maxwell, University of Texas, Dec. 1971;
Bureau of Economic Geology)

CHAPTER ONE

Jess E. Hanes, a good-looking gentleman in his mid-sixties, stood on the veranda of his motel room watching the sunrise. Its brilliant streaks of light fingered out between thin layers of rain clouds into the deep blue western sky. The Odessa, Texas morning was clear of sand and air pollution.

Jess was a typical Texan, thinly built, 180 pounds, sun-weathered face, five feet ten inches tall barefooted, and graying at the temples with permanent smile wrinkles at the corner of his eyes, and a good set of his own teeth. His grandfather, a dentist down in Crane, was credited for keeping his grandchildren's teeth in good condition.

When Jess smiled, he smiled all over. But, when he was angry, his brown eyes became beady and piercing. He was slow tempered and had mellowed somewhat after retiring from the U.S. Air Force. But again, when he was mad, he was mad all over.

It was a mild 60 degrees, and the smell of the rain freshened the September morning, making him want to stretch. Jess set his hot cup of black coffee next to a Gideon Bible on the balcony table. He had finished his morning scripture reading and prayer time. Raising his arms, he reached up stretching as far as he could, sucking in the fresh air. Leaning against the railing, he grasped it tightly flexing the muscles in his arms. A cool breeze caused goose bumps on his bare forearms.

Jess had packed long-sleeved, western shirts because temperatures could be a little chilly further southwest at higher altitudes. *He just might have to change shirts if the sun did not start warming things up...* the short-sleeved shirt he wore was thin and a favorite of Marie Ann's; he missed her at his side.

There was very little traffic at that time of the morning, but truckers had come alive in their big rigs at the enormous Lazy 20 Truck Stop across the interstate from the motel. They were heading out to continue their travels. Black diesel smoke left traces in the heavy moist air. Many of the other trucks were from the oil fields, busy carrying their crews and equipment to work.

The wind was calm with no dust in the west. A few water puddles remained from the light morning shower. Overall, it looked to Jess as if it was going to be another clear day for flying.

Taking another sip of coffee and turning around, Jess leaned back against the railing, watching the local satellite weather report on the TV in his room. It showed the rain-front had passed, and nothing was coming from the west to hinder his flying for that morning.

The telephone began to ring. He strolled back inside, turned off the TV with the remote control, and sat on the bed. He had been waiting to hear from one of his twin nephews in Midland, Jack Randel.

Brushing back his short brown hair from off his forehead, he picked up the phone. "Good morning!" Jess said in his native Texas accent.

No answer, just a low-pitched hum, "Hello, anyone there?" Still no answer, "Guess not!" he said out loud, and laid the phone back in its cradle. No sooner had he put the phone down, it rang again.

"Yes!"

"Uncle Jess? Why did you hang up on me?" the voice asked him.

"Nobody there to talk to that I could hear!" Jess responded, "So why talk to a dead phone?"

"Sorry, Uncle Jess! This cellular phone of mine only works half of the time." His voice faded and came back, "This is Jack, sorry about that! I'll have to get a digital cell phone to stop this

2

cutting out from happening. Anyway, are you ready for a big western breakfast with Texas size biscuits and all the trimmings?"

"Sure, when and where?"

"I'll be out front with my pickup truck in five minutes," Jack said.

"Great, see ya!"

Jess turned off the coffee pot, poured out the remaining coffee in the bathroom sink and drank the last swallow from the cup. Picking up his flight bag and room key, he put on his Texas Tech ball cap and stepped into the hall closing the door behind him.

He was looking forward to seeing his nephew again, even though it would only be during breakfast. Neither of his nephews had been in town the previous evening.

Jess wanted one of nephews to fly down to the Big Bend country with him for a few days on research, but they couldn't take the time off now. Instead, they had been busy Texas Rangers, always looking for the bad guys. Like they say, "One riot, one Ranger!"

Jack had given Jess a classic book about the Rangers, *Captain Bill McDonald: Texas Ranger* by A. B. Paine. The captain's creed was: "No man in the wrong, can stand up against a fellow that's in the right, and keeps on a-comin'!"

In the twin's younger years, Charles and Jack had spent many hours with their Uncle Jess searching through the west Texas areas for Apache and Comanche Indian relics and talking to the Native Americans about their ancestors. Many of their trips followed the Indian Trails from Big Spring to the famous Horse Head Crossing on the Pecos River, and then on to Marathon and Boquillas.

Their research had continued down the Chihuahua Trail from Presidio to Ft. Stockton, to Del Rio, and across to San Antonio, a few times. They were trying to find additional information on Charles and Jack's great, great grandfather, Blue Feather, from their father's side of the family. He was a full blood Arapaho Indian who the Comanche kidnapped at a young age on the Platte River, taking him south to Texas during their annual migration across the Rio Grande River into Mexico. He became one of the many tribal Comanche chiefs in his later years. Through the years, the twins had an increasing interest in Indian affairs.

The morning's breakfast with Jack was brief because he had to take Jess to the airport and get to the ranger's office. Charles was to come from his Odessa office later and meet his Uncle Jess for lunch at the terminal restaurant, and then see him off.

Jess had a couple of hours to spend in the Confederate Air Force Museum at the airport. He obtained maintenance information on his Pilatus PC-6 aircraft from one of the mechanics working on the museum's B-29. The mechanic had spent many hours working on the same type PC-6 in Vietnam. Then Jess met Charles at the terminal restaurant for lunch.

#

Charles and Jess had a good talk while eating, and now they were pre-flighting Jess' aircraft.

"How's the research coming on your Granddad Hanes' ventures down in the Big Bend country?" Charles asked Jess.

"Slow, very slow."

"Just curious and nosey," Charles squinted his eyes from the bright morning sun reflecting off the tarmac. "Thought I'd ask, because I know you've been at it a long time. And, . . . Aye!" He banged his head against a tie-down eyebolt on the underside of the wing strut when he stepped around the big tire going to the open side door. Rubbing the hurt spot, he frowned and quietly moaned, so Jess would not hear.

Charles Randal, over six feet tall and solidly built, looked down at Jess. He changed his line of conversation, still squinting his eyes, "Uncle Jess, make sure you keep one good eye open and

4

your powder dry. Okay?" He continued to rub his head, "There's a lot of drug dealing in the southwest counties. It's so bad that the innocent tourists are being used for transporting it. You've got a sharp aircraft here! They'd sure like to get their hands on a cargo hauler like this one for hopping over the Rio Grande with drugs and illegals."

While Jess busied himself rearranging the flight gear up front, he said, "You're right! It is designed for maximum weight loads of 6,195 pounds, plus it can take off, and land, on a dime with that heavy load." He unrolled the netting, spread it out over the cargo and hooked it in place. Then he stepped back, "Look at all that stuff I've packed back there. It doesn't weigh anywhere close to max. Half of it, I won't need; but you never know! Right?" he said to Charles, laughing at himself for hauling so much equipment.

Charles leaned around Jess and stuck his head in the aircraft's doorway, pushing the pilot seat forward. He snickered and began to laugh, shaking his head. The six rear-passenger seats had been removed which provided additional space to the already spacious cargo compartment. The carpeted floor was covered with a heavy canvas tarp with the equipment and camping gear lying on top of the canvas. A plastic netting secured everything from being tossed around all over the place.

"Think you forgot anything?"

"Nope, don't think so," Jess replied.

Charles pointed at the metal detectors under the webbing, "Going to be treasure hunting for relics or prospecting? I'd sure like to be snooping around with you again! It's fun!"

"Probably both! If you can get away while I'm down there, you know you're welcome," Jess said while putting his map and other paperwork in order. "I would like to follow some of the trails that lead to Mexico and search them. Never know when you might find a place where the travelers camped . . . Indians,

Mexicans, or the early travelers, heading west to California. I want to research some specific areas where they crossed the Rio Grande, camping on both sides. That's where smaller villages have disappeared over the years."

Charles rubbed his chin, contemplating his next remark, "I was hoping to see Aunt Marie."

Jess smiled when his nephew spoke of his wife, "Her Mom took ill and needed some assistance. I sure miss her." His eyes filled up thinking of her, while moving a few items in the aircraft. It was lonely without her.

Charles closed his eyes and thought, then spoke, "Yes Sir! I know you do, Uncle Jess. You're always traveling together," patting his Uncle's shoulder.

"M.J. flew her up to northern Indiana," Jess replied.

Charles had a puzzled look on his face, not remembering the name.

"You remember, our other nephew?" Jess said. "Mick J. Slater, who owns that charter service out of Indianapolis International?"

"Okay! Now, I remember," he said.

"Marie Ann may come out here later, if her Mom gets better. My research may take awhile."

Charles knew his aunt and uncle were very close to each other. He didn't want to carry the subject any further, "I'm scheduled to attend a district lecture on Wednesday. Sorry, but I can't go with you on this trip to Marfa. I'll take another rain-check."

"You've got it. How many rain checks will that make now? At least a dozen," Jess said as he moved a few items around behind the right front seat. "Hand me that flight bag, please. I better make sure what I need will be within arms reach, once I'm flying."

Jess laid it on the tarmac in the shade of the wing, knelt down next to it, unzipped the bag and began rummaging around in it.

He pulled out his knee board with all of his pilot's essentials and opened it: sectional maps of the area he would be flying in; E6B computer; airport directory; Global Positioning System (GPS); a hard copy of the aircraft's check list; numerous pencils; and a scratch pad for notes. He laid it on the pilot's seat next to his headset.

"Let me see now," Jess said, going back over his flight checklist. "35mm camera, film, tripod, a loaded 8mm video camera, blank video tapes, weeks worth of clothes, writing stuff, laptop computer, floppy disc, batteries, cellular phone, a copy of Granddad Hanes' book, and . . ."

Charles interrupted, expressing his desire to help, "Think you'll finish your research about Texas being in the Civil War before the winter storms start coming?"

"Nope! Don't think so this year," Jess said. "I've still got a long way to go, especially in the libraries and field research around Marfa and Alpine. You can be a big help to me in both areas, if you're still interested. And, when you have the time off!"

"Interested? Yeah, I would spend all my vacation running around with you if I could. But, the Major has put it on hold for a couple of months." He wiped the sweat from his wet face with his handkerchief. The sun was making every reflecting metal a heat source. "We are still working on a big problem along the border south of El Paso. That's another reason I would like to go along . . . a second set of eyes. You can never be too cautious down there!"

"You're right, wish you could go! But, I'll be all right! My research will take a long time. It looks like a drawn out affair," Jess said, turning to Charles poking him in the ribs with a bony finger. "I'll call you. Eventually, I'll need you to translate

Spanish for me. There's a lot of people to interview who knew Granddad Hanes."

Jess closed his flight bag and handed it up to Charles to put behind the pilot's seat, "Secure that netting over the equipment for me, please."

They stepped out from under the wing into the hot morning sun, and Jess finished his preflight check of the aircraft with Charles following his every move.

"Received more letters about Granddad Hanes from a professor he knew in Alpine," Jess said, walking behind the aircraft's tail as he checked the rudder and elevators movements.

Charles grunted his acknowledgement and replied as if he really did not hear Jess' comment, "Did you bring your guns? I don't see them!"

"Rifle and .45 revolver," Jess said. "They are in that hard case under the netting. I shouldn't need them until I'm on foot near the Big Bend."

"You still carry that old .45 Long Colt revolver?" Charles teased.

"Yes, and a new Colt 1911 .45 auto. But, I don't care for the .44 magnums you guys carry. It's too heavy for me."

Laughing, Charles patted his sidearm, "I don't notice the weight anymore like I use to. Using it on the range everyday has kept me in shape, plus this new holster has helped me carry it easier. Especially on horseback."

"Yeah! I'll keep toting that oldie, wouldn't leave home without it. Bringing that .30-.30 Winchester rifle was a good idea in case those javelina or peccary hogs become a nuisance. Which reminds me, I didn't see my binoculars, did you?"

"Just a minute, Uncle Jess," Charles said. "I think you left them on the front seat of my truck. Be right back."

He strolled over to the blue Chevy pickup parked behind the aircraft. As Jess finished his preflight around the aircraft, he noticed the light breeze had stopped and felt the sun's reflected heat increasing from the surface of the tarmac. He remembered it was suppose to get up to 80 degrees later in the afternoon with no forecast of bad weather. It felt hotter to Jess. But, it did mean he might have turbulence at lower altitudes from heat rising from the warmed ground.

Leaning on the folded back of the pilot's seat, Jess inventoried the items under the netting again, using his homemade checklist. Whispering to himself, "Deep Wilderness Emergency first aid kit in place and easy to get to; emergency Locator Transmitter (ELT) in its mounts and armed; there's the portable transceiver and GPS; rope and four military food rations (MRE's); the cloth helmet for the video camera and camera; 8mm video tapes; bedroll and two solar blankets; three White's metal detectors. And finally, two full gallon water containers strapped down and a large canteen fastened to a web belt hanging over the back of the copilot's seat."

Charles stooped and walked under the trailing edge of the wing flaps on the right side of the aircraft and leaned inside the cargo door opening, "Here! Where do you want this, Uncle Jess?" he asked, interrupting the inventory check and handing the binoculars to Jess.

Pointing towards the co-pilot's seat, "Slide them under the netting, behind the seat. I'll need them on the way to Marfa. I'm not flying by instruments down there. It's clear, and I'll only be eighteen hundred feet or so above the ground, until I get to the Davis Mountains - that's if the turbulence isn't too bad. I enjoy the scenery crossing the mountain range. I may do some canyon snooping."

Charles removed a small transceiver radio from his waistband with its holster and handed it to Jess, "I forgot to tell you, Jack will be in the Terlingua and Lajitas area tonight." Pointing at one selector switch, "Contact him on channel one. It's already set."

He spoke with concern in his voice, "Since September 11, 2001, our borders have tightened up. I have already let them know you're headed for the border."

Jess nodded in reply.

"I remembered you're having problems with that com/nav radio on the instrument panel," Charles said.

"Yes! Thanks for remembering," Jess said reaching over and slapping the instrument panel VHF/UHF radios. "If I bang on it enough, it clears up. Probably a loose wire or solder joint somewhere," he said, smiling. "Of course, that banging on it helps! I've got that backup portable transceiver, anyway, plus this one you gave me." He shrugged his shoulders and motioned with his hands as if there was nothing to be worried about. Then he said, "There's a good radioman down in Marfa. I'll take them out and leave them with him until I need to fly out."

Jess whispered to himself while wiping his glasses clean with his red bandana, "These Texas Rangers are sharp; they don't seem to miss a thing." He continued smiling to himself, as he scanned the aeronautical map. He saw Presidio on the map and his mind wondered, "I thought his brother was still in Presidio. It doesn't matter, I'll catch him somewhere for dinner some night."

Putting his bandana in his hip pocket, Jess accepted the transceiver from Charles, "This will come in handy. What's on these other channels?"

The young ranger removed his own transceiver radio from the gun belt holster, leaned inside the cockpit behind the right seat, and then pointed at the channel selector switch, "These are special frequency channels for the rangers in the southwest Texas area. They are linked with scrambled satellite communications, so no matter where you are located, you'll have a radio hookup. It's even good deep in the canyons." He slid the radio back into its holster and buckled it in place. "Plus, it will be confidential. Only ranger units will have a receiver that will decode your transmissions."

Jess nodded his understanding.

They reviewed Jess' flight schedule, and when he would be in Alpine, Marfa and Lajitas. Charles took his light tan Stetson hat off, wiped his forehead and placed it over his pistol in its holster. He leaned his forearm against the side of the aircraft peering inside. Jess stepped back under the wing staying out of the direct sun. It was getting hotter.

"If you can't raise Jack on channel one, call for "TR-ONE" on either of the other two channels and tell them who you are. They will relay your message. He is supposed to be in the Terlingua and Lajitas area for a couple of weeks."

"Great!" Jess replied, "Now I won't feel so isolated. Got a charger for it?"

He went back to the truck for the charger and had to answer a call on his radio. Nodding his head, he smiled, and Jess heard him say, "Sure I'll tell him." With his exceptionally long stride, Charles was back with Jess under the wing. "Jack says to tell you to take it easy, and his prayers are with you."

"That was thoughtful of him. Sorry you guys can't come along. Thanks for the lunch and the radio," Jess said, shaking hands with Charles and receiving a firm grip.

The usual custom of teasing for the two nephews was to pull their uncle towards them when shaking hands, trying to catch him off-guard. Jess had already braced for the tug and waved a finger at Charles with the other hand, "Not this time. You have to get up earlier than this to catch me."

"I'll get you one of these day, Uncle Jess! Don't forget now, you're always welcome around here, anytime. Living alone gets to me, and I always enjoy our trips together."

"I wouldn't have invited you if I didn't enjoy your company too," Jess said, giving Charles a gentlemanly hug.

Charles put his Stetson back on, closed the doors on the right side of the aircraft and insured they locked properly. He backed out from under the front of the right wing as Jess stepped up on the left oversized tire, opened the narrow door and slipped into the pilot's seat, strapping on his shoulder and lap harness. Charles walked around the front of the aircraft doing a visual inspection and stood next to the left tire where Jess could see him. Jess motioned him to remove the chocks from the two landing gear tires.

In a whisper, "This is going to be a great trip," Jess said. "No clocks to watch, no pressures, no stress, just researching at my own pace, enjoying interviews, and visiting with people. But, I won't forget my sweet Marie Ann. Lord Jesus, continue to keep Your protecting arms around her and her Mom. Give M.J. a clear mind and judgment in his flying."

Thinking, *My nephews, Charles and Jack, are quite the law enforcement officers.*

Jess left his pilot's door partially opened for air ventilation. He began calling off the aircraft's checklist. Charles gave Jess thumbs up, signaling it was safe to start the engine. Then, he went to his pickup truck, driving it from behind the plane and around past the left wing tip; parked the pickup and walked back in front of the wingtip to scan the taxi area and under the aircraft for anything in the way. They signaled thumbs-up to each other, and Jess turned the master power switch 'on'; both wing tank gauges showed full; fuel pump on for four seconds, then off; throttle control set; propeller control set . . . Jess continued the check list.

Putting on the headset, looking out the windows all the way around the inside cockpit to make sure no one was near, Jess yelled, "Clear!" out the door opening, and not hearing a reply or seeing anyone in front or next to the plane, he turned the ignition switch to 'on'. The engine caught after one revolution of the propeller and roared to life. After checking his instruments and gauges, he called the tower and moved out to their indicated taxiway.

A light breeze from the west caused the need for slight trim adjustments as he pointed the nose into the late September sky. Most of the West Texas unsettled weather was over, and he could expect a relaxing trip to Alpine, and then on to Marfa.

Once Jess obtained the altitude he had requested from the Flight Service Station (FSS), he leveled off and trimmed the aircraft. He then did a clearing visual check for any other aircraft near him. Finding none, he filed necessary papers and guides into his flight bag and put it on the floor behind the seat next to him.

Relaxing, Jess thought about the conversation at breakfast with Jack, and then again with Charles at the airport while loading the aircraft. Running the morning events over in his mind brought him uneasiness.

Jess' thoughts returned from Charles to flying when light turbulence bounced his aircraft around, then smoothed out. It was just enough bouncing to make him pay attention to his flying. Letting the aircraft fly itself after setting the trim again, he relaxed and put off further thoughts about problems that might arise in the Big Bend country. He checked the sectional flight map, and marked the time he passed over Crane. He had only been in the air twenty minutes.

"Time: thirteen hundred (1:00PM) hours over Crane, and change course for Imperial, should be there in ten minutes. Heading indicator matches the magnetic compass, and Nav 1 set for Alpine's VOR."

I'm not only enjoying this, thinking to himself, *it's good to get back up here away from the rat race down there.*

The Pecos River, 1,800 feet below, looked like a small rope that had been dropped from his height. It had no special course as it wondered toward the Rio Grande, except for its southerly direction weaving in and out of all points of the compass, like it was lost trying to find its way.

The water tower at Imperial should be over there to the right, just south of the Pecos River, Jess thought. *I remember when Dad made me taste that brackish river water as a boy.* "Phew! Takes my breath away thinking about it," Jess said out loud, laughing to himself.

He liked his rebuilt Pilatus PC-6 military aircraft. It saw service in the Vietnam War. He reached over the stick and patted the top of the instrument panel, thinking, *With this new paint and engine, you handle like a dream. I'll be putting you through your paces on this trip. We'll probably be landing and taking off in the shortest distance imaginable. The test pilot at the factory suggested I practice as much as possible on the shortest distance possible getting off the ground. Wow! At the factory, I was airborne in seven seconds from a dead stop. Landing, we stopped in less than three hundred and fifty feet, and that's going to improve the more I fly you. I plan setting you down in some isolated areas during this research trip, so that should prove exciting for both of us.*

"Your special tires will come in handy for that," Jess said looking out the window at them.

Checking his watch, speed indicator, altitude and heading, Jess marked his sectional map again. "Great, we're still on time. Now a little right rudder to stay in a coordinated turn and a smidgen bank to the left, bringing your nose around to 225 degrees, keeping you on the horizon as we turn. Now, a little rudder trim to stay on that heading."

The land passed smoothly below. Jess could clearly see to the horizon. The sun was beginning to shine through the windscreen, heating up the cabin. He moved the elevator trim slightly to keep the nose of the aircraft down for a level flight. Then he pulled the knob to let more outside air in.

"The next way-point on the map is Ft. Stockton, twenty-four miles down Texas Country Road 1053, at 140 mph, we should cross there in 10.3 minutes. Check the map again, Jess. What did you write down for ETA?"

Making sure there were no aircraft to the left or right, he looked at the sectional map again. *Right on the button for time to Ft. Stockton, as long as we don't pick up any cross or head wind. I can't see any dust blowing on those open fields or pastures. So far, so good!*

"I should be in Alpine in less than an hour for the night, and on to Marfa tomorrow morning." Jess picked up the habit, years ago, talking to himself or the Lord, when alone. But, talking to his aircraft was usually his way of talking to the Lord too! "Texas, this time of year, is usually burnt from the sun and brown from the lack of moisture. But, this year it's like an oasis, everything so green. This will be your first trip down here, what do you think about it so far?"

Not really expecting an answer from his aircraft, he continued, "I can see the Davis Mountains straight ahead, dark and ominous, sixty miles south of Ft. Stockton. No haze today, which is surprising with all the rain we've been having."

Jess checked off Ft. Stockton on the map. It passed below as he crossed Interstate 10 going west to the junction of Interstate 20 at Van Horn. Whispering, "Two roads out of there, going south. And, then the left one to the east is Texas 285; the one on the right is 385. I need to follow Interstate 10 west until Texas 67 comes in from the south.

15

"If I remember right, Burt's Gasoline & Oil station should be at that intersection, with a short dirt airstrip. No hangars! Just a cleared strip of land for small aircraft, maybe crop dusters use it for refueling. No aircraft to our left or right coming out of Ft. Stockton, better give notification that we're in the area."

Jess turned up the volume on his headset and checked the frequency again, then transmitted, "Ft. Stockton traffic. Pilatus Nancy 4422 Lima, three miles east. Passing over Ft. Stockton at 2000, west bound. Any traffic, please advise!"

"Pilatus, Nancy 4422 Lima, Ft. Stockton Unicom," came a voice on the radio. "No traffic to report around here. Have a good flight, Sir."

"Nancy 4422 Lima will follow highway 67 to 90 and over to Alpine for the night. Thank you! Talk with you later!" Jess replied.

"Copy 67 to 90 to Alpine for the night. Out!"

There's your turn south Jess, get on it, thinking to himself. *There's still no hangar at that dirt strip. Now, check the map for Alpine. 57 miles to go, no problem. Mark off Ft. Stockton's time, right on again. The GPS is showing my route to be the same, so enjoy the flight, Mr. Hanes.*

Jess was approaching two mountains that were on each side of his course to Alpine. *On the left will be the Glass Mountains and the Davis Mountains on the right. I better call Alpine for weather. Wind between these two mountains would be dangerous this afternoon if thermal updrafts caught us.*

He dialed in the frequency on the Com 1 radio, "Alpine Unicom, this is Pilatus Porter PC6, Nancy 4422 Lima at twenty-five hundred AGL. North of you about 20 miles. You have a copy?"

"Yes, sir! I sure do, heard you talk to Ft. Stockton, and I have you on the scope. Clear weather between us. Wind is zero, maximum visibility, pressure thirty-point-two-zero and holding."

"Copy clear, wind zero, visibility max, pressure holding at thirty-point-two-zero," Jess replied. "What are wind conditions between these two mountain ranges I'm headed for at two thousand?"

"No report, but it should not be too rough. There may be a headwind in about an hour, but you should be here by then."

"Copy! I'll call again when I see the airport!"

Jess heard two clicks on the headset, giving him an affirmative response. Thinking, *I'll be on the ground in about fifteen minutes.*

Everything seemed to be going good and an uneventful leg of his flight. Jess could not see thunderclouds to the west or south, "Thank you, Lord Jesus, for the good weather. I don't want to race with storms today, just don't feel like being tossed around."

There's the flashing beacon on top of Blue Mountain, call in altitude change, "Alpine traffic. Nancy 4422 Lima changing to approach altitude."

"Use runway two three, straight in. No traffic reported. You're clear for landing on left two three. Winds calm. Barometric pressure three-zero-point-two-nine. Clear to the horizon with no clouds. Welcome back, Mr. Hanes."

"Copy. Approach straight in . . . runway two three and thank you," Jess replied, and then set his barometric pressure to three-zero-point-two-nine on the altimeter.

'For 2000 feet above the ground, altitude 6,515 feet . . . Good, right on the button! The altitude at the Alpine Airport is 4515' above sea level,' Jess thought to himself. *'Wonder who that was talking to me on the radio? I really can't remember knowing anyone down here? Wind should be no problem and altimeter is correct,'* Jess rehearsed.

After landing, chalking the wheels, and tying down the wings, Jess took a walk around his aircraft. The PC-6 looked great in the afternoon sun. The wax shine made the white with blue trim glisten. He had the olive drab (O.D.) military green removed. Grabbing his flight bag, he headed for the terminal building and called for a taxicab. While on the phone, Jess could not see anyone at the ticket desk, and the lobby was empty.

He remembered it would take twenty minutes for the cab to arrive, so he looked in the weather room, no one around. They did not have a control tower, but the Unicom radios were behind the ticket desk with an old WWII radarscope.

"Is anybody home?" Jess called out.

Walking over to the large picture window, he couldn't see anyone around the tied-down aircraft on the ramp, and there were no cars in the parking lot. That's funny, maybe the attendant lives out here, and he has everything catered.

"Mr. Hanes, I'm Joseph Spire, owner, traffic controller, and operator of this ATC." Jess jumped like he had been shot. He didn't see where the guy had come from. The attendant offered his hand.

Surprised, Jess stepped back from him, "Didn't see you coming! I thought everyone had gone home."

"Nope! Just in the little boy's room. Heard you call out, but you must not have heard me, sorry."

Jess shook the guy's hand.

"I'll call you a cab if you're not leaving tonight."

"I called a few minutes ago. They should be here shortly."

Jess walked toward the front door of the lobby, "How did you know who I was?"

The guy leaned on the counter top with his elbow, watching Jess, "Oh, yes! Well! I have collected aircraft I.D.'s for years, and you were here four years ago passing through. I was a senior at Sul Ross University working here in the summer months."

"But this is not the aircraft I had back then. I wasn't flying this Pilatus PC-6 four years ago. I had an old . . .

18

"Tripacer, Nancy 1231 Zebra," Joseph said. "Yes, and I have both aircraft listed in my notebook. Here, take a look," he said as he handed Jess a heavy reference book.

It was thicker than a Webster dictionary and had small pieces of scrap paper stuck between most of its pages. Some of them fell to the floor.

"I haven't got all of the I.D.'s listed yet, your Pilatus Porter is my last note. I used my computer on the Internet to cross-reference information. I can find just about every I.D. on any aircraft in the U.S. and Canada," he said with pride.

"When you talked to Ft. Stockton, I copied your I.D. and got on the Internet. In two minutes, I knew whose aircraft it was, and where it was registered. Just guessed you were flying it, and went to my book and there you were back in June of 1998."

Jess stood there with his mouth opened in disbelief, "Quite a hobby you have here!" He began to laugh and shook Joseph's hand again, "Well, I'll be!"

Picking up the heavy volume, he handed it to Jess. Jess almost dropped it, not realizing how heavy it was. "It's probably a handy book to have around with all of the aircraft you have stopping here . . . and, a listing of pilots you have talked to on the radio. Yes! Nice hobby."

"Thank you, Sir," he said smiling. "Mr. Hanes, I've talked to everyone of them."

"You should get someone at the University to publish and print this for you."

Jess was interrupted by a taxi horn, "Please top off the Porter, 100 Low Lead!" He waved, thanked Joseph and left for town.

The lady driver only asked Jess where he wanted to go, and that was all she said for thirty minutes until arriving at the Settler's Hotel. She was in no hurry.

The weeds, grass, flowers and trees were flourishing, much prettier than when he had been there a few years back. Even the flowerbeds around the courthouse were in full bloom.

His stay would be downtown on this trip. He was tired of the fast life of the motel circuit. It was his first time staying in the old 1873 Settler's Hotel.

"Five bucks, Mister!" she ordered.

Jess got out, set his handbag and suitcase on the sidewalk, turned around and handed her the money through the front door window opening. She snatched the ten-dollar bill out of his hand and drove off muttering to herself about the big city folks.

"Where's my change?" he hollered, stepping out into the street. "Hey, Taxi! Stop! Come back here!" Shaking his fist at her, he muttered something under his breath, "Lord, take care of that situation, please!" and then stepped back up on the sidewalk.

With his hands on his hips and trying to calm down, Jess was speechless. *She's too far away to get the taxi number. I'll get my change and then some, when I find her. Payday isn't always on Friday! Whatever that means!*

Inside the hotel lobby were three cowboys standing near the big bay window overlooking the street, laughing. At the reservation desk, Jess turned around to glare at them. They were pointing at him. A tap on his shoulder turned him back to the desk. A tall, well-dressed Mexican was smiling at him. A tag over his jacket pocket read, "Settler's Hotel Manager", with no name.

"May I help you, *Señor*?" he said smiling. "You permitted us to have the dull afternoon broken at the expense of your embarrassment. Your room is free tonight."

"I usually don't get that upset," he turned and pointed toward the front double doors. "But, what she did caught me off guard. Do you know who she is?"

"Yes, and let me give you her telephone number. You may need to call her again, if you do not rent an automobile."

Continuing to smile, he said, "She does that often. Those cowboys had a bet she would do it to you."

He gave Jess the room key and the telephone number with no name. The manager laughed under his breath as he answered the desk telephone.

"No name?" Jess asked and motioned with his hand.

"You will not need a name, *Señor*," he said with his hand over the telephone mouthpiece. "She is our only woman taxi driver in Alpine! Just ask for her!"

The manager snapped his fingers at the seated bellboy next to the hotel's lone elevator and pointed to Jess' bags.

The little Mexican bellboy led Jess up the plush, black oak winding staircase to the second floor balcony that opened to the lobby below.

Jess wondered if the elevator was broken. But, no problem, he needed the exercise from flying so long.

The bellboy opened the room door and laid Jess' flight bag on the bed and the suitcase on a small bench. Then, he crossed the room to large glass doors, opening them to the outside. Jess tipped him, and he left with a nod of thanks.

The room was exceptionally large, compared to the motel rooms on the interstates. The old Settler's Hotel still used the late eighteen hundred's sturdy furniture-of-fashion, with plenty of sitting space. A thick Persian rug with a pattern from the Middle East covered the shiny hardwood floor.

This room must still be used for meetings, too. Look at all the antiques - divans, desk and tables, Jess was impressed with the expensive old furnishings. *The high ceiling keeps it cool in here with the nice breeze coming in through the open veranda doors. That would help keep the moisture down.* The white lacey drapes moved in the light breeze, parting at the bottom.

He walked between the sheer drapes and stepped out onto the veranda. It opened toward the courthouse yard across the street to the west. The sun was about to drop behind the mountains, and its rays began to shoot through the blue sky. Even though it was only afternoon hours, the shadows of the mountains partially covered the hotel.

I can tell I'm still in Texas with all the pickups parked at the curb around the courthouse and across the street to the east of it. That's either a bar or a good eating place, or both. I'll have to check it out.

Digging through his flight bag, Jess found the shaving kit and took it to the bathroom. "Wow, look at that! I'll have to take a bath in that tonight and soak." *That old-style tub on legs looks deep enough to swim in. I haven't seen one of these since I stayed with my grandparents on their ranch south of Crane. First things first! Chow!*

After supper at the hotel restaurant, Jess walked the sidewalk around the square block surrounding the courthouse and window shopped at the stores. *At least the big malls haven't shut down this nice downtown area.*

Jess waved at the hotel manager when he passed the counter going back to his room for the night. The soaking hot bath in the deep, old white ceramic tub was worth the wait. He slept soundly.

CHAPTER TWO

Five blocks from the Settler's Hotel was the T-Top Restaurant where ranchers, ranch hands, and oil field roustabouts got the best breakfast west of the Pecos River. At five-thirty, Jess still had to wait for a seat, which was in a booth next to one of the front windows. There was noise with morning chatter and the smell of cigarette smoke, freshly brewed coffee, eggs and bacon frying, and steak with biscuits and gravy. One of the cooks in the kitchen had a radio on, listening to country-western music.

The waitress took Jess' usual order of two eggs over easy, steak medium rare, biscuits and gravy, American fries, coffee and grapefruit juice.

That order should hold me until I get to Marfa, Jess thought. *But, I had better get an orange and apple. They're stacked over there on the counter next to the cash register.*

The early morning crowd left before Jess got his order filled . . . Then local office workers and labor groups began to arrive, mixed with college students and faculty. The breakfast chatter began again, but in a higher pitch and faster conversations. It wasn't long, and they were finished eating, forty-five minutes at the most.

He just finished his last fork full of biscuits and gray, when his waitress gave him the third cup of coffee, asking if he needed anything else. She looked familiar, but Jess didn't know anyone here, so he politely said, no. She put the bill for his meal next to the water glass, and then stepped back.

Jess laid down a ten-dollar bill on top of the meal receipt.

Just as he did, he grabbed it back and looked up at her again. *You bet I know her!*

She gave him a big smile and began to laugh. "Your breakfast is on the house, this morning, Mr. Hanes!" With her arms spread

23

wide, "I own this place! Had you foaming at the mouth last night, didn't I?"

Jess started to get up in protest, but she gently put her hand on his shoulder and held him in the booth. One of the men from the kitchen grill came over next to her, "Is this the gentleman you told me about at the hotel last night?"

She nodded, "Yes, he's the one."

Jess scooted away from them on the booth's seat with his back to the window. The cook held out his hand, "Don't get excited, she does that to all the incoming from the airport . . . unless she knows them, Mr. Hanes."

Of course, Jess had another one of those dumb looks on his face, because they both started laughing, and he did not shake the guy's hand.

"This has become a town joke on everyone that comes in new, needing a taxi from the airport. Horris, the hotel manager was here for our midnight supper, he told us who you were," he stuck out his hand again, "I'm second in command in this here eating establishment, Mr. Hanes. This here is Gladys, my wife. I'm Tom Ramp."

Jess tried to smile as he scooted across the seat, and rose to shake hands.

"Keep your seat, sir," he said grabbing Jess' hand. "Your room and breakfast are taken care of today, on us, because you came here for chow. We welcome you to Alpine."

"Well, thank you for your abrupt warm welcome. It certainly took me by surprise," Jess said laughing.

"We grew up around here and thought we would liven things up a bit when people would fly in and stay around," Tom said. "Gladys is the only one that answers calls for taxi pickup at the airport. We apologize, and hope there are no hard feelings."

"Fine, there's no problem now!" Jess replied putting the ten-dollar bill in his shirt pocket. "But, how did you know I would come here for breakfast, or for any meal as far as that goes?"

"We would have made sure you got here for one meal before you left; we have eyes all over," Gladys said.

"Okay, I'll watch my step from now on! By the way," Jess asked, "who runs the cabs back to the airport? I'll need to get my things at the hotel and head out there in about an hour."

"We do!" Tom smiled broadly, "In an hour, that's about nine thirty?" Looking at his watch, "I'll have one of our taxis pick you up. The driver will call you from the hotel desk when he arrives."

Jess got up and shook Gladys' hand, "Thanks again for the welcome to Alpine," they all laughed. Then, Jess headed for the hotel. The brisk walk back got his blood circulating, and he took two stairs steps at a time going up to his room.

CHAPTER THREE

After spending time with the Lord Jesus in prayer and reading the Holy Bible, placed in his room by the Gideons, Jess reviewed his plans for the day. *I should have asked Tom and Gladys Ramp about Professor John Stapleton, maybe Horris downstairs knows him. The professor has been around these parts since after World War II, teaching at Sul Ross University. He's retired now, living on a ranch south of here. He was one of Granddad's old mining buddies. The professor sent me this letter last week, saying he needed to talk about something he found that belongs to Granddad Hanes.*

Looking at his watch and mumbling to himself, "I'd better get downstairs for that taxi ride to the airport. It's nine-twenty now, so pack up, let's get this show on the road."

I can take my time checking the aircraft and take some notes before leaving. I don't need to be at Professor Stapleton's place until two. After fueling, I could even take a nap on the bedroll in the shade of the plane's wing. Now, dog-gone if that don't sound invitin'!

Later this evening, I'll fly to Marfa, then on over to Presidio for the night; if my visit with the professor isn't too long. A couple of hours at his ranch should be enough.

Leading Jess to the lobby's front revolving glass doors, Horris said, "Everything has been taken care of Mr. Hanes," with a snappy salute, *"Adios Señor!* Come back, *por favor."*

"Óptimo, adiós Señor!" Jess said with the little Spanish he thought meant 'excellent'.

#

Jess asked the taxi driver if he knew Professor Stapleton. He nodded, yes, and with broken English, "The old man west of town?" The driver's Spanish accent was thick, which reminded Jess again he needed to brush up on his Spanish.

"*Si, Señor!* If the 'old man' taught at Sul Ross University?" Jess answered.

"*Si*, he retired long ago. He sick now!"

Jess coughed as dust from the dirt road came in the window of the back seat. "This isn't the road we took into town. Where are you headed?"

No reply from the front seat.

"How long has he been sick?" Jess asked. "I got a letter from him only last week."

This is unexpected bad news, and from a stranger. The professor is an important link in my research on mines in the Big Bend country south of here.

"He been sick long time," he answered as they turned through a gate and crossed the active runway to the aircraft parking area.

This guy drives like a wild man high on drugs, Jess thought.

Approaching the aircraft at full speed, *"Señor?"* He questioned and motioned with both hands off the steering wheel, as to where Jess' airplane was parked.

Jess yelled as they crossed the active runway again, "Watch for landing aircraft!"

"Que? Donde uno? Señor?" he asked again, spreading his arms in a wide arc over the dashboard toward the parked aircraft – then grabbed the steering wheel.

Jess leaned between the front seats and motioned toward the white and blue Pilatus, "The two-wheel, tail dragger, blue and white! It's a good thing this isn't a busy airport this afternoon. We could be in trouble crossing an active runway like that."

The way he darts between the parked aircraft, this taxi driver knows his way around. But, back home, the airport security would be all over him by now, Jess thought.

The taxi driver slid to a stop behind the Pilatus. Jess held tight to a door strap to keep from being tossed into the front seat. When the dust settled, he was looking into the barrel of what could have been a cannon.

Jess froze! *A stickup! I can see the silver slug in the cartridge down the barrel.*

"Mr. Hanes!" He whispered. "Jess, please continue to stay against the back seat and put your hands on your kneecaps."

What happened to the slurred Spanish accent? What's this all about? I'm not in the habit of having the 'bitter-end' of a gun pointing at me! Especially, right in my face! Jess did not panic, but stayed calm. *This guy is smiling like the canary that swallowed the cat. Lord Jesus, take care of this situation!*

The taxi driver's expression changed as he glanced past Jess, as if someone behind them was about to pounce.

The hole at the business end of the gun looked like a truck tunnel to Jess. He was going to speak, but the driver put his finger to his lips and motioned Jess to sit still. Taking his I.D. wallet from his shirt pocket, he let its flap open and gave Jess time to read it.

"Mexican Federal Agent, Chihuahua, Mexico: Donald Ramos Simms," Jess said. It was all he could read. The sweat ran down his forehead blurring his vision and stung, plus his thinking wasn't clear like it should have been in a panic situation. For some reason, Jess' mouth was too dry to speak.

He doesn't have any jurisdiction in the U.S. . . . Jess' thoughts began to run wild as the Mexican agent motioned him out of the car, then holstered his automatic as he grabbed Jess' arm. Jess turned to throw a punch, and he wasn't there. The agent had quickly moved to the rear of the taxi and opened the trunk. Jess got out on the opposite side away from the driver.

Agent Simms held up Jess' flight bag for him to carry. Then, he nodded toward the aircraft, and Jess followed cautiously. They stopped under the shade of its wing. The sun reflected off the hot metal, and the coolness of the shade felt good, plus a breeze began to rustle the red streamers on the propeller and exhaust covers.

Jess gave the agent a harsh look and dropped his bag under the fuselage. He was becoming very angry at this type of treatment from a law official.

"Mr. Hanes, please try to relax while I endeavor to explain what is happening," Agent Simms said, wiping the sweat from his neck and face with a handkerchief.

Jess folded his arms, "I certainly would hope so. It's not every day I get a gun stuffed up my nose. What's going on?"

"I need your immediate help," he said taking off his sunglasses and wiping his face with the handkerchief.

Jess was thinking, *'This guy can't really be doing this, and the thought of being hijacked is causing me to twitch a little. Why would he flash his gun, shove it in my face, and then flash his badge? Lord Jesus, something isn't quite right about this whole thing, and I need some answers.'*

"Please open the door to your aircraft and put your bag inside," he demanded. "We are being watched. Rather, I'm being watched. I have a feeling you may be here for the same reason I'm investigating for Professor Stapleton. I have reason to believe the taxi is bugged to listen to my conversations with people I pick up."

"Really!" Jess said. "That still doesn't explain your gun in my face."

Agent Simms took a deep breath, "That was to get your attention, in order to shut your mouth long enough to get you out

29

of the taxi. I'm on to something on the professor's ranch. He has hired me to solve some problems out there." He shifted his weight against the side of the fuselage back of the wing. For a big man, he was having a hard time breathing in the heat. "I am working with the Texas Rangers."

Jess wiped his face on his short sleeve shirt, watching Simms every move. *If he gives me a reason, I'll have to do something drastic. Lord Jesus! What, I don't know right now.*

"We are far enough away from the taxi for talking, so I'll hurry with my request." Simms leaned away from the aircraft, squinting his eyes and putting his sunglasses back on. "I've been watching visitors in and out of the airport, and those coming and going to the areas around his ranch. There seems to be a lot of traffic in his area with aircraft, four-wheel drive vehicles and horseback riders at night."

Simms stood up straight with his hands on his hips, "The noises close to his ranch house at night sound like trucks and helicopters. They are never around when I'm out there, and I'm not working alone. But, we still can't get a fix on them."

"What does this have to do with me?" Jess asked, pulling his campstool out of the back of the plane and setting in the shade. Simms declined the use of one. *This could take awhile*, Jess thought with a frown on his face, then folded his arms again.

"I lied about his sickness to get your mind off what I was trying to do," spreading his arms to express his frustrations, "and I wanted . . . " His dark face turned as white as the side of the aircraft. He stumbled backwards against it, sinking to his knees.

Jess thought he was having a heat stroke and jumped to grab his arms, letting him down under the fuselage for shade. Jess didn't realize what had happened until he saw blood oozing between Simms fingers, where he had grasped his side. Blood was smeared on the side of the aircraft where he slid down.

Jess felt his pulse, and it was beating hard and fast. *He's been shot and I didn't hear anything.*

Jess laid next to him on the ground, looking in the direction the bullet should have come from. *High hills in that direction,* he surveyed the area to the west, *and a ravine with large cottonwood trees. We need some protection from that direction.*

He grabbed Simms and pulled one of his arms around Jess' neck, dragging him down into a ditch back of a storage shed behind the aircraft. *Someone must have been a long way off or used a silencer. This guy's not looking good at all.*

Jess ripped open the front of Simms' shirt and stuffed his own wet handkerchief into the gaping bullet hole in Simms front side.

"This looks like the bullet was tumbling when it hit," Jess said, and rolled Simms' against his leg and found the exit hole. "This doesn't look too bad. The slug ripped completely through, and took part of you with it."

Jess grabbed Simms hand, "Give me your hand. Hold this handkerchief in place, and I'll use yours to plug the hole in your back. Then I'll get help!"

The hole in the back swallowed the handkerchief, so Jess stuffed Simms' shirttail into it as well. *That seems to stop the excessive bleeding,* Jess thought, pushing more of the shirt into the hole. He made Simms as comfortable as possible before standing up.

"Let me catch my breath," Simms said. "I've been shot before in Vietnam. Man! I sure have more pain now than I remember back then. Can't be I'm older!" Simms tried to straighten up off the ground, but stayed down. "Here, take my gun! Use it if you have to. They will kill us both if they have another chance."

"Who? Who is, *'they'*?" Jess asked.

Simms was beginning to cough up blood, which meant internal bleeding.

That wound didn't look that bad, Jess thought as he ripped open Simms' shirt. *Sure enough! There's a small hole below his left nipple oozing bubbles of blood.*

He used the other part of Simms' shirttail to plug the hole. His back, at the same level, showed no blood soaked through his shirt. *Lord, the slug is still inside his chest cavity, doing its damage. Lord Jesus, cancel that thought. No more damage!*

"I'm not going to last long," Simms sputtered. "In my jacket pocket are notes of my investigation for the professor. He hired me to find out who was on his ranch, but I found out more than that."

Jess nodded and waited for him to say more, but he passed out cold. He shoved an empty oil drum behind Simms, making a good backrest to keep the cloth in the bloody holes. He then slid two empty drums behind the empty one to hold it from sliding, and to provide some protection from other rifle shots.

The storage shed gave Jess enough cover to survey the area across the runway from where the shots came. He could not see anyone with a gun anywhere or anyone suspicious.

"They must have used either a sniper rifle or a long range varmint rifle," Jess said.

Now, what am I going to do for help? Wait a minute. Two shots at the same time, maybe two people fired together, who knows? My cellular phone is in the aircraft at least twenty yards away. I can make it.

Running back to Simms with the cell phone in his pocket, Jess could almost feel hot slugs slapping him in the back. He tripped and fell headlong past the oil drum Simms was propped against, rolled over next to him and dialed 911. While the phone went through it paces, Jess reached up and checked Simms' pulse. He waited for someone to answer, no ring back or recording. Simms' pulse was good, but weak.

Leaning against the oil drum next to Simms, Jess looked at the phone and dialed 911 again, noticing the antenna was not pulled out, he thought, *"No wonder, dummy!"*

"This is a recording for 911. You must use a local number for emergency calls, thank you." By then, Jess was about ready to throw the thing away. *Keep calm Jess, get your wits about you. You're shaking like a leaf. I need to get an ambulance out here, and now!*

Jess put the gun back in Simms' holster and stood up. *What's this all about, now? I can't believe this is happening to me again! I can't get involved in another shooting like back in Morocco. Plus, this will delay my research about Granddad Hanes.*

"Jess!" He yelled at himself. "He'll bleed to death before you ever figure out all of this!"

Jess looked around, nothing seemed out of place except the Mexican agent's lifeless form next to the barrel. Taking a chance again, he ran from behind the shed for the plane, dumped out the contents of his flight bag on the floor and grabbed the Texas Ranger radio. He kept looking around while strapping his gun in its holster around his waist.

As Jess ran over to the taxi, an aircraft landed and parked next to the terminal building. The passengers and pilot went inside and did not see him waving, or hear his hollering.

In the taxi, Jess spotted the two-way radio's handmic and began calling, "This is an emergency! Man shot at the airport! Anyone out there! Dispatch! This is an emergency!"

While waiting for a reply, Jess searched through Simms' jacket for his notes, finding the writing pad and address book. He stuffed them into his empty hip pocket along with Simms' I.D. wallet.

"Repeat that last message about someone shot at the airport. Who is this speaking?" she asked.

"This is Jess E. Hanes at the airport! Am I talking to Gladys?"

"Yes, Mr. Hanes, what do you need?"

"Send the police and an ambulance to the airport, now! I'm at the storage shed across the runway next to a white and blue aircraft. Hurry! This driver of yours will bleed to death! Over and out!"

"I understand!"

Running back over to the taxi driver, Jess was wondering who Donald Ramos Simms was? Is this a fake I.D., or is he for real? He squatted next to him, "Mr. Simms, I'm going to check your wounds again. Help is on the way."

No reply, but his bleeding had stopped, and his pulse seemed steadier than before. Good! Thank you Lord! Maybe he'll make it after all. Lord Jesus, please take care of his injuries.

Rio Grande River
Lajitas

CHAPTER FOUR

"Yes, we know about the problem Professor Stapleton was having," Brewster County Sheriff Baker said to Jess. The sheriff was looking at Simms' wounds. They were about to move Simms on the stretcher into the ambulance.

"Hey, Jones! You finished here?" Motioning with his hand at his deputy, and then to the emergency medical technician, "Okay! Get him in and over to the hospital, pronto!"

Looking at his notes about the shooting, he turned to Jess, "Now, Mr. Hanes, let's look at your aircraft. I'd like to have my men take photos. Show me again where you stood when Simms was shot."

Walking to the plane, he handed Jess' identification, pilot license and logbook to him. He impressed Jess as a thorough investigator, not only a county sheriff, but also a man of political significance. The sheriff knelt down next to the fuselage where the two holes were located in the side and checked the holes with a gauge for size. One slug had gone through the cargo sliding door and through both sides of the fuselage. The second slug made the same size hole as the first, six inches below the other, but from a different angle. One of his deputies pushed two long stainless steel rods through the two holes and out the other side.

"Let's go to the other side of the plane and get a bearing on where the slugs ended up," Sheriff Baker said. "Both are .308 slugs."

"Wait a minute! Two slugs went through the fuselage?" Jess put his hands on the rods protruding from the side of the aircraft. "I could find only one exit hole in the agents back…how did this second hole get here?"

"The doc will check him out further and make sure he doesn't have more holes in him," the sheriff replied.

The rods pointed approximately to the same spot, about a mile across to the nearest foothill, from where Jess thought the shots had come from. Sheriff Baker nodded. He was getting ready to ask a deputy for binoculars, when Jess handed him a pair from inside the plane.

Sheriff Baker pointed, "Jones, you and Evans go up on that hill over there and make a sweep along the ridge on this top side." Turning to Jess, "That is called, 'Lover's Lane.' We run off a lot of college kids in the evenings. Too many muggings up there at night."

He handed the binoculars back to Jess, "Thanks! That's a nice pair. Need to get a more powerful one, too." Then he asked for the deputy's camera, knelt down and took a picture toward the hill. "Jones, find any slugs over here?"

The deputy sheriff shook his head, no.

"Sheriff Baker, try these binoculars by using one eyepiece, the one you can focus with the center adjustment. I used it this way in the military and got some good snapshots. You should be able to get a good close photo of the hill from here."

He tried to look through the camera and focus the binoculars, but could not keep them together long enough to take a picture. Jess motioned to lay it on the top of the fuselage, letting him know that he would hold it steady for the sheriff.

"Thanks. I'll have to remember that little trick and use it again. Maybe my brother-in-law can make a jig of some type to do the same holding job." He handed the binoculars to Jess, "So again, what is your business here with Professor Stapleton, all the way from the hill country of Austin?"

Jess took the other campstool from the aircraft, offering him a seat. They sat in the shade of a big cottonwood tree. Its shadow had moved across the taxiway, covering the planes, cooling things down. "Don't have any iced tea to offer you, sorry!" he said and then, continued, "but, to answer your question... I'm researching my grandfather's activities during the time that he lived further down in the Big Bend area… in the 30's. He passed away some thirty years ago. I have an appointment to interview the professor this afternoon at two o'clock."

Looking at his watch, it was after two already, "Dog-gone it! I'm late," Jess said. "He sent me some letters about Granddad Hanes some weeks ago, and I was to visit with him at his ranch today." Jess stood and folded the campstool. "I'm late now. I suppose I better call him on my cellular phone."

"Sure, if you don't mind my listening to your own conversation? But you may get a bad reception down in this part of the state… too many mountains between cell phone towers."

"No problem, Sheriff!"

Jess extended the antenna as they walked back toward the aircraft. He took a pocket phone directory out of the flight bag in the baggage cabin and searched for the professor's number.

"What exactly did your grandfather do for a living down in the Big Bend during the 30's?" Sheriff Baker asked. "There wasn't much going on in those days other than ranching or mining."

Jess pushed the antenna back in place and laid the cell phone on the floor of the aircraft. "He was involved in more than what I had known about or ever expected. He was an on-the-road salesman… whatever he could pick up to sell. Remember, during the WWII years, things like silk stockings, real estate, and curios to the white man along the Rio Grande; these were his trade. He mined for silver, gold and cinnabar. You know, quicksilver down in the Terlingua area when the mines were in operation?"

Sheriff Baker looked like he was getting drowsy sitting there with his eyes almost closed, "He must have been a loner to come down here?"

"You're right, Sheriff, he called himself the Hermit, among other names. He even drove mule wagons for the mines on his first job. I did a lot of historical research on Indian diggings for the University of Texas. It's somewhere around Paisano Peak and Calamity Creek."

Swallowing a couple of mouthfuls of water, Jess continued, "I remember as a kid, he would take me out in the sand hills of Monahans to go hunting for Indian relics."

"Sounds as if you two were close," the sheriff commented.

"It was during WWII when my parents were involved with the war effort... he would take care of me for a week or so. Yes, we were close pals."

One of the county deputies came toward them with his dog, "Sam's ready, Sheriff."

"Mind if we search your aircraft for drugs? You never know who was out here last night while you were at the Settler's Hotel."

"Help yourself. Open both doors so you can get some air through there," Jess said resting on his campstool.

The deputy led his dog through, around, under and over every inch that it could search. Inside, behind the front seats where the back seats were missing, the dog stopped at one of the holes in the side of the aircraft where a bullet had entered.

"Well, look at this, Sheriff. You want this in a plastic bag?"

He leaned in the pilot's side, looking at what the deputy was pointing at. He grinned and nodded, "Yeah, better take that along, too. But, I don't think Mr. Simms will be needing that piece of flesh."

The bullet had exited Simms' body and carried a piece of his flesh through the hole in the aluminum side. Then it caught on the inside of the insulation; it just hung there. The police dog sat looking at it with a questioning expression on its face.

"The aircraft is clean, Sheriff," the deputy said. Afterwards, he left in a county police van. The sheriff motioned Jess to go with him to his car.

Reaching inside the trunk of his vehicle, Sheriff Baker handed Jess his Colt .45 automatic, "Here's your pistol. I would put those other guns that are in the plane under lock and key; especially, if you leave them out here."

The two men shook hands, "Try to keep in contact; I may come up with some interesting facts about the shooting. Have a safe flight if you go out to the ranch; or, a nice stay at the Settlers Hotel, tonight."

"Thanks," Jess replied.

He waved goodbye to the sheriff, turned and walked back to his aircraft. Folding the campstools and placing them back into the aircraft, Jess extended the antenna on his cell phone and called the professor. Jess sat inside the open cargo door entrance in the shade. It was getting warmer.

Jess explained the delay to Professor Stapleton, who understood what had happened and said he would expect Jess later that afternoon by car, which Jess had planned to rent from the Settler's Hotel.

He turned, studying the two holes in the aircraft. "How come there's two holes, but Simms only had two in and one out?" Then, he went to the taxicab.

Jess called Gladys and told her he would deliver the cab to the Settler's Hotel. He put his briefcase in the passenger's seat and headed to town.

CHAPTER FIVE

It was at least four hours to sunset. Jess drove west out of Alpine on US 90 to the Twin Peaks location and then, south about fifteen miles on a winding, paved county road. The drive was good therapy, allowing him time to rehearse the events of the morning at the restaurant and the shooting at the airport. He had to turn on the air conditioner; the car's dark blue color attracted the sun, causing it to be extremely hot without the cool air blowing.

The rugged mountains in their own mysterious ways seemed to swallow the road winding through the deep valley, barren except for spotted growths of cedar, mesquite, tumble weed, cactus, agave and yucca. The sun cast its shadow over the valley except for brief cuts in the cliffs where it was blinding to drive toward, causing Jess to pull down the visor.

The ancient stories told by the Comanche, Apache and the Caddo Indians uncovered the forced migration to the area Jess was traveling. Prior to the U.S. Government placing Indians on reservations, either the enemy Indian tribes or the white man forced them to survive in the southwest rough country of Texas. Many stories told by their ancestors of the bearded white man and black soldiers forcing tribal movement further from the north and east. Jess had come to enjoy stories about the native Indians of the southwest, and especially white man's settling in the Big Bend country.

He began to relax while driving the empty traveled road to the professor's ranch house.

Abruptly, the road angled to the right with a steep incline wrapped around the faces of sheer cliffs. In low gear, he let the car's engine break its forward motion, taking it down and around hairpin turns, toward a distant canyon valley fifteen hundred feet below. The reddish gray cast of the cliffs with their shadows made the walls look deeper than they actually were.

Jess could see a line of cottonwood, willow and cedar trees along the edge of a creek meandering through the valley. It was the only green vegetation he could see from his altitude. A ranch house and barns, not far from the creek, looked only a rock's throw away from the east line of cliffs behind them. A dirt airstrip paralleled the creek across from the barns, running east to west.

Jess thought, *Perhaps one of the barns stored an aircraft. That must be the professor's ranch.*

In the distance, the valley opened toward low desert plains to the west; to the south, the Chisos Mountains of the Big Bend rose like a fortress from the desert floor. Off in the far distance, a blue silhouette of another mountain range could be seen, the Sierra Madre Mountains in old Mexico.

Jess could hardly take in the vastness before him. "What a breath taking view in all directions!" he said to himself.

The paved road became level in the valley where it passed the entrance to the ranch. Jess could not see the ranch house because it was down beyond small rolling hills, but he could still see the treetops. Turning off the county road, crossing a cattle guard with five feet high brick walls on both sides, he continued onto a smooth graveled drive.

Professor Stapleton's ranch house was located on a slow rising valley floor from west to east. The rimmed rocked cliffs to the north kept the sun's heat in the valley, but the cooler east winds dropped the temperature in the evening hours.

The cloud of dust behind Jess' approach to the ranch announced his arrival to the front of the large, remodeled, two-story white ranch house. The old style covered porch extended across the full south front and around the west and the east side of the house. It was an ideal picture for any country magazine of ranch homes, sturdy and livable. The barns and corrals to the east of the house had a fresh coat of red and white paint. They boldly stood out against the grayish brown cliffs behind them.

The interview Jess had prepared with the professor should cover how well Professor Stapleton had known his Granddad Hanes, and if the professor had any correspondence with him before he died in the late nineteen forties.

Wish I had had the time to read Agent Simms' notes before coming out here, too late now. I'm sure he knows someone's here, the dogs at the barn are barking. Jess knocked at the door a couple of times, no answer. Passing the porch swing, he went to another door at the other end of the porch, which continued along the west side of the house. Again, there was no answer to Jess' knock.

Maybe he's out in the back or over at the barns.

Jess walked down the west porch steps to the yard and around the edge of the porch parallel with the south front where he met a large, vicious looking, snarling dog.

The dog held its ground and Jess froze in his steps waiting for the next move. Out of the corner of Jess' left eye, he saw someone moving towards him, but he kept both eyes on the dog.

Lord, I would hate to kill it! A good watchdog is hard to come by! But, if it attacks!

A deep voice from the shadows yelled, "Stranger! Do not move! Stand where you are! I have a rifle pointed at you," the man said with a European accent.

Right out of the movies, word for word. But, what accent is that? Italian, German!

Jess could see the man who yelled at him limping with a cane in one hand, and an automatic rifle aimed at Jess cradled under the man's other arm, "State your business!"

He was a tall, lanky gentleman in his mid-eighties with a weather-tanned face like most west Texas ranchers. He reminded

Jess of his mother's father who was a rancher during World War II.

Giving Jess a stern look waiting for an answer, he took another step toward him. When the man moved, his dog made a couple more advances toward Jess, close enough that he could touch the top of his head with an out-stretched arm. Jess did not want to take his eyes off the eyes of the dog. *Sure as I do, he'll be on me. We're almost eyeball-to-eyeball, and I don't want to blink. I don't want to get bit.*

"Professor Stapleton! I'm Jess Hanes! Called you earlier!"

"Snake! Barn!" he yelled over the other dogs barking out back of the house. Jess was glad those dogs weren't with this one.

"Snake, I said get to the barn! Snake!" he took a step toward the dog swung his cane at its backside, missed. The dog knew that the boss had spoken, and the next swat, would hit the mark. Wagging its tail, the black mongrel licked Jess' hand and retreated toward the barn.

"Well! I have never witnessed that before," he said shuffling closer to Jess. "Now, can you produce any identification proving who you are? My eyesight is not what it once was. Move your hands slowly. I am a dead shot with this rifle! Especially at this range," he warned.

"Yes, Sir! I have my ID in my left hip pocket. You can check with Sheriff Baker in town. He left the airport the same time that I did." Slowly taking it from his hip pocket, Jess laid his ID on the porch floor and stepped backwards away from it.

"Now, move further away please!" He almost lost his balance reaching for Jess' ID across the flowerbed. Professor Stapleton never took his eyes from Jess and moved away from the flowerbed.

"Mr. Hanes, move up on the porch ahead of me and keep your hands where I can see them." Jess could hear Professor Stapleton coming up the steps behind him. The professor stumbled and let out a loud moan when he hit the ground. He had fallen sideways into the empty flowerbed. Jess turned around to see the rifle in the yard, but only the professor's feet on the edge of the steps.

Jess ran over to the edge of the porch, "Are you alright, Professor?" He jumped into the flowerbed and offered his hand, "Can I help you up?"

"No! I can get up by myself, thank you! I missed that second step and figured this was the softest place to fall," he said, while rising. Shaking the dirt and leaves off, he got to his knees and then stood.

"I will throw that damnable cane away yet! It almost killed me again! I am getting too dependent upon it. If my daughter had not insisted, I would not be using it at all!" Smiling, he extended his hand to Jess.

"Jess, it is good to finally meet you, face to face. You look like a 'Hanes'... your dad and his brothers for sure." He leaned into Jess' grip, "Have not lost my grip on things yet, but you can help me up these steps, please."

Finally, on the porch, Jess realized he did not have his wallet, "You dropped my wallet. May I go get it?"

"Certainly!" he said. "I will wait for you, and while you are there, bring me that rifle. Make certain it is still on safety... Please!"

On the porch again, Jess followed him into a large front room with an old fashion fan hanging from a high cathedral ceiling. A huge stone fireplace in the far corner had a purple marble mantle, and two large kerosene lamps on each end. Next to the heavy wooden door was a large front window covering the ceiling to the floor, which Professor Stapleton opened.

One bay picture window gave a panoramic view of the west to the mountains in Mexico. The hardwood floor was covered with an Indian-patterned woven rug. The room had to be at least

45

twenty degrees cooler than what it was on the porch, with just the south windows open for a breeze.

"You have air conditioning out here, Professor?"

"No, too expensive! Too noisy, plus I do not need it. I can manage to cool off if I am too hot," he said lighting his pipe and having a seat next to the porch windows. The old rocking chair rails creaked when he leaned back and began to rock slowly.

"Ah, yes! There will be a good breeze this evening," he said with a heavy accent, but with very distinct English. "If you care to smoke, you may do so!"

"No, thank you," Jess replied, "I quit back in the seventies. But, I do like the smell of good pipe tobacco. In fact, it makes my mouth water. When I get around tobacco shops, my taste buds begin to flow, can't help it."

"I know what you mean," he said as he settled down for a long afternoon talk. "Nothing can compare to an excellent pipe with a superior blend of tobacco."

Along the three front walls of the room, between the opened, screened windows, were walnut shelves with antique clocks of all sizes and shapes. In the four corners of the room stood tall, stately grandfather clocks, striking the deep quarter hour and hourly Westminster chiming tones. Their loud, uneven, ticking together, soon became unnoticed after the conversation rambled from his beautiful home to his favorite dog, Snake.

"You have a excellent collection of clocks, "Jess said. "My father-in-law makes grandfather clocks from solid oak and walnut planks. He has collected clocks for over fifty years."

"Thank you," the professor replied. "They are exceptional, are they not? I accumulated these noisy pieces of history for about that same length of time. Some of them, I acquired from the old country, Europe, on my many travels. I have no inkling what is in my inventory, but the count is well over one hundred."

He knocked out the burnt tobacco from his pipe into an old fashion ashtray table next to his rocking chair.

"Do you drink iced tea?" he asked as he stood.

Jess nodded, "Yes, Sir."

"Tell me what the sheriff was doing at the airport. You know him?" He went into the kitchen and came back with two, tall, frosted glasses of tea, "Excuse me, do you use sugar or lemon? I can take the lemon slice out if you prefer."

"No sugar, but I do like lemon or lime. This is great, thank you, Professor."

"Please drop the professor title," he replied. "We have been friends by letter and through your grandfather for many years. My name is Jonathan. Preferably, my friends call me, 'John'." Squinting at Jess with a nod, "Yes, I consider you one of my friends. I do apologize for my rude welcome. I have problems here on the ranch with unwanted visitors, which I will share with you later."

John sat his tea glass on the hardwood floor next to the ashtray and stuffed fresh tobacco from its pouch into an oval-shaped bowl pipe. It was a different pipe than he smoked earlier. While this activity was taking place, he restarted his slow rocking in his comfortable, wooden rocker. Jonathan Stapleton was very active, but at this moment in time, he was a man of leisure with his life collections around him.

Not only the clocks throughout his home, but rows of shelves lined his study, right inside the porch door. Jonathan gave Jess a tour, displaying proudly his numerous books that would make any library envious. Jess was tempted to ask permission to look through them, but not now, maybe later. Jess scrutinized the room of its contents as Jonathan pointed out every detail, and then he noticed a doorway into another room lined with bookshelves. John had a life's fortune in literature at his fingertips, and Jess knew he could spend hours just thumbing through them all.

They walked back to the front room and sat in their rocking chairs.

"We have been side-tracked by the pleasures of peace and quietness, so back to the events at hand," John said.

"Yes," Jess replied, "you asked about the county sheriff! No, I don't know him. I only met him today at the airport." He began to tell John about his arrival, spending the night, and the taxi ride to the airport.

After another swallow of the delicious iced tea, Jess continued about the shooting of the Mexican agent, and how he had told Jess about working for the professor.

"Who did you say he was?" he asked angrily in disbelief with a shocked look on his face.

"The name on his identification was Simms, a Donald Ramos Simms."

John stopped rocking and pushed himself to the edge of the seat, tipping the rocker forward, and set the iced tea glass on the floor next to the ashtray stand. He frowned while running this information over in his mind, tapping his fingers across the top of his knees.

"Please hand me that portable phone next to you. This will not be a private conversation! Sit still and take notes!"

Professor Stapleton spoke like he was directing a college student, and then dialed a local number. Jess could hear it ringing, "Sheriff's department, Sergeant Higgins speaking."

The expression on his face became firm business, and his tone of voice was with authority. "Sergeant Higgins, Sheriff Baker, please! Professor Stapleton calling, this is an emergency!"

"Just a minute, Professor! He's just arrived. Sheriff!" The sergeant yelled, waving the phone over his head. "It's for you! Professor Stapleton!"

John frowned while holding the telephone away from his ear. "Yelling like that, he must have been a mile away!" Placing the phone to his ear again, "I'll obtain straight answers for us."

After a short pause, they could hear noise in the background from the telephone and the office door slamming shut.

"Professor, how is everything out there at the ranch?" he asked. The volume was turned up on the telephone so that Jess could hear the sheriff clearly.

"What's this about Agent Simms being shot at the airport this morning?"

"Yes, Sir! That's right," the sheriff said. "Mr. Hanes must be with you now?"

"He just told me about the whole sordid situation. What have you ascertained from the investigation of the matter? I terminated his hire last week for being a slacker! He may have tried to hustle Mr. Hanes the same way he tried hustling me."

Jess was surprised at the cold attitude he had toward Agent Simms, wondering what the real problems were.

"I haven't found much of anything at this time, just getting back in the office," Sheriff Baker replied. "Three other cases today, plus this one. So, I'll stay on top of the matter and handle it personally. There will be a report for you every morning if you wish."

"That is not necessary. Let me know what develops, and why he was shot and by whom."

Jess stood up and moved his rocker closer to Professor John, "Ask how Agent Simms is getting along, and the name of the hospital where they took him."

"What is the latest condition on Agent Simms, Sheriff?" John asked.

"I don't really know! He was flown to St. David's Hospital in El Paso for special surgery," the sheriff said. "That was at the request of another state agency."

"Thank you! I will be calling for updates," the professor said, and then turned the remote telephone off and handed it to Jess.

He pushed back into his large rocker, lit his pipe, took a few puffs to get it going good, and reached down for the iced tea glass. Leaning back again, he took a long sip of tea. Holding the pipe between his teeth, he puffed a few more times and contemplated what had happened.

Jess felt like he could help in answering some of his questions, but he didn't want to break John's train-of-thought. The comfortable breeze, quietness, his tobacco scent, iced tea and easiness with Jess' presents, caused a calm to settle over them both. *After what had happened today, it was a pleasure to relax again,* Jess thought to himself.

CHAPTER SIX

"This is Captain Charles Randel, Texas Ranger in the Midland Office, calling for Captain Jack Randel."

A reply from the other end, "He is not here, Captain."

Moving the Venetian blind blades apart with a finger, Charles glanced out the office building from the seventh floor, "Have him contact me ASAP! It's about our Uncle Jess down in Alpine."

"It shouldn't be long, twenty minutes or so. I'll make certain that he gets your message, Captain. He went to the restroom."

Leaving the message with the Ranger down south working with Jack; his brother, Charles walked away from the transmitter scratching his tickling nose. *What has Uncle Jess gotten himself into now,* he was thinking. *Hope it's not connected with his Moroccan trip from a few years ago or September eleventh?*

He went back to the fax machine and tore off the message he had received a few minutes earlier, 'Attention: Captain Randel. Airport shooting of Agent Simms near Jess E. Hanes' aircraft. Alpine, Texas… Contact, Sheriff Baker, Brewster county.'

"Uncle Jess has witnessed another shooting?" Charles said to himself. "How in the world does he manage to always be at the wrong place at the wrong time?"

Walking over to the wall map of the West Texas District, he talked to himself, "I can rent a helicopter and be there in a few hours. I have plenty of vacation time on the books. I better do it, because he'll need a bodyguard now. I can cover this on my own time."

"Captain Randal, what's up?"

Not aware of the news that Charles had received, a young ranger walked in and sat down in the chair next to Charles' desk.

Not turning around, Charles held up one finger, "Just a minute, please!"

A long period of silence studying the wall map, he turned and tossed keys to Lieutenant Roger Hicks, "Take two M16 rifles and a riot shotgun from the storage room. Has the border gear been re-supplied from last shift?"

"Yes Sir! Where's the war, Captain?" Nodding an anxious reply, "The gear is in my truck."

"Big Bend country," Charles replied, "and, it's hot tamales down there."

With a worried look on his face, Charles wrote a list of additional field gear, signed it and handed it to the lieutenant. "Get this issued to you, and get our field pickup truck with a horse trailer set-up. Pick up our horses at the corral, and have them outfitted and ready. You'll leave as soon as I get authorization from the Major for you."

"Yes, Sir, but where am I going, and where are you off to now?"

"That information is confidential," Charles replied. "I'm flying down to meet Captain Jack Randel at Alpine."

The lieutenant left the office as Charles talked to Major Hawkins in El Paso on a voice scrambled secure telephone system.

"Major, this is Captain Charles Randel in Midland. Please put your phone on scramble."

"Go ahead. What's up, Charles?"

Trying to hold down his emotions, "Remember my Uncle Jess Hanes and his Moroccan adventure a few years ago? He has again, according to the message from the Brewster County Sheriff in Alpine, been a witness to a shooting. It involves Agent '*Licito Dimino.*' I don't have a lot of details at this time, but I'm requesting annual leave to go down and support him."

Silence on the line from El Paso, then, "How did your Uncle Jess manage to do this again?"

"My very words, Sir!"

"You have full authorization as of the end of this conversation, and it will be sent to all field offices. You'll get a message in writing to that effect. Let me know what you need, and I'll get the Governor's assistance. Take the two new Ranger helicopters in Midland. I'll send a release to you."

"Thank you, Sir. They will be handy. I'm sending Lieutenant Hicks down with horses and trailer; we may need them," Charles said. "Captain Jack Randel is still near Terlinga and Presidio. So, he'll be available for support."

Major Hawkins replied, "Fine, you do what is deemed necessary; you're in charge of this assignment. Which reminds me, you're not to take annual leave. This is business as usual and our team member, Simms, is in trouble with Mr. Hanes involved."

The fax machine in Charles' office started receiving a message, "Just a minute, Major. Something is coming in on the fax; it may relate to the Alpine situation."

"I'm holding!"

Charles' telephone cord was stretched to its limits as he reached and tore the message from the machine. "Yes, Sir. It's from Brewster County Sheriff Baker in Alpine. Simms is in need of emergency surgery. Should I have them fly him to El Paso, St. David's Hospital? It's closer than Austin!"

"Do it! We need him! He has all the information about the problems down there. Got to go now, the Governor's meeting is in fifteen minutes. Good luck, Son!"

"Thanks, Major. I'll keep in touch."

CHAPTER SEVEN

Professor Stapleton left the room while Jess was checking the books on the shelves. History had always held his attention, so he picked out one on the Civil War engagements at Franklin, Tennessee. Turning with his back to the outside light from the windows, he noticed a basket of detailed knitting near one of the grandfather clocks.

Jess closed the book, placed it under his arm, and picked up the knitting. When he did, one of the needles fell out and made a loud racket as it hit the floor and bounced, and bounced and bounced again, coming to rest against his boot. The Professor began laughing in the other room.

"Hope I didn't mess this up," Jess said.

Coming back in the room with photos and a bundle of letters, John said, "There is no way you have messed up anything. I have taken knitting as therapy to keep my fingers limber. It helps work out the pain of arthritis. It is one of my many hobbies which keeps me occupied since Doris died."

He pulled a coffee table between the two rockers and laid the photos and letters in the middle. Jess picked up the needle and handed him the knitting bundle.

"What's it going to be," Jess asked.

"Well, I really do not know this time. I am knitting and purling." He smiled over his bifocals. "It may turn out to be an Afghan spread or a cover for one of those pillows on the divan over there. I cannot say on that piece. As you can see, I have just started it. Now, is not that silly and childish for my age?" John said, rocking and puffing his pipe.

Jess chuckled. He understood why Granddad Hanes' liked John... so laid back, "Nope, I don't think so. If it's what pleases you out here alone, do it. Who's going to complain about not feeding the chickens or milking the cows?"

Laughing heartily, "Yes! Especially, when I do not have either one!"

Where have I detected that accent before? It is definitely European, maybe German or Dutch. But, from where? Hey, I made a 'funny' for him, how did that happen? Jess put the knitting back in the basket and pointed over to the items on the coffee table.

"We have much to talk about and many decisions to make," John said spreading the old black and white photos on the table. He began sharing prospecting and deer hunting trips that he had experienced with Jess' Granddad Hanes. He picked through the letters looking for special ones to read, while relating their situations.

"I still remember and enjoyed the many stories your Granddad wrote about the Big Bend country. They would excite me enough, I would go down and prospect with him. Many times in his letters he would tell me, 'Don't grade my spelling or sentence structure like you do them fancy college boys, just read it.'"

Smiling, he lit his pipe again, filling the room with its sweet scent, "I was happy to receive your printed copy of other stories and letters of his in book form. That was a nice Christmas present you gave to his grandchildren, and I appreciated the copy as well."

Looking as if he had just remembered something, he left the room telling Jess, "By the way, before I forget it again, I have been meaning to send you something for a long time. I have one of his letters," snickering to himself. "No one knew about it for years, not until recently."

John spryly walked to the windows, without his cane, and lowered the bamboo curtains to the bottom of the windowsills.

The breeze pushed them away at the bottom, and they lightly slapped back against the window frame, making a hollow banging sound. He locked the front door and nodded for Jess to follow him.

Turning around, pausing, listening, he retrieved his cane. John opened the large, etched glass front door of a huge grandfather clock next to the staircase. Stopping the pendulum from swinging, he moved the minute and hour hands to four o'clock. It struck the normal four times for the hour. He reached inside behind the Swiss workings of the clock and released a lever. A soft click could be heard as the whole clock case moved away from the wall.

He glanced over his shoulder at Jess and then toward the front door, listening, and then with a twinkle in his eye, turned to the opening in the wall, behind the grandfather clock.

Motioning with his finger for Jess to follow, he said, "Remember, this is our secret, just you and me. What I have to show you may in the future involve the both of us with the federal government."

Jess nodded and followed reluctantly into a huge walk-in vault under the stairs with two safes, one atop the other. It looked like the inside of a bank vault room.

"Could have fooled me," Jess said with his mouth open in surprise, "This is something else, very nice, dry and secure."

There were rows of books and papers stacked upon stacks to the ceiling of the vault. He reached into one stack and handed Jess an envelope with no address on it.

Jess had that normal puzzled look on his face.

"I have been waiting a long time to give you this," John said. "I thought that I would be dead first, and that you would not get it," he said glancing at the envelope.

It had turned brown from age and felt brittle handling it. Jess turned it over, and his name was on it. 'Jess E. Hanes, from your

Grandfather Hanes.' It was handwritten, with an old-fashioned ink pen. The envelope was heavy at one end, weighted by a small key inside. It had its imprint on both sides of the envelope.

"Better light out there," John said, motioning Jess back into the front room.

Jess turned to walk back past the clock and noticed a sophisticated alarm system mounted in the corner of it at the floor. The system couldn't be seen from a front view of the clock, even if one were standing over it looking down. Back in the room, John closed his secrets away and pointed to another door at the side of the clock. It opened to stairs down into the basement where he wanted Jess to follow him again.

This gentleman grows more mysterious at each turn of his living room. Jess started to open the envelope before going down in the basement.

John requested, "Wait! Wait before you look at it, please."

Jess could see the staircase had not been used for a long time because dead spiders were still in their webs hanging from the hand railing to the floor. Dust was at least half-an-inch deep on the stairs, and billowed from under their shoes as they eased their way to the basement floor.

The empty, musty basement was lit dimly by a small bulb covered with dirt. From the floor above, cold, bare, stone walls jutted out, and on the dirt floor, was a lonely solitaire object - - an old antique pedal sewing machine in the middle of the room. Its canvas cover had layers of dust… years of collecting and being untouched. The design on the foot pedals were buried level in dust.

Jess was still clinging lightly to the old crusted envelope with as much tenderness as possible. Not knowing what it was all about, he turned in his dusty tracks looking at the four empty rock walls. No pipes in the floor above, only the electric wire to the bulb, and no windows to the outside. The vault's cement floor upstairs was at least four feet thick.

He surmised, *'This basement would be a safe place from storms and tornadoes or to hide anything else that would not go into the safe.'*

CHAPTER EIGHT

The small county sheriff's office was busy with activity: personnel on telephones, others interrogating suspects, officers escorting prisoners to the cells in the back, idle talk between officers and secretaries.

The front desk officer on duty answered a telephone call, "Brewster County Sheriff's Department, Corporal Jones speaking."

"Sheriff Baker please, Captain Charles Randal, Texas Ranger's office calling from Midland," a soft feminine voice announced.

Corporal Jones replied, "Yes, he's here. Hang on please and I'll call him. Hey Sheriff! It's the Texas Rangers in Midland on line two."

"Okay! Okay! I'm not in the next county you know," he answered toward the outer office through the glass window of his office. He walked around his desk, across his room and shut the door. Then he pointed at Jones, shook his finger at him and returned to the telephone.

"Sheriff Baker here."

The nice soft voice said, "Captain Charles Randal is on the line. Captain Charles Randal, this is Sheriff Baker in Alpine on the line for you."

Baker looked at his telephone receiver and thought, *'I don't believe what I'm hearing.'* He waited for a few seconds and said, "This is Sheriff Baker go ahead."

"Sorry, Sheriff, new secretary started today. I'll try to make this short. I read your report on the airport shooting and Jess Hanes' involvement. Is he still there?"

"Yes, he is out at Professor Stapleton's ranch as we speak. He had some business with the professor in relation to his grandfather. Why do you ask? Problems? Know him?"

"He's my uncle, Sheriff. I need some assistance to insure his safety, as well as the professor's safety. It all relates to Simms being shot. Also, did you get Simms rerouted to El Paso?"

"Yes!" he said. "But, the hospital flew him to Austin. They couldn't handle his injury in El Paso, which shocked me! I thought they could handle anything, especially with all the military in the area." He hesitated. "Anyway, you have our support. What do you need from me?"

"Uncle Jess is a semi-retired government agent with the Overseas Investigations Agency and CIA, plus a bunch of other things. He still has the government's most sensitive secret clearance. So, he is cleared for *Licito Dimino*."

"That's nice to know. It's great we don't have a green civilian on our hands," the sheriff said.

"I'll explain more when I get there in a few hours. Until then, can you make a social call out to the ranch with good reliable backup?"

"Sure we can, no problem. I'll be out there in thirty minutes."

Charles replied, "Great, I'll need your most trusted men to be with you. However, keep that number low - - top priority and confidential, no media is to know! I have another Ranger on his way to you now, with horses."

Sheriff Baker looked up, glancing out the window into the other offices. Corporal Jones was listening on the extension, "Captain, we will comply!" the sheriff said, and hung up the phone.

"Jones, get your butt in here!" he yelled so loud it startled everyone outside his office. Jones almost dropped the phone, but gently placed it in its cradle.

"I'll put you in one of those cells back there. How many times are we going to have this talk, Jones?" He yelled standing outside his door, waiting for Jones to hustle passed him.

"You don't listen worth a damn to my orders, do you? How many times do you have to be told not to listen to other people's conversations on the phone? Do you understand? You are not to listen to my phone conversations! Or anyone else's!" He shouted, like the old drill sergeant he once was. Looking up, he noticed that he was in the white face of his new recruit, almost nose to nose.

Sheriff Baker was thinking, *Jones could be the leak in my sheriff's department.*

"But Cap, I thought it was important from the Texas Rangers," he said sheepishly.

"Damn it, Jones, don't call me Cap. I'm Sheriff Baker to you! Do you understand?" Throwing up his hands and shaking his head, "What is happening to this younger generation? Where is your common sense?"

The younger generation stood stiff as a board, at attention, not wanting to say another word. He was scared that the sheriff would fire him, and he wanted to stay.

"Never mind what else I'm thinking!" Sheriff Baker said. "No more listening in on phone calls. Got it! No more! In fact, you are not to answer the phone if someone else is in the office. Understand?" His face was getting redder with each word. "Get out of my office! Send in Sergeants Blaine and Shanks!"

Jones just stood in place, frozen to the spot.

"Jones!"

"Yes, Sir! Right now, Sir!" he said stepping around the sheriff on his way out of the office.

CHAPTER NINE

Governor Sticker nodded impatiently to Texas Ranger, Major Hawkins, as they entered the conference room at the Texas Ranger Regional Office, "I'm behind schedule, Major! Let's get this decision over with now. You see, I'm due to leave for Austin in an hour."

Shaking hands, the major motioned toward a large Texas map on the cedar-paneled wall behind his desk.

"As you know, Governor, the Lajitas, Marfa, Terlingua and Presidio areas of southwest Texas are open ranges of cattle country along the Rio Grande, as well as the Davis and Santiago Mountains," he said, pointing to the Big Bend country on the map. "The Rio Grande runs down the border between us and Mexico, along here, south passed Brewster and Presidio counties." Using his white pointer stick, he continued, "We are having great problems with illegal migrants, drugs, dangerous waste and cattle rustling all through this area."

Governor Sticker interrupted with a cough, "Major, I don't need a review of the matter, and I'm damn sure that I don't need a Texas geography lesson. Get on with it!" Impatiently, he purposely looked at the wall clock, and then motioned the major to continue.

Major Hawkins smiled to himself while facing the map. He thought, *'Just what I wanted the Governor to do, make an impatient authorization for my request,'* and then he pressed on, "Thousands of acres of unfenced prairies and mountains stretch as far as the eyes can see. This area," pointing again to Brewster County, "of west Texas has distances of eighty to a hundred miles between towns. The law enforcement agencies cannot cover this adequately and still be effective."

The major moved to the side of his desk, "There is a growing concern among the land owners, who are very strong supporters of yours, that the protection needed by them is not available. Tourist trade has fallen off in these areas because of the increasing drug traffic, illegal foreign and Mexican immigrants, and hostile Texans taking the law into their own hands. Economical growth is decreasing at a frightening rate."

Calmly as the major could, knowing he was running out of time with the governor, he said forcefully, "And, my hottest aggravation of all is that Texas is losing the lives of its own people and transients. I haven't been able to stop that from happening. You know as well as I do, that there is an increase of shooting across the Rio Grande from both sides." He wadded up a piece of scrap paper with notes on it, throwing it into a wastepaper basket. "We need more funding and more men... not only for the Texas Rangers, but for the county sheriff departments and Border Patrol down there."

"Even with the boosting of forces since 9-11, we are weak!" With a finger in the air, "The state police are not even accounted for down there!" Red in the face, he turned to the governor, who had taken a seat on the major's desk corner. "This is wide open country and there are few bodies to cover it."

"Bottom line, Major!"

Going to the map on the wall again, the major traced the United States border on the Texas border, "Immediately, we specifically need coverage in this area between Langtry and up to Presidio, in the Big Bend country."

"Major!" Almost with a shout, standing up and spreading his arms, "What do you want from me? The government has doubled the Border Patrol and I.N.S.! What do you want? I'm running out of time here. Besides, that is a federal park down there, not state!"

"I need an open-ended authorization to use what is available to stop these problems. Special helicopters in Midland are ready to leave now, and a satellite link has been set up with Washington and Interpol. I didn't want to go behind your back to get this accomplished." He was about to lose his patience with the governor, "That is why I've delayed and pressured you here and now. You can activate the National Guard and Reservist along the border!"

Stomping his foot and facing his aide, the Governor said, "Why wasn't I informed of this problem prior to now? Why weren't these matters brought to my attention before I took office? I've been in office only one year, and I'm drowning with demands! Where's the break in my communications?" With his hands on his hips, he continued, "Major, you have my authorization and full cooperation. My assistant will fax you a written copy from my aircraft, and it will be done before we get to Austin! Right?" He turned, looking at his two aides. They nodded their heads, yes. "Good!" Turning to the major, "I'll give you my contacts in Washington, as well."

He headed for the double doors of the major's office, "Keep me informed daily on this and call me on the hot line. I want to hear from you personally!"

"Yes, Sir! And, don't forget Governor... no news media!"

The Governor was almost out of earshot and did not reply to the major's last statement. *Fine, if this hits the news, the criminals will have a head start on us. He better keep his aides in control, or we'll really have problems.*

Smiling to himself again, *Glad I didn't vote for him.* The major picked up his phone, pressed the scrambler button and dialed Midland. "Captain, hit it! Try to keep your uncle out of this as much as possible. Draft him into the Rangers, if necessary! Report to me every night, no matter the time!"

Captain Charles Randel replied, "We are on the way, Major! Thank you!"

CHAPTER TEN

Jess turned to Professor Stapleton with a questioning look and asked, "This old sewing machine sure is in good shape. Does it work?"

"Yes, it does, Jess. It worked better than my wife's modern one upstairs in her sewing room. God bless her soul, I sure miss her being by my side. Although she has been gone all these years, I feel like I can call out to her in the kitchen, and she should answer." He was almost to the point of tears.

Leaning toward the professor, "I'm sorry, John. I didn't mean to upset you," Jess said. "You know, I've experienced that too... missing my wife, Marie Ann, although she is just up in Indiana on a visit. They leave a big vacuum in our lives, when they're gone, don't they?"

Professor Stapleton nodded his head, "You did not upset me," he sniffled. "I did it myself. I have been doing that more frequently."

Jess ran his fingers along the top edge of the sewing machine, feeling the oily residue of a furniture polish. *I like antiques, but I'm not too interested in this sewing machine. What does he want to show me down here? This basement reminds me of a tomb.*

"Jess, that letter was hidden under this bottom drawer. It was taped under here, let me show you," he said as he pulled the drawer out of the sewing cabinet, pointing to a dark spot where the wood had not yet faded.

The deteriorated brown envelope matched the faded marks on the drawer bottom. A scribbled note on the wood drawer bottom read, "Whoever finds this letter, please give it to my Grandson Jess E. Hanes, Sanfor, Texas. Signed, 'Stumpy', C.J. Hanes, 1946."

"This letter is so brittle, I'm afraid it may tear if I spread it open. 1946? I was only six years old. How did you come by this sewing machine, Professor? I mean John."

"I was waiting for you to read the letter, maybe it tells about the machine. I have not read it! So, when you finish, I will tell you the story."

Jess smiled, "You mean curiosity didn't get the best of you?"

"Restraint! It was not any of my business. But, you must read..." the professor hesitated, listening.

Professor Stapleton suddenly turned when they heard the dogs barking, "Get upstairs! I am behind you," he ordered as he pointed with his cane. "Put that letter inside the clock behind its works. We will talk about it later, when we will not be interrupted," he said, climbing the stairs. Breathing heavily, "Its secret has been kept this long. It will keep a bit longer."

When Jess came out into the living room again, after placing the letter behind the clock works, the outside breeze had stopped, and he could feel the coolness of the basement vanish. He pulled cobwebs from between his fingers, from when he had brushed through them coming up the stairs.

Professor Stapleton was silent as he appeared in the front room, motioning Jess to wait before closing the glass door on the grandfather clock. He peered outside through one of the porch windows. A cloud of dust, from a vehicle approaching at high speed, could be seen on the lane leading to the ranch house.

"Jess, close the clock door now, and bring me my rifle," he ordered.

Jess did as he was told. While closing the door, he saw a security alarm switch. He hesitated, looking at it through the glass door, *Well I'll be, didn't notice that intrusion switch mounted at the bottom of the clock case - missed that earlier. Anyway, it must have been off, because John didn't get an alarm.* He hurried to the rifle.

Where did John get this fully automatic M16? Legally, anyone can buy one of these, if, they have a federal stamp for it. So, what's the big deal, Jess? He picked it up, and made sure the safety was on, and then approached the professor with it.

John pointed to another porch window, "You used one of those in Vietnam, so hold onto it. I do not know who is out there. They will appear from behind those salt cedar bushes... about now."

Jess could see a white jeep bumping down the winding lane toward the ranch house. It had a Brewster County Sheriff's emblem on the doors, with the typical red and blue lights on top.

"It is Sheriff Baker's jeep, and he is alone. We can go out on the porch," John said.

Jess leaned the rifle against the porch banister as the jeep came to a halt in front. Sheriff Baker waved before getting out, opened the door and stood on the outside talking on his radio.

"Professor, is everything alright out here?" he asked pointing to the rifle.

Leaning on the banister, Jess replied, "Certainly! No problems, Sheriff."

Sheriff Baker tossed the radio's hand mic onto the seat, shut the door and went up on the porch. Jess was wondering; *'Does he have news about the taxi driver who was shot?'*

"Got some of that good ole West Texas sun tea, Professor?" asked the sheriff. "Sure would help this parched throat of mine," he said taking off his white straw Stetson hat.

"Sure, come on inside," John said getting up from his porch rocker.

The sheriff waved his hand, "Thanks anyway, Professor, but I need to stay out here on the porch so that I can hear my police radio."

"No problem, I can bring the tea out here, want more Jess?"

He nodded, "Sure, that was great. Can I help?" John waved, no. "Again, no sugar, please. A slice of that lemon would do just fine, thanks."

John propped his cane against the screen door casing and went inside.

The sheriff leaned toward Jess, "Quickly, Jess! I don't want to disturb the professor any more than he is already. We've got company coming in from Odessa about the shooting at the airport. They should be here around sunset, in thirty minutes or so. I'm here on business, so help me visit with the professor until your two nephews get here by helicopter."

"Charles and Jack? Why?"

The sheriff cut Jess off as Professor Stapleton came out onto the porch with a pitcher of lemon slices floating in iced tea. He handed the sheriff a tall glass with ice cubes and filled it, then poured more tea for Jess.

"More ice," he asked Jess.

"Nope, this will be enough."

He sat next to Jess on the porch swing, "Best drink around these parts," and drank from his glass.

Sheriff Baker sat on the banisher with one leg cocked across the top, exposing his brown high-top western boots, "Seems our Mexican agent taxi driver has an interesting background, Professor. How well did you know Agent Simms, and for how long?"

John pointed to a wicker chair, "Pull up a chair, Sheriff, and we will discuss this whole matter. I have not been able to go into detail with you for a long time."

#

The tranquil evening in the valley far west of the professor's ranch was suddenly disturbed by two Texas Ranger, black Bell

206 Jet Ranger III helicopters skimming southwest, close above the cactus. Their backwash blew up dust from the desert floor, as they turned east toward the distant mountains. They stayed well clear of the military flight operations area, north of Presidio.

Following a deep ravine in the valley, Captain Jack Randal who was in the lead, flipped a switch on the control panel for 'hush rotor' operation. Captain Charles Randal, in the following helicopter, did the same, as if some unseen cord tied them together.

They maintained radio silence throughout the complete trip from Odessa to east of Presidio, where Charles picked up Jack with the second helicopter. Jack flew the second helicopter, as pilot-in-command, following his brother toward the ranch, keeping their altitude well below radar detection.

They were both Marines in Vietnam and Desert Storm, flying Cobra gunship helicopters and Harrier jets; spending many hours flying above jungle tree tops and desert floors, and then higher altitudes to stay out of the range of small arms fire, Anti-Aircraft-Artillery (AAA), and Surface-to-Air (SAM) Missiles.

Both rangers agreed, describing their mission, "But! This mission is at home! A different kind of mission was being fought here, but it is still war. War is war, whether in a foreign country or in your own back yard. It was no different, lives were at stake, and the bad guys have dug in now."

Prior to the present event with their Uncle Jess, the Texas Rangers had set up a temporary command post near Presidio on the Rio Grande River. They were having a hard task preventing a takeover of Brewster and Presidio counties by the drug cartels, drug runners, cattle rustling and illegal entry of aliens. There was also an increase of illegal chemicals and waste materials being moved into Mexico from the U.S. side of the river.

The battle lines were being drawn, again.

Castelon, Texas

CHAPTER ELEVEN

Castolon, a short distance up on higher ground from the Rio Grande River, in the Big Bend country, was a small quiet trading post village with an unpaved dirt street and mostly abandoned adobe buildings. Like other small villages on the border, it had a fluctuating population. Through the years, it had ranged from zero to thirty. The trading post was the only active business.

The little village seemed empty, except for two old-timers in the shade of a thatched porch roof, leaning back in wooden wicker-seated chairs against the adobe wall. Almost asleep, they calmly watched two stray dogs scouting for food.

It was late afternoon with small swirling dust-devil whirlwinds in the dusty road, moving down toward the river. The dogs chased a jackrabbit into a hole under a prickly pear cactus in the shadow of the porch roof. Barking, they circled the cactus like a band of Indians on the warpath. They did not bark long in the heat, and decided to lay sprawled in front of the hole, panting with their tongues hanging out - almost in the dirt.

A half-a-mile or so down at the river, tall willow, cottonwood, and birch trees grew along its dusty banks. Unfortunately, that was the only shade to be found for miles. Neither man nor beast stayed in the sun long when it was high in the sky; shade would be the only place to survive the direct rays of heat. The shadows grew longer as the sun began to lower.

The barking of the dogs and the tree leaves rustling were the only noises heard, not much activity for close to sundown. A gust of wind blew tumbleweeds down the road toward the river, which did not get the men's attention.

Back up in the canyon, across the river into Mexico, a beat-up old pickup truck could be heard. The old vehicle made its way through the empty street of *Ejido de Santa Helena*. Turning south along the river, the noisy truck made its way down the dusty gravel road toward the muddy river. The *Sierra Ponce* high canyon walls echoed its approach.

It slowed and turned into a narrow gully that cut through the grayish red sandstone down to the riverbank. Concealed by tall salt-cedar brushes, huge sotol plants, mesquite and cactus, the pickup stopped and backed under their cover. The truck was hidden from the Texas side of the river and from anyone on the road they backed off of, on the Mexican side.

Two men, Mexican government officials, sat waiting with the pickup truck doors open. Talking low and nervously, they glanced over their shoulders through the truck's back window to see if anyone had followed them. Knowing their arrival was broadcast all the way to El Paso, they were jittery. Especially now that it was no longer a secret.

Every ten minutes, the light brown uniformed official on the passenger side would step out on the running board, and peer through the brush with binoculars toward the far riverbank on the U.S. side. Then he would search up the road to the Park Ranger Station. He seemed very impatient and sat down again in the truck.

After an hour, the driver tapped on the back window of the truck, signaling men hid in its bed. It was time.

Under the trunnion cover, four men unsnapped it and rose up, looked around, and then they jumped over the side with automatic weapons. Their dark camouflage faces and military clothes blended into the black background shadows. The men noiselessly disappeared into the shadows of the cliff although dust trailed up behind them, hanging in the salt-cedar shrubs and underbrush. The sun was behind the high peaks of the cliffs casting its long dark shadow across the river, slowly covering Castolon. In the distance, showing up the land, were the mysterious Chisos (Ghost) Mountains.

Lieutenant Frando Lopus of the Mexican Federal Police talked in a low voice to his companion in the passenger's seat of the pickup. Dust had collected on the windshield, preventing any view in that direction. They had to either stand in the bed of the truck, or, on top of the cab, to see over the underbrush. Climbing around on the pickup made too much noise, so they sat inside the hot cab with the doors open. No wind stirred in the shadows, causing the heat to linger from the surface of the pickup truck.

Mosquitoes were on the move, finding the two idle men in the truck. The cab light was removed to help keep pests from swarming around it.

"What is the latest information you have on this agent of yours?" the passenger asked sternly.

"He will be here on time tonight, *Señor!* He is our most reliable contact in Texas, and he has never failed me. He will have more specific information on the storage location of the drugs and be able to tell us in which direction of the chemical waste is coming."

Quietness was almost deafening until the bullfrogs along the river began their croaking. Their concert echoed back up the canyon, and others replied from across the river. The current of the river was so quiet, it could not be heard.

"What time is it now?" asked the lieutenant.

"We have been here an hour and it's only seven o'clock. Why are we here so early? We have an hour or more to wait!" he said, briskly questioning his passenger.

"It is hard enough traveling in this old wreck, but it is worse traveling these roads after dark. I wanted to get set early, before sundown," the lieutenant said and changed the subject. "I hope that they bring cameras and video equipment for tonight. The Texas Rangers will be arranging that with my contact. I think Ranger Randel will be along, too. He's good with the special electronic equipment we need for these night raids."

The sun had set, and the large orange moon began its slow rise behind the *Sierra Del Carmen* Mountains, east of the *Chisos* Mountains, casting its eerie reflections across the mountainous Big Bend country.

CHAPTER TWELVE

Jess, Professor Stapleton and Sheriff Baker sat on the front porch of the professor's ranch home, silently watching the sunset. They were close enough to hear the sheriff's jeep radio. A long hour passed with few words, no radio traffic, and the shadows of the western mountain range increased their reach towards the ranch.

"To answer your question of how well I knew Agent Simms; let me ask this first! How is he?" Professor Stapleton asked the sheriff, breaking the silence.

"I really don't know. He was flown Medivac from El Paso to Austin," replied Sheriff Baker.

"Wonder why he was shot and by whom?" Jess asked.

"We may get those answers sooner than we think," the sheriff answered.

The professor stretched his arms above his head and yawned, "He was doing an investigation for me here on the ranch. I have had a hundred head of cattle stolen, and there are trucks and strange noises that wake me at night. The sound echoes off these canyon walls, and I could not track them effectively with my binoculars. I hired Agent Simms to find out what was going on," shrugging his shoulders, "but I fired him because he was not producing any results."

"Evidently, he was getting too close to somebody. They shot him, and could have hit me," Jess said. "Don't you have ranch hands to acquire your information and to protect your range?"

"I do have part-time employees here. I needed an outside investigator," he replied.

The dog, Snake, lay against the porch railing between Jess' chair and the professor's rocker. His ears suddenly perked up and he raised his head. The dog yawned, wagged his tail and put his nose back down between his front paws.

The sheriff nodded toward the bunkhouse in the back, "Where are they now, Professor? I haven't seen anybody moving around out there doing chores."

"I dismissed them for a few days," he answered the sheriff.

Funny, you'd think a rancher with rustling problems would have all his men here, plus more... maybe even be running shifts around the clock. None of my business, Jess thought. *So, let it go!*

"That must be why you met me with the rifle and ole Snake here?" Jess reached down and scratched Snake a couple of times behind the ears; his tail swished the dusty porch.

"There have been too many weird happenings the last few weeks, then there was this shooting. I am leery of strangers, although you called ahead to let me know you were coming."

Snake sat up, turning his head toward the western valley; ears turning like radar dishes listening for intruders. Moaning while he looked at the professor, the dog looked back out into the dark shadows of the mountains. The sun had almost set behind them.

"I only knew Simms since he reported to my office two months ago," said Sheriff Baker. "He let me know that he was working undercover as a taxi driver. The man didn't elaborate on any details, other than his showing me his authorization from the governor's office, Border Patrol and Texas Rangers. I didn't know he was working for you, Professor. How did you contact him?"

The breeze stopped across the porch area where the sun had warmed all day, causing the temperature to increase. Jess took another swallow of the cold iced tea, letting it slowly flow down his throat. The sweat rolled into his sideburns, and he could feel it on the back of his neck. He soaked up the salty liquid with his white handkerchief, then folded it the long way and wrapped it around the iced tea glass. His famous neck ache was starting again, so he placed the cold damp handkerchief around the back of his hot neck.

"He was the brother of one of my students in Ethnology at the university." They could tell by the tone of the professor's voice that there were to be no more questions.

Crickets and locust sang from the mesquite trees and sagebrush. Jess leaned forward in his chair, "John, that letter you wanted me to read, may I get it?"

"Sure, Jess. You know where it is."

Jess stood and started toward the door, stopped, thinking he heard something in the distance just as Snake awoke. Sniffing the air with a deep husky growl, Snake walked to the edge of the front porch steps. He turned and ran to the west porch steps. Still growling, the ridge of hair on his back stood straight up in the air.

'I'm glad we may have become friends because your growl put goose bumps and chills up and down my spine. He's not looking at me, not this time,' Jess thought as he watched Snake.

"Sheriff, listen!" the professor said, while standing. He looked in the same direction Snake was growling toward. "That noise! It sounds like the unusual noise that I have heard at night."

Jess walked to the edge of the porch steps and listened intently toward the west. Snake licked his hand and ran into the yard barking.

"Sheriff," Jess said, "that's no truck! It's the beating of helicopter blades."

"Are you sure?" The professor asked, as he and the sheriff walked over next to Jess. They all had to lift their hands to shade their eyes from the glaring sun. It was setting behind the far mountain ranges.

"Jess, you're right!" Sheriff Baker said, "Your two nephews will be landing here shortly."

"Nephews?" the professor bluntly asked. He yelled at Snake, but the dog ignored him. He whistled, using his two little fingers between his lips, and Snake immediately came to him. He then fastened him to a leash.

In the distance, two black shapes suddenly rose out of a ravine from the dark shadows of the mountains into the sunlight. Jess had never seen two helicopters fly so quickly and so quietly. They had almost arrived at the ranch house, when they heard sounds.

"Why are they coming here, Sheriff?" The professor asked.

He avoided answering the question, "Can they land over there by the garage in the grass?" the sheriff asked, pointing in that direction.

Professor Stapleton nodded, 'yes.' The sheriff moved off the porch and over to the large open grassy area between the barns and the garage. He held his hands up over his head as the two helicopters slowed to a hover next to each other. He motioned them to settle on the lawn. Cut grass and twigs blew in all directions from the prop wash; the three men had to turn their backs.

They reminded Jess of a helicopter years ago on a TV series, shiny ebony black, sleek slender fuselage, looking like a porpoise from the side. The swishing noise of the propeller blades began to slow as the pilots turned off the engines.

In all the excitement and distraction of the helicopters landing, two black vehicles were not seen coming down the road toward the ranch.

CHAPTER THIRTEEN

Inside the abandoned *Chisos Mariposa* (Ghost Butterfly) mine, near Lajitas, (Little Flags,) air flowed through the many tunnels and shafts making eerie sounds causing two illegal Mexican immigrants to be nervous. They were guarding the entrance to the old silver mine, which was being used for a temporary distribution point for drug contraband. The weird mysterious sounds of the interior musty shafts persisted their moaning and whistling.

Local superstitions said the mine held the spirits of twenty-three white men and five Apache Indians. They lost their lives hiding in the mine after stealing silver from the Comanches who trapped them and burned their bodies somewhere in one of the many deep shafts.

This legend kept the two men from entering further than the hidden opening of the mine. In addition, a fowl, overpowering smell of something dead caused them to linger at the entrance for fresh air. A skunk or rabbit must have crawled back inside and died.

One of them walked outside and searched the valley below with binoculars. The spotter scanned the brown, barren, sage land to the south, toward the Santa Helena Canyon entrance. There, the Rio Grande River cut through the high mesas of the *Sierra Ponce* on the Texas side, and the *Mesa de Anguila,* on the Mexican side. He slowly checked every light that he could see in the dark shadows of the mountains and mesas. Nothing seemed to be moving; he was getting tired of waiting. They had already been there two nights with little food and water.

His partner, inside the mine entrance, nervously puffed a *cigarillo*. The flicker of a kerosene lantern caused a wavy shadow on the mine's wall. He kicked at a rock on the dirt floor swearing in Spanish, and kicked at it again. This time, it flew through the air and ricocheted off the wall. It bounced along the floor of the main shaft. Taking a long draw on his *cigarillo,* he walked outside and stood next to his friend, where his *cigarillo* glowed like a torch in the twilight. He took another long drag on it, and his face shown from the reflection.

While looking through the binoculars, in the corner of the spotter's eye, the sudden light of his partner's *cigarillo* made him flinch away. He swore and slapped the *cigarillo* from his partner's mouth. Talking loudly, he pushed him back into the mine entrance and shoved him against the cold musty wall. He walked back outside, swearing as he went, mumbling to himself, and continued to search the wide valley.

The spotter stopped looking, put one hand on his hip shaking his head, "*Estupido hombre!*"

Headlights on the highway caught his attention. He put the binoculars back up to his eyes. A few vehicles on the highway between Lajitas and Terlingua could be seen as they traveled up and down the gullies, ravines and small hills. The night was clear with the moon low on the horizon and stars shining brightly. Nothing seemed out of the ordinary, so he reentered the mine and gasped at the awful odor.

"Give me another *cigarillo,* stupid!" he said in English. "Something's dead in here!"

Their talk echoed in the mine as they lit their smokes with the flame from the top of the lantern mantle. The men puffed a few long drags and let the smoke slowly flow from their mouths and nostrils to help kill the dead stench.

"We go deeper and find silver bars. We be rich and not bother with drugs. We be rich, Mexican peóns before Americans return," the shorter one said. "No, wait for them!"

"Shut up," his partner replied sharply. "Boss would hunt us down and kill us." Puffing harder on his *cigarillo*, "He will pay good money so we can go north. Remember, we have our families waiting for us in Pecos to take them north for jobs. *Mucho norte*, away from the border! *Ganar muchisimo dinero.* We must have *dinero* now, to pay for families!"

He paced the mine floor from wall to wall, puffing harder on the short *cigarillo* to keep it lit until the hot ash burnt his lips. Dropping it to the floor, he blew the thick smoke toward the light of the lantern and with his fingers, demanded another. This one he lit from his partner's *cigarillo*.

#

Two deputies in a Brewster County Sheriff's cruiser were heading north from Study Butte on Texas State Highway 118. It was too dark to continue without headlights; so on the lights came. The deputies were traveling at a slow speed, looking for illegal immigrants. The two had settled back hoping for a long uneventful evening.

The western mountain range shadows quickly darkened the valley highway when the sun went down as they headed for Alpine. No sooner had the lights flashed up the road, when a large, fast moving tanker truck appeared south bound around a blind curve with no lights. The truck was straddling the double white lines when the bright headlights caught the driver in the eyes.

The front left bumper of the truck hit the left front of the cruiser with a glancing blow, causing the car to spin. The rear of the sheriff's car was thrown under the dual wheels of the truck, crushing the trunk and the back roof of the car. The truck's dual wheels bounced into the air, and then hit the pavement, jackknifing the tanker trailer. The whole rig careened toward the edge of a deep rugged canyon on the right side of the road. The trailer's dual wheel axles caught the sheriff's car, dragging it over the edge into the creek bed below.

The trailer's internal tanks exploded upon impact throwing the sheriff's car up the creek. The truck and trailer were smothered with one large red and orange fireball which rose straight up, high out of the canyon. The black smoke rapidly rose higher as additional explosions from the truck's fuel tanks ignited. The trailer tank compartments continued to individually erupt, spewing liquid fire for yards around the burning twisted metal.

The explosion appeared to be a small-scale atomic explosion, as the smoke continued to rise from the darkness of the canyon into the bright moonlight. It kept boiling upward to thousands of feet.

#

Twenty miles south of the truck wreck, across the river from Castolon, the Mexican federal agent and his government official stood in front of their pickup truck, both looking to the north across the Rio Grande. They were still waiting to meet with the Texas Rangers and the undercover Mexican Agent.

Suddenly, a booming sound echoing from across the river reverberating off the flat face of the walls of the canyon above them.

"Where was that explosion?" asked Lieutenant Lopus.

"Over this way, Lieutenant, toward Study Butte. It is probably a sonic boom from the American Air Force jets flying in this area. They play their war games north of Presidio," his companion said.

"No! I know a sonic boom, when I hear one, and that was an explosion from up at Study Butte. In fact, it sounded more as if it were a mine explosion!"

Going around to the driver's side of his pickup, he grabbed the radio mic, "Maverick Ranger Station, this is Lieutenant Lopus, Mexican Federal Police, do you copy?"

Long pause, "Go ahead, *Amigo*, this is Jake. Be quick, I have a problem over here!"

"Did you hear that explosion a few seconds ago?"

"Yes, it was up 118 towards Alpine. Almost blew me off my horse," Jake replied. "I'll call you back when I get up this hill!"

"I understand!"

National park ranger, Jake Wilson, spurred his Appaloosa horse, Tango, up the hill around cactus, boulders, thick cedar and mesquite trees to the top.

"Up, Tango! We're almost there," he urged.

Looking north from the top, Jake could see fire with the moonlight silhouetting the black billowing smoke. It was too dark to see much of anything more than explosions in the fire.

"We heard the explosion down here across from Castolon, Jake. How bad is it?" asked the impatient lieutenant.

Looking through his binoculars, Jake keyed the radio, "I can't tell from here, but I'll get some help up there for you. I'll keep in touch."

Going back to the pickup with his passenger, Lopus frowned, "This is bad, another delay! That will stop our contraband from crossing tonight. There will be U.S. authorities swarming all over the Big Bend country."

He slammed his fist on the hood of the truck as he passed by, "This area is beginning to be a noticeable place again. We can't catch these people if they don't deliver the contraband."

"*Amigo*! Did you hear something like a rumble?" asked Antonio in Spanish, one of the Mexican men at the Chisos Mariposa mine.

Shaking his head, "No! I did not hear anything. All I have heard for the last two days is your mouth and the moaning of this mine," Hermandez complained.

"Wait! Feel that? Grounds shaking! Get out! Now!"

They ran out of the hidden mine opening into the moonlight. The earth below them rumbled, and the mine roared from its depths. Up from its shafts and out through the entrance bellowed a thick cloud of dust. They stood in the open, clinging to an old wooden post, not knowing which way to run. The shaking of the ground crept to a halt as the mine's entrance clouded with blowing dust covering and choking the two men.

"I go back to Mexico! This country do not like me!" Antonio yelled. frightened.

"No! What about our families?" Hernandez asked.

Shuffling his feet and moving further away from the mine, "I am no good to them dead!" Antonio said.

Hermandez grabbed his companion's arm, "But we need that money for them, no matter what it takes! I say we wait here until they come for this shipment."

"Promise to leave and not do this no more?"

"Yes, I promise! On my mother's grave, I promise."

"Your mother doesn't have a grave, she not dead!"

Getting more upset with his friend, "Come on, you know what I mean. We will leave when they pay us, Okay? No more drugs!"

Hermandez thought to himself, '*Although Antonio is my brother-in-law, I will not leave him stranded or take him back to Mexico.*'

Antonio moved away from Hermandez, turned his back and looked at the bright moon. '*I am afraid to continue with this drug business. I want to go back to Mexico. But, that is no good either!* He shook his head, *I must provide a better life for my family, so further north we must go.*'

"Okay!" Antonio screamed.

"Come on then, get those flashlights in the pickup so that we can check the wooden boxes, they might be broken. Boss will skin us alive if they are damaged or open."

Reaching out and grabbing Antonio's arm, Hermandez sticking out his hand to him, "*Amistad*? Friendship?"

"*Si, Amigo! Siempre!*"

They grabbed each other around the neck and kissed each other's cheek. Friends, they were! Always!

Running to the truck, the men found the flashlights and returned to the mine entrance.

Hermandez hesitated, "Do not go in mine! Where are my glasses?"

Antonio shrugged in the moonlight, "You no wear glasses! Do you?"

"No! No! The boss's binoculars," he replied. "I dropped them coming out of the mine."

"I no want to go back," Antonio whined.

"Stay out here. Keep flashlight off because someone may have seen us already. I will be back, and no smoking either," he said, going into the dusty mine. "Phew! Smell that? Worse than before earthquake."

They did not know that the rotten smell was natural gasses from the ground formations inside the mineshafts, which could ignite from lighting a lantern. It smelled worse than before the rumbling, which meant more natural gas fumes were seeping into the mine.

Dust still swirled in the air but had thinned enough to use the flashlight. Hermandez covered his face with his handkerchief to keep the dust and stink from bothering him. He finally made his way over the rubble and huge boulders that had fallen. The shaft where the drugs were stacked had collapsed, closing it up to within a few feet from the top. The air exiting through the small opening came out with great force, clearing the dust from the outer opening of the mine.

"Ah! *Chihuahua!*" exclaimed Hermandez, making the sign of the cross across his chest. "God buried it all!"

He ran out of the mine and got into the pickup with Antonio, telling him what he had found. After he calmed down, they decided to go back in the mine and uncover the hemp-roped bags of drugs. By the time it was all uncovered, and moved to the front of the mine entrance, both men had sweated through their clothes.

They could barely pull themselves back into the truck. Neither one spoke as they stretched and went to sleep.

CHAPTER FOURTEEN

The Presidio Sunset Motel was the only motel in town with a swimming pool along the Rio Grande River north of Lajitas. The same evening of the truck wreck, the night was quiet except for people coming in and out of the cocktail lounge area near the pool. Its underwater lights danced shadows through the rippled emerald water on the walls of the tall private fence, which surrounded three sides of the pool's patio area.

Three men sat at a table across the pool from four women sitting along the pool's edge. Their beautiful, long, tanned legs hung over the side of the pool, dangling their feet in the warm water. The sun had heated it. They were lovely women right out of fashion magazines wearing their scanty bikinis; a bit over-dressed for the small Texas border town.

The men ignored the women while talking in low voices, leaning on their elbows toward each other in order not to be overheard arguing, pointing accusing fingers. With Bermuda shorts, loud, colored Hawaiian shirts, skin white as snow, they stuck out like a sore thumb - strangers on the border. Looking and acting too stylish for this west Texas town, the big city dudes were out of place.

One was a broad-shouldered bearded blonde who continued to prod, "Look here, Tony! Are you sure that second tanker left on time? I'll need both those shipments over into Mexico tonight!" He looked like a wrestler with all his bulging muscles.

"Ace, no sweat! A piece of cake!" Tony, the fat man said confidently, puffing on his big cigar. His muscle-bulging bodyguard squinted his eyes and stared at the longhaired blonde. "We had our best driver leaving out of Odessa last night at eleven with the second shipment. There's plenty of time to get to the border. Your money will be in the Dallas bank tomorrow morning."

"You both better be right, or you'll be belly-up in that muddy Rio Grande tomorrow night," Ace said, shaking a finger at Tony. "You'd better have my money! Cash! In my hands by tomorrow! No banking deals!" Gritting his teeth, "Got that? You don't get your dope until that cash is right here," jabbing his palm. "I'll need that money for another international load of drugs coming into Lajitas tomorrow."

It was as if he was talking to a brick wall. Of the two men, neither had expressed acknowledgment of Ace's demands or his intimidation. Tony continued puffing on his cigar. Ace's bodyguard stood nervously behind Ace, glaring back across the table. There was no mutual trust displayed at this meeting.

Not looking at him, Tony said disgustedly, "Okay! You're the boss!"

The big blonde held up two fingers, "Chemicals to Castolon and drugs to Lajitas. The Mexicans..."

Tony cut him off, "Don't talk so loud." Pointing his bony finger at Ace, "You're taking a big chance hauling through the federal park area, more eyes watching," he said with a northern Chicago accent. "Besides, I don't want to know anything about your operations and you're sure not going to know mine!"

He pushed drink glasses and an ashtray to the side with one sweep of his arm, "Too many people involved already! Too many links in the chain connecting me with you and your contacts! Don't threaten me, Ace! You ain't nobody that I can't do without! You'll get your money when I get mine! No sooner, no later!"

Tony stood up and tossed his cigar over his shoulder into the swimming pool, not taking his eyes off of Ace. He and his bodyguard entered the lounge. Ace shoved the table and its umbrella away from him, stood and swaggered toward the women, escorting them to their poolside motel rooms.

CHAPTER FIFTEEN

Smoke and fumes filled the deep canyon and rose out of the gorge to thousands of feet, blowing north toward Alpine. The trailer tank continued to blaze and smolder. Tires of the truck and trailer had melted into molten rubber mounds in the dry sagebrush and buffalo grass, catching it on fire.

The brightness of the fire and sporadic explosions exposed the ravine creek bed reflecting off its high cliffs and the higher canyon walls. The mangled county sheriff's car was upended against the wall of the ravine. It was standing on its rear end wedged sideways into a limestone crevice, as if a giant had pressed it into the wall.

Inside the crushed cruiser, two deputies, Marc Thompson and Bob Stacey, could barely be seen. One deputy clung to the bottom of the front seat because it was upside down on the back seat. The combined seats hung half out the hole where the rear window once was located.

"Marc!" he moaned, fearing to move. "Marc! Can you hear me? Where are you, Marc?"

"Right under you, Bob," he whispered. "You're on top of me! Move slow and easy. I can hardly breathe! I feel you moving your weight, take it easy!"

Marc tried moving his left arm, but it was pinned between the back seat and the trunk lid, "My arm's stuck under me. I can move my legs and right arm, but I'm pinned. My weight's holding the seat down on my arm."

They both groaned when either officer moved. Some of the smoke from the fire would swirl over them, causing them to cough. Their eyes burned and watered. The twisted metal of the cruiser would rub together, scraping itself against the hard crevice. There was a danger of it loosening, falling to the rocky bed below.

Marc moved his legs, "Great!" he said. "I can move! Hold still Bob, this may hurt. I might be able to get out from underneath. I'm pulling my knees up to my chest to try lifting you." Grunting and gritting his teeth, "Maybe I can slide out from under you."

"Okay!" he moaned, "Do it!"

Marc slowly began raising the seat above him and the trunk lid pressed into his arm, causing the front seat to tip. Bob lost his grip and slipped off the seat, hit the trunk and fell to the ground.

"Dang it all! I'm in a bed of fire ants," Bob howled, squirming around. He looked up at the hanging car as he tried knocking off ants, "Marc, can you move at all?" he tried to yell over the noise of another tank explosion. Its concussion made the car move again, and sprayed dirt and thick black soot over them.

"Yeah, I'm moving the seat; no problem now! I'm sliding out, can't hold on much longer," falling on top of Bob, they both moaned and groaned.

"My arm's broken," Marc began to moan louder, going into shock.

He laid his left forearm across his thigh, "At least it ain't bleeding, but look at the protruding bone. I'm going to faint, Bob... Bo...!" Trying to catch himself, he fell against the rear fender of the hanging car.

Bob scooted over to him and laid him out flat, pulling him away from the wrecked vehicle. He propped Marc's feet up on a large rock. The broken arm looked bad. He was certain that if first aid was not administered quickly, Marc could lose the arm.

"Marc! If you can hear me, take some long deep breaths," he said checking for a pulse and watching as Marc began breathing deeply.

"I'll have to splint your arm, but not right now. You're too close to going into shock. I'm going to lay it across your chest. It's gonna hurt... hold on Buddy."

He slowly lifted the broken arm and laid it on Marc's chest, with no yell from him. "I'm unbuttoning your shirt, and I'm gonna slide your hand and arm inside and button it again. Talk to me Marc, talk to me! Remember what we were taught in first aide? Tell me how to do this! Maybe that will keep you awake, okay?"

Marc opened his burning eyes, "Sure is a clear night. Look at all those stars up there. Big Dipper, Milky Way..."

Boom! Bright orange and red flames shot skyward. Another explosion shook them and echoed through the gorge and mountains around them, knocking Bob against a bolder. Shaken, he moved back to Marc's side.

"Looks like that's going to burn for awhile. I wonder what's in it that keeps burning. Sure smells like chemicals or aviation fuel," Bob said, while looking up toward the highway. "Keep talking to me Marc. You're going to be all right. I'm sure that help will be on the way. Ranger Jake is out here somewhere. He can't miss seeing this fire and smoke."

The two deputies had only a short wait; cars began stopping, and people were looking for a way down into the gorge.

CHAPTER SIXTEEN

That same evening, after the Brewster County Sheriff had introduced the two Texas Rangers to Professor Stapleton, Jess broke into a questionable smile, "Jack? Charles? What are you two characters doing flying those beauties? Man alive, they're sharp! That's all I can say!"

"That's a first! I've never, ever, seen Uncle Jess speechless. How are you doing Uncle Jess?" Jack asked as he shook Jess' hand and wrapped his left arm around his neck.

Charles and his brother, Jack, were twins, but built differently. Jack was like a tree stump, six foot and stocky, "You've been pumping iron again?" Jess asked squeezing Jack's biceps.

"No, not since I've been down here in the Big Bend country. I lost weight running around, hiking and riding horses. My patrol is more primitive than Charles' stationary desk," Jack kidded.

Charles was an inch taller but not as bulky as Jack. He flexed his arm muscles for his Uncle Jess to compare, "I'm still thicker than he is! Got a tape measure?"

Before either one could answer, two black vans silently parked at the front of the house. Six men moved from each vehicle and swiftly surrounded the ranch house and the helicopters. They carried automatic weapons and wore desert battle dress uniforms, BDU's. Sheriff Baker's SWAT unit had arrived to back up the Rangers.

Professor Stapleton walked past Jack; "I better turn some lights on around the yard before you start shooting at each other."

"No! Please, no more lights than what you already have," said Jack. Leave everything, as it normally should be. We can see." Motioning the SWAT team to join them, he continued, "It's getting late, and Charles is behind time meeting with Mexican officials at a drug drop near Castolon."

Pointing to the ravine behind the helicopters, "Sheriff, move some of your men to the crest of that hill so they can get a clear view down that gorge. We may get visitors on horseback."

Jess was taking this all in like an observer at a military maneuver, with his arms folded in front, smiling to himself. *I once held these two wet-diaper, smelly butt babies in my arms together. They sure have grown into a couple of efficient team leaders, very proud of them.*

Charles turned to Jess; "I was to meet with your taxi driver tonight at Castolon, Uncle Jess. But, you know what happened to him?"

"This is becoming a very long day with all of this excitement." Jess nodded, "Yes, you're right! I know what happened to Agent Simms. But, what's all of this to do with him, you two and Professor Stapleton?"

Sheriff Baker moved close to Jess and interrupted, "Mr. Hanes, it may take awhile to explain all of this. We all have been working together on this special drug project. The Rangers, CIA, and Professor Stapleton, all about the same time, contacted me. They were all in contact with Agent Simms in different ways, and then you got in the middle of the action."

Charles and Jack put their arms around Jess' shoulders and in unison, "He's always in the middle of the action!"

The three of them laughed, remembering the Morocco incident, but the others did not know about their inside story. Charles said, "Uncle Jess has the canine ability to sniff out excitement, no matter where he goes." They let go of him, and Charles started quietly talking to the sheriff with their backs to the rest of the group.

Jack turned to Jess, "In short, Charles was to direct a drug bust along the Rio Grande with the help of Mexican Federals and

94

Agent Simms. We have other problems of illegal transport of chemical waste, dangerous acids and petroleum into Mexico around here." They sat on the floor of the helicopter with their feet hanging out. Sheriff Baker was directing his men, and Professor Stapleton leaned against the side of the helicopter to listen to Jack.

"It's been polluting the water supplies near some small villages on both sides of the Rio Grande. We have videos of Mexican families using the discarded empty barrels and containers for storing drinking water."

Jess was beginning to understand; *'This puzzle is slowly fitting together. Evidently, Agent Simms got too close to somebody in his investigation, and they shot him.'*

"Many tanker loads are coming to the border from refineries in Colorado, New Mexico, Oklahoma, as well as from here in the west Texas oil fields. It was bad enough with the increase of drug traffic, but with the added traffic of waste transferring through here, we are shorthanded in law enforcement," Jack said.

Professor Stapleton seemed as surprised as Jess and listened intently to the conversation, thinking, *It seemed this was becoming a lengthy report of the situation. I wonder why they are lingering here so long with the engines of the helicopters still running. The blades have stopped turning, but engines are running.*

"Agent Simms was placed here by us for the professor to hire," Charles said.

Professor Stapleton became very attentive with an astonished look at Charles, "What do you mean? 'Placed here'! I hired him through one of my university students."

"Yes Sir, you did! But, that student was one of our government agents with the CIA," Jack said.

A shocked look came over Professor John Stapleton's face. He frowned and then pulled nervously at his left ear. "CIA? They have their fingers in everything now days!"

Jess could feel Charles' impatience building, "We have to make some quick plan changes. Now! That's why we agreed to meet here at your ranch, Professor." He knelt down and opened a map of the area from Alpine south to the Mexican border.

"Sorry Professor, hope this will not be too inconvenient for you?"

"I suppose not! It's just all so sudden! All these people descending upon my ranch at one time, reminds me of the *Geheime Staatspolizei, Gestapo* SS Troops in World War Two..." catching himself as he continued. "But that was a long time ago, we're in the United States now."

That was an unusual comment, Jess thought. *Why would he compare this activity to the Gestapo? He wouldn't, unless he was there in Germany during the war to experience Hitler's movements. As old as he is, he may have been involved in the war. Wonder if he was a soldier or worked with the underground? Interesting! I'm sure these guys have researched the professor's background. If they haven't, I just might do it myself.*

The professor turned and walked toward the front porch with his cane tucked under his arm as he muttered under his breath, "What's going to happen next?" Shaking his head, he slowly climbed the steps.

Pulling his rocking chair close to the porch railing, he sat on its cushion, took out his pipe, filled it and leaned back, rocking while lighting it. He had a good view of all the activity in his yard.

Leaning close to Sheriff Baker, Charles quietly ordered, "Sheriff, stay with the professor please, and keep your men alert. He might be one of our suspects in all this. There's a lot of activity on his ranch. Don't let anyone interview him, and no news media."

"What about family?" Sheriff Baker asked.

"No problem, just watch them carefully."

Sheriff Baker left them and called to his SWAT team leader. They were far enough from the Rangers that the helicopter's engines covered his conversation.

Squatting down next to Charles, Jess asked, "Why is he a suspect?"

Charles looked around them to see who was close, "I will tell you, but this is strictly confidential, Uncle Jess. Even the sheriff doesn't have this info."

This is getting more exciting by the minute, Jess thought. "Do I have the need to know? Even though I still have a top secret government clearance, doesn't mean I need to know what you're wanting to tell me."

They stood up together, and Charles turned his back toward the helicopter's noise, looking Jess straight in the eyes, "Uncle Jess, if you were not cleared, I'd not be sharing this."

Jess nodded his understanding and stepped closer to him, "Okay, what's this all about?"

"Are you up to some heavy excitement?"

"Sure! You mean there's some more?"

"Professor Stapleton is under a government protection program," Charles said. "Just as you and Aunt Marie are. Only, he has been in the program since World War II. His name is Elmerhurst Stinner, a Jew who escaped the concentration camp at Treblinka. Elmer was one of the scientists the Germans used to build the missiles, like the V-2 rocket. He refused to continue development of the missiles. So, his two young daughters and wife were held in another prison to force him to abide by the SS authorities' demands."

He took hold of Jess' arm and put his mouth close to his ear for him to hear better, "He had first hand knowledge of Hitler's secrets, and because he was a Jew, Hitler had him sent to the concentration camps. Elmer helped dump the camps dead, and then hid in a pile of dead bodies that were to be buried in open graves. The German soldiers had the other prisoners cover the dead bodies with lime and then shoveled dirt over the mass grave." He paused, "Once you two become better acquainted, ask him about it."

"I will, but later. This isn't really the time for us to get that involved. Maybe, before I go back home to the ranch."

"Captain," someone yelled from the helicopter, "Park Ranger Jake Wilson calling!"

"Which one of us do you want?" Charles yelled back.

Jack hollered, "I'll get it," and ran to the helicopter.

#

Jess' mind began racing back to when he first met Agent Simms, "Charles, did you tell Simms about me coming down here?"

Not looking at Jess, "No, sir, Jack may have. I didn't know you were down here from your ranch. Not until he called me this afternoon."

Nodding, Jess left his group and walked to the helicopter Jack had entered and looked inside the cockpit area. *Sure are lot of lights, instruments, switches and knobs, seems more impressive at night with everything lit up.*

"Okay, Jake! Contact Lieutenant Lopus and call off the meeting for tonight. Tell him to meet us for breakfast at the Old Lajitas Restaurant. They serve good biscuits and gravy, and I'm buying. Seven A.M., our time! Okay?"

"I'll be there!" Ranger Wilson replied.

Turning to Jess, with the reflection from the instrument panel lighting on his face, Jack smiled and said, "Dinner and breakfast on us, Uncle Jess! Come on, you can hear this, too!"

"Charles!" Jack called, approaching the huddle of men kneeling around a map on the ground.

"Hello Brother," Charles replied. "What's new?"

Everyone stood up and stretched from kneeling so long. Jack pointed at Charles and nodded, "We can relax a little, but things may start hopping by sunup. One of the sheriff's cars ran into a tanker truck going south on State Road 118. Jake said it was full of chemicals and exploded. He doesn't know who all was injured, yet. A full report will be on the way. He's setting up camp at that sight right now and will be there through the night."

Jack continued, "State Police and the County Sheriff's Departments will handle the cleanup in the morning. The Border Patrol will take up some slack for us tomorrow while we continue our investigations."

Jack turned to Sheriff Baker, "Sorry, Sheriff! I don't know who was in the county patrol car."

The sheriff took his transceiver from its pouch and moved away from the rest of group, waving to his SWAT team leader. Charles and Jack separated the group of men, gave out orders, and took questions.

After a few minutes had passed, exchanging information, Charles hollered, "Okay! Everyone! Sheriff!"

Jack motioned everyone to assemble again, "Set up camp over near the barn for tonight. I'll brief you more in about an hour. Then, take shifts for chow. Get as much rest as possible tonight because I have a feeling we'll need our peak performance tomorrow."

"Captain," Sheriff Baker yelled from his truck, "there were two of my men in that wreck, got to go! I'll keep in touch."

The fire continued to burn in the deep canyon while the Texas Highway Patrol Officers kept the highway clear of on-lookers. Traffic had begun to pile up because it was a Friday evening and tourists were headed for weekend camping in the Big Bend National Park.

"We'll have to carry you out of here on a litter, Marc!" Bob said.

"No! I can climb as long as I don't lose my balance. Give me a hand, Jake," Marc replied, ignoring Bob's offer. He stood with Jake's help, dusted himself off and looked at his splinted arm.

"We will send you a copy of our report, Jake. Will you be at the Park Ranger Station all day?" Marc asked, trying to steady himself walking.

"I'll probably be up here for awhile with the Texas Rangers. Tell Sheriff Baker I'll get him details about all this ASAP," Jake said. "You guys take it easy and let me know if you need anything."

The two deputies helped each other up toward the highway, and Jake returned to the burning truck. They were going to let it burn out. The fire department had no foam to smother the fire.

Jake hollered at the volunteer fire department crew, "You guys sure got here in double quick time tonight, Chief!"

"Yes Sir, we sure did, didn't we! They broke our station record," the Chief said. "They all headed for the station when everyone heard the explosion, and was ready to roll when I got there. That cut down our response time!" The Chief continued, "There isn't much we can do with our pumper, except keep the grass wet. This tanker was hauling all kinds of chemicals and petroleum mixed. Hope it doesn't contaminate the air or this protected wildlife area."

Jake stood next to the Chief and put his head back, looking up at the smoke continuing to billow into the cloudless sky. The smoke was being pushed east, about two thousand feet up, straight across the valley between Christmas Mountain and the Chisos Mountain range, over Panther Junction towards Mexico. From Jake's location, the moon was blotted out completely.

"I'll have the office call the Department of Natural Resources, DNR, about this cloud of smoke," Jake said. "It could be hazardous downwind. I'll set up a six-man tent on that east rise there between the road and the ridge for a command post. I'll also stick around with you guys until you leave, and wait for the investigators from Midland or El Paso. If you need anything, you know I'm around here somewhere, radio or in the tent!"

"Okay, Jake! See ya," the chief said.

CHAPTER SEVENTEEN

Lieutenant Lopus sighed, "We have had two set-backs already tonight. First, our contact was shot this morning at the Alpine airport. Second, the truck shipment of chemicals and drugs was wrecked. The driver was at high speed south of Alpine and collided with a County Sheriff's car. All the evidence we needed is still burning, as you can see. And, that was the explosion we heard earlier, not a jet aircraft."

The lieutenant opened the pickup door and hunted for his water container on the front seat in the shade of the moonlight. Finding it, he climbed into the truck bed and leaned across the cab roof on his elbows. Taking a long swig of water from a plastic bottle, he then looked through the binoculars toward the black smoke rising from Study Butte.

His companion asked, "What are your plans now?"

The lieutenant replied, reluctant to share details, "I'm scheduled to meet with the Rangers in the morning. Which means, we may have to cancel these plans and start all over."

The other men who came with the lieutenant began to assemble at the pickup. They all seemed disappointed the task had not been completed and would have to return later.

One of his senior men spoke up, "Lieutenant Lopus, we are equipped to stay as long as you need us. We will make camp back in that box canyon and wait."

Lopus considered the request for a few minutes, reached down through the door window laying the binoculars on the seat. Still standing in the bed of the truck, he moved around the canvas-covered equipment and sat on the wheel well.

"Okay men! Stay alert!" Lopus said in Spanish. "There could be more than one truck. So far, we haven't spotted any contraband coming or going. Trucks that size should not be hard to spot, even though we're not having good luck."

The lieutenant's companion moved to the pickup and leaned against the opened passenger's door. He lit a cigarette and turned his back to the others. From his pocket, he pulled out a small note pad and a map. "Lieutenant! Come over here," he demanded over his shoulder.

"Yes, Sir?" he questioned, and then stood, walked to the back of the cab and leaned over its edge above the door. He turned on his flashlight, shining it on the map his companion was holding.

"We are making every effort to support you on this drug arrest. Mainly, because of the high creditability of the Texas Rangers," his companion said quietly. "But, is your agent able to continue his investigation?"

The lieutenant shuffled his feet and placed one boot on the bed railing to brace himself, "No Sir! Not at this time. You heard on the radio he had been shot this morning. I do not know his condition, but I will find out in the morning. And no, I have no replacement for him, except myself!"

Lopus knew this was not pleasing to his companion. He did not want to discuss any more detail, "Commissioner Rodiquez, I will take full responsibility for his vacancy. I, myself, will take his place. I will leave for Alpine now to contact the Texas Rangers. This will not be transmitted by radio."

"Good! Take your best men. I will be in Mexico City tomorrow morning," the commissioner said. "Have one of your men drive me to the airstrip. I will await your message to return here."

He wrote in his note pad and gave the map to Lieutenant Lopus. Getting in the pickup, he turned and whispered, "Get results, Lopus, or I will replace you!"

The young lieutenant snapped a salute as the commissioner slammed the truck door, which echoed across the Rio Grande

River. He immediately turned in his seat toward the driver's door, swearing something under his breath.

The lieutenant turned, "Sergeant!" and motioned to one of the soldiers. Then he leaned down to him and whispered his orders, "Take the commissioner to his aircraft and return speedily as you can. We must make plans tonight."

The old pickup roared out of the canyon away from the muddy Rio Grande, throwing gravel and dust behind it.

After the sergeant returned, Lopus discussed the new plans for the coming day. "This will be brief, so listen good, Sergeant! One hour after sunset, go across to Castalon in civilian clothes. Have each man follow you at fifteen minute intervals." He paused thinking what needed to be done, "A bus will be there for Alpine passengers at 10:00 tonight. I will arrange for the four of you at Castalon for the bus. Everyone board the bus. I will also follow in another vehicle later. Meet me at the airport in Alpine at 2:00 tomorrow afternoon. Don't talk to anyone unless you are forced to have a conversation. Act like a *peon*," he said. "Here are two more radios - *Adios Amigos*!"

The sergeant talked with his hands as he spoke, "We will be ready lieutenant! What should I do about Customs Agents and the Border Patrol?"

"Show them your credentials. They will not give you any problem," he said.

CHAPTER EIGHTEEN

The silver mine was quiet, and the two illegal Mexican guards slept soundly in their pickup. A coyote howled in the distance, waking Hermandez with a start.

"Wake up! We both went to sleep," he said in Spanish, excitedly.

His brother-in-law, Antonio, yawned, "I was sleepy and could not hold my eyes open."

"We are lucky the boss is not here," Hermandez said. "What is the time?" He yawned too, and looked at his watch with the flashlight, "It is after midnight! Where is the boss? Hand me those binoculars."

They got out of the pickup, "I no see any lights near," Antonio said. "Red and blue flashing over on the road at Study Butte. Not moving."

Hermandez continued to look toward the south with the binoculars and then to the east where the explosion had taken place. Even though they did not hear it, the mine had reacted to the concussion from the ground waves and some of the tunnels collapsed. The dust had settled during the night and an unusual silence from the mine was noticeable.

"Quiet around here," Antonio said folding his arms around himself. "I feel evil near this mine. Scary!"

Hermandez turned toward him, mocking him, "You are never happy? Always crying like an old lady, 'The mine scares me with its moaning!', and now, 'It's too quiet'." He threw up his hands in the dark, "Go back to sleep! I'll watch until the boss gets here."

CHAPTER NINETEEN

Jess tried to sleep, but all the excitement of the previous day kept him puzzled. *Lord, what does it all mean, and how do they connect? The shooting of the special agent, truck exploding with chemicals and petroleum, my Texas Ranger nephews being involved... and that 'letter' from Grandpa Hanes in the sewing machine?*

He sat up in bed. *In all the commotion, I forgot about the letter Professor Stapleton had shown me. It was nice of him to offer me a room here at the ranch. I didn't have to go back into Alpine.*

Slipping quietly out of bed, Jess dressed and walked softly down the hallway to the head of the stairs that lead down into the living room. He heard voices as he approached the kitchen, "You guys can't sleep either? Coffee's on?"

"Help yourself, Jess," the professor said. "Hot mine, will you please? Your nephews brought me up-to-date about you, Jess. You have been quite the adventurer the last few years."

Jess nodded his reply.

"Sorry to hear Marie Ann could not come with you. Do not fail to let me meet her," he said.

Jess sat next to Jack, sipping the freshly brewed coffee, "Thank you, Professor. I certainly miss her not being with me, and the first chance we get, you'll meet her."

"They are always together, Professor," Jack said.

"You're right!' Jess said. "We're very seldom apart, especially since my trip to Morocco and then the September 11th terrorists attack." He took another sip of the coffee, "But her ailing mother needed her for a few days. She may come down next week." He smiled at the professor, stood and poured his cup full. "Like the old saying, about not missing someone. We don't, until they are no longer around." Lifting his cup to John, "As you certainly know too well! It's true!"

John agreed and nodded.

Jess sat back at the table, "I'll call her when I get back to the hotel."

"Ya know? My wife has been gone over thirty years. I still miss her presence," the professor replied.

Charles came in from the back yard with an empty coffee cup, "May I have another cup?"

John pointed at the pot on the stove. Charles helped himself and sat next to Jess. "Weather report is good. Suppose to be a high of eighty-five degrees today. No rain though.

"You will find most of the people down here do business with the tourists and complain about the weather. They do not want the rain. They say it hurts the trade," John said, shaking his head. "The rain would be nice for the grass on this ranch. I have an enormous amount of funds going to purchase feed for my livestock."

Jess cleared his throat, wanting to change the subject, "If these two nephews take after their father and grandfather like I did mine, they'll become adventurers, too. I took after my Grandpa Hanes. Remember, he was the treasure hunter and world traveler?" Chewing on a toothpick, he continued, "Anyway, about that letter he left with you, Professor, for me? Did you tell these two about it and where it was found?"

He shook his head, "No, I have not told anyone about it. That is up to you, once you have read it."

"Good! We'll have to do that before you guys leave," Jess said, pointing at Charles.

Jack turned to the map they had laid open on the kitchen table and continued to study it. "We have about a thirty minute run from here to Lajatas by helicopter," he said. "The sun will be up in an hour, so we should be well on our way before then."

"I'm ready, but what do you want me to do? I don't have any details," Jess said.

Jack started to fold the map. "We will fill you in on our way. First we need to swear you in and pin this Texas Ranger badge on you." He handed the map to Charles and took a Texas Ranger badge from his vest pocket. "Major's orders from El Paso, papers are on the way to Austin."

"You mean I'm drafted?" Jess asked.

"Yes, Sir! You're right!" Charles said, trying to keep a straight face, "You're not on the payroll! This is free on your part. It's all out of your pocket."

Laughing, Charles got up and put his arm around Jess' neck, "You're worth every penny, Uncle Jess. The major said you're on the payroll as a Captain, as of this morning. That means you don't out rank us." He laughed, snickering like a horse. Finally, he controlled his emotions; "We wanted you on our side, not the CIA. They think they have all the answers for down here. They might try recruiting your services."

"Never worked with family or Rangers in law enforcement. This is a first for me. Let me get my gear out of the car, and I'll be ready except for firearms. They should still be in my aircraft at Alpine," Jess said, smiling from ear to ear. The wrinkles from his eyes were moist from the emotions he felt, *I'm needed by the Texas Rangers; and now, working with my Ranger nephews! Wow!*

Charles replied, "We have the weapons you'll need. Do you have your video camera? There will be beautiful views of Santa Helena Canyon and the Chisos Mountains."

Jess started out to his rented car as the telephone in the kitchen rang. Jack shouted, "Uncle Jess, Sheriff's on the phone."

Jess dropped his bag on the front porch and entered the living room. As he picked up the telephone, Jack said, "I'll be on the extension in the kitchen."

Jess gave him thumbs up and took the receiver off the hook, "Morning, Sheriff. What's on your mind this early?"

"Jess, can you come to town this morning?" he asked. "I need some more info on the shooting at the airport and want to bring you up-to-date on the case."

Jess stretched the telephone cable far enough to see into the kitchen... Jack gave him the okay. Jess frowned a little and sat in the chair next to the telephone table.

"I suppose so, Sheriff. Just hate to miss a chance of riding in the ranger's helicopter," Jess said.

Charles laughed, "Uncle Jess, you'll get your chance. Breakfast at Lajitas would have been 'a kick' with you around. We'll miss that!"

"I'll take a 'rain check' on that breakfast at Lajitas. Okay? Will this afternoon be soon enough?" Jess asked. "I'll be driving up."

"See you then," the sheriff said.

#

Both helicopters lifted off the yard and swung around heading toward the border. They disappeared in the distant canyon. The sheriff's crew departed in their black cars.

"Jess, before we are interrupted again, let me get that letter for you," the professor said. They went back into the kitchen where he had left the letter's envelope on the counter. There was an empty coffee cup on top of the letter.

"Now, who put this here?" The professor said in an angry tone. Turning to Jess, he handed the envelope with a coffee cup ring on it, "Sorry! Did the coffee go through onto the letter inside?"

They sat at the table and the professor poured more coffee for them both, while Jess held the envelope between two fingers, looking at it closely for damage. He wanted to examine the letter.

Professor Stapleton stood and put his hands on his hips, "How about an old fashion ranch breakfast? I know it is late, but you will need breakfast for the trip to town; two eggs, over easy, a big pork chop, biscuits, gravy and American fries. How does that sound?"

"That sounds great! Professor, can I help?"

"No way, Jess! You are a guest in my home, so relax. And please, you do not have to be so formal. John, is better," the professor said. "Go ahead, look in the envelope... it is your letter. I am anxious to know what he has to say."

John opened the refrigerator, took out the morning breakfast menu and started cooking. The kitchen filled with the aroma of biscuits and pork chops. Jess felt his stomach rumbling from hunger. *If the professor is Jewish, how does he get away with eating pork?*

Jess opened his pocketknife and inserted the blade at the edge of the envelope. It had not been opened. Holding it up to the light so he could see through it, he then saw a dark outline of a single key. He carefully sliced the edge of the envelope open, and then eased the two folded pages out, letting the key slide out of its years of imprint between the pages.

Jess offered a short prayer, *No coffee stain! Thank you Lord!* The back of the last page had small maps drawn on it, and the letter began on the first page.

April 23, 1943

Long before you were born, Jess, I spent many years here in the Big Bend country - mining for gold, silver and asoga. (Spanish for quicksilver, cinnabar - mercury.) I was very successful at times with my claims. But, but back in '32, I lacked a lawyer and/or money. I lost them. The old abandon Amarillo Mariposa (Yellow Butterfly) mine was the most rewarding, not only with gold, but also historically. The mine has natural caverns, which I think is the southern part of the New Mexico Carlsbad Caverns.

The reason for writing this is my health is not good, and I have enemies that want what I have.

Your Father is now off to the war against Hitler, and your Mother is building bombers in Ft. Worth. Dr. John Stapleton is my newest and closest friend down here - he will be given this information.

The Amarillo Mariposa Mines #12 & #23 are confidential subjects and secrets for you to research after you are retired. Then, you can devote more time to their research.

I do not know what your life will be in the years to come, but Professor Stapleton will give this to you or your first son, if you are not living. The old sewing machine is his now. Tell him, in the back of the center drawer is a hidden space with his reward. There are twelve, San Francisco minted, 1856, $20.00 gold coins.

His personal secrets will die with me. Perhaps, he will share them with you. God bless you, Grandson of mine. Jess, your Granddad Hanes loves you.

Jess Wright Hanes, Sr.
P.O. Box 218
Terlingua, Texas
Papers in: Alpine 1st State Bank Of Texas
Lock box #31

Survey #12-63	Survey #23-63
Brewster County Mine	Presidio County Mine
Claim #12	Claim #23

Jess turned the last page over to maps on the back, "John, look at this letter."

"Let us eat first; it is ready. The letter does look interesting," John said, not reading it.

Suddenly, there was a shuffle of shoes on the back porch, "Knock, knock! Breakfast smells good!" A woman's voice came through the kitchen screen door, and it opened.

"Come in, Sweetheart," John called out. "You are in time."

The young lady walked over to him at the stove and planted a kiss on his cheek. Then reaching past him, she took a slice of crisp bacon from a plate on the stove.

"That is good and thick," smacking her lips. "Best bacon in the county," she said with a smile and turned facing Jess at the table.

"You have not met Jess Hanes," John motioned her over to the table.

Jess stood, and extended his hand. Thinking to himself, *'She sure is a beautiful redheaded with a big smile, and perfect straight teeth. She's probably his daughter LeAnn. She must be part of his family to walk right inside like that. I guess that she could be in her mid-fifties, about five foot seven or eight...a slender well-proportioned woman. With her tight blue jeans, bright yellow western short-sleeved shirt and light brown boots, she would be hard for a man to miss.'*

"Jess! LeAnn Stapleton, my only living child."

"Good morning. I have heard a lot about you from your father's correspondence. How is your first name spelled?" Jess asked.

"Please sit down, Jess," she said, shaking his hand. "One word. L-e, capital A, two small n's."

Jess repeated, "Big L, small e, big A, two small n's?"

"Correct!"

"Wow! I passed my spelling test for the day," Jess kidded.

LeAnn ignored his remark, "Daddy, do you have enough for me, too?"

Jess pulled a chair away from the table for her to sit in, then sat down. She looked Jess straight in the eye with a warm smile, exposing evenly matched white teeth. Jess was not accustomed to close female scrutiny, except from Marie Ann. LeAnn was very obviously looking him over.

She reached over and placed her hand on top of his, and with a soft Texas accent, "Sorry, Jess! Didn't mean to make you uncomfortable." Fluttering her eyelashes, "Daddy says I'm too forward with people I'm attracted to. Promise to be on my best behavior." She patted the top of his hand, "He has told me a lot about you, too! And, about Marie Ann!" Her inflection was more than just being friendly. Jess hoped she was not coming-on to him.

Jess returned her smile and locked eyes with her. He lifted her hand and planted a tender kiss on it, while continuing his eye contact. "I'm honored to meet you, LeAnn. Are your bodyguards outside? You know, you are a very beautiful lady!" Jess said with as much Texas charm as he could muster.

She blushed and broke her eye contact with him, looking up at her Dad as he put a plate of breakfast in front of her. Jess continued to hold her hand, even though she tried to remove it, and then he propped his arm on the table.

"Careful you two! You will melt the butter," John said.

Jess patted the top of her hand and released it. The three laughed and attacked breakfast like they had not eaten all week.

"Jess, I have never seen a man do what you just did to her!" John said. "You made her blush. She is somewhat the flirt!"

"Daddy! Now, that's enough," she said laughing.

"Marie Ann calls me an old flirt too!" Jess said and pushed his chair back from the kitchen table. They all laughed.

"Have you heard from the children this week?" The professor asked.

"Nope! Not a thing."

Jess had completely forgotten the letter he put next to his plate, until he reached for his coffee. Folding it, he placed it back in the envelope with the key and carefully stuck it in his shirt pocket.

After finishing breakfast with polite conversation, Jess pushed back from the table and stretched. He noticed John had not eaten any pork at all with his breakfast and dismissed his thoughts about Jewish laws. "That sure was great, John. You missed your calling. Open a ranch restaurant in Lajitas, and big city folks would flock there to sample your fine cooking."

"I could open one right here, and you two could fly in the customers from all over West Texas... Professor Stapleton's Ranch Steak House!" John said with his arms spread, a dishtowel in one hand and a skillet in the other.

"Sure, Dad! That would work. Let me see, we could..." she started a list of attractions for the restaurant.

"Enough you two. We have other important subjects to talk about. Your letter, Jess," he said.

"Yes, John!" Jess said. "You're right. We need to talk about Grandpa Hanes." He waved his hands no, and stood up. "But, right now, no! First, I must leave for Alpine. I'll be back out after talking to the sheriff. I promised to be there early this afternoon."

"Fine, I am not teaching this semester, and I am ahead of schedule on my chores," John said, wiping his mouth with a cloth napkin. "Sweetheart, you are stuck with the old man this afternoon. By the way, I did not hear Snake bark. How did you get past him?"

"Your guard knows me well enough, plus we're in love!" she said.

"I will have to talk to that canine," John said.

LeAnn turned to Jess, "What's this about your Grandfather Hanes? I've sure heard a lot about him from Daddy."

John walked over and put his arm around LeAnn's shoulder, "It is fine, Jess. She knows about your letter in event of my death."

Jess reached for another warm biscuit and smeared butter across both sections of it. Then, he added fig preserves on them.

After swallowing the first bite, "When I get back from the sheriff's office, we can talk. Right now, I better be heading that way." He pointed to his coffee cup, "Mind if I take a cup of coffee with me?"

LeAnn handed it to him and poured more coffee.

Moving away from the table carrying the bottom half of the biscuit and cup in one hand, Jess turned and reached for another biscuit, "May I have another one to take with me. Those are the biggest and best tasting I have ever eaten. Don't tell Marie Ann!"

"Flattery will get you the remainder of them," LeAnn said. "Don't forget, they are used for chocking aircraft when they are a day old. I made the dough for those biscuits two days ago. We'll have to feed and stir that sourdough tonight, so it will be ready for breakfast tomorrow."

John laughed, "Do not forget to quarter that small potato to put in the sourdough. It will need to be fed today. I am afraid to open the refrigerator where she keeps it." Motioning with his arms, "It grows and grows and grows. It may grab me someday when I open the door, and you will never hear from me again."

They laughed, and she kiddingly slapped him on the arm with her napkin.

"I keep telling her it will grow better when it is warm," John said. "Keep it covered in that crock, and put it out on the screened-in porch."

"But, Dad! You know I don't want it to grow too fast. Out on the porch it would push the crock lid off and take over the house," LeAnn said, laughing.

Jess thought, '*They seem to have a great relationship, that's fantastic.*'

"Excuse me please? Better get going," Jess said as he moved to the screen door. "Thanks for the biscuits; they will help me survive the long trip to Alpine. Which reminds me, is there a strip of ground close by to land my aircraft here?"

"Dad has a good dirt strip behind the barn," she said. "It is that flat area which goes up into the box canyon. It should be long enough."

"I think we measured it to be five thousand feet," John said.

"May I drive out there and check it?" Looking at his watch, Jess swallowed another mouth full of biscuit, "I'd better hustle."

Carrying a sack of biscuits, they walked Jess to the porch edge, and Snake followed him to the car. He waited for the door to open and hopped inside the car.

"Well now! Does this mean we are friends?" Jess asked.

John called from the porch, "That is another first around here. He does not take to strangers very quickly. Not until now!" He waved, "Take him out there with you and drop him off on the way back."

"See you two later," Jess waved as they headed toward the barn.

CHAPTER TWENTY

The Texas Rangers and Mexican crew returned to the helicopters at a small hangar across the highway from the restaurant.

Their supervisors stayed behind to formulate new details for handling the illegal immigrants, drug traffic, rustling and murder along the Texas border in the Lajitas area. Charles, Jack, Jake, Lieutenant Lopus and the Border Patrol officer, Captain Hector Gonzales, had finished breakfast and moved to an empty booth in the back of the Lajitas restaurant.

"What is the latest on Agent Simms?" Gonzales asked. "Will he recover?"

"We haven't heard this morning, but I'll call in before we leave and find out," Jack said.

"He was our key to the whole mess. I will take his place, myself," Lopus said.

"May I ask who we are talking about?" Jake asked.

"Agent Simms was our Mexican government agent working this side of the border in the Big Bend counties of Brewster and Presidio," Charles said, nervously twirling a shiny 1862 American silver dollar between his fingers. It was his good luck piece. "As you know we are all having problems with drugs, waste dumping and illegals. Both sides of the border!" Then he looked at Jack and nodded.

Jack motioned the conversation to quiet down, and directed his conversation directly to the National Parks Ranger Jake Wilson, "Simms was working as a cab driver in Alpine and a ranch hand on some of the ranches north of here. We have additional information on a gentleman who is under government protective custody. He has been a witness to some of these border activities on his ranch." Tapping the table with his empty coffee cup, he paused and raised it for their waitress to fill. He continued after she went back to the cash register, "The government is letting us handle the investigation with the state and local police. I hope that it will not require us calling in the federal agencies. They are overloaded, as it is. This is why your boss gave orders for you to assist, representing the Federal Park."

"There is a leak of information from Mexico, and from this side, as to what we are trying to do," Charles said. "Money speaks loudly along the border, and good law enforcement officers are getting bribed. Some have had their families beaten, harassed and threatened with death."

Lieutenant Lopus tapped his fingers on the table nervously, "This is the third time we have been stymied with apprehension or arrests. It is enough to cause a man to break the law and shoot the illegals on sight! No questions asked!"

"But, we all know that can't be done, legally. Only if our lives are in jeopardy," Charles said. Folding his hands and leaning his elbows on the table, he looked at Lopus sternly, "I agree it would be easier. But, we have to live with ourselves too. Some of the law enforcements' morals match the criminals' and are becoming so seared, so bad, they can't see right from wrong. Some people just don't care! And, that affects us directly! That's when innocent people get killed."

They sat there in their own deep thoughts, trying to come up with plans to outsmart the international drug cartel. They knew one of the biggest problems the lawman encountered was that prosecutors would not take a smuggling case unless the law enforcement officers got at least three of the smuggled aliens to be material witnesses.

The waitress brought coffee, "Freshly brewed, gentleman!" They shook their heads, no, and she then left them with the thermos pot of coffee.

Charles continued, "Like Hector said, 'Never mind the fact that two B.P. officers saw the aliens come out of the brush, jump into an awaiting vehicle, and drive in front of them. When stopped by the B.P., all the aliens would not admit to be smuggled by a U.S. Citizen or anyone else.'"

Jake picked up on Charles' point and leaned closer to the others around the table, "Unless we can get three or more of the aliens to be material witnesses, we have no case. And then, the U.S. citizen goes free. Any other time, if a law enforcement officer sees a crime committed, that is all that is needed. He or she does not need to get three or more of the accomplices to testify against you."

Jack put his hands behind his head and leaned back in his chair, "You know, if we could pass legislation that would enable law enforcement like us to write citations and fine the U.S. citizens for each alien or drug in the vehicle, maybe that would help curb the smuggling. They charge $700 to over $3,500 per person to smuggle aliens from Mexico to Houston."

"Yea, and more than that is made on the Asian drug traffic into the central part of the U.S. because we can't stop it here," Jake said squinting his eyes, putting deep wrinkles into his tanned face. "Did you hear about the homemade twin engine aircraft that flew 500 pounds of coke from Mexico to Detroit, non-stop? Now that takes a large amount of money to back that kind of operation, and we can't fight it here locally. Not successfully!"

"Well guys! What we can do, let's do it!" Charles said forcefully, getting restless and needing to get outside. He was tired of just talking and not solving anything.

"I know!" Jack said, "We lucked out on the truck accident. The patrolmen were not seriously hurt and no smuggled waste chemical got into Mexico. But, we still have not found the holding point for the drugs. They don't use the same place each time, and with so much area to cover... Now, if we find that, and if," he put up both hands making a quotation sign with his fingers, "we could find it all together - drugs, aliens, tankers and some of the head cartel?"

"Yeah, a big 'if'!" Jake said. "Also, remember! Nobody was found in the truck wreck. The Border Patrol is supposed to bring their dogs today and search the area. Right, Gonzales?"

"Ya! I'll make sure that is done," Gonzales said.

"I'll have to get back in the park tomorrow," Jake said. "So, I'll contact you guys later tonight by radio, on the outcome."

Jack looked at Charles for his approval, "I'm sending one chopper back north and will keep the other one at the ranch. We can work three teams at one time now. Charles, once you get your horses and gear, you can cover closer to Castalon and Lajitas. I'll cover between Alpine, Marfa, and down this way by chopper." Pointing at the lieutenant, "You can continue on the other side as you see fit. We can coordinate our efforts again by radio with you." Nodding to Jake, "Keep your eyes open and let us know what you come up with." Spreading his arms, Jack said, "Suggestions, anyone?"

There were none.

"I'll keep my men and horses here at Lajitas to start with," Charles continued. "We'll stay in the pickups and pull the horse trailers until we need them. We have three trucks over at the hangar. Don't forget to use the 'scrambled' channels on the radios. We don't want the bad guys to get the jump on us. They also have state-of-the-art electronics equipment."

"Wouldn't surprise me if they used satellite communications," Jake said. "Ya, I know they do and El Paso should be able to monitor them, but if they do, why don't they filter it down to us?" He shook his head.

"Jake, we have a radio for you in the helicopter," Charles said as he scooted out of the booth. "We'll need your assistance in the park."

"Great! I'll be on my way. Be careful, you guys!" Jake said, and shook everyone's hand.

Jake, Charles and Gonzales headed out the front door after paying for their breakfast. Lopus and Jack were still talking in the booth. Jack had purposely asked him to stay behind.

"Let's wait and go out in a few minutes," Jack said. "There is no need for Jake to hear the rest of this conversation. He is trustworthy, but he doesn't need to know about our leak of information." Nodding to the lieutenant, "Who is your number one suspect in Mexico?"

Lopus cleared his throat. Sitting sideways in his chair and with a lowered voice, "Commissioner Rodiquez has been on my list for a long time. He is power conscious and money hungry. His government income does not match his lifestyle. He has long absences, somewhere in the Middle East and here in this country, which does not match his job responsibilities... or his monthly pay."

He turned his back to the adobe wall, "I also suspect he had Don Simms setup at the airport." While tapping his index finger on the table for emphasis, he said, "Before I forget! Captain Jack, please apologize to your uncle for Mexico. He could have been shot at the same time Agent Simms was. I would like to meet him to tell him that myself."

"We can make arrangements for you to meet him," Jack said. "Ya! He was lucky, or rather, the good Lord was watching over him."

"Amen! Jesus had His hand on your uncle," Lopus said while crossing his heart with his hand.

"Yes, He did," replied Jack with a broad smile. "Even so, I'm glad Uncle Jess is down here. He can be a big help if we need quick support."

"He retired after thirty years in the Air Force. You remember, Cambodia, Vietnam, Panama, Desert Storm, and then Sarajevo, Bosnia, Yugoslavia?"

The lieutenant nodded, yes.

"He's been around," Jack said. "I think he's still on call from the federal government. He was drafted into the Texas Rangers the other evening! That's confidential!"

"From what you express about him, they have made a sound choice. I can tell, you are close to your Uncle Jess," Lopus said with a frown of caution. "Don't let that closeness cloud your decisions in this battle."

Jack nodded his understanding with a smile. "You can say that again!" He paused and folded his hands, "Anyway, to finish our discussion, we have a hotel in Presidio under surveillance. There are some high rollers in town from Las Vegas and Chicago. Sometimes, I think those mobsters are more on a status kick than hungry for money. The big flashy cars with out-of-state plates make them stand out like a sore thumb." Wiping a water spot left from his water glass with a napkin, "There may be a link between that group and your commissioner. Can you get me documents or written info on him? Does he have South American or Asian connections? We will need his full name, birthplace, and schooling if any. You know, whatever you can get. I'll check with Interpol, Washington and our headquarters in Midland."

Lopus shook Jack's hand and stood up, "This will continue to be my priority. I'm excited about the outcome. Keep in contact."

"*Buen viaje, amigo!*" Jack said. "Let's go! I'm anxious to get back on track."

When the two men got outside, Charles saw them and gave one finger-fisted circle above his head for the co-pilots to start the helicopters. The two Texas Rangers jogged to their helicopters as Lieutenant Lopus headed toward the Rio Grande River. Six

Mexican men, who looked like they had just left the dusty road, straggled in behind him.

CHAPTER TWENTY-ONE

Commissioner Rodiquez's frown became a cruel looking smile, exposing crooked stained teeth. He was using his Mexican government position as commissioner for a front to his drug/firearms traffic dealings with Arab terrorists and the mobsters in Chicago and Vegas. Rodiquez was a skinny five-foot eight, and with his western boots on, he looked taller. He wore a stylish western business suit, which made him look out of place in the small Mexican town.

He jammed a *cigarro* into the corner of his mouth and puffed excitedly. Then, with one long draw, inhaled and exhaled the thick smoke through his nose. He moved away from the second floor villa window thinking, *A deposit of an extra two million American dollars in my secret bank account in Bogotá, Columbia, will certainly be nice. If Lieutenant Lopus does not continue to mess things up in Texas, I'll have that money today. Then, I will leave for Columbia tomorrow and then Algeria.*

He patted a large black duffle bag and then scooted it under the back of his desk. *This eight million dollars added to my deposit will leave me a comfortable cushion of ten million American dollars to spend on the French Riviera.* He was pleased with himself.

Taking another deep drag from his *cigarro*, he again, slowly let the smoke flow from his nostrils while pacing the floor. Intensely thinking, *'Although my shot did not kill Agent Simms, and the truck's cargo did not make it into Mexico, drug money will still be flowing. The drugs should be on the way north into Arizona by sundown. The Americans can choke on it as far as I am concerned. My main cover, Lieutenant Lopus, has worked out wonderfully. As long as I can keep him from getting too nosey, everything will be fine.'*

He moved back to the open shuttered window which had no screen, and blew a smoke ring out into the still air, thinking, *'These green Yankee dollars will be in my hands tonight if all continues to go well. Next time, I will do it right under their nose, even if Simms lives.'*

Noise from the room outside his office drew his attention. Before he could get to the door, it was violently swung open by two military Arab men. This caused him to stagger backward into the edge of his huge desk. They glared at him, and then eyed the room for anyone else. A tall, well-dressed Arabic speaking military officer, with a smirk of a smile, limped into the room. He towered above Rodiquez.

The people in the outer office, confused by the abrupt intrusion, fled into the hall yelling for security. The two Arab soldiers with automatic weapons closed the door and stood in the outer office waiting for the officer to come out.

In Commissioner Rodiquez's office, the tall officer pointed at him with a long weathered finger. Rodiquez spoke first in Spanish, swore, and then demanded, "What is the meaning of this rude intrusion, and who are you?" Moving behind his desk, he opened a drawer to reach for a small automatic UZI submachine gun.

"That is not necessary my friend!" Still pointing at the commissioner, the officer replied in Spanish, "I am General Alvarez." He calmly walked toward the commissioner with a limp, "I am not armed at the moment! I mean you no harm, unless you demand it."

Smiling, his eyes narrowed and the smile turned to a sneer, "Please come to this side of your desk, so we may talk more politely about your drug money."

"What drug money?" Rodiquez asked as he sat on the edge of his desk. Thinking, *This ugly foreigner will not intimidate me any longer,* "Who are you? Who sent you?"

"You do not listen very well!" Alvarez was getting impatient with the commissioner, "Is not my Spanish clear enough for you?" He slammed his fist on the desk next to the commissioner. "I do not have time for lengthy explanations for infidels. Ten million American dollars! Cash! You were to deliver it across the border yesterday! I am to take it from you to purchase weapons, firearms, and missiles." He slammed his fist on the desktop, again, "Call your contact in Mexico City – now!"

The wrong thing came out of the commissioner's mouth, "Get out of here! I will call my security if you do not leave!"

"What security? I see no security!" Alvarez pointed a shaking finger. "Perhaps further persuasion is required! Look out that window, to your left! Observe the men on top of that building with rifles. And, across the street! Now!" He shouted, "Sit down!" He said shoving the commissioner's desk chair toward him, "I am running out of time and patience with you!"

"I do not have any money for you or anyone else, much less drug money," Rodiquez said. This giant of a man was beginning to frighten him.

"Call this number," Alvarez said writing a telephone number on the desk pad, then shoved the phone at him. "You are nothing! You are just a small man in international trade. Call! So, I can leave this stinking office of yours."

Again, Rodiquez said the wrong thing, "No!"

The general moved faster than expected of a man his size. Grabbing the commissioner by the shoulder, spinning him around, the general grabbed the seat of Alvarez's pants, and lifted half of the commissioner's flailing body out the window. He was pinned to the windowsill by the general's body size and strength.

"We are only two floors from the ground, but you will be dead before you hit it. Where is the drug money?" he yelled.

"I do not have it yet!" Trying to catch his breath, "I will have the money tonight. I do not have it now!"

Pulling the commissioner back in, Alvarez brushed him off, straightened his tie for him, and handed him a handkerchief. "You are bleeding, Mr. Commissioner." Pointing to his own ear, he said, "It is the left ear. I would hate to see a nice suit ruined with all that blood. Perhaps, I should cut it off and stuff it in your mouth?"

Again the commissioner was pushed, this time to his desk, but Alvarez had already reached past him and had the Uzi weapon, "Please! Use the telephone!" He pressed the barrel against the commissioner's neck, and nodded toward the telephone.

Rodiquez made the phone call, obtained instructions, and was then escorted by the Arabs out the back entrance and to a waiting cattle truck. He hesitated getting in and was rewarded a rifle butt to the back of the head. Falling halfway through the trailer's open door, one Arab grabbed his collar and pulled him all the way inside. He lay in a pile of fresh cow manure.

"We do like traveling in style," Alvarez said.

The truck left for the little airport outside of town, where a C130 cargo aircraft was waiting. Rodiquez was pushed out of the cattle trailer onto the gravel runway, where he slowly sat up as the truck left the area.

Seeing the aircraft, "That aircraft is too large for flying this close to the Texas border. Radar will pick it up and..." He was slapped in the side of the head by one of the general's men. Two of them lifted the commissioner by the shoulders and pushed him to the aircraft.

General Alvarez only smiled and looked away.

Mule Ear Peaks
Big Bend National Park

CHAPTER TWENTY-TWO

Jess stood up to leave the Brewster County Sheriff's office in Alpine and extended his hand to Sheriff Baker.

"Thanks for coming in, Jess." He shook hands with Jess. "This should take care of all the red-tape paper work. By the way, we just received news from doctors in Austin. They say Agent Simms is recovering from his operation faster than expected. He is in good health and should be back in a week or so."

"That is good to hear. He was a mess the last time we saw him," Jess said while signing the papers. "Which reminds me! I forgot a note pad of his in all the excitement. It's in my hotel room. Do you need it?"

Sheriff Baker shrugged his shoulders, put his hands on his gun belt, "I don't think so. Let me look at it later. I've some running to do about that truck wreck. Thanks again, Jess."

"You're welcome, Sheriff. I'll be staying at the ranch tonight in my aircraft. I'm doing research in Marfa, Presidio and Terlingua. If you need me, contact either Professor Stapleton or the Texas Rangers. Someone will know where I am."

After checking out of the Settler's Hotel, Gladys' Taxi Service took Jess to the airport. She was full of all kinds of questions, which Jess avoided answering directly. He suspected everyone in town knew his business with the law.

At the airport, Jess loaded the Pilatus PC-6 aircraft, opened all the windows and doors, patched the holes on both sides of the fuselage, had it refueled, preflighted it and made his flight plans from the sectional aeronautical chart of the local Big Bend area.

Jess spread the chart on the ground under the wing of the aircraft and knelt to refresh his memory of where he wanted to fly before it got dark. He had six hours before sunset. A nice breeze came out of the north making it seem cooler.

He kept thinking over the past events, '*What a crazy three days! I wonder if I will encounter any other surprises before this day finally ends. Anyway, my map shows State Road 118 down to Study Butte and up to the ranch - eighty miles down and sixty back to the ranch.*

The Amarillo Mariposa Mine is not on my sectional, but it's on one of Grandpa Hanes' hand-drawn maps. The other mines are located on the Texas Archeological Survey map of the Big Bend, Terlingua and Lajitas areas.'

#

Study Butte was directly south of Alpine, but Jess did not plan on a straight flight. The rugged country of Southwest Texas was too unusual for him to just fly over and not get down low to investigate its rarities, especially if it would be a great view to record on video.

He had been cleared with the FAA for flying in the ADIZ areas, and cleared with the Border Patrol, Texas Rangers, Texas Air & Army National Guard Units and National Park service. His clearance covered low flights in the Big Bend area from Marfa to Presidio, Marfa to Alpine-Marathon-Haymond-Sanderson, and south to the Rio Grande River. Even the U.S. Air Force had been notified of his scheduled flight plans for the next two months.

He had notified The Center for Big Bend Studies at Sul Ross University of his archeological research intentions in the areas of interest to them. They had been very supportive and interested in his findings.

Jess had videoed farms and ranches to sell to magazines. This trip was to locate some of the remote mines that were not on maps. He had installed a small video camera system. One lens, in the top of the vertical stabilizer, looked forward; one lens viewed the canopy for a view of the pilot from the right wingtip; the third lens viewed forward from the high wing; and the fourth lens was mounted in his helmet. The camera's lenses could be selected individually or all at one time with toggle switches mounted on the instrument panel. There was a five-inch monitor screen mounted next to the switches for him to see the view of each selected camera lens. It had a white flip-up plastic cover for protection from the sun when not in use. Plus, it hid the monitor from prying eyes. The 8mm digital video camera was stored under the pilot's seat for easy access and removal.

He had seen the system used by professional stunt pilot instructors to record their student's progress during flight lessons.

Jess designed his own khaki skull cap/helmet with a video camera strapped in a Velcro pocket at eye level. He could fly and tape whatever he could see by moving his head in that direction. It had a remote zoom and focus function switch for the camera installed on the control stick.

Curiosity was one of Jess' many traits, even though it usually got him into trouble. Some people would consider it being nosey. Often Jess would land where no runways were available, just to check out something that caught his eye when he flew over. Open desert, clear mesas and dry sandbars of a creek or river were always inviting places to land. *A good pilot always watches for clear areas for emergency landings, especially flying at low altitudes. I should practice a few while I'm here.*

#

As Jess flew 300 feet above Adobe Walls Mountain, he could see Christmas Mountain four miles to the left and Wildhorse Mountains eight miles further ahead in the distance. This was the area of Study Butte, where the tanker truck had collided with the county sheriff's car.

He contacted the nearest FSS, which was in El Paso, and they still were monitoring his location with 'flight following' until he dropped to a lower altitude where their radar lost him. He advised them that his flight in the Lajitas and Terlinga areas would be no more than an hour and he would be landing at the professor's ranch.

With two cameras, one under the seat looking down through the bottom porthole and the other in his helmet, Jess could select either one or both to run. He selected the camera lens under the right wing, and it auto focused on Leon Mountain. He then switched to the left wing and focused on Indian Head Mountain. This would give him a wide scan forward from both wings at the same time, sort of a panoramic view.

"Okay," he whispered, "I'm finally ready!"

Thinking quietly, *The monitor indicates the correct date and time; in addition, we're in focus. Location is junction of Texas road 118 and 170 at Study Butte, Texas. Cut back RPM for slow flight of 55 KTS, bank slowly to the right. Yea! There's the junction of the two highways, and there is the wrecked tanker in the ravine! Camera and action!*

With the helmet camera running at the same time, Jess was getting good-recorded views. "Wow! What a burn down there! Look at the ground around what's left of the truck, and the depth of the ravine it crashed. It's still smoldering." Jess locked in the wing lens to stay on the truck as he continued a 45° bank while holding his altitude eight hundred feet above the top of the foothills on both sides of the highway.

He leveled off, synchronized the lens of the camera forward, followed highway 170 west toward Terlingua, and continued taping the view from his helmet. He passed Cigar Mountain on his right. On his left toward the south was a beautiful view of Big Bend National Park, Chisos Mountains and the Terlingua Fault leading to the Santa Elena Canyon. The Rio Grande River cut the canyon some 1,900 feet deep and emptied out on the desert floor making an abrupt 90° southerly turn.

Looking north for a clearing turn, Jess lowered the right wing for circling the mining area near Terlingua, and descended to five hundred feet above the ground in a 360° slow turn. Leveling off again, he headed north when something huge cast a shadow over the aircraft. He knew it was a cloudless day. The Pilatus shuttered, and the nose dropped from the vortex wake of a four engine cargo aircraft passing dangerously close overhead toward Lajitas.

Jess applied full turbo power and pulled up steep to keep from loosing any more altitude. Gritting his teeth from uncomfortable G-force, Jess hollered at the top of his voice, "Where did you come from? Another C130! Desert sand paint job, and I can't see your markings. He's heading straight for Mexico, and I can't catch him! What's your hurry, and where're you going? I gotcha on both cameras! Adjust the lens for your distance... there you are! I have a sharp picture, but still no markings on that aircraft! Where have I seen this before?"

Jess continued to climb to three thousand feet, contacted the El Paso FSS about what happened, then angled down toward the C130 Hercules cargo aircraft, which had started a wide slow circle northwest of Lajitas. "I've still got you on video! I'm going through two thousand; he must be under a hundred feet, right on the deck. Hope the automatic telescopic zoom lens stays focused and gets a good shot of all this if I can hold my head still enough. Got everything focused on him now! This will be great! I can't look at the monitor and him, too! Hopefully, my digital camera will take out all this shaking around. I'm doing 160 knots and he's leaving me in the dust heading into Mexico."

Coming out of the shallow dive, leveling at two hundred feet, Jess began to climb and turned back north to keep from getting too close to the Rio Grande River at the Texas-Mexican border.

He could still see the aircraft as he rose to six thousand feet above the ground. It all happened in about fifteen minutes time.

The cargo plane crossed over Lajitas as Jess watched from his higher altitude. It climbed steeply and continued into Mexico, west bound.

Jess took a deep breath, "That was certainly a surprise. Wonder if it was a Mexican aircraft? With all the tensions down here because of September 11th, I'm surprised he wasn't on radar." He turned off his video cameras.

Slowing his speed to 55 knots, he took the portable transceiver Charles had given him from the door pocket. Then, he stuck the antenna out the air vent in his window and called, "This is an emergency. I need to contact Texas Ranger Randel. This is Pilatus PC-6 calling any Texas Ranger in the Big Bend area."

Silence.

"This is an emergency! I need the Texas Rangers! This is Pilatus PC-6."

Silence again.

"Where are they when you need them?"

Jess tried twice more as he headed toward Professor Stapleton's ranch. North of Lajitas, flying fifty feet above the ground, he passed over a panel truck churning up a cloud of dust approaching a mine at Tres Cuevas Mountain (Three Caves). He was thinking, *It must still be a productive mine with all those people standing around the entrance.*

#

A white panel truck with a fictitious name on it in large fancy scrolled letters, ACCENT HEATING and AIR CONDITIONING, was leaving a cloud of dust on the desert road. It slid to a stop next to a new, blue Cadillac at an abandon mine.

The truck's dust settled over the car, truck and the men standing near the mine entrance.

"Let's get out of here! There's too many low flying aircraft," said the white-uniformed truck driver. His fat stomach rubbed the steering wheel.

His t-shirted passenger replied, "Don't think about it! We're here now! So, get with the program and start loading it."

They had come close to ramming the Cadillac, and when the dust settled enough for them to get out of the truck, they could hear yelling and swearing. Someone shouted orders for them to get in the truck and back it up to the mine entrance.

"Who in their right mind would bring a swanky car like that out here in the desert? Someone's trying to make an impression! Stupid city dudes," the driver said. He removed his green ball cap and wiped the sweat off his forehead.

After two Mexicans loaded the truck with the hemp roped burlap sacks of sealed wax packages, a well-dressed man exited the big car and yelled at the truck driver, "Give me a good count on those sacks. Write it down anywhere on this receipt, and I'll compare it with the manifest order."

"I bet these bundles have drugs in them," the driver said to his partner. "No wonder they were so cagey on the phone. If we deliver this in good shape, they said we would get a bonus."

Closing one back door of the panel truck, "Yea! We have to be out of Texas by sunset and we have a long way to go," said his helper from behind the truck. "I don't want to know what we're hauling. We need to get it delivered as soon as possible."

A big man got out of the Cadillac and walked over to the truck, opened the door and took the keys from the ignition, "Nothing leaves until the Commissioner gets here! No money, no drugs! You must understand *Señor*, you will not leave with this shipment until we have the money." After stating that, he exposed a weapon under his suit jacket.

The driver waved his hands in front of him, "All I know is the money will be here in an hour by helicopter."

Another well-dressed Mexican left the car and went into the mine. Two shots echoed through the tunnels and out to the men at the mine's entrance.

"What's going on in there?" the driver asked. "Second thought, I really don't want to know that either! Shut the truck doors! Lock them. We will seal it after the money changes hands."

He climbed into the cab of the truck, reached behind the seat for a collapsible-stocked M16 rifle, and then put it on his lap. His partner got in, rolled down the window and pulled an Uzi submachine gun from under the seat.

"That chopper better get here on time," his helper said. "Or, we may not get out of here. Wonder who got shot in the cave?"

"That's no cave! That's an old abandon mercury mine," the driver said. "Chisos Mariposa. Know what that means in Spanish?"

"No! Don't know any Spanish."

"Ghost Butterfly. The old story they tell at Van Horn is there are evil spirits of Indians living in the depths of the mine. Sounds mysterious don't it?"

"How come you know so much about this part of the country? You're from Chicago," the driver's partner said.

"I spent some time south of here at Laredo in the Air Force. I use to come out here to the Big Bend to hunt Mule Deer or spend the weekend roaming around. Those were the good old days," the driver laughed and rolled his window down. "That breeze feels good." He yawned and stretched his arms, "Looks like we've got a long wait with these people. I'm going to close my eyes and nap until the chopper gets here."

They both slumped in their seats with their eyes closed. One of them began to snore.

136

CHAPTER TWENTY-THREE

Earlier than expected, Jess landed on the dirt airstrip at Professor Stapleton's ranch, and taxied to the barn. The professor and his daughter LeAnn heard him circle and were at the barn before he turned the engine off. She had two sets of tire chocks ready. After Jess fully stopped and the propeller quit spinning, she put them in front and back of the main gear tires.

Jess opened the pilot's door, "Hi, there! Got iced tea at this airport?"

"Sure we do, come on! We'll have lunch shortly!" she replied. "It won't cost you much!"

"How you doing, John?" Jess asked when he opened the cargo door on the Pilatus from inside.

"Fine, fine!" he said and slowly walked around Jess' aircraft, looking it over very carefully.

LeAnn and the professor finally got around to Jess' side of the aircraft where he sat on the floor with his legs hanging out the cargo entrance. John pointed at the two blue patches over bullet holes.

"Those are the holes punched by high powered rifle slugs that went through Agent Simms' body," Jess said.

John shook his head, "I hope he is not permanently disabled."

"Me, too!" Jess replied.

The two stood back a few feet, and she spread her arms wide, looking at the Pilatus, "Now this is a huge expensive piece of transportation! And, it's slow too!"

"Not really!" Jess smiled opening the section of the cargo door wider and locking it in place. "When you consider, I can come and go most anywhere in good or bad weather with all my state-of-the-art electronics. Plus, I can see the country better at lower altitudes and speed. I can almost transport a baby whale,"

Jess said laughing. "It will cruise at 130 knots fully loaded with no strain."

"How many seats can you put back here?" John asked looking inside from the cargo door entrance.

LeAnn motioned with her hand asking Jess if she could get inside. He nodded his approval, jumped from the cargo opening to the ground, and then held his folded hands together for her. Up she went and he then helped her father inside. Stooping, they moved forward and sat in the pilot and copilot's seats.

"Back here," Jess said, pointing at the seat mounting locations on the floor. "I can put three rows of seats, three across. Nine passengers total, which does not include the pilot and co-pilot." He pulled the aircraft's manual out of a pouch behind the co-pilot's seat. "With this Pratt & Whitney turboprop engine, I can carry a lot of weight." Flipping through the pages, "Actually, around 3,373 pounds above its empty weight of 2,800 pounds. This gives a maximum takeoff weight of 6,173 pounds."

"So, with all the seats out, except these two in front, you can carry a bunch of cargo." LeAnn concluded.

"I have only carried a maximum load once, which put no strain on this old bird. I have the original logs from when the Air Force purchased this for Vietnam. Since then, it was factory refurbished with new engine, electronics, windscreen, doors, windows and insulated interior."

Jess spoke like a proud pilot would about his aircraft, "I went over to the factory in Switzerland and flew it back. I know what Lindbergh went through, but I had good navigational aides. It was a long flight, with stops in Paris, London, and then Aberdeen, Scotland. From there, to the small islands north... the Shetland Islands! I took on a full load of fuel in the regular wing tanks, two tanks hanging under the wings, and three rubber bladder tanks back here on the floor. Those five items I sent back to the factory."

"I wager that was expensive on top of the aircraft cost. How many gallons did you have in those five tanks?" John asked.

"A total of 384 gallons, which included the aircraft integral fuel tanks full, at approximately $3.75 per gallon in Switzerland. A total weight would have been that times six pounds per gallon... equals... rounding it off, six times 400, would be 2,400 pounds of fuel."

LeAnn put her finger in the air, "You were well over your gross weight limit! Especially, with everything else you would have had as extra weight!"

"Yes, it was close. But, it would burn off the further I flew," he said. "There wasn't any problem getting off the ground." He shook his head, "I wouldn't do it again!"

They continued discussing the technical aspects of the PC-6. LeAnn thoroughly inspected each instrument and equipment mounted on the flight panel. John just listened, taking in his daughter's knowledge of aircraft.

He asked again, "What did this gangly single engine aircraft cost you?"

Jess leaned against the interior wall, "Now, would you believe, it all was a gift? It did not cost me a thing, not even the insurance. It is a gift from the King of Morocco. I'll have to tell you about that adventure sometime," Jess said.

"Aw, no way! Come on!" LeAnn said. "You've got to be kidding me."

"No! He is not kidding." John said all knowingly. "It is a fantastic story. Jess, you should author a book about it."

"I have kept journals on all my travels, but I'm not a writer," Jess said.

"You can get someone to take your journals and write your story for you. In fact, that is what I do," LeAnn said.

"Really! I'll certainly keep that in mind."

She put her hands together and entwined her fingers, pointing at Jess with her index fingers pressed together, "Please call me, Le. Most of my friends do."

"I can do that," he replied.

John cleared his throat; "It irritates me when Americans cut the English language to pieces like that!" He looked directly at LeAnn, "Such as; shortening 24 hours a day, seven days a week... to 24-7. American English is becoming a coded language."

"Yes, Daddy!" She replied, and kidded him, "It's a cultural thing!"

Jess jumped back to the ground and heard a low growl from under the aircraft. It was Snake stretched out and watching Jess. He wanted some attention. He was panting from the heat with his tongue hanging out the side of his mouth. His tail wagged so hard it was hitting the ground on both sides of his body.

"Come here feller! I'll scratch'cha between your ears," Jess said. The dog moved next to him and leaned against his leg, waiting for more scratching.

"By the way," Jess said. "I need to contact the sheriff or the Texas Rangers. As you can tell, I'm easily sidetracked when I'm not flying." Smacking his head with the palm of his hand, "It's an emergency. I should have tried again before I landed. Le," he pointed, "hand me that radio in the pouch of right seat, please." LeAnn looked puzzled about Jess having to call.

He finally contacted the Rangers and passed along the information about the C-130 aircraft headed for Mexico. He explained what had happened with the C130, and then about the crowd of people at the Chisos Mariposa mine. They locked his aircraft and walked to the house.

LeAnn chased after Snake, picking up a piece of tree bark and throwing it for him to fetch. She turned to Jess, "I sure would like to fly your plane. I mean fly with you sometime!"

"Great, no problem. Just let me know." Jess said. "You're welcome to come along too, Professor."

"No!" He curtly replied. "I do not like flying in small aircraft."

She kidded, "Now, a few minutes ago, you agreed that was a huge aircraft."

He just looked at her with a sly twinkle in his eye, shaking his head, "I cannot out maneuver or escape with anything!"

"You have a pilot's license?" Jess asked.

She nodded, "Sure I do! Twin and single engine commercial, instruments, acrobatics and glider!" she said with a broad smile. "Last count I had over 3,200 hours total time."

"That's two up on me. I don't have two of those endorsements," Jess said. "I've never been in a glider and no acrobatics."

Walking up on the back porch, John said, "This all is definitely more than I experienced. Never will I be in an aircraft that flies crazy like she does with those maneuvers. I have no idea what my total flying time is, haven't added them for a few years."

"I've never flown anything else, just tail draggers," she said as they entered the kitchen. "Never flown one as big as your Pilatus."

"I can certify you in the P6 and for complex aircraft, if you want it," Jess said. "I'm still a CF-double-I."

"When? Sometime soon, I hope," she said and then pointed at her father. "But, first! Let me get dinner on the table. We can talk about this later. I'm hungry."

Wrinkling his forehead, John asked, "What is CFII?"

"Certified Flight Instructor with Instruments," LeAnn answered.

CHAPTER TWENTY-FOUR

At the Chisos Mariposa mine, both groups had gathered to transfer the drugs and money. Everyone was on edge because the deadline for the exchange had passed, and no money. The unusual moaning wind continued to whistle in the inner shafts of the mine, which added to the heightening of tensions. They were all standing inside the entrance out of the direct morning sunshine.

The three, well-dressed men from the big city were outwardly uncomfortable in the close-walled mine. The driver of the truck and his companion stayed back in the shadows, created by the air movements across the flame of kerosene oil lanterns hanging from overhead beams of the mine. They all cast black silhouettes on the walls. The city guys shaded their eyes from the bright sunlight after leaving the entrance of the mine.

Inside the mine, "These big shots from the north sure think their something in their fancy clothes and big car. I'll be glad when the boss gets here with the money, so we can get this load on the road," Sam said. His whispering echoed in the mine. "I don't trust these guys. Wish we didn't need the other gang's money and could just stay a small gang. The more we get into the bigger gang, the more people to mistrust. I don't like strangers." He rubbed his stomach and turned his back to Johnny. "I'm sure getting hungry. Think I'll get my lunch sack."

"Ah!" He stepped back looking at the dirt floor, "Johnny! Remember those shots we heard? Someone was dragged back there. Look at these heel marks in the dirt." Sam turned around and his buddy was gone, "Johnny, where did you go?"

Looking into the dark mine tunnel, he could not see his buddy.

"It ain't safe in here with no flashlight! Where are you?"

Johnny called from the darkness, "Sam, get one of those lanterns and come in here."

Johnny's small pocket flashlight led Sam to him holding the lantern, "Where did you get that tiny thing?"

"I had it on my key ring," Johnny answered. "Look here! These two Mexicans are all tied up. I thought somebody got shot, but there ain't no blood anywhere," Johnny said. "They are both alive!"

The two illegal Mexican immigrants, hired by Commissioner Rodiquez, who had been watching over the drug cache for three days were wide-eyed and scared. They had tape across their lips and could not yell for help.

Sam removed the tape and neither Mexican spoke to him or Johnny, but whispered in Spanish to each other. They were frightened their lives were about to end.

"Boss will be mad! He had these two hired by somebody in Mexico to stay here with this stuff. We'd better cut them loose," Sam said.

Johnny pulled a bowie knife from his boot and tried to convince the two he meant them no harm. After they were free, the four cautiously approached the inside of the mine entrance. The three city dudes were in the Cadillac, not noticing the four leaving the mine.

Sam and Johnny pointed their guns at the men in the car, and Johnny yelled, "Hey you guys! Don't move a muscle. Slowly put your hands behind your heads. We're supposed to be working together to get these drugs up north. Why tie up our hired help? These Mexicans were watching over the stuff inside." He and Sam stayed between the guys in the car and the Mexicans.

The large Mexican driver behind the steering wheel in the Cadillac sneered, "Watch your mouth truck driver. We couldn't understand their language! They looked to me like they were going to load the drugs in their pickup truck. His Spanish was so poor, I couldn't talk to him."

"You big city dwellers can't speak your own language to these two guys? Boy, that's dumb!" Sam remarked with a laugh. "What do you think we are here for? Mining gold?"

"Like we told you!" One of the rough talking men from inside the car, said, "Watch that mouth of yours, trucker, or I'll have your tongue cut out!"

Johnny shouted, "Okay! Okay! Back off! This isn't getting us anywhere. Both our bosses will get here with the money, and we can get this over with and out of here. All this macho stuff will do is get us all killed."

He turned and pointed for the two Mexicans to get in their pickup truck, "Nobody's going anywhere right now."

No sooner had he shut his mouth, a C130 cargo aircraft flew low above them making an approach for a short field landing on the dirt runway at Lajitas. They did not want to use the new paved runway four and a half miles out of town. The men at the mine stood wide-eyed after they ducked for cover from the low flying aircraft.

The little border community of Lajitas was located on the Rio Grande River, a crossing to and from Mexico. A military fort was built in 1915 by the U.S. Army to stop invaders like Poncho Villa. The village had not grown much, but recently a few modern businesses had been built: motels, gas stations, restaurants, river tour offices and pack mules for hire.

The aircraft made a loud roar as the four turboprop engines reversed to slow the aircraft on the runway. It stopped and began to back up. The aircrew stood on the rear-loading ramp as it was lowered about three feet above the ground. The aircraft continued to backup all the way to the east end of the runway. Two engines shut down while the other two continued to idle. The military aircrew wore battle dress uniforms of desert light tan and carried automatic weapons.

A small, dark gray helicopter landed close to the huge cargo aircraft. Two men from the Chicago mobsters got out and slowly walked toward the back ramp. Three men, General Alvarez with his bodyguard and Commissioner Rodiquez were on the cargo ramp of the aircraft. They jumped off as it was being lowered to the ground and approached the two from the helicopter.

One of the men from the helicopter said, "General Alvarez, your money as promised!" and then handed two attaché cases to Alvarez and nothing to Rodiquez. No other words were spoken as Alvarez and his bodyguard turned toward his large aircraft.

"Alvarez! Where is my money?" Rodiquez yelled as they walked away from him.

He was the go-between, between Alvarez and the drug dealers, and wanted his part of the drug money. Alvarez and his men walked up the ramp and further into the aircraft, ignoring Rodiquez. The men on the ramp pointed their weapons at the commissioner, preventing him from getting back on the ramp. The ramp was raised off the ground, leaving the commissioner behind. He ran and jumped, grabbing the edge of the ramp. One of the soldiers stepped on his fingers, causing Rodiquez to drop to the ground.

The aircraft's two silent engines came alive as they matched the high-pitch roar of the other two. The men disappeared inside as the ramp closed, and the aircraft was soon in the air, leaving the commissioner in a cloud of dust. He knelt and bent over with his backside to the windblast, covering his eyes and face with his arms to keep the small gravel from hitting him.

The helicopter bounced on its skids as the two men from Chicago got back inside. It scooted across the gravel in the backwash of the larger aircraft. It was not damaged, but the pilot had a rough time keeping it on the ground. The blast of wind subsided, and the helicopter rose in the air, spraying the commissioner again with dust and gravel. He shook his fist at the men in the helicopter as it left for the mine. The large cargo aircraft skimmed low across Lajitas and disappeared into Mexico.

This activity lasted only ten minutes, but it was enough to stir up the border authorities and Texas Rangers in town.

The men at the mine watched the helicopter approach and land in an open area behind the Cadillac. Two men got out as the rotor blades of the helicopter began to spin faster, blowing dust and gravel again, then departed toward the mountains in the north, leaving the two men behind.

There were smiling faces from everyone at the Mariposa mine. Both of the gangs' bosses had arrived and all seemed well. The whole group went into the entrance of the mine to get out of the hot sun and dust.

"Anyone have cold water?" asked one to the bosses.

The big Mexicans driving the Cadillac said, "There is iced tea in the car."

"I have an ice water jug in the big truck for anyone who don't like tea," said Johnny.

"Great! You men have served us well," said the well-dressed man from the helicopter, who seemed to be in charge. "Get the water, and I'll have your pay ready," he said, turning to the other boss and then nodding his approval.

He then reached into the inside of his jacket vest pocket and pulled out two stacks of hundred dollar bills, "Johnny, divide this up among everyone, and we'll get this stuff loaded."

"It's loaded boss, and the inventory is correct!" Johnny replied.

"That's great! Now!" Turning to the two Mexican men who had watched over the drugs in the mine, "It took awhile to find this small hole-in-the-ground yesterday. It's closer to that village than I would have chosen, but it has all worked out."

"*Señor*, shipment was buried by the mine. Ground shook and dust made us come outside," Hermandez said. "We dug it out and loaded in the white truck."

He handed them both an envelope with instructions and money to get north. "Your green cards are in these two envelopes with five hundred dollars each. Take the cards out and put them in your wallet, right now!"

He waited until they had put their wallets back into their pant's pocket. "Now, on your way!" He said with a wave of his hand, "Your families are waiting for you up north."

The two Mexicans shook his hand as he said, "I'll contact you again some time in the future for your assistance."

"*¡Si, Señor! ¡Gracias! ¡Estoy muy agradecido!*"

The two got in their old pickup and left a cloud of dust behind them leaving the mine area.

#

"Captain, the pickup is leaving with those two Mexicans who were in the mine all week," said a voice on the radio. "Did you hear that C130 land and takeoff?"

Captain Jack Randel replied, "Okay! Let them shut the truck doors again, and then we'll get them all outside the mine. Yes, we all heard and saw both aircraft."

"I counted eight total at the mine," Park Ranger Jake Wilson said. "Wish we could get your brother Charles or your Uncle Jess on these radios. They should hear us using this satellite link."

"They may not have them turned on right now," Jack replied. "If they are on this channel, they will hear us and answer back."

"Let's get down in that dry creek bed below the mine and head up there," Jake said. "It will take about fifteen minutes to get there from here."

Jack called, "You other two Texas Rangers above the mine entrance, keep covered for right now! If they come our way, we should be able to keep them from getting to the highway."

"Yes, Sir!" came the reply.

Automatic gunshots echoed through the canyon from the mine. The two Rangers above the mine had been spotted and were being fired on. The two drivers with the big van truck jumped out of the back and ran down a steep slope to the dry creek bed below. It was the same creek bed where Jake and Jack were.

"Jack, listen!" Jake pointed up the creek.

Jack jumped behind a thick bush of salt cedar and knelt down with his gun drawn. Jake ran across to the other side of the creek bed drawing his sidearm, and then waited behind a large boulder. He peered out and saw the two drivers heading his way. He held up two fingers to Jack and pointed up the creek. Jack nodded in reply.

Sam, out of breath, hollered ahead of him, "I can't run in these new cowboy boots! Slow down!"

Johnny bent over with his hands on his knees, breathing hard too, "Okay! Okay! I'm out of wind, anyway." Finally catching his breath, "How come? Tell me how come? I always want a cigarette after exerting myself like this?"

"It doesn't make sense, does it?" Sam replied wheezing, "I really don't know because I don't smoke, remember? But, I'm so out of shape; I'm as exhausted as you are!"

"You're carrying more weight than I am though," Johnny assumed.

"Don't get upset with me!" Sam replied as he straightened up. "I'm just winded and not getting enough blood to my brain to think good. But, we got to get out of here to a phone or steal a car before those Rangers catch us."

Sam laughed and patted his front pocket, "At least we got paid before the shooting started. Well, anyway, once we get back to that cold beer and cool air-conditioning, we'll both feel better. This dust and heat is about to get to me!"

"You didn't grab our lunch!" Johnny slapped his dusty hat against his pants leg and sat down under a mesquite tree for shade. With his head down, he breathed a deep sigh, trying to get more air. "That's alright, I couldn't eat right now anyway!"

Jake and Jack both walked out from their hiding places, surprising the other pair.

Pointing their guns, Jack sharply spoke, "Don't get up! Texas Rangers! You're under arrest! Sit nice and still and everything will be alright!"

Two minutes was all it took to handcuff them together and read them their 'Miranda Rights.' "This wasn't tough at all. I didn't fire a shot!" Jake said holstering his Colt .45 automatic pistol. "No gun cleaning tonight!"

Jack put his sidearm back in its holster, "I've got some short rope in my saddle bag to hobble these two. I don't want them to wonder off and hurt themselves. These city dudes won't last long out here." Heading for his horse, "We'll take a look at the mine when I get them tied."

"I ain't no city dude," Johnny said out of breath. "I live in the country back home."

Jack just looked at him and did not say anything, leaving the prisoners with Jake. While getting to his horse, he surveyed the area, *No one in sight. The Cadillac looks empty and no one near the mine entrance. They must have gone inside! Where did my other Rangers go?*

Jack rode his horse over to Jake, with Jake's horse in tow, "I couldn't see anyone from up there where the horses were. What do you suggest, Jake?" Jack asked, getting off his horse. He hobbled the two captives in the shade of a mesquite tree, and then tied them to it. The two Rangers walked away from their captives and whispered between themselves.

Jake nodded toward the mine, "See those timbers stacked next to the mine opening?"

"Yea!"

"I can get to them from around the other side of the hill in about ten minutes walking time." Jake suggested, "From there, I should be able to see your other two Texas Rangers."

Jack didn't take his eyes off the mine opening and jabbed his thumb into Jake's side, "Do it, and be safe! We're not out here to be dead heroes. When you get there, I'll come up behind the Cadillac and insure no one is inside it."

Leaving the two horses tied under a rock overhang in the shade and the two prisoners tied to the tree, they slowly made their way up the rocky hill toward the mine. The afternoon sun cut the chill out of the dry air.

CHAPTER TWENTY-FIVE

Lunch was over back at the ranch. Jess and Professor Stapleton discussed the location of old mines near Terlingua and Lajitas. They had spread hand-drawn geographical maps made by Granddad Hanes on the dining room table. LeAnn was reading aloud the instructions from Granddad Hanes' letter, which had been attached underneath the sewing machine. They were comparing the smaller old letter maps to the new larger ones they had brought in from Jess' aircraft.

"Your Granddad indicates there are four entrances to that Butterfly mine. One was partially shut by a cave-in, November of 1912. One opening was a vertical shaft to lower drinking water down in buckets. Look at this! What do these symbols mean?" she asked, pointing to a sketch in the letter.

John took off his glasses and looked at the page she handed him, "Puzzling to me! The sketches must be something the miners or prospectors would use to be secretive with their information. They are not Egyptian or Greek hieroglyphics. What do you think, Jess?"

"They may be Apache Indian symbols," LeAnn suggested.

"That is a good possibility, Sweetheart. I think you are correct," John said smiling, and then nodded his head in agreement. "If we cannot figure them out, I know good anthropologists and archaeologists at the Sol Ross University Big Bend Studies who can interpret this."

Jess looked at his Granddad's notes, "Well, they look like Indian markings to me, too. He studied their history in West Texas and could also read and speak their language. Now, look at this group of note symbols, they're for miners. Like this square 'c' marking for a tunnel; this 'ORO' is gold nearby; sunburst is another one for mines or cross pick and shovel. I'll start a new list of these." He then handed the pages back to LeAnn. "Some of those other markings certainly look like Indian signs."

"Dad, my research book is still in your library from graduate school, the one on Texas Indians. Be right back." She poured them more iced tea and left the room.

"When he lived down here," Jess said, "off and on in the nineteen twenties and thirties, his research was quite extensive. I have often wondered what happened to all his notes and files. I would hope he would have kept them in a safe place. No one in our family knows where that would be." He paused, "I remember a big book! At that young age, it was a big book! At least, 14 inches by 20 inches and four inches thick – heavy musty smell." He reached for his note pad, "John, I remember it had a multicolored drawing in the center page... a large circle with sharp points to the outside and funny codes or language on it. Granddad Hanes said it was from the Holy Bible. How did I remember that?" Looking up at John, he shook his head.

John stepped back from the table, thinking out loud. "I have an idea of what Jess' Holy Bible was, the old scriptures of the Sixth and Seventh Books of Moses from the Arcan Mosaic Books of the Cabala and the Talmud scriptures of Moses, for the good and well-being of mankind." He paused, and then said, "Mephistopheles!" Laughing, he continued, "Such big words! Should I spell it for you?"

Everyone shook their heads, '*no.*'

"In medieval legend, a devil to whom Faust, or Faustus, sold his soul for riches and power: a leading character in Goethe's Faust- Gounod's opera. A crafty, powerful, malevolent devil; a diabolical person – so says the Webster Dictionary."

"Wow! What was that you quoted?" Jess asked, leaning back in the chair looking across the table at John.

"Just something I remember from working on my PHD one summer, back in 1940 at Zurich. Evil spirits that lead humans to valuable treasures." He trembled, "It still gives me the shivers. I did not spend a great amount of time on that research, just enough to finish that paper on medieval legends."

Jess smiled and moved one of the old maps, "Well, look here! On the backside of this map, there are more sketches and explanations of markings." Looking over to where LeAnn had been sitting, "She must have taken the letter. I bet some of these sketches will match the ones in his letter."

Jess studied the maps and sketches. Professor Stapleton watched him makes notes, "You do not need an interpreter. That is a very thorough job you have accomplished." He chuckled and stood up, "You are full of surprises, Jess."

Jess looked up, "Thank you, John." He turned back to the map, "We can't mistake this one." Jess pointed at the map.

Skull and crossbones were drawn on a creek, north of the mine opening for the water shaft. "Bad water? Of course, these over here are simple miners' signs," Jess said, pointing to other symbols. "Where did they get drinking water if that location was bad? Or was the water used for drinking, maybe for washing out their diggings? Then where did it drain off, or did it soak in? I'm thinking of mercury problems in the ground and drinking water. Questions, always questions!"

John patted Jess on the shoulder, "That is life! It is always full of unanswered questions. That keeps us sharp, trying to figure out the answers. You are doing a fantastic job. I'm just an observer."

"Hey, I need all the help I can get. So, don't be a silent observer, your years of experience is invaluable, Professor."

"You know how to give confidence to an old man!"

Jess stood up and walked over to John. He put his arm around the professor's shoulders, "Thanks. But, really, it's just speaking the facts, as I know them. You and me, we make a good team. Even if I don't speak the correct Queen's English, we understand each other.

"Let's fly down to Lajitas tomorrow morning and investigate some of these mines. I should be able to rent a car there at the hotel."

"That would be great," LeAnn said, coming back in the dining room. "I'll get a chance to fly your aircraft."

"LeAnn! Do not be so forward!" the professor said sternly.

"But, Dad! I..."

Jess held up his hand to quiet her, "That is fine with me. You can fly. You," nodding at the professor, "and I will use the maps and be spotters."

"No, Sir! Absolutely not! Not I!" The professor said again, "I do not like small aircraft and even though I like looking at yours, no small ones for riding in, please."

"Okay! Some people just rather keep their feet on the ground, no problem. I'll leave for town now and fuel up. We'll need a few supplies, too." Jess rolled up the maps, "I should be here around sunrise, six thirty or so. I need to talk to the sheriff when I get to town about that C130 aircraft I saw earlier. He might know about it already."

LeAnn handed Jess the letter from his granddad, "You have a date. I'll be ready and waiting at the barn."

They waved to Jess as he lifted off the dirt strip in the Pilatus Porter aircraft. Leveling off at a thousand feet altitude, he slowed to cruise speed and made a 45° bank, and then leveled the wings as he came around to a 180° course back toward the ranch house. He passed over wagging the rudder and tipping his wings to the two figures below. Climbing to 2,000 feet above the ground, he followed the road back up to the Alpine airport.

The clear morning sky was crispy which made it good flying weather. It was 8:30 A.M.

#

"Charles, can you hear me?" Jack asked on the hand-held transceiver radio.

"Texas Ranger, Code One. Does anyone have a copy? This is Ranger Jack Randel."

Silence again.

"Jack, this is Charles! Where've you been?"

"I've been calling you, too!" Jack replied. "Hey! Jake and I are at the Chisos Mariposa mine north of Lajitas. Can you hear me alright?"

"Yes, I can now! I'm on the helicopter radio, go ahead," Charles said.

"I've got some high activity down here. We have two already in handcuffs and at least five or more up at the mine." Jack said. "We are down the creek ridge in front of the mine opening. One large panel truck, a Cadillac and a small helicopter are on the flat next to the mine. What've you got?"

"We have an Air Force AWAC aircraft out of San Antonio watching all movements in the Big Bend area." Charles replied. "He's keeping track of that C130 that almost got Uncle Jess. He should be at the ranch by now. Do you need me there with you?"

"Yes! A.S.A.P.! How many men do you have?" Jack asked.

"Two, plus me! We are on the way," replied Charles as they lifted from the ground in the Texas Ranger helicopter. "I'll land at the mine if there's room!"

"Negative on landing at the mine. Not enough room. Lajitas would be better."

"Roger, on Lajitas," Charles replied.

#

After leaving the ranch, Jess turned on the video camera in his helmet and flew the Porter PC-6 aircraft in a wide circle increasing the speed to over 100 knots. He made further adjustments and settled back for a fun flight to Alpine. The automatic weather broadcast at Alpine and Marfa airports sounded good, so he reset the altimeter to the correct barometric pressure. That would insure his altimeter indicated the correct altitude readout on the instrument. He contacted the tower in Alpine to let them know his intentions in the area around Lajitas before flying into their airspace.

Jess switched fuel tanks, from the left wing to the right wing. Both tanks were low of fuel, so he planned to refuel in Alpine. But, he had enough fuel to do what he wanted and make it to the airport with thirty minutes of flight time left in the tank.

Following the arid valley, he turned southeast and flew toward two high outcropping of jagged rock in the distance. The sectional aeronautical chart showed them to be the Devil's Backbone.

They were referred to as indigenous intrusions, called dikes, pushed up through the earth. Cracks in the layers of sedimentary surface rocks broke open, and molten lava pushed up into and out of the cracks. He focused the video camera on them, and then flew between the two formations.

"Someone sure picked the right name for this site, Devil's Backbone." Jess scanned the instrument panel and then the horizon for other aircraft.

The unusual land had remarkable abrupt changes, which kept his eyes wondering, trying to reflect on all of it. At times, Jess did not know what to video first. He circled clockwise and turned around circling counter-clockwise videoing the ground formations.

"That's worth ten minutes of flight time. Just another fantastic view of Texas Big Bend country... another free commercial," Jess said turning off the video camera.

He noticed a trail of dust moving southward and banked as he leveled off at 1,000 feet above the ground. He turned on the video camera again because he was following a black helicopter below him, which was pulling away. His aircraft maximum speed of 161 mph (177 kts) would not catch the faster helicopter. The turboprop engine could not pull the big heavy aircraft any faster.

"Must be a Texas Ranger, could be one of the twins," Jess said reaching for the portable transceiver. "Texas Rangers, Charles or Jack? Do you have a copy on your ole Uncle Jess?"

He looked at the transceiver window, "What frequency did he give me to use? Switch to channel one. TR1, do you have a copy?"

No reply. Jess opened the air vent window and stuck the antenna outside and transmitted again.

"TR1! Jack do you hear me?"

"Whoever that is trying to transmit, try again," came a voice over the radio.

"Is that you, Charles?"

"Yes, Uncle Jess?"

"Is that you making the sand storm? Course heading one eight zero?"

"Yes! Is that you following me?" Charles asked, "If so, please do not transmit again. Continue to follow and land when I do."

"Okay, I can do that," Jess said to himself. Thinking that was an unusual request, Jess continued to follow above and behind the helicopter. "Well, no matter. Change number one hundred and one, coming up! And, the day is not over. I'm right behind you young man, lead the way," Jess muttered to himself. They landed at the Lajitas dirt airstrip.

Charles hustled over to Jess as he shut down the Porter's engine. He wore a bulletproof vest with Texas Ranger printed on it – actually, more like a military flak vest and he carried an M16 automatic rifle. The helicopter's engines were still running, waiting for Charles to return.

"Where's the war?" Jess hollered getting out of the aircraft.

"Uncle Jess, stay here at the airstrip. We are going up to the Mariposa mine to support Jack and the other Rangers. These are the only vests we have. Otherwise, you could go along. If we need additional backup, we'll call on Channel Two of your transceiver. The bad guys are monitoring Channel One. Channel two is scrambled," Charles said.

"Before you rush off, I had a narrow escape this morning down here. A C130 almost got me as it made a low level pass and disappeared into Mexico," Jess said.

"Yes, we know! Our spotters, the balloon radar at Marfa and satellite pictures told us all about it. Stay here! We'll talk later," Charles said patting Jess on the shoulder and then hurried back to his helicopter.

In a cloud of dust, Jess watched them head for the abandon Chisos Mariposa mine at the foot of Tres Cuevas Mountain, about four miles north of the airport. He turned and opened the cargo door of the Porter and removed the safety netting over the equipment. Quickly attaching a telephoto zoom lens to the full size video camera, he grabbed a tripod. Moving under the shade of the right wing, he mounted the camera on the tripod and hurriedly focused on the distant helicopter. He could see the mine also, "There's the truck I saw this morning and it's blocking my view of the mine entrance. Two men above the entrance and two more down the road, all wearing armored vest," Jess said, speaking loud enough for the video camera's mic to pick up his voice. "They must be after drug smugglers or illegals from Mexico."

Startled, Jess jumped back. Something cold was pressing against his neck under his left ear. His first reaction was to swat at it with his hand.

"Do not make any unnecessary moves! Keep your hands on that camera. Feel this barrel at your neck?" whispered a determined voice with a Spanish accent, and then Jess heard a click of the safety being released or reset.

Jess felt the guy's other hand frisking him for weapons, finding none. He grabbed Jess' hair and slammed him against the fuselage of the aircraft. The guy was slightly taller than Jess and out weighed him thirty pounds or more. He was also a heavy breather. From the moving around and leaning against Jess, he knew the guy was frantically looking around. The man's pungent body cologne with his heavy sweating almost made Jess sick to his stomach.

"What do you want with me?" Jess asked gruffly.

"I want you and your aircraft! Get in!" He yelled into Jess' ear and shoved him toward the pilot's door.

"Climb in and buckle up! I can reach you from back here," he said, slamming the cargo door behind him. "Shut your door!" he demanded to Jess.

Commissioner Rodiquez stepped on Jess' netted cargo, moving between the pilot and copilot's seats pressing his gun against Jess' ribs. He jabbed the barrel hard, taking away Jess' breath, "Buckle up, I said! And close that door!" Glaring at him, he swore at Jess in Spanish.

"I'm almost out of fuel," Jess said pointing to the fuel gauge. "I didn't top it off here!" He slammed his door shut. "Hope you don't want to go far."

"Mexico is not very far! Get this thing started, now!" Jabbing Jess again in the ribs with the gun, he commanded, "Follow the river north, but stay on the other side close to the water."

"I can't do that! It's not legal for me to fly across the river into Mexico without approval from the FAA and Border Patrol. I haven't submitted a flight plan or called..."

Rodiquez punched Jess in the mouth, "Shut up, you...!" He was swearing again in Spanish.

Jess knew if he stalled long enough, playing the stupid pilot part, the Texas Rangers might notice him being highjacked.

"I'm just a dumb photo pilot, looking for work," Jess said gritting his teeth. A trickle of blood flowed from a split in his upper lip.

The guy swung again hitting Jess with a glancing blow to the cheek and right ear, "No more talking! Buckle up and get this aircraft started." He stuck the gun barrel in Jess' ear, "Now!"

Jess buckled up and grabbed the aircraft checklist, beginning the series of starting procedures. He could do the checklist by memory, but he continued to delay – and prayed, *Father in Heaven, I'm in your hands and claim victory over this man. In Jesus name!* Finally, he turned on the master switch for the battery, and then the ignition switch to start. The turbine engine came alive, belched some smoke and came up to speed. Glancing over the instrument and gauges for oil pressure, rpm of the engine, he released the brakes and pushed the control in enough to make the aircraft move.

Jess retracted the flaps so the rocks from the gravel runway would not damage them, spun the aircraft around to the right and held the brakes. He put on his headset and murmured a prayer into the boom mic, "Lord Jesus, again we're in Your loving hands."

He pushed the throttle control lever all the way forward, noticed the gauges were in the green and the annunciator panel was clear of red lights. Then, he released the brakes. The big aircraft jerked forward; the three bladed propeller bit into the air. The air speed increased, and they were off the ground in a short distance.

Steeply banking the aircraft to the northeast, Jess then leveled the wings and flew at a low altitude over the Mariposa mine, where the Texas Rangers were located. He banked again, sharply back toward the river and followed it to the south. The aircraft gained speed as Jess flew it down toward the surface of the Rio Grande. He was hoping the abrupt turns would cause his unwelcome highjacker to become disoriented.

Jess pulled up twenty feet above the water, G-stressing his passenger. He maintained a level flight heading south where the canyon walls towered high above the white-watered river. The canyon walls become increasingly narrow the further down the river.

Jess had never river rafted from Lajitas to the mouth of the Santa Helena Canyon, but he remembered his sister's tales and the old surveyor's accounts about its narrowness. It was where a man could spread his arms and touch the canyon walls. One hand would be on Mexico and the other on Texas.

Here we go, Lord! Whether my passenger is ready are not! Jess thought to himself, watching the canyon walls rapidly grew in height as the aircraft approached.

"You dressed for your funeral?" Jess said laughing.

"You crazy, Gringo! You cannot go this way!"

Jess began abrupt maneuvers of his aircraft, yelling at the man, "You want to shoot me?" Gritting his teeth, "Now, it's my turn! I'll take a chance you won't shoot! If you do, you'll not make the trip out of this canyon alive!"

Ahead of them, the canyon walls narrowed drastically. Jess jerked the aircraft into a vertical 90° knife-edge bank, (right wing down and the left wing high, vertically), holding the fuselage horizontal in a straight flight through the canyon. He was flying blindly, trying to stay clear of the jutting cliff boulders. They felt the G-force pressure increase. The turbo engine screamed and strained at the unusual attitude of the aircraft.

Jess' unwanted passenger screamed. Rodiquez looked out his window under the wing toward its tip, straight down to the Rio Grande River, some twenty feet below. He did not have strength in his neck to move his head to look up at Jess. Had he opened his door, he would have fallen to his death. The wing tip was not far from the water.

His passenger dropped the gun, which wedged under his seat, and then held onto the inside door handle next to his side. He was white and wide-eyed at the circumstances he had created, frozen in his seat. Staring straight ahead, he began squinting his eyes tightly and then closed them for what was coming.

In less than a minute into this maneuver, Jess could see the canyon walls widen at a higher altitude and crabbed the aircraft upward. Its turbo engine screamed and moaned in that unusual attitude of climb. It was not designed for acrobatic flying. Everything seemed in slow motion as the aircraft fought higher up the side of the cliff, almost to a stall speed.

After the long thirty second climb, Jess finally reached space enough to level the wings. He let the nose drop down as the stall warning horn came on to gain speed. The nose fell like a rock, and he jerked the yoke back, bringing the nose to level flight, regaining control with the increased airspeed. They were very close to being back down in the narrow canyon. He wanted to let the aircraft go into a spin, but there was not enough altitude. He pulled back on the prop control for a slower speed. Then, he looked at his passenger. The guy was about to throw up.

Jess finally flew out above the canyon walls and was a hundred feet over the tops of the cliffs. He made a slow turn to the west into the wind for a short landing on the rough Mexican soil. Easing the tail-dragger down on the rough ground, he brought it to a halt as fast as he could. He pulled back on the yoke and slammed on the brakes, releasing the left brake, which spun the aircraft around bringing it back 180° into the wind and shut down the engine. This quick stop and spinning on one wheel caused more pressure on his passenger's body because of the seat and shoulder harness.

Jess yanked off his headset and was unbuckled almost before the aircraft stopped moving. He pushed his seat all the way back, opened his narrow pilot's door, grabbed the door opening and jumped to the first wheel strut step. He swung around on the step and reached across under his seat for the passenger's gun, but the guy was still conscious enough to realize what Jess was about to do. He was faster than Jess had given him credit and had the gun first.

Motioning Jess down and away from the aircraft, the guy fell out feet first from the high cockpit to the ground, and threw up his insides. Then, dry heaves started. His legs became rubbery and he collapsed to his knees, burying the gun in the dirt, but still gripping it tightly.

Jess was glad the guy got out before relieving himself of all that mess. *Now*, he thought, *what to do about that gun? He could have shot me!* Jess eyed the guy to see if he had an advantage of getting the gun away, and then stepped toward him.

Rodiquez fell back on his left elbow into the dirt and quickly pointed the gun at Jess. Cussing in Spanish, he motioned Jess to get back in the aircraft.

Jess left the pilot's door open as he strapped in and turned on the battery power. His passenger got in behind him through the cargo door, jammed the gun against his neck, and slid across to the other seat next to Jess.

Reaching toward the right instrument panel, Jess tapped the fuel gauge, "Haven't we been through this once before? Get that gun off my neck! It's not going to help you if I'm dead. I've already told you, we're low on fuel! Look at that fuel gauge, it's showing both tanks are empty." He reached over and tapped the gauge again.

The guy was persistent in pressing the gun barrel against Jess' neck, "Get it started!"

Jess talked through the aircraft's checklist for taking off, which he held in his left hand. He was trying to think what to do next. Praying under his breath, "Lord Jesus, now what do I do?"

"What did you say?"

"I was praying for help!"

"Don't get smart with me!" He hit Jess' right ear and cheek with the barrel of the automatic. This time, the barrel's sight cut open Jess' cheek below the right ear. Blood slowly trailed down his neck under his shirt collar, turning it dark brown. It had cut so clean Jess did not feel the cut, only the tickle of the blood on the hair of his neck. He put his hand up to brush it away and had his hand knocked down.

"Keep your hands on the controls. Go! *Vámonos! Pronto!*"

Jess did not know what to do, but to fly, "Here we go, again, Lord Jesus!"

Jess set the controls for Short Take-off and Landing (STOL) conditions and maximum power. The turbine engine roared to life, and the aircraft shuddered and strained to move forward. Jess released the brakes. The three propeller blades chewed into the air, and the pressure forced the two back into their seats. He kept the aircraft headed into the wind, the steerable tail wheel immediately lifted from the ground. They could see the edge of the canyon cliff not more than a thousand yards ahead of them as the aircraft's large low-inflated tires bounced them over rocks and cactus. Estimating he was airborne in less than 600 feet, Jess realized that was a record for him in the PC-6. They were immediately up one hundred feet and crossed into the opening of the canyon. The ground disappeared below them down to the Rio Grande River 1,800 feet below in the canyon.

A sudden updraft from the canyon hit the aircraft broadside and upward two hundred feet higher. Jess banked into the wind shift, which brought them parallel over the river, just as a fast downdraft pushed them below and between the canyon's rims again. The engine sputtered and died. Jess mentally went through the 'engine out' procedures. The engine would not restart.

"I told you so! No fuel!" Jess yelled, pointing to the fuel gauges as the prop stopped turning. He feathered the prop, turning it into the wind. "No place to go! Just down!"

Maintaining a slow glide speed of 60 knots, Jess continued to look for a place to land, but there were no nice beaches on the river. He turned his radio to emergency frequency 121.5 and then transponder to 7500. On the side panel next to his left hand was the emergency locator transmitter remote switch, which he turned on, causing a red light to light on its panel.

"Now, we are ready to crash land this aircraft, if necessary!"

The wind across the propellers and cowling, his passenger's heavy breathing were the only noises to be heard. Jess pointed to his passenger's door. "Open your door! Tighten your seat belt and shoulder harness," he commanded, while he did his own. His passenger obeyed without hesitation.

"Hope you're prayed up, Mister! This is our final landing," Jess said, as he continued to look for a place to land. "Where do you safely crash land when canyon walls are within a few yards of the wings and they are straight down to the water?"

Jess had never had problems with his PC-6. Even though he had many hours of practicing emergency procedures, the 'real thing' was now here. Everything came second nature for the emergency, which did not leave time to think of what could happen. Fear and anxiety were not present in Jess; he was too busy. Many of his reactions were now from memory of the checklist for getting on the ground as safely as possible. He had never had to crash land an aircraft. Bail out, yes!

"Lord Jesus! Here we go!"

He banked the glide around a bend in the canyon, and there was the opening of the Santa Elena Canyon, a mile ahead of them. The head wind was keeping them up, but it was slowing them down as well. Now, Jess could see the Chisos Mountains across the open plains directly ahead of them through the opening of the canyon walls, but the desert itself was not all flat. Mesquite trees, boulders, deep ravines and dry rugged creek beds which once emptied their waters into the Rio Grande came into view. Then, huge cactus and yucca plants popped up, everything except nice soft sand dunes of desert. He lowered the nose again to keep the glide airspeed correct. In doing that, he was losing altitude rapidly.

As they broke out of the canyon over the arid parched plains, Jess grabbed the hand mic, **"MAYDAY! MAYDAY! MAYDAY! PORTER PC-6! 738 NANCY VICTOR! SANTA ELENA! CASTOLON! ENGINE OUT! NO FUEL! TRANSPONDER SEVEN-FIVE-ZERO-ZERO."**

He continued to scan the area ahead and below them for a good spot to land, and then pointed, "See that creek bed on the left, I'll try for there!" Jess said, as he fought to keep the aircraft from stalling. "It's the Terlingua Creek!" The speed had dropped to 50 knots, eight below stall speed without flaps. He wanted to stay up as long as possible, and only use the flaps to get down fast for a short landing. It certainly did not look promising for a smooth set down.

And, there were no updrafts from the warm ground to help keep them up because they were gliding in the afternoon shadows of the canyon walls.

CHAPTER TWENTY-SIX

The drug dealers had all been rounded up, except the one in the aircraft with Jess and the two Mexicans who were at the Mariposa mine during the night. Their pickup had broken down on a back road north of Terlingua and they had disappeared.

At the Lajitas airstrip, the Rangers talked to the Mexican authorities as they all walked to the end of the runway where Jess' equipment was left behind. They were comparing information from both sides of the Rio Grande River.

"This is your Uncle's video camera?" Lieutenant Lopus asked pointing to Jess' video camera on the tripod.

Jack nodded and walked over to it, peering into the eyepiece. "Yes, it's still running! Look at this you guys!" He pointed at the red indicator on the camera. It was still mounted on the tripod where Jess had left it under the aircraft's wing. His accessory bag was covered with dust.

"I'm surprised it didn't blow over when he took off," the lieutenant said.

"Hey! All we have to do is stop it and rewind. He was recording us over there at the mine," Jack said pointing as he looked through the eyepiece.

He stopped the recording and pushed the rewind button. While it was rewinding Jack pulled out the small screen from the video camera's side. The rewind light shut off, and Jack pushed the play button.

A low battery light began to flash. "That's just great! Low batteries," Jack said, turning the camera off. "Let's take it to the helicopter and plug it into the cigarette lighter."

Lieutenant Lopus grabbed the camcorder bag. He and Charles continued sharing information while walking with Jack and the other Rangers toward the helicopter. They were all concerned about Jess.

"We have been tracking that C130 that landed here. It's now somewhere on the ground across from Del Rio, in Coahuila, Mexico, some hundred miles or so," Charles said to Lopus. "I haven't looked on a sectional map to find the location. We should do that shortly."

The lieutenant frowned, putting his hands on his hips and squinting his eyes looking at Charles and Jack, while looking into the sun. He shaded his eyes with his hand in order to see their faces. The sun was directly behind the two Rangers.

"There must have been an exchange of money, but such a large aircraft for just that," Lopus said, shaking his head. "There must have been *mucho* drugs or equipment to need that cargo hauler."

Charles hooked up the cable to a small portable VCR/TV in the helicopter and power plug to the cigarette lighter. Then he inserted the cassette from the camcorder. It began to run. The picture was crisp and colorful, which surprised Lieutenant Lopus.

The lieutenant was amazed at the scenery of the Big Bend country, "How can your Uncle fly his plane and take such good pictures?"

Jack motioned with his hands, "Jess has done this for years. He has a smaller remote camera mounted on his helmet. Whatever he's looking at, he can record by flicking a switch on the aircraft's control stick."

"I'll fast forward to get to the view of the mine," Charles said. "We can watch the first part later."

"Now with this bigger video camera and larger lens, we should have some close-ups of our operation," Jack said.

Viewing the mine's activity on the small television surprised them all. It was sharp and clear, plus good sound.

Charles clamped his hands, "This is great, no written reports for this drug bust. It's all right there."

"Stop and back up the cassette. Listen to the voice in the background! Someone's talking to Uncle Jess," Jack said. "I'll turn up the volume on the TV set."

"Ho! Ho!" Lieutenant Lopus said, "I know that voice! Keep it playing."

As they listened, the commotion on the screen at the mine became less important. Looking over his shoulder toward the Rio Grande River, Jack said, "His plane didn't go north like he was instructed. Look at that, it circled the mine and came back across the airstrip and headed toward the river."

"I remember now! It went south, down the river. I looked up just at the time I heard him pass the ravine we were in," said Jake Wilson, the Big Bend Park Ranger.

"You're right! Now that you mention it, so did I," Jack said. "He dove down toward the river and headed south. He can't go far, it's too narrow."

"That was Commissioner Rodiquez in the aircraft with your Uncle Jess," said Lieutenant Lopus. "We have been working together on this drug activity," he said, clenching his fist in the air. "He is my security leak!"

Jack turned to Charles, "We don't need both helicopters here." He began digging in his pants pocket. "Flip for it!"

"Okay!"

"Here's my quarter," flipping it in the air. "You call it!"

"Heads!"

"Tails! You lose, brother!" Jack said, grabbing his helmet on the pilots seat. "See ya later! You want to go Lieutenant?"

He replied with a big smile, "*Si!*"

The air search began as the Rangers and Texas Border Patrol coordinated the sector from Lajitas south to the Castolon Ranger Station on the banks of the Rio Grande River. There were no reports of a small aircraft down at all. It was only a twenty-mile flight to the Ranger Station, so they figured Jess must have flown into Mexico. So far, there were no radar reports of aircraft, other than the information on the C130.

CHAPTER TWENTY-SEVEN

At Professor Stapleton's ranch, he was sitting in a bench swing admiring the clear view of the distant mountains and puffing on his pipe. Up toward the main road, he saw a vehicle head down to the ranch, leaving a cloud of dust hanging in the air.

Sheriff Baker drove in, parked and got out. He began rubbing the back of his neck while walking to the porch, "Professor! Has Jess been here yet?" He said as he walked up the porch steps two at a time. "I'm expecting him for signing these papers about the shooting at the airport."

"No he is not around here," Professor Stapleton said, rapping his knuckles against his forehead. "He was to meet you and then return here to the ranch later this afternoon with some groceries. Darn, I forgot to have him add bacon on that list"

"We must have miss communicated," the sheriff said, still rubbing his neck. "I thought he would be here."

The professor pointed at the sheriff with his pipe, "You have a sore neck muscle?"

"No, Sir! Just a habit of doing that when I'm trying to think." He turned toward his vehicle, "Hold on a minute Professor, someone is calling our dispatch." He returned to his car.

Listening to the reports of Jess Hanes' aircraft missing, he turned on the outside speaker. They heard the area of the search. Sheriff Baker said, "There has been a highjacking of Jess with his plane. I'll keep you informed. Bye!" he said and then got back into the Brewster County Sheriff's Department vehicle.

"Wait! Can I be of assistance, Sheriff?" The professor hollered from the porch.

"No, Sir! Not at this time," said the sheriff. "Maybe later! Got to go!"

LeAnn waved at him, as she came out on the porch to see what the noise was all about, "Please keep us informed!"

"Sure will! See you two later," he said backing out into the driveway. He waved back, turned on his red lights and left, leaving a cloud of dust as he headed for Alpine.

They waved again, but there was not any way he could see them for the dust hanging in the air. "Sure is dry! What happened to Jess?" the Professor asked.

LeAnn nodded her agreement that it was dry, but made no comment about Jess. She circled her arms around her father's one arm, leaning her face against his shoulder. They walked together across the porch to the front door. He shook his head as the two entered the living room, letting LeAnn enter first.

In the kitchen, she poured iced tea for them both. Seated at the dinette in the west wing of the kitchen, they both stared out a large picture window, watching the willow tree's shadows lengthen, pondering what they could do for Jess. Neither spoke for a long while.

Professor Stapleton was thinking: *I know very little detailed information about Jess, only what Jess' Grandfather Hanes shared prior to his death, fifty years ago. The letter he had left for Jess, found in the sewing machine, is still a mystery. Jess had not studied it completely. Then, his two Texas Ranger nephews; Jess witnessing the Mexican Agents shooting; the county sheriff's cruiser and truck collision; helicopters on my ranch, and now Jess missing in his aircraft.*

Not only that, but LeAnn has taken serious notice of Jess; of course, he is a married man. His wife may be out here later this week... At least they struck cords of the same interest earlier this morning. I will have to watch this relationship very closely. They have so much of the same interests. Since her husband died at a young age of thirty-seven, she has been lonely. Then, her mother died three years ago.

He reached over and held her hand; she responded with a warm smile, "Yes, Daddy, I was praying for Jess. I'm wondering if there is any way we can be of help? Surely there will be an involved air search, plus his nephews will have the Rangers and Border Patrol alerted. I don't want to be in the way, but I feel I should do something and not sit here sipping my iced tea. We should wait for a little while before calling his wife." She hesitated, "What's wrong with me... I'm a major in the Civil Air Patrol! What am I doing sitting here?"

LeAnn slipped from her father's hand and walked to the counter for more tea, "Didn't Jess say he was landing at Lajitas airstrip, and then going to the Mariposa mine?"

"Yes! That was his plan," he replied.

"Well! Then, I'll take the back ranch road down to Terlingua and over to the mine. No, now think! Use the plane," she said setting her glass down on the table. "Daddy, I'll take my plane. It's topped off with fuel. Plus, there is still a full survival backpack in the saddle room. Would you throw a few sandwiches together for me, please?" she said heading out the back kitchen door toward the barn. "Grab a couple of apples and two canteens of water, and a couple of those military food rations. You know, MRE's?"

Out the kitchen door she went, "I'll taxi up to the back door," running with Snake right beside her, barking.

Professor Stapleton smiled, "That is my daughter! There she goes again! No planning, just confident she can be of help."

LeAnn taxied her Cessna 180, with the short take off and landing system installed (STOL) to the back of the ranch house, and the professor opened the passenger door, handing her the supplies she requested.

"Thanks, Daddy! I'll be flying over Lajitas and following the river north to Presidio. Then, I'll double back to the mine... if I don't find Jess. I'll stay in radio contact with you. Every half hour both of us should check the emergency frequency, 121.5. I'll be back sometime after sundown," she blew him a kiss.

"Be careful, and do not take any risks!"

"See ya later, Daddy," she said, as she shut the door and waited for him to move away from the aircraft. She spun it around with the backwash of the propeller, using the tail wheel. Then she added full power and blew a cloud of dust behind her, hiding the barn and corrals. In a short distance, she was airborne.

#

Texas Rangers Jack and Charles Randel had heard Jess' "MAYDAY" emergency broadcast but lost the last part of his transmission. The distant flight safety service in El Paso did not hear his transponder signal about being highjacked, but his Emergency Locator Transmitter (ELT) signal was strong before it stopped. The signal only lasted five seconds, not long enough to get a fix on his location.

They only knew of his southerly course down the Rio Grand River canyon from Lajitas. Coordinating the search and rescue activity until the U.S. Air Force arrived was not progressing as fast as the Rangers wanted. Too much red tape with all the agencies involved: Texas Rangers, Border Patrol, Brewster and Presidio County Sheriffs' departments, and now the Civil Air Patrol out of Marfa, and the U.S. Air Force with the Federal Aviation Administration representatives on the way.

Also, they were concerned with the Mexican authorities on the other side of the river. At least one of the men, Commissioner Rodiquez, was involved with the highjacking. He had been identified from the videotaping. The aircraft population at the gravel airstrip in Lajitas grew through the late afternoon hours. The Rangers had set up a command post at the only hangar and an outpost down river at Santa Elena Canyon and on the river at Lajitas. The Big Bend National Park Rangers had called up their reserve personnel and had disbursed them through the area. The Rangers wanted to find Jess before sunset and before the FBI and CIA got involved.

CHAPTER TWENTY-EIGHT

The Terlingua Creek bed turned out not to be the place to attempt a forced landing. Jess had glided north out of the Santa Elena Canyon over the creek where it emptied into the Rio Grande River. He did not spend a long time making his decision. The creek had too many large rocks and boulders; he immediately turned southeast for the Castalon area where he knew there was a landing strip and a Park Ranger station. He was losing altitude fast trying to keep the airspeed up.

Every time the glide speed dropped, Jess had to lower the aircraft's nose to regain that speed, which in turn lost precious altitude. It was a long six miles straight ahead to Castalon. Now, he knew it was too far; he had made the wrong decision.

It was familiar territory, so he knew he could continue his descent for at least a couple more miles to pick a better landing area. The wind turbulence from the hot air rising from the basin prairie of the Big Bend, west of the Chisos Mountains, funneled into the opening of the canyon, cooled and caused down drafts and headwinds. Even so, Jess had figured he should reach Castalon if he could pick up the lifting hot air off the canyon walls to the west and from the flat barren land.

His sick unwanted passenger, Commissioner Rodiquez, was still having visual problems from the prior landing on top of the canyon. The man was weak and had again dropped the handgun, which had scooted under the cargo netting back in the cargo compartment. Jess stayed confident of his flying ability and response of his aircraft.

"Hey, talk to me! What's your name?" Jess hollered.

Before realizing his reply, "Commissioner Rodiquez! Get me on the ground before we crash somewhere!"

"Help me look for a place to land. Open beach on the river, a road, dry creek bed, something!"

"I can't see good! I'm dizzy!" His face was pale and he was gasping for air.

"Don't vomit in my aircraft! You'll clean it up!" Jess firmly replied. "Commissioner of what?"

"If you don't get me down, I'll cut your throat!" He said pulling a knife from his pocket. Before he could open the blade, he vomited, dropping the knife. He covered his mouth with both hands; vomit spewed between his fingers and sprayed the door window next to him. It hit with such force it splattered back over him.

"Lord Jesus, help! I've got a crazed maniac on my hands who's wild-eyed and sick." Jess opened his door window to force wind through the cabin, "Keep your door open! Open your window! Now!" He mentally checked gauges and instruments and continued to scan the country before them and to the side for an opening to land on.

Jess tried to judge his time left in the air. '*It has been a long ten minutes gliding. This aircraft isn't designed to stay aloft this long without losing a lot of altitude. Thank you, Lord Jesus!*'

The propeller was not spinning, so he tried one more time to start the engine on gas fumes. The battery spun the propellers, but the engine would not fire or start. The fuel pump switch was turned on, and he could hear it running. His fuel gauge showed empty, but maybe enough unused fuel could be in the tanks. He reached to try the start button again, when an updraft pushed them to 1,400 feet and toward the 1,500-foot canyon wall on the right. The open plains were to the left, and the river below.

Lord Jesus, work this out for us. I'm out of answers. Jess prayed as he banked slowly to his left, trying to keep the same altitude. He began quoting scriptures from Psalm 91, out loud, "He that hideth in the secret place of the most High, shall abide under the shadow of the Almighty. I will say of the Lord, He is my refuge, my fortress, my God; in Him will I trust. Surely He will deliver us from the snare of the fouler and from the noisome pestilence."

Jess' passenger was in a daze, not paying attention to what Jess was saying, and the commissioner's knuckles were white from gripping the seat arm rests.

I know that you've continually watched over me, Jess prayed, *but now I'm asking for Your special help for both of us.*

Jess had never stayed in the glide condition at low altitudes as long as today. Away from the canyon wall and river, he leveled the aircraft's wings on a northeastern course. The Mule Ear peaks came into view straight ahead in the distance, beyond them were the high peaks of the Chisos Mountains. They had lost over a thousand feet of altitude.

No more than 400 feet above the ground, Jess tried the starter again. The engine sputtered and blew flame from the exhaust. The engine was flooded with fuel, but Jess continued to press the start button, and swapped hands reaching to turn the fuel pump off. The propeller continued to 'free wheel', and then the engine fired again, making the propeller spin faster. Jess pushed the propeller control forward as he worked the mixture control back and forth until the engine began to run. Releasing the start switch and continuing the manipulation of the controls, Jess was able to keep the engine firing, but roughly. The aircraft was steadily gaining altitude, and finally the engine began to run smoothly, another three hundred feet gained.

Jess let out a shout, startling his passenger, "Thank you, Lord Jesus!"

The altimeter slowly indicated 950 feet above the barren land below. Jess continued looking for a place to land; his passenger was still dazed and in shock. The only paved road was extremely hilly and behind him to the right, too low to turn around for that.

The higher altitude gave him a better look at the terrain. The sun was casting longer shadows across the plains, giving up the false sense of smooth land.

The engine quit again. Jess was letting this get to him, and he became impatient searching for a place to land. He knew there was a paved road going from the Big Bend park station westward around the Chisos Mountains and turning toward Castolon. He turned in his seat to look back to the left, and the shadows of the cliffs across the Rio Grande had covered where he thought Castolon should be. But, he could still see the Mule Ear peaks off his left wing, which meant the road was about 90° to the left. He slowly banked again, keeping his gliding speed; now he could feel a tail wind pushing.

Jess transmitted on the radio another "**MAYDAY - SEVEN-FIVE-ZERO-ZERO**" emergency signal with his location, then took off his headset to concentrate on his airspeed and any open space to get down on directly ahead.

Suddenly, from above, a large aircraft passed within 50' of Jess and the commissioner! He never saw it coming, only when it nearly missed them. He fought to control his aircraft from the wake turbulence produced by the large aircraft. The larger C130 climbed, banked and headed for Mexico. Jess was dangerously out of control and getting very close to the ground. He saw a dry creek bed to the left and carefully banked towards it.

He whispered, "That could be Alamo Creek. It's not very wide."

The lower he got to the ground, he knew the dry creek was not the best place to land an aircraft - it was covered with large rocks and boulders.

"Another bad decision!" He eased back the yoke, flaring the aircraft for touchdown, unlocked his door and yelled, "Keep your door open as far as it will go and hold on!"

Casa Grande
7,235 feet
Big Bend National Park

CHAPTER TWENTY-NINE

"The FBI have problems with their aircraft in Alpine, and want us to pick them up," one of the Rangers reported to Ranger Charles Randel.

Charles nodded acknowledgment of the message and shouted to his brother Jack, "Ranger Jack! Over here!" His tone of voice caught Jack's attention, and returned a wave of the hand. As he walked over to Charles, he pointed at the number of aircraft on the field next to the Ranger's helicopter at the hangar.

"We need to get authority to shut down this airport. The media will crowd in here tying up the airspace and field parking," Jack said in a disgusted manner.

Jack pointed at a junior Texas Ranger at the reception table set up in their command post, "Find Sheriff Baker on the phone, ASAP!"

"Yes, Sir!" he replied.

"The Sheriff knows the local FAA people. We need immediate contact with them. Now, what did you want, Charles?" he said, turning to his brother.

"The FBI has 'requested', not demanded, an aircraft to pick them up at Alpine. Theirs is grounded," Charles said.

Jack frowned and guided Charles away from the others, "We need to keep good relations with them because Uncle Jess is getting deeper involved. Send our helicopter up there and have them top it off with fuel before coming back."

Charles put his hands on his hips and nodded, "Good idea. I don't want to use this fuel here in those overhead tanks next to the hangar. I suspect moisture from condensation may be in them. They sit in the sun all the time."

"I'll relay this to Major Hankins in El Paso," Jack said, shaking his head, "And, I agree about those tanks. I'm surprised they aren't covered over, protected from the hot sun."

"By the way," Charles said with a low voice. "I'll delay the FBI longer so we can find Uncle Jess before they arrive! I'll tell the pilot to come back the scenic route."

Jack gave him 'thumbs up', and they both went back to their individual responsibilities.

#

LeAnn had obtained permission to fly in the restricted border areas of Presidio, Lajitas, Big Bend State Park and the Study Butte area to Castalon since Jess' rescue had begun. This came from the FAA Flight Service in El Paso and Albuquerque Center for the Military Operations Area (MOA) and Air Defense Identification Zone (ADIZ), which she would be flying. All borders of the United States have the ADIZ areas for flight restrictions.

As a member of the Brewster/Presidio counties Civil Air Patrol, she informed them she was the advance CAP searching for the downed aircraft.

LeAnn's red and white Cessna 180 glistened in the bright late afternoon sun when she would bank around questionable objects on the ground. With two aircraft radios and a hand held transceiver, she could monitor three frequencies at one time. One was tuned to the emergency 121.5, listening for Jess' ELT transmissions.

She tried two frequencies she had overheard Rangers Charles and Jack discussing to be used in the Big Bend area. No communication traffic on either frequency, so she transmitted, "Ranger Randel, Cessna 180, 8001 Quebec Uniform, calling

Ranger Randel. I am the advanced Civil Air Patrol en route to Castalon, over!"

No answer. She transmitted again, identifying herself, and waited.

"LeAnn, 8001 Quebec Uniform," came a voice.

"Yes!"

"This is Park Ranger Jake Wilson. Texas Ranger Charles Randel is coming to the radio."

"8001 Quebec Uniform, Roger."

"Go ahead, LeAnn," Charles said.

"I'm your advanced Civil Air Patrol. I am now crossing Terlingua, heading for Castalon. Have you any transmissions from Jess?"

"We heard a short 'Mayday' earlier, but nothing since then. No fix on his location. He was flying south over the river from Lajitas at water level toward Santa Elena Canyon. Hijacker on board," Charles said.

"I understand! Is he armed?"

"Yes! We always assume that!"

"I'll start above Santa Elena Canyon opening where the river turns 90° to the south, and search around there," LeAnn replied, as she gained altitude for topping the canyon ridge.

"Great! We will be sending others to help and will give you advance notice. Continue to monitor this frequency. Be careful, over and out," Charles replied.

LeAnn adjusted the aircraft's radios to the Rangers' frequency, and left the portable on the emergency frequency. She was getting thirsty and reached behind the right front seat for one of her canteens. After a couple of swallows, she laid it on the seat.

Whispering, "Jess, where are you? Talk to me, Jess." She quietly prayed.

Out of the corner of her eye, she noticed a large plane pulling up into a steep climb. It was a four-engine cargo aircraft; she identified it as a C130, and then noted the time and GPS location. It appeared to have just missed a smaller aircraft.

"That's Jess' aircraft!"

The large aircraft was heading in her direction; she was between it and Mexico. LeAnn put her Cessna into a steep right wingover dive to get out of the other aircraft's way. She came out of her spiral barely one hundred feet above the ground.

Leveling off, she transmitted, "Texas Rangers! Texas Rangers! This is an emergency! A light tan C130 just missed hitting a smaller aircraft, which looked like Jess'! The larger aircraft almost got me as it gained altitude heading for Mexico, over Castalon. No markings! I can still see it! Over!"

"Cessna 8001, where are you?" a voice asked.

"Northwest of Castalon. GPS coordinate: one-zero-three-degrees three-zero-minutes-west. Two-niner-degrees one-zero minutes north. Copy!"

The Rangers repeated her GPS location and she replied, "That's a copy! Roger, that is correct!"

"Have you seen Jess' aircraft?"

LeAnn was puffing, holding her breath while in a steep turn, "I'm in a steep bank coming around to find that aircraft I saw. It did look like his Porter PC-6. I got disoriented in getting out of that guy's way. I'm searching!"

Shouting aloud in the cockpit of her airplane, "Jess, where did you go? God, help us find him!"

LeAnn slowed her aircraft to a speed below stall speed. With the speed stall warning horn blaring in her ear, she increased her speed just enough for it to turn off, and kept her Cessna at an even two hundred feet above the ground. She had plenty of power to gain altitude if needed, but she wanted to be low and slow to scan the ground for any sign of life or aircraft.

"Cessna 8001 Quebec Uniform," Jack called. "We will have two more aircraft in your area in 30 minutes to assist. Keep talking to us every five minutes or so."

"Cessna 8001. Roger that!"

She opened her door window and locked it in place. It was becoming unbearable with the low sun heating up the cabin. The canyon wall shadows were rapidly increasing toward the area where she was searching. She knew the search would be called off after dark. Steadily holding her altitude, LeAnn turned her head and leaned her forehead against the top of the window frame, squinting into the sun, which was shaded by the left wing. No sign of Jess' airplane.

LeAnn continued flying figure-eight maneuvers northwest of Castolon, where she hoped Jess would be. Banking to the right, she slowly turned back toward the east, looking out the right window for any sign of another airplane or men walking. The noise of the aircraft flushed five mule deer from heavy mesquite brush; their dust cloud hung in the air, tracing their exit. She leveled the wings and searched out her window. Still no sight of the two men, and the radio was silent. The only noise was the prop, engine and the wind passing the window.

On the horizon to the northwest, two helicopters flew toward LeAnn. She did not see them for concentrating so hard staring at the ground below her and watching her instruments.

"Hello, LeAnn! We will be there in five! Have you seen anything at all?" Charles asked.

"Negative! Just mule deer and a few jackrabbits. I last saw Jess when that C130 almost collided with him and then with me. In the confusion getting out of his way, I lost sight of Jess in this area I'm covering."

She banked slowly again, to the east. "I'm covering a square mile or so, twice. Then cut it in two. I'll do an adjacent square between the river and me, after this leg. Copy?"

"Got your next square in sight! We will work north of you," Jack said. All three aircraft crews slowly flew their assigned areas without communicating.

"Jack! Can you still hear me? You're five minutes has come and gone," LeAnn said, listening hard for a reply. "If you're on the ground, can you hear me?"

No reply, just steady noise of the radio's squelch in the background.

Both of the Texas Ranger brothers had a helicopter and were covering the areas on both sides of LeAnn.

"I called off the other aircraft until morning," Jack said. "Everyone is being put up at Lajitas. There is an aviation fuel tanker on its way from Marfa by morning. No cost to you."

"Thanks, but I can fuel at the ranch. I need to get back there tonight. I'll be at Lajitas before sunup for breakfast," LeAnn said, just a little bit aggravated and disappointed of not finding Jess.

They continued searching for another hour, and then departed for their separate night locations. There were no further sightings or communications with Jess that night.

CHAPTER THIRTY

Jess' large turboprop aircraft bounced over huge rocks in the canyon's dry bed, causing the left wing to catch the face of a canyon wall, shearing it off at the wing strut. There was no danger of a large fuel explosion when the tank ripped open because there was only the small amount of residual fuel in the tanks, which evaporated when it hit the air. But, the aircraft jackknifed and cart wheeled into the face of the canyon wall: nose down, tail high. The tail slammed against the wall and bounced away. Then, it tittered and smashed hard upside down on the dry riverbed, breaking the fuselage open aft of the wings. Some of Jess' cargo tumbled out.

Jess was dazed for a moment, but regained his senses. Upside down, he put one hand on the ceiling of the aircraft and held onto the seat belt as he unbuckled, easing himself down onto the ceiling. He kicked the jammed door open and then jumped from the aircraft. He ducked under the nose and went around to the passenger's side to get Commissioner Rodiquez out. The door was wedged open under the bent wing, and the commissioner didn't have any problems stumbling out.

Jess' unwanted passenger jumped away from him. Sick from fright, airsickness and confusion, he fell to his hands and knees with dry heaves from trying to vomit.

Jess let him finish and then lifted him to his feet by his right shoulder, "You have a mess to clean up! Look at my aircraft!"

The commissioner was not steady on his feet, and his face was bleached like the rocky canyon bed sand he was trying to stand on. Jess guided him to the pilot's side of the airplane, making him sit on the large aircraft tire lying on the ground.

"Just stay right there. I'll get you some water," Jess said, yanking the damaged cargo door open.

"Why am I being so nice to him?" Jess said to himself. "He just hijacked me and caused me to wreck my aircraft! Lord, under these circumstances, it's sure hard to have compassion for this guy."

Jess picked up his .45 auto in its holster on the ground and buckled it around his waist. Then put two full extra ammo magazines in his shirt pockets. He moved jumbled cargo, bedroll, metal detectors, tools, and finally uncovered a six-pack of 24-ounce plastic water bottles. They had not been damaged.

"Hey!" Jess yelled at the commissioner, and then tossed a bottle to him. He surprisingly caught it. Jess wanted to stay away from the man until they both calmed down.

"I don't know what your problem was or is!" Jess said. "But, I'm not interested. I'm heading up this expedition, and I call the shots from now on!" The commissioner looked at Jess in a dazed manner, not understanding, just sat there staring at him. "If you don't like it, you can find your way back to wherever you came. I'm going to find high ground to make camp."

Jess climbed further into the wrecked aircraft and found the Texas Ranger transceiver that wound up in the cargo compartment. He hung it on his belt next to a long blade bolo knife in its scabbard. He gathered small survival equipment and stuffed it all into a backpack with a large canteen of water. He grabbed his crushed camping hat and snugly put it on his head. The old gun holster and ammo belt with the old five-shot colt .45 in it fit nicely on the opposite hip around his waist. Now, he had a gun on each hip. Jess backed out of the wrecked aircraft and tucked the rifle under his arm.

Turning around to look for his passenger, he stooped picking up the backpack. The guy was still having dry heaves.

Jess was thinking about their rescue, *Wonder if that Emergency Locator Transmitter (ELT) activated when we crashed? Wait, you turned it on in the air. If it's working, it shouldn't be long before someone shows up.* He laid the rifle against a rock and the backpack next to it.

He then climbed up through the pilot's door. Moving wreckage out of the way, he reached the instrument panel. Prior to the crash landing, he had turned the Com radio to the emergency frequency, calling for help. Then he had turned everything off before the messy crash landing. He turned the battery power on, which supplied power to the instrument panel, and then turned on the avionics switch.

The equipment hanging around his waist kept catching on wreckage of the aircraft, causing Jess to get aggravated. Fussing under his breath, he paused and took a deep breath. Then he sniffed the air. *'It's a little late to be sniffing for fuel fumes!* Jess thought to himself.*'

"Dog-gone-it!" Jess said discussed. "No power from the battery to run the radios. And, my GPS is smashed!" He wanted to listen for the emergency locating transmitter tone, which would have activated upon impact. The GPS would mark his exact location. *The Texas Ranger transceiver radio is damaged and dead. Now what? Guess we will just wait for help! Maybe the ELT is activated.*

"Lord, what do I do now?" Jess asked. *Let me see? I can use my handy-dandy all-purpose tool and cut through the side fuselage. It's only lightweight aluminum.*

He made his way over to the tail section, took the Leatherman Tool from its leather pouch on his belt and began cutting a hole where the ELT would be. *Sure enough, there it is – still in its rack. That didn't take long.* He straightened up and put his left hand on the butt of the old Colt .45. *Transmitter light isn't on!* He operated the transmit switch on the ELT. The light didn't light. "Now what?"

He turned and shouted, "Satan, get away from me in Jesus name! I don't belong to you!" His voice echoed between the canyon walls. "Thank you Lord! I had to get that out!"

After turning the power switch off at the instrument panel, Jess eased his way back out of the wreck, again. Turning around, he saw the commissioner staggering across the dusty canyon bed. He was not plotting a straight course, trying to walk around large vegetation.

"Hey, Commissioner! Where ya' going?" Jess hollered, and then sat on a boulder watching the dazed man. He felt a little woozy himself. He took one of the water bottles out of the backpack and took a long swallow. Then, he stood and swung the backpack over his shoulders.

I hope I don't need all this stuff. But, never know!

"Over here, Commissioner!"

The commissioner slowly turned around and waved at Jess, smiled and stumbled back toward him. He was not careful where he stepped and continued to stumble over small cactus and *sotol*, falling through a *candelilla* wax plant. He got up, brushed himself off and waved to Jess again, almost like he had been drinking.

Must have a concussion, Jess thought. *I'd better help him. Don't think he's stable enough to give me any problem physically, but need to keep a close watch; he could be in a bad way.*

Jess grabbed him by the arm and swung it over and above the backpack. Then, with his free hand gripped the commissioner's pants belt in the back to help keep him stable. He found a temporary place for them on higher ground to set up camp, just in case of a flash flood. Surging water from up stream could sweep the aircraft all the way to the Rio Grande River.

Propping the commissioner against a dried mesquite tree stump, Jess took off his backpack and pulled an emergency tarp from it. He made a little windbreak for the commissioner and took the water container from him pouring some over the commissioner's head and face. The commissioner responded with a gasp and shook his head, lifting his hands together for more. Jess filled the commissioner's palms with water. Then, he splashed his face with it.

"That is good water! May I have some to drink?" he asked, looking up at Jess through wet hair.

"Sure, this bottle is yours to use," Jess said handing him the water bottle. "Don't drink too much! It might make you sicker. You'll need it later. We may be here for a couple days."

The sun was down behind the mountains to the west in Mexico, and the shadows were making it cold. The wind came up, causing them both to shiver. Jess was not high enough on the hill to see any distant landmarks.

"Sit there and don't move! I'll get some firewood, be right back."

Jess found large dead *Agave* or *Maguay* plants and cut them in two-foot lengths; then carried them back to their makeshift camp. The wind was becoming stronger, causing Jess to scan the vast openness for better shelter. There was a large outcropping of limestone a hundred yards or so from their camp; that would provide better protection. The sun was still shining on the west side of the top of the protruding limestone hills. It was an uphill climb.

"Hey, Commissioner! Give me a hand getting this all together. We need to move up there to that limestone wall. It should protect us from this wind."

"Yes! That is a good idea," he replied and continued mumbling something in Spanish.

They gathered everything, plus the dried logs from another dried *Agave* plant Jess had cut. He remembered stories of using the live plant's roots for food, after roasting it. The thick pointed leaves could be made into Tequila, which he didn't know how to concoct. The roots would be an unusual treat to fill in, if necessary, because he only had a three-day food supply for two people in the survival kit.

Having to rough the elements was not anything new for Jess. He tried to always travel with the thought of emergencies arising. Plus, desert and mountain survival was not a problem for him; he had special training in the U.S. military and additional training in Morocco a few years back with Interpol agents.

Jess did not expect this outing to be more than a day or so. They would stay close to the aircraft wreckage for rescue. In the morning, he would setup a smoking fire. The rangers would certainly find them.

"How does that overhang next to the large prickly pear cactus look for shelter? Would it be out of this wind?" Jess asked the commissioner. They were both a little out of breath and stopped to rest from their short hike up to the outcropping of limestone.

Commissioner Rodiquez just nodded his approval and collapsed to one knee. He put up his hand, telling Jess he was all right and waved him to continue. He slowly got back up, unsteady on his feet and followed Jess.

Jess made camp under the overhang and built a small fire, which reflected their silhouettes on the wall of limestone behind them. He tied the emergency tarp to the overhang and laid large rocks along the bottom to keep the wind from whipping it. The tarp closed in one side making a triangle shape room with its one edge as an entrance. It helped keep the heat of the fire from escaping so quickly. They both enjoyed its comfort.

"There is a bedroll in the wreckage and some more camping gear. I'll go get it, be right back. Will you be okay?" Jess asked.

"If I stay warm, I will be okay. I will keep the fire burning," he replied with a heavy Spanish accent and moved the *Agave* logs around in the fire.

I better cut some more wood on the way back. What we have now will not last all night, Jess thought as he swung the backpack on, picked up the rifle and headed down toward the wreck. *I sure manage to get myself in some of the most ridiculous situations. I could write a book!*

"Ya! You're always making threats to write a book and never do it," he said out loud to himself. "Here we go again, having a one-sided conversation with me, myself and I." Laughing to himself, "Can't lose this way!"

Stumbling on down the hill, he continued mumbling to himself, "Wonder if either of the twins have their radios on. Don't see or hear any aircraft." He stopped and surveyed his vast surroundings.

The sun was down and the stars were so bright, he could almost see his way by their light. He couldn't remember if the moon would be out. Jess turned on his mini flashlight.

\#

Jess' unwanted companion huddled close to the limestone wall, which was still warm from the setting sun. With his legs and arms crossed, the commissioner leaned toward the fire. His front side was toward the hot coals of the *Agave* logs that seemed to crack endlessly. Sparks floated up to the overhang; hitting it they would disappear. Not thinking of anything specific, he hummed a familiar Mexican song from his childhood, not remembering the words.

The commissioner put his head on his folded arms and then rocked back and forth, thinking, '*Why must I do these horrible things to myself and to others? I lost my family because of my wicked ways. I am a no good peon.*' Tears came and he moaned deeply. '*If I had only listened to my little mother! She prayed for me, but I did not care. What am I to do?*' He suddenly quieted,

193

looked up and listened to whatever startled him. *'Is it the pilot coming back? Or, is there an animal out there? I have no gun. He has a rifle and sidearm. Maybe I can use the firewood.'* He unfolded his legs and arms reaching for a hot log in the fire. Then he moved back into the corner of the shelter. *'I do not hear anything now, so I must be imagining things. I am so tired and sleepy. I'll just lean back against the wall and shut my eyes. Rest! I need rest!'*

#

The sweet aroma of cooking woke Commissioner Rodiquez. He pushed his head out from under a warm bedroll Jess had covered him with looking at Jess in surprise. He had the tarp partially open and the commissioner could see the sunrays warming the western mountain peaks. He looked back at what Jess had stuck to a stick over the fire with a questionable expression.

Jess pulled a stick wrapped with strips of bacon from the fire and moved the bacon closer to the commissioner's nose. His eyes widened and a broad smile came across his face. He sat up and stretched his arms. Jess offered him the hot strips of bacon; he took one off the stick. He juggled the strip from hand to hand, trying to cool it before putting it in his mouth.

"Hum, yes!" He smacked his lips and wiped his mouth on his shirtsleeve. Then, he saw the coffee on the hot fire in a camping tin. "You have biscuits and gravy?"

"I'm glad you're feeling better and awake with a good sense of humor," Jess replied, handing him a warm biscuit. "Had some of this stuff in the aircraft; thought we would enjoy it this morning. What do you think?"

"I am most surprised by your hospitality. What is your name?" He stuck out his hand to Jess, "I am Commissioner

Rodiquez, from Chihuahua, Mexico. What were you doing at the Lajitas airport?"

"The same question for you? Why were you there and why did you hijack me?" Jess said with a glare in his eye. "I was taking pictures! What about you?"

"Do not raise your voice with me! I am Commissioner..."

Jess pointed his finger at the commissioner, "Don't give me that bull! You're in the United States now, not Mexico! And, you're in a heap of trouble! The Texas Rangers and Border Patrol are out looking for you because you took me by force!"

Fear came across the commissioner's face, "I apologize, and I am sorry..."

"Hold it right there!" Jess said shaking his finger in Rodiquez face. "I will accept your apology, but being sorry doesn't cut it now. You got involved with some wrong people and now you're running for your life. Whoever it was almost rammed us in the air with that C130. It's too late to be feeling remorse over the situation." Jess stood up, "Here have some more bacon and biscuits. We're not gonna waste this food, eat up!" And handed the astonished commissioner a small jar of peanut butter and jam, with a plastic knife to dig it out. "I always have that for emergencies. No not the knife! The sweets!"

Lord, what am I going to do with this guy. He said that he hasn't done anything wrong. I don't believe him. I could pop him in the nose for hijacking me; he could have caused both our deaths and injuries. My aircraft is destroyed, but I know it can be replaced. Don't mean to complain like this, Lord. I am thankful to be alive, but what about this guy! As a Texas Ranger, I should read him his rights and arrest him... that would make it official. I probably should handcuff him.

Jess spoke softly to himself, "I know You have given me the power to defeat terror and fear. So, in Jesus Christ's name and through the power of His blood that was shed for us, I bind you Satan. No death, no more injuries or damage. Get out of here!"

"Did you speak to me?" asked the commissioner, looking at Jess.

Jess shook his head, "No! I'm talking to someone else."

With a questioning look, he turned around searching for the person Jess had been talking to, and then back toward Jess shrugging his shoulders.

Jess pointed toward the sky, "Heaven!" and smiled.

"You pray?"

Jess nodded, yes.

"Good to pray!" the commissioner replied and made the sign of the cross, watching Jess closely.

After I get a good smoking fire started, Jess thought to himself, *I better find out what the commissioner's problem is.*

Jess squatted next to a stack of dried wood and struck a match to it. He had placed rocks around the fire to protect against it spreading. In a few minutes, it was blazing. Then, he took the ears from prickly pear cactuses and sliced them in pieces, tossing the green plant into the hot fire. It began to make thick and gray smoke. Then, he took an arm full of dry sagebrush and tossed it on the fire. He had smoke rising straight up hundreds of feet.

"There! Let's finish breakfast and wrap everything up. It won't be long before we are rescued," Jess said sitting down next to the commissioner, letting out a tired sigh.

"You are correct!" Rodiquez said. "I am a criminal hiding behind the law of my state Chihuahua, Mexico. I have been trading guns for drugs with foreign countries, bringing them across the river into the United States. The aircraft left with both, the guns and my money. I deserve that!" He looked at Jess, "Why am I telling you this? You are not a priest!"

"Confession is good for the soul!" Jess handed him another biscuit, "Eat your breakfast! There is plenty. We can talk about this after we have finished eating. Drink a lot of water. We'll need it before this day is over," Jess commanded and leaned against the warm limestone wall.

From their location, Jess figured they were somewhere close to Castolon. He could see the Santa Helena canyon and the Terlingua fault. *Which means, the Chisos Mountain range is behind us on the other side of the limestone overhang. Lajitas is a long way off, perhaps too far for the rangers to see the smoke. But, the Big Bend National Park Rangers are around somewhere, even at Castolon. Surely, someone will see the smoke.*

Jess went back to the smoking fire and added more dried grass to make it smoke more. He didn't want to smother the fire, but wanted to get more smoke into the air.

Then everything went black for Jess.

#

Commissioner Rodiquez dropped the *Agave* log he had hit Jess in the back of the head with, "Sorry, *amigo*! Whoever you are! I must get to Mexico," he said in Spanish.

He picked up Jess' .30-.30 rifle and a plastic bottle of water, slowly poured the water on the fire Jess had built and watched the red coals disappear. The smoke turned white and then a dirty gray after he kicked dirt and ashes onto the dead fire. When he was satisfied it would not continue to burn, he turned and shuffled down into the canyon where the aircraft had crashed. He could follow the canyon all the way to the Rio Grande River. He knew it would not take long to wade or swim across.

The commissioner hummed some Mexican song as he trudged passed the aircraft, not even looking at it. He climbed out of the riverbed and walked the canyon ridge until he had to climb down to the canyon floor again. The rocks were hard for him to walk on and stay balanced; he was constantly falling to one knee.

Two hours had passed and the commissioner was only a mile down the canyon when he ran out of drinking water. He did not take an extra container nor conserved what he had.

He swore in Spanish, throwing the empty plastic bottle at a cactus growing out of the canyon wall. He stopped, held up the rifle he had been carrying, and injected a live round into the breech.

How straight does this shoot? Aiming at one big ear of a cactus, he sighted a red cactus apple growing out the edge of the ear. Slowly pulling the trigger, it fired, knocking off the apple. He smiled to himself; *I am not a bad shot after all. But, why do I need this rifle? It is too heavy to carry.* He walked under a mesquite tree, leaned the rifle against the trunk and sat down in the sand next to it.

It is getting too hot and no water. Suddenly, a noise from behind startled him, "*Que?*"

He turned to look behind him and saw two wild, black, longhaired pigs staring at him, about fifty feet away. The hair was bristled up on their backs. He knew they were feared in this part of the country, Javelina Peccary hogs. They had been known to tear up men on foot to protect their young.

The bigger Peccary snorted and then kicked up dust with its fore hoofs, like a mad bull would do. The ridge of hair continued to stand up on its back. The commissioner moved around to keep the tree between them and him. The mesquite tree was not very big, but big enough to hold him off the ground away from the tusked beast. They charged as he stood up to climb the tree with thorns.

Rodiquez jumped as high as he could to grab the biggest branch closest to him, pulling his boots up against the trunk of the tree. When he grabbed the branch, two long thorns pierced the palm of his right hand, protruding out the other side. He could not lift his hand without the danger of falling on the raging pig.

He squirmed around the branch and lodged his one boot in the fork of the branch at the trunk, and then tried to pull it out in order to move higher, but it would not come loose. He found himself in a bad situation with his right hand pierced and his left foot caught.

Screaming and swearing from the pain, he yelled as loud as he could, trying to scare the pigs away. It only made them more agitated and they began butting the small trunk of the mesquite tree. The excitement made them give off a stinking odor. Both pigs foamed at the mouth. Every time they hit the trunk, their two short tusks torn the thin bark off, and then they began to splinter the tree.

The commissioner realized what they were doing and held still. He looked for a way to reach an overhanging willow tree branch that was higher, but he did not dare to move. The group of trees where he was located grew up out of a deep sand bar in the curve of the creek, under the larger willow tree. The high canyon walls did not give him any way of escaping on foot, even if he could climb to the larger tree.

With all the strength he could muster, he yanked his hand up and away from the long needles on the branch. Now, the blood flowed like a water faucet. He held his hand under his left armpit, trying to stop the bleeding. The monster pigs smelt the blood and dug it from the sand. Again, they snorted, cut at the tree trunk and butted it with their foreheads; each time it swayed and began to lean.

Rodiquez lost grip with his left hand and fell head long toward the two Peccary pigs. His weight caused the tree to bend lower and they began jumping at his face, still foaming from their mouths.

Suddenly, there were gunshots from a crevice in the canyon wall. Jess came out with both his automatic .45 Colt pistol and single action revolver firing away at the pigs. He was a good one hundred feet away. Each shot hit the wild pigs, knocking them down. No sooner were they down, they were back up. The noise of the guns turned them in Jess' direction. He climbed onto a large boulder and continued firing away at the pigs. He emptied both guns and reloaded.

"Commissioner, try to pull yourself up higher. They're not dead yet," Jess hollered.

He reloaded the .45 single action revolver and took careful aim between the eyes of the biggest collared Peccary. It stood about two feet high at the front shoulder, weighing about a hundred and fifty pounds or more. Its coarse, grizzled, black coat had a light gray, almost white, ring or collar around its neck. Jess fired. It dropped over dead. The smaller pig butted the big dead one, trying to get it up. It snorted, foaming at the mouth, looking straight at Jess as he fired again. Another dead shot. Both pigs lay side by side.

"I have never seen wild pigs that close. I could have been killed!" the commissioner said, hanging from the tree by one foot. "I think my leg is broken. I cannot get it loose from the tree."

Jess reloaded his weapons, jumped down, walked over to the pigs, and then shot them both again for good measure. He looked up at the commissioner while reloading again, "Hold on tight! I'll cut you down."

Jess holstered his .45 automatic pistol and walked around the dead pigs, pushing them with his boot, "These two Peccaries look like they may have a disease of some kind, or do they always foam at the mouth when they get mad?"

"I do not know! Leave them alone, and get me down!"

Jess pulled his long bolo knife from its sheath and began chopping at the trunk where the pigs had gnawed. It only took half a dozen whacks for the tree to break, and the commissioner was on the ground.

"Let me cut that branch, and you'll be free."

The commissioner's eyes got big as Jess swung his bolo knife at the branch. "Careful!" He yelled.

Jess looked him in the eye, "I'll try not to hit you! So, be still! Don't look!"

Two cuts from the sharp blade, and Jess was able to crack the branch. The commissioner's leg fell to the ground. He was white as a sheet and close to fainting. Jess soaked his handkerchief with water from his canteen and gave it to the commissioner.

"Wash your face and take some long deep breaths," Jess said cutting open the pants' leg. The bone was pushed up through the skin above the boot top, but no flow of blood. The skin was already black.

"Let me pull you over to that boulder, so you can sit up."

Jess slid him across the sand easily, and propped him up. He looked at the wound again, "Splint it!"

"What you mean? *Qué me estas dicieudo?*"

"I'll have to splint your leg! It's broken bad," Jess said. "There's plenty of dried drift wood around here. I should be able to make a nice splint."

"How do you know so much about first aide?" He asked in pain.

"I had training in the United States Air Force. Don't worry, I'll get you out of here in one piece!" Jess said picking out good sticks for the splint. "Keep talking! It will help take your mind off the pain."

"What is your name?" the commissioner asked.

"Jess Hanes, retired Air Force. Spent twenty-five years in the service."

Jess took off his shirt and undershirt, and then put his top long sleeve shirt back on. With his pocketknife, he made strips of cloth from the undershirt to hold the sticks in place. He motioned the commissioner not to watch. "I will not set the bone; the damage is too great!"

201

Jess frowned as he began splinting the leg, *He may lose this leg from gangrene if I don't get him help. Real quick!*

"I know that name, Jess Hanes. Where are you from? Are you a policeman? Texas Ranger?"

"Nope! Not a policeman," Jess said as he held the sticks and wrapped them in place. "Now, this is going to hurt when I tighten this splint. *Mucho grande!*" He handed the commissioner a stick and eased his boot off the ground a few inches. "Bite that stick. Take your frustrations out on it when I tighten up."

"You ready?" Jess asked.

The commissioner nodded his head, closed his eyes and gripped the stick with his teeth as hard as he could. Jess put his handkerchief and the remainder of his undershirt over the open wound and lightly compressed them, trying not to damage the wound anymore than it was. Then, he slowly tightened the cloth strips around the sticks and knotted them. The commissioner yelled, spit the stick from his mouth and passed out.

Jess had finished strapping the splint and was washing the commissioner's face when he regained consciousness.

"Drink this slowly," Jess told him. "Let me have your shirt. I'm making something to drag you out of here. And, to answer your other question, I'm not a policeman. But, I am a Texas Ranger."

Jess pointed to a tree limb litter he was making, "What do you think of that contraption? I think I can pull you to higher ground, but it may take awhile."

He had taken his buttoned long sleeve shirt off and ran sturdy limb poles through the body part and out the sleeves. He did the same with the commissioner's shirt. Then, he removed his belt from his pants and motioned the commissioner to do the same. Jess looped them around both poles and buckled them together, so the poles would not spread apart any further than the belts would allow. Then, he took nylon rope from his backpack and made other crisscross loops to help carry the weight.

"You should fit in that pretty good. It's not going to be comfortable," Jess said, as he pulled it along side of the commissioner. "Let me lift the weight of your splinted leg, while you roll on your side. I'll put it down on top of your good leg, and then scoot this litter under you. Then, you can roll back over onto it. Okay?"

"*Si! Señor!*" he replied, gritting his teeth again as Jess helped him turn on his side.

Once he was somewhat comfortable on the litter, Jess checked his handguns, again. Knowing Commissioner Rodiquez was not going anywhere, except with him, he handed him the single action revolver. "If you see any more Peccaries, don't wait for me to stop. Start shooting. They have been known to run in groups of six to thirty in this part of the Texas," Jess said.

He picked up his rifle, blew and wiped the sand off, then opened the breech. No rounds of ammo in the rifle, so he filled the magazine with fresh ammunition. Then, he loosened the rifle's leather strap and slung it over his head laying the rifle across his backpack.

Jess stepped between the poles, looked back at his passenger, "You ready for this ride?"

The commissioner did not even look up at him, "*Si, Señor! Vamonos!* I am ready!"

After taking a deep breath, Jess reach down to pick up the poles when a low flying single engine Cessna flew over them and then up the canyon. It was lower than the canyon rim. He got dizzy when he quickly raised his head, staggered and regained his balance.

He ran out into the dry creek bed canyon, just as a Texas Ranger helicopter flew over and made a wide circle and returned.

It landed in the sandy bottom of the canyon, while the Cessna landed on top of the canyon ridge.

"Commissioner, we are rescued!" Jess yelled as he return to the litter.

Jess realized the commissioner had Jess' old Colt pointed at him, and he froze in his tracks. *Lord Jesus! He's in enough trouble!*

Just as Jess was about to raise his hands, the commissioner dumped the ammo out in the palm of his hand. He held the gun out to Jess, butt first, and the ammo in his open hand.

Jess put the gun in its holster on his hip and the ammo in the belt ammo loops. With his hands on his hip, "Do you feel like standing for a few minutes? They may have a stretcher in the helicopter for you to lay on."

He nodded yes and offered his hand to Jess. He put his arm around Jess' neck and leaned against him, taking the weight off the broken left leg

"Before they get here, I want to thank you for trying to take care of me. I have been very bad. Perhaps some day we can talk about this, without being enemies," he said quietly to Jess.

"Well, you will get your chance to tell the Texas Rangers all about it. Once they say it's okay, I'll come see you. I don't know if they will take you to Mexico, or if you'll stay over here in jail," Jess replied, and then tapped on the commissioner's chest with a finger. "Just one more thing. Remember this, Jesus Christ is able to help you anytime. Give your heart and life to Him. If it wasn't for Him, we wouldn't be alive." He slipped his arm around and under the shoulder of the commissioner to help steady him.

The commissioner looked questionably at Jess as two Texas Rangers hustled toward them with guns drawn. *What sort of man is this? I tried to knock his head off and leave him for dead, and then he talks to me about religious things?*

Jess waved for them to put the guns away, "It's good to see you guys! What took you so long?"

Jack and Charles Randel both smiled at their uncle and shook his hand.

"We had to eat breakfast first, you know! Priorities!" Jack said, with a broad grin.

"Uncle Jess, we'll have that Medivac helicopter in here from Lajitas in five minutes," Charles said and radioed his orders.

"By the way, the professor's daughter, LeAnn? She's up on that far canyon rim in her Cessna. We will jump you up there, so you can ride with her. Jack will follow the Medivac chopper to the hospital. I'll ride with the prisoner in the Medivac," Charles said.

"Great! Will the contents of the crash be alright?" Jess asked.

"Yes! The state of Texas will take care of it all. A crew will be here this afternoon to salvage the wreck," Jack said.

"We will get your belongings to you tomorrow. I'm sure we can pull the strings to get you another aircraft. You played a big part in capturing our fugitive," Charles said helping the commissioner onto a stretcher to take him to the Medivac helicopter.

"What about the pigs I had to shoot?" Jess asked.

Jake will take care of that!" Charles replied. "Someone will have a nice pig feast!"

"All aboard," Jack said, when all the doors where shut on the Ranger's helicopter. Jess gave him thumbs up.

It lifted up above to the canyon rim where Jess could see the Mule Ear Peaks at the foot of the Chisos Mountains. He knew exactly where he was now. He had safely crash-landed in the Smokey Creek canyon, further east of Castolon than he had realized.

The helicopter landed next to LeAnn's aircraft where she was waiting under its wing. She ran to Jess through the dust the helicopter stirred up and put her arms around his neck, "Sure happy to see you again, Jess Hanes. Let's go home." She kissed him on the cheek as the helicopter lifted into the air. Both of Jess' nephews were pointing at him and waving.

CHAPTER THIRTY-ONE

The Texas Rangers took the drugs, drug runners and Commissioner Rodiquez to Alpine, turning them over to Brewster County Sheriff Baker. Rangers, Charles and Jack Randel, left Alpine and flew to Professor Stapleton's ranch to interview their Uncle Jess. They were anxious to put the story together concerning the drugs, Jess' crash, the C130 and the videotape they had from Lajitas.

Professor Stapleton paced back and forth across the front porch of his ranch house, sucking on his unlit pipe. Jess and LeAnn sat together on the cedar porch swing waiting for the professor's thoughts on what they had shared with him.

"This country is so wide open here along the border. I am surprised we do not have a full invasion of foreign troops marching through here. The Mexican military come across all along the United States border, at their will – no resistance. They shoot, kill and steal without reprisal, much less the control of drugs and illegal immigrants," John said leaning against the porch rail. He struck a match to light his pipe again, and the ignited head of the match flew off sputtering to the floor. With the toe of his shoe, he smoother the match head, leaving a black smudge.

"We are lucky here on our ranch not to have had more intruders than we have had," John went on to say. "Even though the Mexicans owned this country at one time, it is not theirs now. They come over here illegally and birth their children. Who, by being born here, are given American citizenship and birthrights? In turn, their mother can receive free benefits." He finally got his pipe fired up and puffed away. "Then, the whole family arrives and are given citizenship papers and do not speak any English at all. And, they can even vote!" John stood up straight, "When I came from Austria to this country, during the height of World

War II, I had to learn English before I got my American citizenship papers!" Slapping his hip, "Who made these changes? Did we get to vote about this? Absolutely not!"

"Dad, don't get your dander up! Remember your high blood pressure," LeAnn said.

"Be damned with the blood pressure!" He replied, waving a hand at LeAnn. "I do not mean, 'damning you', Sweetheart!" Getting red in the face, "But, I will get aggravated with the last administration when I chose to do so, young lady!" Smiling at her he reached for an empty apple crate behind the porch swing. "That is my American spirit to protest when I please. Perhaps, I should use this apple crate instead of a soapbox? Anyway, we did finally rid ourselves of those eight years of outrageous, flagrant liars in Washington." Sucking on his unlit pipe, "Maybe this Texan we have in the White House for a president will straighten them out!" He struck another match and puffed away on his pipe.

While the three laughed, the professor turned and pointed up the hill toward the main road, "Sounds like someone is coming."

"I think my twin nephews were planning to be here around four, knowing them, just in time for supper," Jess said, gently elbowing LeAnn. "I appreciate you having us over this evening, especially after my ordeal the last few days."

LeAnn eyed her father, as he spoke, "A team of mules would not have kept her from having you here tonight. We are both overjoyed having you alive and with us." He walked over and patted Jess on the shoulder. Sitting on a stool next to them, he waved at the Hummer as it pulled up to the porch parking space.

The two Texas Ranger nephews of Jess' hopped out and waved back. Both were smiling and Charles held up a thick folder, "Got your video camera in the trunk, this video tape and a bunch of photos."

"It's almost four! What time do you folks eat around here?" Jack asked coming up on the porch. "I have some hot pizza in the trunk. Does everyone like pizza with everything on it, except anchovies?"

LeAnn stood up, put her hands on her hips, "How did you keep them hot all the way from Alpine?"

"I picked up special carriers to keep them warm. Supposed to keep things hot for a couple of hours," he replied. "Just hope they're not soggy."

"I asked him what we were going to do with all those pizzas, especially if no one liked them," Charles said. "He just shrugged and said, 'Guess we'll have a cold pizza breakfast at the hotel in the morning.'"

"Go get them! We about starved waiting for you two," the professor said, putting out his pipe. "I'll get the soda pops from the back porch."

"Need some help?" Charles asked.

"Nope! But, you can come along," he replied.

LeAnn motioned for the other two when they came on the porch with the pizzas, "Come on inside. We can set a table in Dad's den. He has a big screen TV in there to watch the news on satellite. It will be more relaxing in there for everyone, especially after all the excitement of the last few days."

"We're right behind ya, Ma'am," Jack said, waving Jess in front of him to follow her through the door.

LeAnn turned to take a closer look at Jack as he entered. She gave him a big smile and put her arm through his, walking together into the room. '*I wonder how old he is?*' she thought to herself. '*Fantastic looking man!*'

Jack felt the unusual pressure of her against his arm, '*Yes, Ma'am, I'm right here!*' He also thought to himself. '*I can't get any closer!*'

"Gee! Thank ya, young feller," Jess said. "It's nice to have nephews showing respect once in a while."

"Any time for soon-to-be senior citizens," he replied laughing.

"All right, you two! Cool it!" LeAnn said turning Jack's arm loose. "We don't want to start discriminating the young and the old. That wouldn't be politically correct, would it?" She again smiled at Jack, ignoring Charles.

Charles noticed how the two were attracted to each other, right off. Thinking, *Now this could be Jack's downfall. It's the first time I've seen this happen to him. It reminds me of Madi when we first met in Austin when Uncle Jess was in Morocco.*

Jess said, "Charles, don't let me forget to call your Aunt Marie Ann after this is over. I need to talk to her after we eat about when we can expect her. They are two hours ahead of us in Indiana. She's visiting her mom up there."

"Sure thing, Uncle Jess," he replied. "It will be great to see her again. Is M.J. flying her down here?"

"I assume he will," Jess said. "Otherwise, I'll have to fly up to El Paso to pick her up at the airport."

They all hustled, moved furniture around, ate, washed dishes and settled down to watch the video of yesterday's events. The first view was of the Texas Rangers going to the Mariposa mine, then the voice of Jess' hijacker and finally them taking off. As Jess had taxied the aircraft, the video camera got a good focused shot of his passenger in the right seat. It was Commissioner Rodiquez as he turned to look back toward Lajitas with a gun pointed at Jess. The aircraft moved out of view and could be seen in the distance making a banking turn over the mine, heading back toward Lajitas. The sound was good enough to identify Rodiquez' voice before they got in the aircraft. All during the thirty minutes of viewing, they all clapped and were happy for the evidence.

Everyone finally settled down and looked at Jess. He was quietly thinking, *'Should I ask them all of the questions that I have? Might as well, I trust them.'*

"There are a lot of questions I have that are not answered. Let me talk them out, and then perhaps, I will be able to try to answer them as we go. If I can't, maybe you can." Jess got up and picked out a pencil and pad by the telephone, "Mind if we use this, Professor?"

"Go right ahead," he replied.

Jess handed them to LeAnn, who was sitting with Jack, "Would you write some of this down for me? We can go over them once I get them talked out." He walked over to the professor and sat on the edge of the divan next to him, thinking.

With his fingers on one hand stretched up, he started to count, "Let's do some brainstorming. First of all, at Alpine airport, the shooting of Agent Don Simms, and his involvement with you, Professor. Secondly, meeting you here at the ranch, John... shortly there after, you two Texas Rangers showing up. Thirdly, the two county sheriff deputies are in a wreck."

Counting on his fingers again, "Four! The tanker truck explosion that rocked the area. Then number five, the drugs at the Chisos Mariposa mine, where I was to do some research, and then I was hijacked."

Pointing to LeAnn, he said, "Finally, meeting you here at the ranch. Later, you rescuing me after flying for two days of looking."

"And now, here! What have I forgotten?" Jess said looking at everybody.

It was quiet for a few minutes. Then, LeAnn asked, "What happened from the time that you took off, until the time that we found you?"

"Before I answer you, I have one more thing. Where's that C130? Where did it come from and where did it go? Evidently,

Commissioner Rodiquez was connected to those people in some way, right?" Jess asked, and took another sip of iced tea.

"Yes," Charles said, handing Jess a Texas Ranger confidential folder. "We have his statement. Here is a copy for you to look over because it has information relating to your adventure in Morocco. Someone you knew over there."

"Really? Who was that?"

Jack answered, "General Alvarez! That Arab from the Middle-East."

"Wait, just one minute!" Jess' face turned red, eyes narrowed and he blurted out, almost spilling his iced tea, "I buried him inside that mine! All entrances were sealed with missile explosions and dynamite! He couldn't have gotten out alive! No way!" Jess shook his head; he was instantly mad. He turned away from the group. Slamming his fist on the kitchen counter top, he screamed, "And, how did he get promoted to General? He was supposed to be dead!"

It was quiet for a few minutes while Jess tried to absorb what was just laid in his lap. *'Lord Jesus, control my thoughts and my mouth!'*

"There is no way he is still alive!" Jess walked over to the big picture window to the west with his hands on his hips. "I saw him crawl back into that mine entrance after I had blown his knee cap off with my .45 auto! Then, an avalanche covered the entrance with boulders from the mountain above it. I even flew back over and launched missiles to close the openings at the other end of the mine! Plus, that was a shear drop at that end, anyway! He couldn't have climbed out of there either! His knee was shattered! He couldn't walk! He dragged his bad leg getting into the mine before it collapsed over him!"

LeAnn, the professor and Jess' nephews were all wide-eyed at his comments. They were speechless.

Jess turned to them, "How do you know it was him? And, what is he doing here in Texas? Mexico?" Waving his hands, "How could this be? Certainly, he knows nothing of my presence here? Does he?" Looking at his nephews with his hands on his hips, and with a puzzled look on his face, "Well, does he know? Anyone, know?"

"I'm not certain about that, Uncle Jess," Jack said, with earnest. "But, he has been flying across the border off and on for a long time. He is the only one using a C130. He has different colored ones, never using the same color of aircraft twice."

Charles stood next to his uncle; "We haven't had aircraft in the air to stop him, or anyone that knew where he fueled his aircraft in Mexico. He has been running drugs along the border for at least the last four years from Brownsville to Tijuana."

Jack stood, stretched and walked over next to the professor on the divan, "The last few weeks, we haven't been able to keep him on radar or satellite for any length of time. I don't know if that aircraft has radar absorbent paint or electronic countermeasures (ECM.) That information has not been fed to us by the military. But, his identification has just come from Commissioner Rodiquez today."

"You better get him safely undercover somewhere," Jess suggested with a pointed finger at his nephews. "He is a marked man, now that he has dealt with Alvarez. If Alvarez knew that I was around here, your lives would be in danger, too."

Jess sat on the hearth in front of the fireplace, shaking his head, "He probably still has a million in gold for my head! Everyone around me is in danger!" He was almost at the point of tears and prayed, *'Jesus, this is too much in one day. What do we do now? I remember your Word in St. John 15:27 'Peace I leave with you, My peace I give unto you: not as the world giveth, give I unto you. Let not your heart be troubled, neither be afraid.' Lord, settle my heart from fear before I continue!'* He looked up and stood.

"You should put the commissioner under your protection plan. He is your key witness," Jess suggested. "Also, contact the Moroccan authorities for 'mug' shots of this Alvarez."

"We have, and we will, Uncle Jess!" Charles said, then looked at Jack and nodded. "Now, don't worry about him. We'll take care of his safety before leaving here tonight."

"Right now!" Jack said, taking out his cell phone and going into the living room. They could hear him talking to someone, but not clearly.

Charles went over to his Uncle Jess, where LeAnn had already moved to his side and knelt down on one knee in front of him. "I don't know why that C130 tried to knock you out of the sky, unless they knew the commissioner was in on it. I don't think that they knew you were the pilot. You're still under the government's protection plan now, right?"

Putting his hand over his mouth, "Oops! Sorry!" Charles slapped his forehead and squinted his eyes shut, "I sure blew that, Uncle Jess. I'm sorry!"

"Jess Hanes is not your real name?" LeAnn asked, astonished.

"Yes! That is his real name, Sweetheart. I have known him, or about him, since he was born in Dallas," the professor said to his daughter. "I knew his granddad, the man who lived down here in the Big Bend country for years."

"That's right, Dad! J.C. Hanes… or, was it C.J. Hanes?" LeAnn said. "Wasn't he the old prospector working the Terlingua mines? All of this has my mind in a whirl. Jess, you'll have to tell me about this guy and your Moroccan adventure. Please?"

"You'll have to read the book, first!" Jess winked at LeAnn, "And, that project is a long way away. For now, let's get this problem solved about Alvarez," he said, nodding to Charles with a finger across his lips. Everyone got quiet waiting for him to speak.

"First, to answer your question LeAnn about what happened from the time that I took off at Lajitas, until you all rescued us, it was like this..." Jess rehearsed the events for them all.

Then, Jess pointed to Charles, "To answer your question, no! We're no longer under the federal protection plan, not since 9-11.

"I'm having a flash back of September 11," Jess said. "There was another C130, which dropped white powder at the ranch and tore up a security aircraft near the hangar. I wonder if that was Alvarez!"

"We received information from the Austin Ranger Office about that, but never heard anymore," Charles said. "We'll find out if there is a connection." Turning toward Jack, "I'm sure Jack is talking to the Major in El Paso. He's using a scrambler device that he has put on your telephone, Professor. The cell phone can't be securely scrambled," he said, pressing the side of his nose with a finger, thinking. He continued thinking aloud, "If necessary, we'll get the Army and Air National Guard's support on this, with ground troops and aircraft. They are already in this area because of September 11. We'll need them to set their portable ground radars along this stretch of the border with satellite links. Bringing in more troops on the border may cause suspicion of an act of war with the Mexican military." He poured another glass of tea and offered everyone else some. "They have been crossing over long enough in my opinion. We need to put a stop to it."

Charles spread a map of the bordering states on the table and went on to say, "The new Texas Governor is anxious to make points against the drug trade crossing the Rio Grande." Nodding his head toward Jess, "This Alvarez has been around here too often this week to be going that far into Mexico. You know something? I bet we can set a trap for him and catch him right there in Lajitas. He has already landed and taken off from there

215

twice, right?" Charles asked, looking at Jess and Jack who had finished his phone call.

"Yes, and he left without paying the commissioner his fair share for the firearms he acquired," Jack said sitting close to LeAnn. She scooted closer to him. Someone in the room snickered because they were acting like a couple of teenagers.

"That's another reason that Commissioner Rodiquez jumped you at the airport, Uncle Jess," Jack said. "He needed a way back into Mexico."

"Guess I messed your plans up for good," Jess said, pausing. "By the way, I'll be the bait for the trap that you explained. Me!" Jess said, folding his arms with a determined set of his jaw.

"No! You've been involved more than you ever needed to be, Uncle Jess." Jack said emphatically. He waved his hands, no!

Jess copied Jack, waved his hands, no! "Wait now! Just hear me out!" He put more ice in his tea, and took a sip, "Professor, may I stay on the ranch? Not here in your home, but out on the range somewhere, just until we can talk this out. I'll get everything out of my room."

"I don't know, Uncle Jess," Charles said, agreeing with his brother.

"Sure, Jess! I know just the place for you to hide," the professor said.

"Nope! I will pick the place," Jess said. "And, only these two Rangers will know where I'll be. I can keep in contact using the Rangers transceivers. They are scrambled, too." Turning to LeAnn and the professor, "But, to keep you two safe, I don't want you to know where I am. If I need supplies, LeAnn will know where to drop them from her aircraft."

"We have most of your equipment in the truck out front. Your aircraft was stripped clean by the Rangers," Charles said. "There is a small tent out there, too."

"I will start a list of things needed out in the rough, and you can take one of our horses," Professor Stapleton offered.

"That's great! How does this sound to everyone?" Jess asked. Everyone nodded affirmative, knowing they would not be able to change his mind.

"Fantastic, John! That will work fine with the horse. Now, you two Rangers have charge of this investigation, not me. So, continue," Jess said folding his hands.

"Uncle Jess, if you're out of line, we'll tell you point blank. So far, it sounds feasible," Jack said, smiling. "Now, how do you suggest us using you as bait?"

Jess, with a questioning look at the professor and LeAnn, said, "Would you two start getting stuff together for me, please? I don't think that it would be wise for you to hear these details."

"Good idea, Jess. We will get to it right now. This is exciting!" Professor Stapleton was up and prepared to do whatever was needed to help. He turned around, "Holler if anyone wants more pizza, and I will heat it." They left the room, while Jess and his two nephews worked out a trap for Alvarez.

#

After a week of preparation with the Texas Rangers, Brewster and Presidio County Sheriff's Department, Border Patrol and the National Guard Units from the western counties of Texas, the additional anti-terrorists forces were unofficially activated to keep the news media from snooping around.

These special anti-terrorist ground units slowly filtered into Brewster and Presidio counties in personally owned vehicles and in civilian clothes in order not to attract attention in a curious and prying community.

Twenty-six of these small units of six-men-each, operated portable, highly accurate, state-of-the-art electronics that would detect intruder targets crossing the border, day or night on the ground and in the air. The sophisticated equipment transmitted an uplink signal to a satellite, which down-linked to monitors secretly located in Lajitas. The units were placed along the Rio Grande River to cover from McNary in the north to Del Rio in the south.

Both Charles and Jack were the rank of Major in the Air Force Reserve out of El Paso. They were put in command of the operation representing the Texas Rangers and the military. All law enforcement units reported to them.

CHAPTER THIRTY-TWO

In the course of three days, two men from each unit of the military and law enforcement met for breakfast, dinner or supper at different restaurants and diners in Lajitas and Study Butte. They were given verbal instructions with a packet of photos and maps. Charles and Jack swapped turns at these locations to not draw attention. The packets were to be used to flush out anyone who was connected with Commissioner Rodiquez and General Alvarez.

The packet of information also had photos of Jess, Commissioner Rodiquez, General Alvarez, a description of the C130 aircraft and the drug dealers that were not apprehended at the Chisos Mariposa mine.

It was planned for the following Saturday evening to have a couple of the undercover Border Patrol stage a drunken brawl at a Lajitas *cantina*. They were to talk loudly about not getting paid for a job they had done for a drug smuggler, and about some pilot getting away with one of their shipments from Mexico. Supposedly, they did not have money to pay for another aircraft drop of drugs. Names were loosely mentioned, and Jess' was to be called all kinds of names in English and Spanish. They planned to get so out of hand the county police would have to be called to haul them away.

This was to be done by the same two men in other saloons, *taberna* and bars at Alpine, Marfa, Presidio, Study Butte, Lajitas, Terlingua and in Chihuahua, Mexico, over a two week period to stir up the drug traders.

The main point of interest was the pilot, Jess, and his location at the Lajitas airport where he had relocated from the ranch. He was located in an old stucco house and corral near the Rio Grande River. It was on high ground partially hidden from aircraft by an overhanging ledge and hidden on the ground by huge boulders, not far from the west end of the runway. The house was within walking distance from his rented Cessna 172 aircraft tied down under an open-sided hangar. Hopefully, the law enforcement would be able to use him as bait to get the drug traffickers.

Jess was comparing notes with Lieutenant Frando Lopus for Charles and Jack relating to the shooting of Donald Ramos Simms, the Mexican agent, at the Alpine airport. That shooting started the whole series of events; almost like the domino effect.

"Do you know what Agent Simms' physical condition is?" Jess asked. "Has he been released from the hospital?" He poured the others another glass of iced tea, "I forgot all about him with all this other mess happening."

"I am happy you asked," Lopus said and took another long sip of tea. "Simms is supposed to be reassigned to the Texas Border Patrol and Sheriff Baker. Ex-commissioner Rodiquez was setting me up when Simms got shot. I found out it was either Rodiquez or one of the drug dealers from El Paso. I suspect the commissioner was feeling pressure from his drug supplier after that truck tanker blew up."

Jess reviewed his notes as Lopus entered the info on his laptop computer. "The commissioner did not get his exchange of drugs, drug money or the automatic weapon delivery. The examination of that burnt tanker out on highway 118 had both drugs and firearms in it. Rodiquez lost out all the way around. No wonder they left him behind." To make a point, he tapped his finger a couple of times on the table, "But! They got away with a huge amount of American cash."

Jess leaned his elbows on the table and folded his arms, "You and I can I.D. Alvarez, and so can the commissioner. We have three witnesses as to who is dealing in contraband." He pointed at Lopus and frowned, "You, the commissioner and me. I'm sure we have a price on our heads, and Alvarez probably increased the amount for me. Back in Morocco, he had a price tag of a million in gold for my head. Money does funny things to people, and it certainly can shorten the lives of witnesses."

Lopus nodded his head in response, "You know, I think we should take a second look at our location here in Lajitas." He circled the area on the map. "We are in a trap back here among these rocks, and that cave out back is no place to run for safety."

"You're right! I've thought about that, too." Jess said. "The river is the only way out. But, we don't have a boat available right now."

"I have one in my truck," Lopus said. "It is one of those inflatable rafts for four people. It is the same type used for rides down the river. I bought it at an Army surplus in El Paso. It also has stored survival gear." Then, he pointed a finger in the air; "I did not answer you about Agent Simms' condition. I apologize, sorry!"

Jess waved off the comment, "No apology need. Why don't we take a look at that raft and tote it back to the river? I'm sure we can find a place to hide it."

"I will get cabin fever if we stay in here much longer," Lopus said as they went out the back door of the house. They were in the shadows of an overhanging cliff while walking around to the front of the garage.

"Agent Simms' wounds healed in fast order. I think he wears a bulletproof vest all the time now. I suppose we should be doing the same thing, especially now that we are marked men," Lopus said.

They continued to talk while removing the yellow raft from the pickup. It took both of them to lift it to the ground. "Let me get that wheelbarrow in the garage to move this," Jess said. He turned to go into the garage when a low flying aircraft passed over them headed toward the river and then into Mexico. Both ducked for cover, which was very little. Jess ran further into the garage, and Lopus slid under the corner of the porch. They did not hear it coming or see it, for the boulders blocked their view and its noise.

Jess shouted at Lopus, "You alright?"

"Yes!"

They came out to the front of the truck, "Guess we are a little jumpy!" Jess said.

Leaning against the fender of the truck, "And, why not?" Lopus said brushing himself off.

"I wonder what type of vest the Texas Rangers can get for us from the National Guard guys." Jess said. "They should have some extras. Hopefully, they're the type we'll be able to wear clothing over, so we don't stick out like sore thumbs."

"We'll put this in the garage for now," Lopus said. "I'll make a few telephone calls about the vests. They are not issued in our state in Mexico. We have to purchase them with our own money."

They moved the raft inside and both entered the house. Arrangements were made for the vests, which were to be delivered within the hour. The two men discussed further escape plans and possibilities to bait General Alvarez to their location.

Suddenly, there was a loud crash outside, sounding like the roof was starting to cave. They both rushed out the back, looking up in time to see a hang glider disappear toward the river. Jess looked back to the house roof in time to see a white cloud of dust settling on it.

"Someone has marked the roof with white powder! Let's get out of here, LT.," Jess shouted. They ran inside the house for equipment they had been using.

Lopus grabbed his radio, holding it up, "Radio!"

"Got mine, too! Go!" Jess hollered and headed out the garage door behind Lopus as he jumped into his pickup and sped off toward downtown Lajitas.

Their plans had been to separate during the daylight hours if jumped and stay together at night. Lopus would head back into Mexico, and Jess would hide close to the river.

Jess found his way through the salt cedars, mesquite, purple prickly pear cactus and beargrass. He pushed through tall stalks of *Carrizo* cane, whose leaves rustling in the wind covered his noisy movements. He wanted to keep hidden as much as possible and search the base of the high hills behind the house next to the Rio Grande. At the same time, he wanted to stay hidden from the Mexican side of the river, where whoever it was flying the hang-glider had to have landed.

He stopped every so often to look across the river. He could not see any movement, but continued to be cautious because he would have to leave the cover of the vegetation of the river in order to climb its banks to higher ground. The day prior, he and Lopus had scouted the trail he was to be taking.

Finally, he reached the high point they had picked for a better view of the road leading up through the hills to the house. It was a perfect view of the closed runway from the west end. Jess could not see any traffic on the highway, which ran parallel with the runway, and no one was on foot.

Catching his breath, Jess used the radio Charles had given him, "Ranger one, this is Uncle. Do you copy?"

"Copy you, Uncle!"

"We had a scare at the house. Have split up, as planned."

"Roger that, Uncle. Standby!"

"I'll be right here!" Jess replied. *I sure hope Lopus made it to Mexico without trouble. He sure is a nice young man. Lord Jesus, protect him.* "Now what, Lord?" Jess spoke softly to himself, "We left the garage door open! Oh well, the Lord will have to take care of that, too."

He plugged an earpiece into his left ear so the radio could not be heard, except by him. He continued to search below him and across the valley with his binoculars. Jess thought he heard something behind him making noise in the underbrush. He hunkered down and slowly turned to look. Nothing. Holding his breath in order to hear better, he strained to peer through the high weeds which covered him.

"Hello, Uncle! Ranger one."

It startled Jess so much, he jerked up off his stomach onto his right elbow as though he had been stung. He slowly laid back down, whispering, "Uncle here!"

"Uncle, speak a little louder."

"Can't speak louder! Someone is too close!" Jess whispered as sternly as he could.

"I understand, Uncle. Call me when you're safe. There are three Army National Guard men coming to you. They are in desert BDU's. Copy?"

Jess clicked his mic switch twice in reply. *Maybe they are who I heard. Let me take a look. He stayed low on his knees, turned and peered through the dry thick underbrush, looking up the hill behind him.* Hardly breathing, he listened for any unusual noise of movement. *Only in the movies, movement can't be heard! If someone's close I'll hear them.* With his binoculars he searched the hill and down toward the Rio Grande River. The beach, foothills and canyon walls in Mexico did not reveal any movement. Then, the sun reflected off an object high on a far cliff top, overlooking the river and Lajitas from Mexico. Jess focused on the spot. He could not make out what was causing the reflection. Intently, he kept the spot in sight as he stretched out on his stomach, extended his legs on the ground behind him and rested his elbows on a clump of grass to steady the binoculars.

A puff of smoke appeared, leaving a trail straight toward him. For a split second, he froze, not computing what he was looking at. But, his instinct reacted, and he rolled down the incline to his right under a huge boulder overhang. Then, a tremendous explosion rocked the whole area, echoing through the canyons.

Someone fired a missile at me from Mexico!

Jess was showered with rock, dust and fragments of shattered boulders. One dislodged and rolled against the boulder overhang Jess was under. Holding his breath, eyes shut, hands covering the back of his head, he held still. If he moved the boulder might crush him. It was not on him, but it had shoved rocks against his side making it snug under the overhang. Slowly opening his eyes, he could not see for all the dust that was stirred up from the explosion. He cupped his hands over his mouth in order to take in air without breathing in a lot of dust. He spit and sputtered until he could clear his throat and nose.

He waited a few minutes and squirmed out from under the overhang. Jess leaned against the boulder that had rolled down the hill, knowing it was too large for him to move from its spot. It would be there until the next earthquake.

"What are you standing here for, Dummy? They could fire another missile!" Jess hollered at himself.

The boulder protected him from being seen from Mexico. He slowly moved around the boulder where he would have a straight run downhill and be able to stay out of sight from across the river. A hand grabbed his shoulder just as he was about to run.

"Mister Hanes!" the voice behind him shouted.

The voice and hand on his shoulder put shock into Jess; he almost lost control of strength in his legs. Two Army specialists leaned on the boulder behind him. One had a firm grip on Jess' shoulder. "Sorry, Sir! I didn't mean to startle you so bad. Are you alright?" The Master Sergeant asked, carefully studying Jess' face.

Jess put his hand on top of the sergeant's, "Thanks! Yes. Let me take a deep breath," which he did. "On top of the explosion and almost getting crushed...then you grabbed me!" Jess was white as a sheet, "You scared the spit right out of me!" He put his head between his hand, "Lord, I'm getting too old for this."

"Sorry! But, we have to move out." He let go of Jess and motioned him to follow them. "This isn't a good spot to linger."

They moved into the tall underbrush and melted into the shadows of the hills. Slowly moving from spot to spot of protection, they came upon an Army Hummer. It had a radar antenna on top, which was in operation, with two men inside. There were two other Army personnel on guard, crouching on both sides of the vehicle looking toward the Mexican border.

The Sergeant opened the back door, "Any more targets?"

"No, Sarge!"

"Mr. Hanes, we lost track of your Mexican policeman across the border," the sergeant said, as he removed his helmet and wiped the sweat from his forehead. Then, he applied light-green camouflage paste on his face. "At least he was safe going over the river by boat."

"You did a good job of keeping cover. We did not see you until you turned around in the brush. Your binoculars lens gave you away," he said, smiling.

"That's what saved me from the missile!" Jess motioned with his hand toward Mexico, "I saw a sun reflection off that canyon cliff across the river. Happened to be looking at it with my binoculars when the missile was fired," Jess said, as the sergeant looked wide-eyed at him.

"Missile?"

"Yes, something like a shoulder mounted missile," Jess replied.

"Hand me the mic, Joe," the sergeant said. "Headquarters! This is Unit 7. We have a serious incident here at Lajitas."

"Unit 7. We heard it. Did you find Mr. Hanes?"

"That is affirmative! He seems to be okay, except for the explosion that just occurred. That was a missile from Mexico and has been identified by Mr. Hanes as a portable hand held."

"That's a violation of the ADIZ between us and Mexico," the voice replied.

"The Air Defense Identification Zone has been breached! Plus! A hostile enemy has fired upon an American citizen, who is a Texas Ranger Captain. Should we return fire, if target is found?" the sergeant asked, shaking his head, no. He knew the answer before he asked.

"If the target is in Mexico, do not return fire! I repeat, do not return fire if target is in Mexico," replied the voice. "Only return fire if target is on this side of the border."

"I understand the order! Do not fire on target in Mexico. Only on this side of the Rio Grande River."

"That is correct, Sergeant Myers. This is Captain Jack Randel, Texas Rangers. We will notify the other units and all law enforcement involved. This is an international violation of borders. Where was the missile fired from?"

"I'll let Mr. Hanes tell you," he replied.

Handing the mic to Jess, the sergeant motioned his men to gather around and listen. He unfolded a ground chart of the Lajitas area, holding it down on the tailgate of the vehicle for Jess to scan.

"Jack, I have a chart of the Lajitas area to refer to. You ready?"

"Give me the works, Uncle Jess."

"Approximate coordinates are 29 degrees 13 minutes north, 103 degrees forty five minutes west. That's a rough estimate. It came from the top of that canyon cliff across the Rio Grande from the cabin," Jess quickly reported.

"We're on it. Stay there with those guys Jess!" Jack requested, and didn't wait for a reply.

"Okay you guys!" Jess said, with his hands on his hips, "Looks like you're baby-sitting."

"No Sir! Major Randel's orders," Sergeant Myers said sternly. "You're one of us. The Top-Sergeant said you were to be given a rifle, ammo, and BDU's when we found you."

He motioned to Corporal Joe for the stack of clothes, "You'll not standout so badly with these on. Your rank is the same as mine, if you don't mind? It's all we have available. I've taken my name tag off the shirt."

"That's fine with me, Sarge!" Jess said, and began to change clothes.

Jess didn't take long to change into the desert BDU's. Battle Dress Uniform, tan camouflage, boots, hat, Kevlar helmet, rank with nametag, he had all that was needed to look like Army special-forces. They even gave him a Beretta 9mm automatic with holster and web belt. Next was a special .308 Springfield sniper rifle.

"Hey! I didn't reenlist!" Jess grunted, with a smile on his face. "I'm retired Navy and Air Force! Twenty-five years."

One of the other men said, "Now we know what's wrong with him! He's one of those guys!" They all laughed, just long enough for one of them to yell, "Large aircraft coming from the east at one hundred feet off the deck, four hundred knots. Ten miles out."

Before he had all the information out of his mouth, the men on the outside of the vehicle had turned around, scanning the country to the east. It was a low-flying, four-engine high-wing aircraft heading for Lajitas.

All the time this was going on, the others were on a sharp lookout for problems afoot, while the two inside the vehicle were watching the radarscope. The sergeant had put on a special listening device headset and was listening toward the area they had picked up Jess.

"Here he comes, a C130," hollered Jess, pointing a little to the right of where the others were looking. The aircraft was hard to see with the Chisos Mountains behind it. It was a light tan color, matching their BDU's. "That's the same one that buzzed me the other day, trying to force me out of the sky."

"We have him on video and locked in on satellite," Joe yelled from inside the truck. "Radar sweeping us from Mexico! Missile lock-on! Get out of here!"

The whole group scattered like a covey of quail for cover. Five seconds later, the radar truck was in small pieces all over the small creek bed that where they were supposed to be hidden. Jess was flat on his back and raised up on one elbow, his helmet was missing. He could see the large cargo aircraft as it flew across Lajitas and continued into Mexico.

"Hey, Sarge! I couldn't turn my radar off fast enough!" The radar operator yelled.

The sergeant did not answer. It took another ten minutes for the men to collect their thoughts and begin a search for everyone. They first checked for injuries to themselves and then the closest man. One soldier was dead and Master Sergeant Myers was injured. Jess was sitting next to him, checking him for wounds. Rolling him over, the sergeant's face was burnt black from the blast. With his helmet, Jess shaded the injured man's eyes and what was left of his face, and then checked for a heartbeat. He was still alive.

"Medic! Need a medic over here!" Jess yelled.

One of the other men ran over to them, and began examining the sergeant.

"Lord, no! This isn't right! Why these guys?" Jess jumped up and began walking toward Lajitas. Sergeant Wright ran over to him and grabbed his arm.

"Mr. Hanes, you can't get out in the open. These guys might be back." He released Jess' arm.

Still in shock from the two close missile explosions, Jess turned around, "You're right! I'm the target! Not you guys!" He had a puzzled look on his face. "How did they know I was right here?" He threw up his hands in disgust and sat down on a rock in the creek bed. Putting his hands up to his face, Jess knocked off his helmet. He grabbed it, and then slammed it to the ground, again.

"Mr. Hanes! Remember this is our plan of attack, using you for bait. It's working!" Acting Sergeant Wright said, "They didn't know you were right here in this creek. When they locked-on my radar signal with their missile radar, I couldn't get mine turned off before they launched."

The sergeant started talking on his portable radio, giving his location from a pocket GPS receiver. The information had filtered back from Mexico that the C130 had landed on or near an abandoned airfield, Rancho Los Juncos, in Chihuahua.

The group moved to Jess' aircraft at the west end of the runway, where he grabbed his flight bag with his sectional and aeronautical charts. They left the Lajitas area in another vehicle from their command post after making sure the sergeant was flown out to the nearest hospital. Jess stayed at the secret command post.

This made one dead and four injured, either directly or indirectly related to Jess since his arrival in the Big Bend country. The situation was beginning to get to him, but he was determined to find the underlying cause of the threat. It seemed Alvarez was still alive and now knew Jess was somewhere in the Lajitas area.

Jess couldn't get it out of his mind, "How and where does Alvarez get his information?"

Back at the secret law enforcement headquarters, Jess cleared an empty card table of glasses and papers in one of the rooms. He took out his sectional aeronautical chart of El Paso and found Lajitas, and then further southwest across the Rio Grande River into Mexico, an abandon airstrip of Rancho Los Juncos near a non-perennial lake.

"Now, what is that? Perennial?" He walked into the transmitter and radar room, "Who has a dictionary?"

Charles stood up, "I have a small one. What you looking for?"

"Perennial!"

Charles could not find it and turned to one of the deputy sheriffs, "Randy, do you know the word, 'perennial'?"

"Yes, sir! It means, 'continual, reoccurring, coming back in a couple of years.' Something like that," he replied, pointing at a prickly pear cactus. "It blooms once every year."

"So, non-perennial would mean, dead," Jess said in a matter-of-fact way.

"Could be, Sir!" Randy said, and turned back to his radarscope.

Jess motioned for Charles and Jack to follow him, "Please close the door behind you, Jack."

"Look at this. If your information is correct, that C130 could have landed either at this airstrip or in this dry salt lake northwest of it." Jess pointed to the map, "If it is there at all, a C130 could land on either one and takeoff."

"You're right," Charles remarked. "This runway is 5,100 feet long, even if it is not usable. The lake measures more than that." His coy laugh was almost like a horse snicker.

"But, we have no authority at this time to check it out," Jack said, looking closer at the chart.

"Why not?" Jess questioned. "I thought the law enforcement had access to Mexico going after criminals, especially those that launch missiles from across the river!"

"We have to be careful and let the Mexican authorities check this out first, and then they must ask for our assistance," Jack replied, disgusted they would have to wait. "It grinds me to no end! All the red tape we have to go through to apprehend someone. Do you realize that Charles and I cannot arrest a drug offender without a witness to the crime? Individually, we need a witness before an arrest is made. Prosecution will not take a smuggling case unless we have at least three of the smuggled aliens as material witnesses. Even if the aliens admit to being smuggled by a United States citizen, we need three or more aliens to be witnesses, otherwise we have no case and the citizen goes free." He continued to rap his fingers on the table, "Which means, each of us can't be a witness for the other. It must be someone other than a law enforcement officer. Damn political red tape!"

"You mean you could not have arrested Commissioner Rodiquez without me as a witness?" Jess asked getting a bit aggravated. "Which also means, you would need witnesses as to who is making these drug runs and launching missiles into the U.S. from across the border? And to throw another wrench into the fire, I can't witness against Rodiquez either; I'm a newly sworn in Texas Ranger! Correct?"

"That's correct," Charles nodded. "Which means you and the commissioner are our two valuable witnesses. But, he will need you as his witness against the other terrorists who were after him."

"That could be a technicality in a trial, which could go either for or against your testimony. All of the U.S. law enforcements' hands have been tied along the border as to apprehending aliens, drug runners and terrorists! Which reminds me!" Jack cleared his throat and looked at Jess, "Give us a short version of your relations with this guy, Alvarez. You're still under government protection from all that mess with him in Morocco, and now he shows up again. Especially, you thinking he was dead!"

Charles said, "On top of that, you're an official Captain of the Texas Rangers!"

"That's right!" Jess said. "But, didn't you guys get the word? The government slacked off having us escorted," Jess smiled and stretched his arms. "If an agent wants to volunteer for a trip on their own time for our protection, they can...and, still be a legal guardian. That's why Madi is with Marie Ann in Indiana."

"Yes, Madi! Now there's a talented sweet lady," Charles said. "We're going to the Grand Canyon next month, if this is settled."

"Sounds like fun," Jack said turning to Jess.

Jess refreshed their memories about his being a witness for the Moroccan government and a few details of what Alvarez was doing in Morocco.

They were interrupted by a knock on the door, "Hey, Captain!"

"Enter!" Jack replied.

"Lieutenant Lopus was found down the Rio Grande on a sand bar. He is alive and needs to be rescued. He is on our side of the river," the messenger said.

"I'll go get him, Charles," Jack said, picking up his paperwork.

They went into the control center to make plans to rescue Lieutenant Lopus. Jack and his helicopter crew departed and Charles walked out with Jess to watch them leave in a truck. Jess took him by the arm and nodded for Charles to come with him, then released his arm.

#

The wind was blowing hard, and Jess wanted to get out of it. He stepped behind one of the large stucco pillars of the porch.

Jess knew what he was about to propose would meet heavy opposition, but he was determined to find Alvarez. With as serious an expression on his face as he could muster up, "I need for you to either volunteer to go with me or give me support with a plan into Mexico. I realize stopping Alvarez will take only a small bite out of the overall problem with drugs coming in, but it would be a big bite out of the problems in this area. He has millions of dollars in gold behind him from the Middle East and millions of users and supporters here in the United States." Hesitating, he looked toward the mountains in Mexico and then began to pace back and forth across the porch. "He is only one out of that large number, but if we cut him out, it would not only satisfy me but put an end to his murderous activities. Too many lives have been lost since I ran into this guy in Morocco."

"Uncle Jess, you're involved enough as it is. My superiors don't know about some of the things you're caught up in down here, yet!" Charles looked around to make sure they were not being overheard, "I can't go into Mexico; I'm a Texas Ranger."

"Yes, I know that! But, what better partner do I need? Remember, so am I!" Jess smiled pointing to himself. "Listen, can you someway get a few days vacation, or leave of absence, or not be a Ranger for a couple of days?"

Charles took off his white Stetson hat and wiped his sweaty brow, "Uncle Jess, you know what you're asking me is not possible?"

"Yes, and it's wrong for me to ask for you to sacrifice your career. That is certainly selfish on my part. I'll do it on my own," he said smiling to himself, knowing he was putting a guilt trip on Charles. "I'm sorry, but what else can I do? That guy is sitting over there in Mexico, scheming up ways to get back over here. And, I can't do anything to stop him. Maybe Jack would do it?" Jess knew he was prodding Charles too far.

Charles smiled and put one arm around his uncle's shoulder, "I love you, Uncle Jess! I know you're grasping at straws right now. But, I can't do it, and neither can you, alone." Turning Jess around to look at the two men walking up the driveway towards them, he continued, "This may be your answer coming here."

They both waved to the men, "Hi, Donald!" Charles was pleased to see the Mexican Federal Agent looking alive and well.

"Well, I'll be!" Jess said, extending his hand to Donald Ramos Simms, the taxi driver who had been shot in Alpine. "It's great to know you're up and around again, Simms!"

"Thank you, Mr. Hanes. I am very healthy now and back on the job. I healed quite fast, which even surprised the doctors." He turned to his companion; "This is my good friend, *Señor* Franado Carlos, from Chihuahua, Mexico. *Señor*, this is Mr. Hanes and Texas Ranger, Captain Randel."

They shook hands and made pleasantries, talking about everything other than what Jess was anxious to get settled. He listened for about ten minutes, then interrupted, "Excuse me, please? Charles, I need to make a decision about our previous conversation, and get going." Nodding to Simms and Carlos, Jess turned to walk back into the headquarters.

"Wait, Uncle Jess!" Charles requested, catching Jess by the elbow.

"Ah, your Uncle?" Simms said, with a smile and shook Charles' hand again, "That is fascinating! Your uncle is quite a man! He saved my life, did you know?"

"No, I wasn't aware of that," Charles replied.

Simms proceeded to tell the story of his undercover work in the Alpine area, and how Jess helped him at the airport. This brought the conversation around to the present situation, which Charles maneuvered into for Jess.

"Are you officially back on the case, and is *Señor* Carlos cleared to listen in on our conversation further?" Charles asked.

"Yes, we are on this case together. He has been working out of our headquarters in Mexico City and now with me in the city of Chihuahua. As Mexico's Director of International Affairs, he knows all the background of the case. This is why he has come with me to be updated," Simms said.

They moved into the small high-ceiling room where Jess and his two nephews had previously been talking. The two men were updated and then Charles turned the conversation over to Jess.

"I have made a request of Charles that I knew ahead of time he couldn't and wouldn't do," Jess said, turning to his aeronautical chart for reference. He pointed to the dry salt lake in the state of Chihuahua. "We have tracked the C130 to this location, and we do not know if it is still there are not. It's dark now, fortunately, our spotters in Mexico are not certain the aircraft is still there, but Mexican radar has not reported any aircraft leaving that area.

"Now, what I am proposing is to fly there with my aircraft and blow up that C130," Jess said with conviction. "It has been a thorn in my side for too long! Legally, I can't cross into Mexico because I'm not a Mexican citizen. Secondly, the American government can't back me up. I would have to be on my own. The less people that know about it, the better!"

"Ah, Mr. Hanes," Carlos said with bitterness in his voice. "We can be of service to you. Our problem is a mutual one, and I am more than happy to assist. You see, this Alvarez has killed my son because he would not help fly the C130 to secret landing strips in Mexico and Brazil." He gestured for Jess' felt highlighter, "May I?" Then, he marked the map, "Not too far from this lake you have circled, down into Coahuila right here!" He highlighted the Aleman Ranch, "In the middle of the night, they were paid in Spanish gold coins for fuel. It almost depleted their fuel tanks filling the C130. Did you realize it has a ferrying distance of over 4,600 miles? Imagine the amount of fuel it would take to top it off. It also had external long range fuel tanks under the wings."

"You sure know a lot about the C130," Jess replied.

"I have ridden many miles and hours in one of those while in the U.S. Army for twenty years," Carlos said. "I have been across both oceans in them, and the C5 and C141's. I'd much rather be in the C5, more room to move around."

"If we wait too much longer, Alvarez will be out of Mexico. We have no idea when he will be back? Right?" Jess looked up at Charles, and questioned with his hands.

"You're correct, sir!" Charles replied. "We don't know."

"I can fly to both those locations, using GPS and IFR in the Cessna 172. Shouldn't have any problems," Jess said, glancing at each of them with his hands on his hips. His smile broaden knowing Carlos was about to support his efforts.

"I own one of the original Beech UC-12A Super King Air, purchased after the Vietnam war from the U.S. Air Force by one of my close friends in Mexico City. It has been my main transportation for ten years," Carlos said. "Are we in business? Most of the surveillance equipment was removed, and I have had state-of-the-art color weather, GPS and ground search radar installed. You have a faster aircraft to work with now. It is at your disposal, Mr. Hanes."

"That's great! What do you think, Charles?" Jess said, like a kid asking permission to take the car on a date.

"Do you have a rating for turboprop twins?" Charles asked.

"Yes, I do. A King Air 200. Probably 1,200 hours, plus, in one," Jess said and reached for his wallet.

"I believe you, Uncle Jess," Charles waved Jess to forget his wallet's evidence. "I'm not the FAA!"

They all chuckled about that comment.

"I'll have you cleared with our law enforcement in a matter of minutes from Austin and El Paso. Do you need to call in your flight plan in advance, or do the Mexican authorities know your whereabouts?" Charles inquired of Carlos.

Jess looked at Simms, who nodded, yes. Simms said, "Charles and I have to go over procedures on this border problem. I should stay here and talk with Ranger Randel, unless you need me to come along?"

Carlos shrugged, "Fine! You should pick up where you left off in Alpine and coordinate with Ranger Randel. Mr. Hanes and I will keep in touch."

"Let me get my gear from the Cessna, and I'm ready," Jess said shaking Charles' hand. He turned and shook hands with the other two, "Sure happy to see you're up and around, Mr. Simms."

"Thank you, Jess," Simms said, inquiring about using first names. "Do you mind?" Simms asked.

"Fine with me, Donald!" Jess replied with a large smile.

"Please, call me Carl," Carlos requested. "Americans have a habit of shortening names. I do not care to be called Fran!"

"Okay. Carl it is," Jess said. "Let's go before it gets too much later in the evening."

"There's fried chicken, biscuits, gravy and beef tamales in the oven. Fresh too!" Charles bragged, "I made the biscuits!"

"Can we use them as weapons?" Jess asked.

Charles threw an eraser at him, bouncing it off the wall behind Jess. They headed for the kitchen, ate and then left for the new runway, four miles away.

CHAPTER THIRTY-THREE

The sun had set behind the mountains in Mexico, and the cool wind had died down. Fog had settled in the low areas around Lajitas, making it an eerie place in the moonlight. The sky was so bright; it was almost like having a security night-light turned on it. They could have driven to the airstrip without headlights.

The Beech UC-12A with its high T-tail stood out above the smaller aircraft next to the hangar. Jess removed his gear from his rented Cessna 172 and carried it to the larger aircraft before going to eat.

As usual, Jess enjoyed the biscuits and gravy, and of course, the fried chicken and beef hot tamales. He was thinking Charles possibly had missed his calling. Jess prayed quietly walking to Carl's aircraft, not only for himself, but also for his two nephews, and all who were involved in stopping Alvarez.

They boarded the Beech VC-12A and headed for Mexico, with Jess in the left seat, at the request of Carl. He wanted to see how well Jess would handle his aircraft. They flew fast and low through the valley toward Rancho Los Juncos, a usable airfield near a salt lake, 60 nautical miles west of Lajitas.

Slowing the aircraft ten miles from the 5,100 feet airstrip, Jess dropped to 300 feet above ground level with all external Nav lights off. Carl and two of his crew used night binoculars in order to scan the area near the airstrip. Nothing was in sight, as they circled a few miles away, and then headed to the dry salt lake to the northwest.

Jess slowed to glide-speed with flaps and landing gear down, but they could not see anything at the lake either. He increased his speed to max-with-gear and flaps-down, and then he retracted the gear. In increments, he retracted the flaps and banked to the southwest, back over the dry lakebed. They still did not find anything resembling an aircraft. He climbed to 1,800 feet above the lake for an overall view, still nothing.

"Okay, Carl! Let's head south to that place in Coahuila, Aleman Ranch, about 85 nautical miles south. It's the closest fuel stop, but the problem is that they are closed this time of night. No one to talk to about the C130, if it isn't there," Jess said.

"At least, we will be able to see if it is there, hopefully before they hear us," Carl replied.

They flew to the Aleman Ranch and did not find the facilities open, nor did they see the C130 aircraft. *Were they too late leaving Lajitas to locate Alvarez in Mexico?* After landing, they spent time on the new digital cell phones Carl used. The cell phone was one which could be used anywhere in the world, using satellite hookups; in addition, transmissions were coded.

Jess and Carl spent the next two weeks searching for clues and returned to Lajitas empty handed. It was not a successful trip, and Jess was mentally and physically drained.

\#

The Rangers had no contact with them until Jess returned from Mexico. The law enforcement and military determined that they would leave their men in place for a month, and then return to normal operations. If the C130 and Alvarez did not return, they would apprehend the lesser drug offenders entering the United States in the Big Bend country during that period.

Jess' nephews, Jack and Charles, suggested Jess return to the Stapleton's ranch for a rest. Professor Stapleton and his daughter LeAnn had convinced Jess to use a bedroom at their ranch home.

\#

After Jess had a couple of days rest at the ranch, he talked Marie Ann into coming out and spending some time with him. She only had small sketches of what had happened to Jess, and he wanted her to meet the professor and his daughter.

LeAnn took a week's vacation in order to stay there to assist her father and Jess, and to meet Marie Ann. LeAnn had become an essential part of his research, not only looking for Alvarez, but in the investigation of the history relating to the Mariposa mine at Lajitas. With her connections with Sul Ross University at Alpine, Texas A & M University in Bryan, and the Texas University in Austin, she had compiled a large stack of paperwork for Jess.

Once Jess had his mind clear of past problems at Lajitas, he settled down with LeAnn's research papers and the letter left by his deceased grandfather Hanes. The Amarillo Mariposa Mine mentioned in the letter, held some interesting history, linking it to LeAnn's investigation.

Jess reviewed her notes on Texas history, where an old Spanish adventurer and explorer continued to be mentioned crossing the Lajitas area, *Alvar Nunez Cabeza de Vaca*. It seems that *de Vaca* was one of the few survivors of a shipwreck in a storm off of Galveston on November 6, 1528. He was a captive of the Indians and there he remained a slave for over six years. He learned many things from the Indians and their customs, and became a trader and a medicine man.

De Vaca escaped the Indians and headed west searching for Spanish colonies, which were on the Pacific coast in Sinaloa, Mexico. How he managed to go so far north, inland, rather than west, the stories vary from being lost and wondering around in all directions, to following Indian trails up into Texas and then southwest through the Big Bend country. Researchers say that *de Vaca* was in Presidio and Brewster counties and stayed for some time near the city of Presidio where there were Indians farming along the Rio Grande River.

LeAnn found another Spanish explorer, *Antionio de Espejo*, who in 1582, traveled from Mexico to where the Rio Conchos and the Rio Grande rivers come together at the city of Presidio. He traveled across the Big Bend guided by Jumanos Indians from near Ojinaga.

The modern day treasure hunter and prospector now searches for the same gold and silver, which attracted adventurers of 500 years ago. The Indians favored the Spanish with items made of same metals, but never disclosed the secrets of their mines.

Early travels of Franciscan and Jesuit monks revealed their interest in riches the Indians concealed for the Church. Then, years of folklore brought more people from the east, seeking the buried wealth that seemed to elude everyone, except for the Indians.

During the early 1900's and during the depression years in Texas, men and women came to the Big Bend to search for silver, gold and cinnabar for mercury (cinnabar: vermilion, mercuric sulfide, HgS, a heavy, bright red mineral, the principle ore of mercury/quick silver.)

It was during this period that the area of Terlingua flourished with companies and individuals mining the red cinnabar rock formations. The Chisos mine was very productive until 1946, when it was closed down because mercury was no longer required by their largest customer, the U.S. government.

Then, further west of Terlingua was Lajitas on the Rio Grande. At Lajitas, there was a Rio Grande River crossing into Mexico of the old Comanche Trail. The Spanish, Mexicans, American Indians, and Americans have used this, ford, for hundreds of years. The history of Lajitas went way back.

In the early 1900's, cinnabar mining began in the area north of Lajitas, at the southern base of the Solitario Mountain, to the Tres Cuevas and Contrabando Mountain areas, Fresno mine and Mariposa mine. But now, in the new century, 2000, no mining was being done in that area and most of the mines were closed, boarded up; except for the Chisos Mariposa mine.

Jess was surprised at how detailed LeAnn's information was and how much it filled in the gaps that he had in his own research. He folded his papers and maps together placing them in folders. The notes that he took from their discussions, he folded and placed them in his shirt pocket for his immediate attention when he was alone.

"I have enjoyed my rest here at your ranch. With all this new information, I feel like a Texas-Indiana Jones," Jess said, standing and stretching. "Now, all I have to do is go to the Amarillo Mariposa Mine and snoop around for awhile. I'll bet there are secrets in that mine that connect the early Indian's gold and silver mining to *de Vaca's* search for the lost cities."

He smiled at them, "Marie Ann will be here in the morning. The three of us should take a short trip to Lajitas and then over to the Mariposa mine." He excused himself and walked out on the front porch.

The professor put his arm around LeAnn's shoulder and pulled her close, "Now what is the matter?"

She had a distant look on her face and leaned her head against his arm, "Daddy, what will he think once he finds out that we are Jews, especially with your German history?"

"So… this is what has you upset?" the professor said, pulling her closer.

LeAnn moved away from her father, "About being a Jewess is another thing. I haven't detected from him a bigoted attitude toward anyone. It's that I'm so touchy about it. I hope that it doesn't show."

"He is sharp and very much a gentleman, so I don't think that will be a problem once it is out in the open and you... rather we, will take some time to explain everything to him... together."

243

"Daddy! Let's wait until Marie Ann has been here a few days," LeAnn said with tears in her eyes, as they walked out on the porch. "I don't want to lose his friendship over my past."

Jess leaned against the porch railing, "Loosing whose friendship over the past?" he asked. "Did I overhear the last of a private conversation between a father and daughter?"

"Not really private!" LeAnn replied. "Well!" trying to think what to say, "You and I will have time to discuss a lot of things once we begin our 'snooping' at Lajitas and the Mariposa Mine." She blushed again. Walking to the banister, with her back to them both, she said, "I want to bring you up-to-date on our family history, and how we came to live in the Big Bend country. Then, I want your opinion about Jack dating me."

"Have at it!" Jess said. "I'm happy for you both."

She walked over to Jess, and put her arms around his neck, "Thank you Jess. I'm honored!" she replied, planted a kiss on his cheek, and then returned to her father's side.

"We'll have to take a break from our snooping for a day or so because I have history that you're not aware of, too," Jess said. "Which, I need to amplify on right now."

The professor and LeAnn turned toward Jess as he spoke, "Remember the large C130 aircraft that almost rammed us and has been illegally flying into Lajitas? That is owned and operated by an international drug and arm's dealer who nearly killed me in Morocco a few years back. I thought I had killed him in Morocco." They both nodded yes, "Well, I'm positive he is our main villain here in this area."

"You said that earlier, but evidently he isn't here now?" the professor asked.

"As far as the authorities know, he isn't." Jess waved his hands in the air with disgust, "But, I have a bad feeling, he is here! I think that he's somewhere here in Texas or Mexico, and somehow, I feel he now knows that I'm here at the ranch."

"This isn't good at all!" LeAnn stopped smiling. All three turned and leaned back against the porch railing, "I've been thinking that the Mariposa Mines have more secrets than drugs, gold and silver."

"I agree!" Jess said, "Remember, the Chisos Mariposa Mine was the location those drug dealers were using for storage. I was told that some of the mine collapsed the other day. It was about the same time that truck exploded over north of Study Butte."

"Now, that's interesting, Jess," LeAnn said. "We should take our mine exploring equipment."

"Good idea," Jess said sipping his tea. "We need to contact the geology department at Sul Ross and the University of Texas. Marie Ann knows people in that department in Austin. Once that we've updated her tomorrow, she can call them."

"Just a minute, Professor Rustaman heads that department at Sul Ross," John said pressing the side of his nose with his cold glass of tea. "I will be right back!"

They spent the remainder of the evening studying the maps and research papers of the mining in the Terlingua area. Jess turned in early, but was unable to sleep peacefully. One time during the night, he awoke and went outside for an hour or so. He sat on the porch steps out the kitchen door. Staring at the stars in the west, he offered quiet prayers for Marie Ann's comfort and safety. He missed her presence.

Lajitas, Texas

CHAPTER THIRTY-FOUR

Marie Ann, Mick and Madi flew into Alpine the following noon. Jess and Charles were there to meet them. LeAnn and Professor Stapleton stayed at the ranch.

They all packed into the converted full size van, Jess had rented, and headed for town. He wanted them to meet the owner and his wife of the T-Top Restaurant, Tom and Gladys Ramp. It was time to eat.

They walked in and Gladys hollered across the counter, "Hey, Mr. Hanes! Got your whole family with ya?"

He smiled and gave her a thumbs up, "Reinforcements!"

After thirty minutes of talking with the owners and going over Jess' introduction to Alpine's taxi service, they finally ordered lunch. After they ate, Mick had to fly back to Indianapolis to be with his *fiancée*. They drove him to the airport, and then left for the ranch. The visit was too short for the two nephews.

It was another hour before they were on the road to the professor's ranch. Jess drove the speed limit, so they could enjoy the scenery of the Big Bend country. During the middle of the afternoon, Jess sighted the valley ranch from the high mountain road.

"Look at that view," he said.

Marie Ann and Madi swooned over the picturesque setting of the ranch. Charles remarked that the ladies would be surprised how the professor kept the old style furnishing in the house, even with the hardwood floors and fireplace.

When they drove up to the porch, Snake met them and would not let them out until Jess told him to sit. He obeyed and licked Jess' hand when he got out of the car. Snake made no advances toward the others, but followed Jess and Marie Ann up onto the porch wagging his tail. Charles and Madi walked hand in hand behind them.

Jack and LeAnn came out on the porch, hand in hand. She turned and hollered back inside, "Hey, Daddy! They are here" They both had big smiles as they crossed the porch to welcome Marie Ann.

"LeAnn, this is Marie Ann," Jess said noticing their smiles from ear to ear.

"I have heard a lot about you Marie Ann," she said, noticeably scrutinizing another female. "It's nice to finally meet Jess' better half." They shook hands, and then LeAnn gave her a hug, "Welcome to our ranch home!"

"Thank you," Marie Ann replied. "It is so pleasant here."

Madi and Charles waved, "Hello everyone! You want bags now, or later?"

"Later," Jack said. "Let's get acquainted first." He hugged his Aunt Marie Ann, and then Madi, who he had known for a few years.

"Madi! LeAnn!" Charles said, letting go of Madi's hand so she and LeAnn could shake hands, and then promptly holding her hand again.

John walked out on the porch, "Well, this is the most company that we have had for a long time." He extended his hand to Marie Ann, "Yes, I know you well by our correspondence!" He stepped back at arms length, "Jess' lovely wife, Marie Ann! You are most welcome to our home. We have rooms for everyone, come inside. Soon, it will get chilly out here this evening."

They continued introductions of the ladies and all settled in the living room. Jack and LeAnn brought out iced tea, coffee and pastries.

"Ladies, do you mind if an old man lights his pipe?" John asked.

No one objected. They all settled down to light conversation, finding out about each other and then Jess excused himself, "John, would you please entertain these lovely ladies, while the three of us Rangers step out on the porch for a few minutes?"

"I would be most happy to be the center of attraction!" he said and stood. "This way ladies; I have wonderful cooking recipes that will delight you."

"Thank you, Sir!" Jess said motioning Jack and Charles to the porch. He grabbed them both by an arm and pulled them into a three-man circle. "How come you two are here this evening? Rangers out of business?"

"Nothing like a nosey uncle!" Charles said and laughed. "I think that Jack has himself a new sweetie! She has been hanging onto him all day!"

"How do you know? You haven't been here," Jack said with a smile. "Anyway, it's no secret! I'm sweet on her, and I think she sort of likes me, too!"

"Okay, you two!" Jess said. "I didn't get you all of the way out here just to question you about your girlfriends." With seriousness in his voice, "Is it safe for these folks to be here on this ranch? Is it safe for Madi and your Aunt Marie Ann?"

Charles nodded to Jack and said, "We have no reason at this time to tell you differently. It is very quiet along the border right now, especially with the military around these parts. It should be safe for a week or two, but you know how that could change in an instant."

"Are you, Aunt Marie Ann, and LeAnn still planning on a trip to Lajitas?" Charles asked. "If so, Jack plans to escort you there, while Madi and I stay here with the professor."

They finished discussing their plans and entered the kitchen where John was giving the ladies a lesson in the proper way to make German chocolate cake from scratch.

"Now! That did not take long, did it? LeAnn!" John said and waved her toward the hot cake on the stove counter.

She began pouring thick fudge icing on the top of the cake and gave the empty bowl to Jack. "Here's a spoon, clean out the bowl, please."

"I'm sweet enough, thank you!" Jess said, and got an elbow from Marie Ann.

"She wasn't talking to you, handsome," she said and winked at LeAnn.

"Fresh coffee coming up… and a slice of warm cake," John said. "Come get it!"

They all got cake and coffee and found a place to sit in the kitchen to eat. Their conversation continued until Jess suggested everyone should get to bed for the next day's adventure.

"Whatever is coming tomorrow, we need a good night's sleep," Jess said. "Where do you want us, John?"

"Men out in the bunk house and the ladies in here," John said. "Linen and towels are out there for you gentlemen, so follow me. Ladies, lock and bolt the doors when we go outside. LeAnn, please show them around and also show them where the weapons are in their rooms. Breakfast at 6:30 sharp! Good night!"

Moans and groans from everyone.

It was not long before the lights were out, and the stillness of the valley took over. A barn owl began to hoot, and a group of coyotes began to yep in the distance. Snake started to howl along with them, and John put him out of the bunkhouse.

"Snake! Go to the barn!"

#

After breakfast, Jess and Marie Ann walked out to the corral to see the horses. He explained what had happened at Alpine and Lajitas.

250

Leaning against the corral fence, he turned to her, "Sweetheart, you know how much I've missed having you with me. I'm sorry for all this messing around again."

"Oh! You've been messing around again?" she replied and pulled him to her. With a sneer and a put-on Texas accent, she said, "Mister, I'm the only filly around these parts you better be messing around with!"

"Yes, Ma'am!" She puckered, and he gave her a long, loving kiss. "You're right frisky this time of the morning."

"How could you forget?"

"Believe me, Love, I haven't!" and kissed her again. Then, he tucked her arm under his, and with the other hand he opened her hand and lay something on her palm.

"What in the world? Did you take this away from one of the twins?" she said while looking at a Texas Ranger badge.

"No, Sweetheart! The state of Texas and the boy's boss in El Paso drafted me! It is somewhat confidential!"

"Jess, you must be kidding me!"

He shook his head with a serious expression, "I'm on the payroll as a full fledge Captain. Same as the boys!"

"Come on, let's take a walk. Let me tell you what has happened and what can happen," Jess said, as they walked out along the airstrip. While he brought her up-to-date, he also told her that he knew about Professor Stapleton's history during World War II, and that he was a prisoner of war in a Jewish camp. The couple stopped in the shade of the barn, out of the view from the ranch house, and embraced each other – and then, prayed together.

#

With Jess driving, Marie Ann in the front passenger seat, Jack and LeAnn in the middle captain chairs, and then Charles and

Madi on the bench/bed seat in the back, they all headed for Lajitas in a full size custom van. It had a small removable card table between the swivel captain chairs and the back seat. The four in the back continued research on the Amarillo Mariposa Mine, while Marie Ann and Jess discussed what Granddad Hanes had left for Jess years before.

She began reading the letter and noticed the missing deposit box key's imprint. She rubbed her finger across it, and then Jess answered her questions about its contents.

"So, this is why we're heading for the bank in Alpine? Did you think about calling to find out about this deposit box?" Marie Ann asked Jess.

"Yes, I did for him," answered LeAnn and handed her a note.

The note had the bank address and the hours of when it was open. Marie Ann read it aloud and Jack said, "That's the bank I have an account with in Midland. I didn't know that they had a branch in Alpine."

"See how easy it is to miss small details, Texas Ranger!" Madi remarked and patted him on the leg.

They all laughed and Marie Ann asked Jess, "Where is the key that was in this letter?" as she examined the aged envelope for the key.

"Right here, Love!" Jess pulled a gold necklace from around his neck and from under his shirt, where the key had been attached by a small key ring. "Safest place that I could come up with for now. Hope the lock on the lock box has not been changed."

"How did I miss seeing that key and chain?" Marie Ann asked.

"I haven't been wearing it all the time, Love."

"I've been away from you far too long!" she said.

"Ya! I agree!" Jess replied, smiling and squeezing her hand.

They continued discussing the maps and the Amarillo Mariposa Mine until they arrived in Alpine at the bank. Marie Ann and Jess entered the bank carrying a large attaché case, while the others stayed in the van. Jess introduced himself and Marie Ann to the bank branch president and then signed papers. He led them into the vault where the safety deposit boxes were kept.

"Who paid the monthly fee for the use of this box over the years my grandfather has been dead?" Jess asked while the bank president used their key for removing the deposit box from its storage location.

"I really do not know, Mr. Hanes," he said removing his key. "But, I will find out before you leave. When you are finished, please return the box to its empty spot." He nodded for Jess to remove the box and motioned them into another room in the vault to examine the contents of the container. It was noticeably heavy for Jess to carry. They were left alone in the room.

Jess inserted his key and looked at Marie Ann, "Here we go!" He lifted the lid and pulled the container over for Marie Ann to watch what he removed. There were the two deeds for the mines, a stack of handwritten papers, maps and two cedar cigar boxes. He took everything out and laid them on the counter next to the container.

The two boxes were awkward and hard to lift because of their content. He scooted them against the counter's back for support because the paper binding had deteriorated from years of storage. A single small nail had to be removed from the front of the cedar lids with his Leatherman tool. When they were open, the cedar wood of the boxes filled the area around them.

Closing his eyes and inhaling deeply, "Hum, smell that cedar! Even after all these years!" Jess said.

They leaned over the boxes and were shocked at what was inside them, "Well, look at that Sweetheart! Have you ever?"

"I've never!"

Inside one box, were twelve tagged Bull Durham tobacco pouches full of gold nuggets. The tags marked the claim, depth and formations/strata of each sample of gold ore pouch. All the information needed for each sample pouch in the box was listed on its own tag wrapped around the pouch and tied with string. The dirty brown tobacco pouches still had the faded yellow drawstrings with the round paper trademark tag with the Bull drawn on it.

"Do you think that it might be a good idea to keep this confidential and not tell the others yet?" Marie Ann said.

"Yes! That's a great idea," Jess replied.

"Let's make the list and read over the deeds before going out to the van," Jess said. "It shouldn't take too much longer."

They opened the other cigar box, which had twelve doeskin pouches full of gold nuggets of assorted sizes. There were six more pouches with the 1850's, San Francisco, $20.00 gold coins.

Jess started the list while Marie Ann made copies of the mine deeds in the bank president's office. They decided to take the box of tobacco pouches with the gold nuggets and the deeds with the list of items with them.

The list was put in Jess' wallet, and a notarized copy was placed in the safety deposit box with the doeskin pouches. They returned the deposit box to the empty space in the banks' safe. After an hour in the bank, they returned to the patiently waiting couples in the van.

"What's up, Uncle Jess?" Charles asked after everyone was settled.

"Pull the inside shades down further," Jess motioned to the couples in the back. "You can see outside, but no one walking by can see what we are doing inside here." He turned in his seat and placed the attaché case on his lap. Marie Ann held the top open for him as he laid all the gold nugget pouches on the small van table between the seats in the back.

Everyone moved closer to the table.

Jess said, "One short story about these tobacco pouches. I remember the many times granddad rolled his own cigarettes from the Bull Durham paper and tobacco pouches; one-handed while on horseback with a stiff breeze blowing."

Jess held up his hands, "This is the truth! I'm a witness!"

Jess continued, "He had his lower left arm, half-way between the elbow and hand, blown off by a shotgun accident back in the early twenties." He acted out the pouring of the tobacco from the pouch, "Granddad Hanes would pull a cigarette paper from the side of the pouch while it was still in his pocket, and then with his index finger in the middle of the paper, fold it and lay it in the curve of his left arm at the elbow."

He smiled, and said, "There was still a stub left for holding the paper in place. Then he took the tobacco pouch, put one side of the draw-stringed opening in his mouth, and with his right hand pulled the pouch open. Then, he tapped the tobacco out into the cigarette paper until it was full. Holding one string between his teeth, he pulled the other one closing the opening of the pouch and then would put it back in his pocket. He rolled the paper with the tobacco into a nice even cigarette and licked the edge to help hold it together, and then moisten both ends so the tobacco would not fall out. Putting the roll-your-own cigarette between his lips, he would strike a match, either on the saddle horn or swapping it on his tight pants and light the cigarette."

"He really didn't have his left hand?" Jack said. "I didn't know that!"

"I didn't either!" Charles said. "He actually mined one handed?"

They were all amazed.

"So, for many years of smoking and collecting these pouches," Jess said, "he put them to use in his prospecting. We have made a list of all this and left it in the safety deposit box for now. We can take these deed copies. The originals are in the bank." Their wide eyes and open mouths expressed unspoken words. Jess said, "Remember, this is confidential!" he said looking each of them straight in the eyes. "Now, before anyone picks up a pouch, let me explain what we have, and then what Marie Ann and I propose. Then we'll head for Lajitas while you examine the pouches and compare them with your maps and essay lists. Once we are there, I'll examine what we have and the geological implications of it all."

Charles, Madi, Jack and LeAnn separated the pouches into four piles of three each. Then, they found the paperwork for each pouch and started their research.

After Jess and Marie Ann explained what they would like to do at Lajitas and the mine as well as what they would like to do with the information from the gold pouches, Jess asked, "Questions, anyone?" and closed the attaché case.

Jack motioned with his hands, "Yea! When do we eat?"

Jess turned in his seat and put on his seat belt. "We'll stop at a fast food place before leaving town and eat on the way. Once there, in the big city of Lajitas, we have rooms for tonight at the hotel. Then, we'll eat a good supper at the restaurant. I'm buying!"

Marie Ann pointed out, "We have three days to get our act together because you Texas Rangers must be back on the job by Monday."

"I forgot about Monday already!" Charles said rubbing his hands together. "See what happens when you're in good company and having fun? I'll vote for a giant burger with onions for lunch!"

All the women liked onions, so everyone agreed. Jess backed the van away from the bank's parking lot and headed for the fast-food strip on Texas 118 south.

CHAPTER THIRTY-FIVE

Jess and his crew were ready after breakfast Saturday morning at sunrise, 5:30 a.m. They had made their last contacts in Lajitas. The two Texas Rangers advised their company of Rangers & Army National Guard troops where they would be with Jess. Also, they would return on Monday morning unless notified differently by radio.

After contacting the owner of the *Amarillo Mariposa* Mine and explaining the research that Jess was doing on his Grandfather Hanes, he gave them written permission to be on the property. If any digging or excavating was to be done, he wanted a detail explanation prior to the work. At that time, he was not interested in gold, silver or quicksilver mining on his land. He was retired and had everything that he needed.

At 6:30, they were headed out of town for the *Tres Cuevas* Mountain area. The mine was located north of the old abandoned Marfa and *Chisos Mariposa* quicksilver mines. Jess had chosen a good sturdy van: a one ton, four-wheel drive and with a heavy-duty suspension. After they left the paved state road and headed north, the ride began to get rough.

Judging the distance of the southern foothills of the *Solitario* Mountain from the road at the Marfa and *Mariposa* mines on the *Tres Cuevas* Mountain, it looked to be ten miles. But, traveling that distance in the van took two hours of up, down, around boulders, crossing washed out gullies and making their own trail; they were ready to make camp and rest.

The entrance to the *Amarillo Mariposa* Mine was just a deep trench with a big hole at one end, which was dug into the southern side of the foothill. It was barely wide enough for two grown men, shoulder-to-shoulder, to pass each other. This was evidence that the Mexican laborers from across the border were of small stature.

Once the camp was in order, everyone seemed anxious to see the interior of the mine. Jess stood up and stretched, "Okay! Grab your flashlights and strap those miner's lamps around your heads." He handed everyone two green magic glow sticks to put in their backpacks. "Remember, we don't want any flares, matches or any thing that may strike a spark. There is always danger of natural gas fumes lingering in mines. Questions?"

They shook their heads, 'no.'

Jess pointed and made a sweeping motion directed at the mine, "Let's check the exterior around the mine entrance for about a hundred yards for any cave-ins or fissures before we go inside!" Leading the way, he asked, "Remember that explosion over at Study Butte? It could have caused ripple effects over here. Be careful!"

They filed in behind Jess down in the trench after the surface search was finished. The men removed the boards nailed across the entrance of the mine. Jess used an old shovel handle to knock down spider webs and bird nests, and then he turned on his miner's headlamp. He stepped into the dark musty mine and searched the dirt floor, ceiling and walls for cave-ins. Jess, next inspected the vertical wood posts holding crossbeams above them in order to keep the walls and ceiling from caving. His boots stirred up dust, which was slowly blown out the entrance by a flow of air from the interior of the mine. The others behind him fanned their faces and coughed from the dust.

"There is a bag of white face masks under the front passenger seat," Marie Ann said. "I'll be right back."

They all came up out of the trench for fresh air. Jess finally finished his coughing, "Sorry about that! We may have to get a portable electric generator to run a fan for sucking the dust out. That would help move it faster."

"Good idea, Jess," Madi said, continuing to cough. "But, we don't have that convenience at the moment!"

"Let's wait for this to clear before going back inside," Jack suggested. "I can have one of the National Guard men bring over both of those items. That way, you'll be able to witness your tax dollars at work!"

"No, we can't get them involved in this! The fewer people, the better. Agreed?" Jess looked at everyone for their reply. "This is not part of their assigned duties or job." They all agreed.

"That is true. But, Uncle Jess; right now I'm their commanding field officer..." with a hesitant sigh, "Just a suggestion!"

"Thanks, but no!" Jess said again. "I can't have any government agency involved with this research on civilian property. Although you two are off duty for a day or so!" He shook his head, "For now, let's wait to bring any equipment of the Army's out here."

"No problem, Uncle Jess," Jack said. "Let me know if you change your mind."

They put on the dust masks and headed into the mine again with Jess in the lead. Once inside, with headlamps on and walking easily to keep the dust down, moisture could be felt on the walls of the horizontal tunnel. He motioned toward the wet walls and ran his gloved hand across it. His gloved-fingers left gouges in the chalky clay mud.

"Keep your mask on for awhile longer. This air is still stale. Smells like bats have been roosting in here too. Watch your step; it may get slippery on this floor." He passed a rope to them, "Attach this rope to each other through the rings on your safety belts."

They came to where the tunnel went left and right. A skull and cross bones symbol was carved into the vertical beam to the tunnel on the right. The left tunnel vertical beam had 'safe' and an arrow carved on it.

Jess refocused on the tunnel beam to the right, "Charles, what indications do you have in the notes for signs in mines? This one usually means 'bad water'."

"We've got our own," LeAnn reminded them.

"You're right," Madi said. "It probably wouldn't be a bad idea to wash our mouths out and take a couple of swallows."

The shuffling of papers echoed in the tunnel, "That sign means, 'do not enter!' But, your granddad has written a note that it may mean opposite from what it indicates! Now what do we do?" Charles asked.

"We could split up, if you care to," Madi suggested with a sniffle of her sinus.

Jess pulled his mask down and turned his lamp across his face so the others could see him, "Good idea! Stay close together and watch out for each other. You rangers watch for traps. If anything looks out of place or unusual, stop and talk about it. Check your notes."

"We should be able to keep in contact with these radios. Use channel 4," Jack suggested.

They tried the radios, which were operable. "Marie Ann and I will take the right tunnel and you four go to the left. About every ten feet, try the radios."

"Roger that, Uncle Jess!" Charles said.

The first fifty feet in both directions revealed nothing, so Jess called on the radio, "Be careful when you come this way! This tunnel has recently collapsed into a larger cavern. There are skeleton remains at this end where the tunnel opens into the large cavern. The remains have Indian artifacts on a ledge." Jess could be heard moving around while talking, "Then, it drops off into a bottomless hole. My flashlight beam does not reach the bottom."

"Jess, don't lean over that... that far! Jess!" Marie Ann hollered at him, as he slipped and slid on his stomach, disappearing over the edge.

She had anticipated this could happen, and taken the slack out of the rope, wrapping it around the nearest beam. Jess did not fall far, but enough when he reached the end of his rope, it knocked the breath out of him. He dangled against the cavern wall until he could breathe well. His weight had jerked Marie Ann against the beam, causing her to lose her grip on the rope. It wedged itself tight around the beam.

"Jess! You alright?"

"Yes, Love! Once I get enough strength to breathe. Can you hold me?"

"Yes!" she said, gritting her teeth after being slammed against the beam. "Can you climb up? I can't pull you up!" Her hands in the canvas work gloves began to cramp.

"I think so!" While dangling on the rope, he banged against the wall of the cavern hole, "I dropped the radio!"

"Don't worry about the radio! Get back up here as fast as you can!" she said, finally getting a better grip on the rope.

Jess' gloves became slimy from the moist sides of the slippery cavern wall. He could not grip the rope tightly enough to pull himself up safely.

Not wanting to alarm Marie Ann any more than what she was already, he promised, "Coming up as fast as I can. Hold on!" Jess wrapped one hand around the rope and released the rope with the other. He put the slippery glove between his teeth and pulled his hand out, grabbing the rope. He pulled himself up on the rope enough to make a loop for his bare hand to hold onto, and then took off the other glove. By this time, both gloves hung from his mouth, giving him a better handgrip on the rope.

He mumbled as loudly as possible, "I'm coming up! I'm coming up!"

"Okay! I've got you!" She replied with tears streaming down her face.

Jess pulled himself up slowly, hand-over-hand, until he reached over the edge gripping the rope. Every muscle in his arms and shoulders strained to pull his weight over onto level ground. He then rolled over on his back, spit out the gloves, and took a deep breath. Marie Ann dropped her rope and ran to him, throwing her arms around his chest.

She was speechless and tears flowed, "Oh! Jess!" she sobbed.

From the depths of the cavern, a voice echoed up to them, "Uncle Jess! We found an old leather saddlebag hanging over a beam along the side of this tunnel. Can we go ahead and open it? It's sure heavy!"

There were no replies from the two laying next to the cavern hole.

"Hello! Uncle Jess! Is everything alright?" Jack called on the radio, and then turned to the other three.

"Try again!" Charles said with a worried frown on this face.

No answer.

Madi gripped his arm, "Let's go!"

"Wait!" Jack replied. "Hello! Can you hear me? If so, key the radio!"

Nothing.

Without a word, the four turned around in unison and fast-walked with the saddlebag over Charles' arm, toward the tunnel Jess and Marie Ann had entered.

"We're headed your way, Uncle Jess!" Jack shouted into the radio.

When they arrived at the cavern opening, Marie Ann was in Jess' arms. They were leaning against a tunnel beam, smiling. He started to get up, but she held him down.

"Relax, Mr. Hanes! We're not running a tight schedule here. Relax!" she said half laughing and crying. "That's what you're always telling me! Relax!"

"What happened? Where's your radio?" Jack asked.

Jess pointed to the cavern pit, "Talk into your radio!"

He hollered, "Hello!" and the pit replied his echo, "Hello!"

The two told the others what had happened and ended the story with pointing to the Indian skeleton, which had relics around its neck. Jess' headlamp reflected from the jeweled *gorg'et*. The bullet-holed skull was the remains of an Apache Indian with a war bonnet around it. Only the band of faded colored beads remained on the thin-leathered stains. The left hand still gripped a tomahawk. Some of the deerskin tunic and leggings were left along with the moccasins. A long knife was still in its sheath next to the left leg.

"Madi, take some good photos of this, will you? Get some close-ups too!" Jess requested. "We need to get this info to Indian Affairs in Marfa."

"Why, Jess?" LeAnn questioned. "Finder's keepers, right?" she asked turning to Jack.

"Not with skeleton remains," Jack replied. "Uncle Jess is right! What we have here is perhaps a crime scene. Is there any other remains in this cavern area?"

Everyone slowly moved their headlamp beams around the edge of the pit toward the opening of the tunnel.

"Jess, look up there!" Marie Ann said as she stood.

Jess took his flood lamp from the backpack Charles was carrying.

He aimed the beam up to where her light was shining on the wall. His lamp illumined another corpse, a Mexican officer hanging from the wall of the cavern. What was holding him in place could not be seen. A lever-action rifle dangled from his waist belt on a leather strap.

"How did he get there?" Madi asked, shining her headlamp beam further up the cavern wall.

Her beam could not reach to the ceiling, but Jess' could. There was another opening, but it was a natural one, not made by miners. The remains of a rotted rope hung a few feet below the edge. She carefully inspected the wall behind the Indian's skull, and then up the wall to her height.

She pointed, "Look here! A .45 caliber slug in this wall." Then, she moved back and took another photo. The flash lighted up the whole cavern.

"Boy, do we have some detectives!" Jess said, shining his flood lamp back to the natural opening above the Mexican officer. "I wonder if he shot the Indian after chasing him in there? I bet the angle of the shot is from that opening down to where this Indian stood. But wait a minute," he said and moved around under the hanging remains. "That's a model 1894 Winchester. It's probably a .30 -.30 caliber, not a .45. Plus, a '94 was made after the Apache were forced out of this area of Texas. This corpse has not deteriorated as much as the Indian's remains."

"I bet he hung there and starved to death," Charles said walking along the edge of the cavern pit to get closer to the hanging soldier.

The corpse hung twenty feet above him. Jack had moved to the edge of the pit, "You two, watch your step. That is slick at the edge where your Uncle Jess slipped inside," Marie Ann warned. "Here, hold onto this rope. It is tied around the beam over there in the tunnel."

Jess handed the floodlight to Jack to shine down into the pit. "There's your radio, smack-dab in the middle of bones. You've got to see this Uncle Jess!"

"Ya, you're right! That is a Winchester .30-.30. I can't tell much about the corpse, too high." Charles said, giving his rope to Jess, so he could peer over the edge.

"Lord, have mercy!" Jess said. The floodlight reflected off gold bars, the size of a loaf of bread. "Marie Ann, gold bars! Stacked knee deep and... one, two, three, four across. Lined up neatly, ten-foot rows! I can't tell if there are any Spanish mintmarks, but there are marks on them," he said, turning to Jack. "Could be Pancho Villa's gold. That is why the Mexican officer is here. Boy! Does my mind wonder!"

"I always said that you should've been a detective," Marie Ann said teasingly.

"I believe our new found detective needs to scrutinize this scene closer," Madi said and waved for Jess to come to her next to the Indian.

She pointed at the Indian's skull and moved away for Jess to look. Jess squatted, and Jack looked over his shoulder. Jess took his small penlight and focused it close to the hole in the forehead of the skull.

"Well, I'll be!" he said and stood up handing the penlight to Jack, moving aside. "Take a look inside this hole!"

Jack examined the hole, "That's a broken arrow shaft, not a bullet hole!" he said and stood up shining the light on the bullet slug in the wall above the Indian. "Now, I wonder where this .45 lead bullet come from... where do you think?"

"The answer might be with the bones and gold in the pit," Jess said.

All this time, LeAnn was quiet. She moved back into the mine tunnel, disappearing in the darkness. The other five had not missed her presence. They were taking photos and taking turns looking at the Indian's remains, peering over the edge down to the bottom below, and mentally comparing what they had found.

"This cavern is not on Granddad Hanes' maps," Marie Ann said, spreading them across her lap as she knelt and leaned against the wall. Shining her headlamp on the tunnel opening, she inquired "That part of the tunnel is not manmade; is it, Jess?"

Charles turned and walked with Jess to the opening. They ran their hands over the tunnel wall surfacing and examined the floor and ceiling. There were no chiseled marks or drill holes, but there were uneven indentations and protrusions that they did not notice when entering the cavern.

"You're right, Aunt Marie Ann! If this broke open from natural causes, where is the debris?" Charles said with his arms spread in a sweeping motion.

Jack pointed, "How did we miss this crack on the floor? It has to be at least a six inch opening." He knelt, bent down and shown his headlamp into the crack. "It must be as deep as that pit. I can't really see an ending to it."

"LeAnn; would you and Jack get that rope ladder out of the van?" Jess asked turning to Jack.

No answer from LeAnn. They all stopped still and flashed their lights around them and over the floor area.

Madi moved cautiously towards the edge, "Did she fall into the pit?" she said, and then carefully looked out and down into the cavern below. "She's not down there!"

"LeAnn!" Jack hollered. His voice echoed in the cavern.

Marie Ann folded the maps and stood, then turned toward the tunnel opening where Jess and Charles were. "Here, use this stronger light," she said, handing it to Jack.

He flashed it into the tunnel and hollered again for LeAnn, but only heard his echoing voice. They all turned to Jess.

"Wind up the ropes, and let's head back to the van. She must have gone outside," Jess said.

Just as they were ready to enter the mine tunnel from the cavern, they felt the ground tremble, and then heard what they thought to be an explosion further in the tunnel.

Jess and Charles motioned the two women to move away from the entrance, "Against the wall of the cavern! Grab this rope," Charles hollered at Jack, and they stretched it.

"Make five small loops and snap them to everyone's safety belt, Jess hollered.

Just as the last loop was snapped in place, "Here it comes!" Jack hollered.

A blast of dirt and rock spewed out of the mine's tunnel into the cavern and the dust filled the open space. Then, it went up and out of the crevice hole in the top above the hanging corpse. Everyone had put their dust masks on, covering their mouths and noses. They felt the ground shake and move under foot. The following moments were like being in a tumbling barrel, as the cavern seemed to turn upside down for them. They could not see, or touch, the wall until they all slammed against it. They lay gasping for air; the breath knocked out of them.

A strong breeze began to flow and circulate in the cavern from the opening above the still hanging soldier's corpse. The wind sucked the dust down into the pit and within five minutes, the cavern was clear enough for the survivors to remove their masks. Slowly, they regained their senses and began to move around on the dusty floor of the cavern. Strong beams of light continued from their headlamps. They checked on each other's condition.

Shaking the dust off and standing, they continued to check each other and their equipment.

Then a laughing female voice came up from the pit, "Is anyone still alive in here? I hope not!"

"That's LeAnn!" Jack said, turning to Jess.

"What did she say?" Jess said, "My ears are still ringing from that roar!"

"I'm not sure!' Madi said.

"Ah!" LeAnn said from down in the bottom of the cavern. "So, there is someone still alive in here! Too bad!"

"I think that we have fallen into a trap," Jess said. "If we have, LeAnn set off that explosion... I think I know why!"

Jess turned to Jack who still held the remainder of the coiled rope, "Take my place here with this first safety loop at this end of the rope. Let me have the coil of rope."

They exchanged, and Jess said, "I'm repelling down to the bottom of the pit to retrieve the radio. You four should be able to hold me."

"Jess, please don't take any chances down there," Marie Ann said. "Make sure the bottom is strong enough to hold your weight!"

"I will, Sweet Lady! Maybe there is a way out from down there where the wind is leaving."

When Jess reached the bottom of the cavern pit, releasing the rope. He let the rope dangle from above and searched for the radio that he had dropped earlier. Finally, he found it under inches of rock and dirt.

He blew it off and looked up to the top of pit, "What channel should I use on this radio? It looks in great shape!"

"Channel one, Uncle Jess!" Jack replied.

Jess knelt down and operated the radio, but received no reply. He then tried the other four channels. Nothing. "Evidently, I can't transmit out of here! I'll try again in a few minutes."

He dusted off one of the gold bars and tried to pick it up by one hand to look at its mint markings. "Hey, you characters up there! You'll never guess whose mint markings are on this gold bar?"

"Mexico!" Marie Ann said.

"No! Spain!" Charles guessed.

Then silence.

"There's two more of you up there!" Jess said.

Suddenly a brilliant beam of light caught Jess in the eyes. He almost dropped the gold bar while shading his eyes with his left hand.

"I can tell you, Mr. Hanes!" A familiar voice came from behind the beam of light, "Germany!"

"LeAnn?" Jess whispered.

"Certainly! Who else?" she said, slowly moving with uncertain steps, to Jess' right toward the dangling rope behind him. He could not see her for the brightness of the light in his eyes, but he knew where she was. Jess did not know that she had a .9mm automatic handgun pointed at him.

"What's going on down there?" Jack yelled, leaning over the pit's edge. His headlamp silhouetted LeAnn against the pit's wall, holding her gun. "LeAnn!"

She squinted and fired her gun at Jack's headlamp. At the flash of her gun firing, Jack slipped on the edge of the pit. The other three held him secure from falling. Now, the light was out of Jess' eyes, but it was hard for him to focus on her. She swung around to point the gun at him and slipped on the dusty gold bars and fell, wedging her foot between them. She moaned, but kept the gun aimed at Jess. He put up his hand to try settling her down.

When he did, she fired at him, off balance. The gold bars shifted and collapsed under her through the bottom of the pit. The bullet hit the hanging corpse above her and dislodged it from the outcropping of rock. It fell into the hole with LeAnn, falling against her. She let out a scream of horror and tried to move away from the corpse. She fired her gun at it until it was empty. Then, she began beating it with the gun, squirming, trying to get away from it. The more she fought the dead soldier, the deeper they sank into the hole. They were up to their waist in the hole, being held in place by the pressing gold bars.

Jess grabbed the rope, "LeAnn!" He stretched out trying to grab her flailing arms. She was in panic! "Don't move! Stay still, or you'll sink more!"

He missed her wrist and knocked the gun from her hand. At first, she pulled away from Jess' extended hand. He then, realized that she was being pulled further down and away from him. She tried to lunge, but she was stuck fast from the waist down. The more she struggled, the deeper she sank. Tears came to her eyes as she yelled for Jess to help her.

Charles was the last one tied to the rope, who was braced behind one of the timbers in the mine tunnel's opening. He held the weight when Jess seized the rope and began jerking on it.

"Uncle Jess, let me help you," Jack said sliding down the rope behind Jess.

As he reached around Jess to help grab LeAnn, Jess had managed to stretch further and grabbed onto the fingers of her right hand. As Jack reached for her wrist, the gold bars gave way below her. Jess lost his grip on her fingers. Jack missed her wrist.

LeAnn and the corpse disappeared into the dark abyss. Her cry faded in the depths of the hole. With all the rumbling and noise, the others could not hear a sound from the bottom. Jack and Jess hung from the rope with the toes of their boots gripping the wall.

Jack with tears and anguish in his voice, "Lord, not this way!"

After the three had pulled Jack and Jess to the top of the pit, the remainder of the bottom disappeared further below, burying the corpse, LeAnn and the gold bars. Neither of their headlamps' beams reached the bottom.

"Uncle Jess! What a horrible way to die!" Jack said as he tried to hold back his emotions. "I don't think that she was ready!"

"Let's get out of here, young man!" Jess said as they climbed hand over hand to the top.

After they caught their breath, Jess said, "We should try finding LeAnn. Through it all, it's possible she's still alive!"

"You're right, Jess," said Marie Ann, leaning against him and kissing him on the cheek.

Charles held Madi's hand, and said, "We'll go get the rope ladder and additional rope if the tunnel is still open."

"Question!" Jess said, and stood up. "Where did she come from and just how did she get in the pit down there? She was standing on this side where the rope is dangling."

Jack insured the rope was securely tied around the tunnel beam, "Hold on, Charles, before you get in the tunnel. I'll repel down and look." Over the side he went, without hesitation.

The four lay on the damp floor and peered over the edge as Jack slid down the rope. With all five headlamps shining down into the pit, the gold bars reflected their lights; the dust had settled. Jack stopped at the level of the pit floor prior to its collapse.

"Can you see LeAnn?" Madi hollered to Jack.

"Just a second," he said, swinging to his right along the wall. "I need to move over to this opening. Then, I'll look."

He disappeared into a hole in the wall. Dust was stirred up and came out of the hole into the pit area, then settled. Jack leaned out of the hole and beamed his headlamp down into the pit below. He slowly panned the light beam across the bottom for LeAnn. The gold bars glisten in the light.

He stopped, "I see her hand. Drop me that other rope!" He extended his rope length with the one from above, and then repelled down to the bottom of the cavern pit.

"We're coming down to the opening, and I'll come on down to you," Jess said. "Charles, you find your way out from that opening and the three of us will help Jack. Okay?"

"Sure, Uncle Jess. I'll be back as soon as I find out where it goes."

The four repelled down to the opening above Jack, and Charles disappeared into the darkness.

"Ladies, stay here and I'll go on down," Jess said, and then repelled down to Jack.

Jack was carefully unburying LeAnn from beneath the rubble and gold bars. She was badly cut, bruised and broken. He checked for a pulse at her neck while putting his ear close to her mouth. Jess continued to uncover her.

"LeAnn," Jack whispered into her ear. "Speak to me! Move a finger! Open your eyes!"

No response. He continued checking her for any sign of life. Her body was cold and her skin was turning dark.

He turned to Jess, while cradling LeAnn's head under his arm, "Uncle Jess, you check her pulse for me. I think that I'm feeling my own. It's too strong."

They both hovered over her, seeking some sort of response.

Jess shook his head, "No! Nothing!"

Jack looked away and up to his Aunt Marie Ann and Madi. He was speechless.

Jess squatted next to him, "Jack, I think that she's gone. It's been thirty minutes or more since this happened. Feel her stomach and under her arms, no warmth at all; no pulse, no breathing." He put his arm around Jack's shoulder, "I'm sorry."

"Me too, Uncle Jess," he replied and lay her head on a gold bar. "I thought I had found a sweet partner!" He stood and tapped Jess on the shoulder, "Let's get out of here."

"We can talk more about this topside," Jess said standing up, and putting his arm around Jack's shoulder. He looked up to the opening where the two ladies were watching, "We're going to have a few words of prayer and then leave."

They all bowed their heads while Jess prayed.

Charles returned with a tarp before they moved LeAnn.

"I thought this would keep her warm, until we could get her out," he said and tossed it down to them.

Madi turned to him with tears in her eyes, "She's gone."

Charles just shook his head, "You should wrap her body anyway, in order to get her out of here. I'll talk to Sheriff Baker in Alpine, about keeping this confidential until we talk to Professor

Stapleton. The sheriff will probably put her in the morgue at Alpine."

"This is so cold and morbid," Marie Ann said, putting her arms around herself, shivering.

"It is cold in here," Madi replied.

They wrapped LeAnn's body tightly in the tarp and tied the rope securely in order to lift it up to the pit opening where she had entered the pit. They carried her to the van. Marie Ann and Madi stayed in the van while the three men returned to the cavern.

After taking closer photos of the gold bars for identification, Jess found her gun under rubble, dust and gold bars where the bottom of the pit had collapsed under LeAnn. He showed it to Jack, who put it in his backpack.

"I'll do a gun check on that later," he said.

"Whoa!" Charles yelled. "Where did that blast of hot air come from?"

Jess stepped to the side in order to let Jack get around him. They were both hit with the heat, preventing them from breathing. The stench of sulfur burnt the inside of their noses and eyes.

"Face mask!" Jess yelled and grabbed Jack by the arm. The whole cavern lit up from an explosion, and the roar was deafening. After their eyes adjusted from the intensity of the flash, they could see where it entered.

"Over there, along the edge of the wall of the pit," Jack said, pointing behind Charles. "Get out of here, it's molten lava!"

Steam began to boil and roar as water sprayed on the molten lava. That part of the pit began to sink, slowly breaking away beneath the floor. Jess and Charles ran up to the higher level of the entrance and waited for Jack to catch up. He had stopped, grabbed a gold bar and heaved it up to them. After he was with them, they turned to watch the whole bottom move with the lava. Jack was the strongest of the three and ran ahead of the other two with the gold bar on his shoulder.

When they got to the van, "Uncle Jess, you drive!" Charles hollered. "You know the way around here better than we do!"

Jack dropped the gold bar on the floor in the back of the van; the ladies did not see what he had. The added weight caused the van to squat, and that caused them to turn around to see what happened. Jess and Charles jumped in the van.

With a startled expression on their faces, Marie Ann finally spoke, "What's wrong now?"

Jess hollered, starting the van, "Jack will explain when he gets inside. We've got to get out of here before the mine explodes or caves!"

No sooner had they sped away on the gravel road the main entrance of the mine bellowed white steam and smoke. Jess watched in the rearview mirror, while the others had turned in their seats to see what was happening. The side of the mountain, where the mine was, sunk into the ground – disappearing from sight.

"Turn around and watch what is happening behind us!" Jess ordered.

"We are!" Marie Ann replied, hanging out the side door window opening with the video camera.

There were rumbles and red-hot lava spewing hundreds of feet in the air. A ground blast rippled from the mine area out under the desert surface toward the speeding van. Marie Ann saw it coming and pulled herself back inside the van to safety. The underground ripple flipped the van's rear off the ground and then the front, sending the van airborne. When it hit the ground again, Jess was able to keep it in control and continued toward Lajitas.

The ripple continued for over a mile. When it had subsided, Jess stopped the van and everyone got out. They took more video and still photos of the eruption's aftermath.

While the others were taking pictures, Charlie called the Texas Ranger headquarters in Lajitas to find out if their equipment was showing an earthquake epicenter at the Solitario Mountain foothills. They repacked the van, laying LeAnn's body on the floor in the middle, between the seats... then, drove to Lajitas.

On the way to the border town, Jess was reminded about things his Granddad Hanes had written about the Amarillo Mariposa Mine, "Marie Ann, among those papers you have on your lap, are there any notes on the depth of the mine? If I remember right, once they got down beyond the 800-foot level, wasn't there something mentioned about how hot the water was? It was seeping in, and the miners were wading in 100° hot water?"

She and Madi leafed through the stack of notes until Marie Ann said, "This says, '...100° hot water under pressure could not be stopped from entering the tunnels and shafts beyond the depth of 800-feet. Those sections were sealed off."

"Here's one," Madi said. "...Something about, 'it was too hot to work while wading in that rotten egg smelling water.' Wonder why it was so hot?"

All three guys answered at one time, "I know!"

"Uncle Jess, you go first," Jack said. "We'll whisper to Aunt Marie Ann."

"The water was heated by lava flows!" Jess said. "And, I bet that is how the water of the Boquillas Hot Springs is heated."

"Yes! I bet that's right," Charles remarked.

It was silent for a while. Jack had put his hand on LeAnn's canvas covering and patted it, and then looked at Madi with tears in his eyes.

They continued tying events together until they stopped at the Texas Ranger headquarters where they found Sheriff Baker. Jack told him about the pit collapsing and the lava. Then, the sheriff took LeAnn's body to Alpine.

CHAPTER THIRTY-SIX

The Texas Rangers, Texas State Police, Federal Marshals and the Texas Army National Guard were still swarming the Lajitas area, because of the terrorist attacks. Satellite communications between terrorists had increased and the national alert was increased to RED. They were not aware of the mine incident, only that an earthquake had occurred.

Jess, Charles, Jack and Madi were the only law enforcement officials who knew about the German gold. The only other people to know about LeAnn's death in the Amarillo Mariposa Mine, was Marie Ann, Sheriff Baker and his special selected deputies from Alpine. The sheriff was not told about LeAnn firing a weapon at them and the gold.

These five witnesses suspected that Professor Stapleton was connected with the German gold, but they had no factual evidence. Charles gave the film taken at the mine to one of his Rangers.

"Sergeant, this film is to be treated with the highest security!" Charles said. "No one is to know where, when or why you are flying to Alpine. Refer them to me, if questions arise. Make certain that you get the photos and negatives back to us at Professor Stapleton's ranch."

Jack added, "Never let this film out of your sight. Stay with the person developing it, and don't let them look at it. Don't surrender the film to anyone but me or Captain Randel." He nodded at the sergeant, "Again, it's imperative that we get the negatives!"

"Yes, Sir! I understand!" the Texas Ranger Sergeant said, with a snappy salute. He turned and headed for the airfield.

The five adventurers left for the Stapleton's ranch.

#

When they arrived at the ranch, a Texas Ranger aircraft had landed. The sergeant met them on the porch of the ranch house as Professor Stapleton came outside. Charles thanked him and reminded him again of the secrecy of the film.

"We will be making our reports and you will be covered on this activity to the ranch," he said, shaking the sergeant's hand. "Thanks. That will be all."

They all watched the aircraft leave and went inside to the kitchen where the professor had a fresh pot of coffee waiting.

"Where is LeAnn? Did she go into Alpine for supplies?" he asked while filling the coffee cups.

They all sat down without a word, not wanting to look at him directly. The silence was deafening.

Finally, Jess stood looking into the eyes of a wise old gentleman who knew something was amiss, "What is wrong, Jess?"

"John, I don't know where to start," he replied to the professor and walked over to him. "We were all in the Amarillo Mariposa Mine when it caved in, which was caused by a lava flow below the mine tunnels." Jess turned to the others, then back to the professor, "This is awful hard for me to say, but LeAnn is dead."

John turned and with trembling hands put the coffee pot back on the burner. He reached for the counter and almost lost his balance. Jess and Charles supported him to a chair at the table. His face was pale, and he began to weep softly.

Jess lightly held John's shoulder, trying to comfort him. Marie Ann and Madi were in tears, holding each other's hands. Jack started to say something and stopped. Charles reached over and clasped Jack's arm, then patted it. They turned to each other and locked eyes; both were at the point of tears, too. Two tough

Texas Rangers emotionally held their peace, waiting to hear from their Uncle Jess.

Jess made a gesture with his open hands towards the ceiling, *Dear Lord Jesus! What to say?* Shaking his head, he squatted next to John, "We, by accident, found the German gold in the cavern. It has vanished in the lava flow."

"My Lord! Did she fall into the lava?"

"No! No!" Jess said waving his hands negatively to help John settled down. "We got her out of the mine before the lava took everything."

"Sheriff Baker took her to a funeral home in Alpine," Charles said softly.

Jess continued with the story of what happened, other than the details of LeAnn with the firearm. There was a long silence with only a few sniffles from the ladies. Jack looked at Jess for approval to speak. Jess nodded.

"I don't know how to go about this, but to be blunt!" Jack wanted to make it as easy as possible, "We must make a report about her death, but not about the German gold. It's gone, except for this... bar!" He stooped over and lifted the gold bar to the top of the table.

John stood up, lightly dusted off the gold bar with the palm of his hand, and pointed to the Nazi mint marks, "My! My! I haven't seen this since 1944!" He sat down, leaned his elbows on the table, and then settled back in the chair.

"Yes, I understand what you must do," John said, wiping his face with his handkerchief. "But, first!" he said standing. "I have a lengthy story to tell. Would one of you ladies take dictation? Or, gentlemen, does anyone have a recorder?"

"Yes, sir!" Jess said. "It's out in the van. I'll go get it."

Marie Ann pushed her chair back, "Jess, I'll get the video recorder."

Madi stood up with Marie Ann; "I'll go out with you, if you don't mind?" They clasped hands and walked out on the front porch to the van. The sun was beginning to set behind the distant mountain ranges, leaving long strips of light to the east and a red sky behind them to the west.

They had the video camera set up, John was ready and both ladies were set to take notes. Jess sat next to John with a long corded microphone.

Turning to John, "Ready?"

He nodded, yes.

Jess switched on the microphone, which started the tape in the video camera. "I am Jess E. Hanes, Texas Ranger Captain, Company E. The two other Rangers that are present are Captains Charles and Jack Randel of the Texas Rangers. Also, U.S. Marshal, Madilene Ash, and my wife, Marie Ann Hanes, are here."

He paused, looked toward John, and then continued, "Professor John Stapleton's daughter was killed in an accident in the area of the Amarillo Mariposa Mine today, November ten, year two thousand and three. A full investigation is being carried out by the Texas Rangers." He placed the microphone in a holder on the table in front of John.

"We are located at Professor Stapleton's ranch, and he has a story to tell," Jess said settling back in his chair.

The professor told in detail about his imprisonment in Nazi prisoner of war camps because of his political stand against Hitler, plus he was a Jew. While being moved from one camp to another, he was privy to secret information about a shipment of Hitler's gold bullion from the mountains near Lyon, Germany, to somewhere in the Swiss Alps. He and a few others escaped from guards between prison camps.

John reunited with the French underground operations, but never forgot the information about Hitler's gold. A year later, before the war ended, he handpicked a small group of men who would fight to take the gold from the German leaders. They knew that their lives would be worthless if caught or later found with the gold. But, taking the gold out of the murderer's hands would be worth the risk.

They succeeded in taking the gold and spent years moving it around in Brazil, then to Venezuela and finally to Mexico. From Chihuahua, they moved the load of gold by mules and burros across to the caverns near Lajitas. One burro a night for two months crossed the Rio Grande River without being noticed by the border authorities. He was not aware of the Amarillo Mariposa Mine being so close to their hiding place.

While John talked, Jess remembered the truck explosion near Study Butte, wondering if it would have caused any collapse in the mines near Lajitas and Terlingua. If so, it may have weakened the tunnels in the mine near the cavern, opening up the area of the mine they were searching.

"So, once the gold was secure in the United States, I was comfortable leaving it alone," John said, and continued. "It was out of Hitler's grasp, and he could no longer use it for his war against humanity. Only LeAnn and I knew of its location."

Talking was helping them all settle down and put the puzzle together. John stood and stretched. "I am close to finishing my story, but I need to visit the little boy's room. Please excuse me."

Jess turned the video camera off. Madi made more coffee and while everyone stretched, Marie Ann poured coffee. While they waited for John to come back in, they rehearsed what had happened the last few days, trying to figure out why LeAnn would confront them with a gun. They had no answers. After half an hour, they were all settled ready for John to finish his story.

"Before John comes back," Jess said. "I hope that you will respect what he is sharing with us. This is not only Jewish history, but it must be terrible to have to hide your bloodline and faith in God."

"Ya! The Jews continually get trampled!" Charles said.

John came into the kitchen smoking his pipe and pulled a counter stool over next to Madi at the table. Jess refocused the video camera and John continued, "It seems that I could not keep all my secrets from LeAnn," John said, and then took a sip of hot coffee. "After my wife and I became legal American citizens, the government put us in their protection program. I had shared information with them about Hitler's Nazi operations in Brazil." He paused, thinking and then continued, "We moved around to different locations every six months. Mainly because we knew that the Nazis were looking for me. Even after the war, they put Jews to the top of their assassination list... LeAnn was born in Houston, and later, we moved here, before she started school. I wanted to be closer to the caverns."

John seemed to be relaxing and then yawned, which caused a couple of the others to do the same. He laughed, "I would do that to LeAnn on purpose, just to make her do the same as you did. Powers of suggestion," he said laughing again.

A scowl came across John's face as he remembered LeAnn was no longer with him. He took another long sip of the hot coffee, and continued, "Prior to teaching at Sul Ross University, back when it was the College of Mines, the United States' government changed all of my university degrees from Germany and England, to names of institutions of higher education over here. The files at those locations in the United States reflected my American credentials. I was never questioned."

"LeAnn was forever asking questions, a curious soul, never taking things at face value. She was always picking things apart, why this, why that... a great thinker!" John tapped his spoon lightly on the edge of his coffee cup, "She graduated with top honors at the University of Texas. She became a great Texas history buff... she liked details of this southwest part of the country." He paused and looked at Jess, "Here I go again, wondering away from the subject!"

Charles clapped his hands, and then everyone joined in, showing their appreciation for what he had shared. "You're tired, Professor. Would you want to stop for this evening?"

"No! I have a mission that I must finish," John said with a smile. "I can tell it all, now! Let me know when you need to change tapes."

Jess nodded, "Right now would be a good time. Take another short break. Anyone have questions?"'

"I'm sure that we will some," Madi said, "after John is finished and we review these tapes." She went to the coffee pot, "Anyone want their coffee warmed?"

No one responded.

"Okay, Professor. You ready?" Jess said motioning with the microphone.

John pulled his pipe from his shirt pocket and emptied it in the ashtray on the table. "Anyone mind? I did not ask earlier!" No one did, "Jack, would you hand me that tobacco pouch on the stand behind you?"

"Yes, sir."

He puffed on his pipe and settled back to finish.

Jess turned on the recorder again, "Continue, Professor."

"LeAnn had found a stack of my research on Hitler's extraction of gold teeth from the prisoners in the war camps, along with other gold items he stole." Measuring with his hands, "Then, he had it all melted into gold ingots." He leaned forward, took small puffs on the pipe and laid it down on the edge of the kitchen table.

"She put bits of information together about Hitler's gold and where he had supposedly hid it. Then she came across newspaper clippings that I had saved. One of which, concerned Jews who had stolen Hitler's gold."

John smiled, "Then, one evening before Mother died, she confronted us both out there on the porch." He pointed with his pipe. "She had that stack of papers and laid them on my lap. 'Papa,' she said, 'this top newspaper clipping is very interesting. The last trace known about Hitler's gold bullion was in Mexico.' She picked up the clipping and handed it to me. 'I tied this in with a receipt for the purchase of mules and burros, and this one for the sale of them.'"

Laughing, he said, "Did she have me in a corner? 'Does this have anything to do with the disappearance of Hitler's gold?' she asked." He snickered, "I do not recollect my exact words, but I told her that she would be the guardian of it one day."

"Lord, have mercy!" Marie Ann said, covering her mouth with her hands. Turning to Madi, she stood up and went out to the porch.

John stood up, leaning on the table with his hands, looking at Jess, "Did I say something wrong?"

"No!" Jess replied and stopped the video camera. "This came as a surprise to us all." He headed for the porch, "We'll be right back."

He went out to Marie Ann and put his arms about her, "Yes, Love! LeAnn was protecting her father's secret. Perhaps she thought we were the enemy, come to take the gold for Hitler's Nazi party." Holding her closer, "They're still an active group in some countries."

"We killed her!" She sobbed against his chest.

"No, Sweetheart! Even if she had not shot at anyone, the floor would have not supported her weight at that spot. Not with the weight of the gold and her, too. Plus, the lava flow took it all."

The others had followed the professor out on the porch. All had clearly heard what Jess had told Marie Ann. John cleared his throat and laid his pipe on the porch swing arm.

Walking over to Jess and Marie Ann, he put his arms around them both. "Now! Now! Young lady," he spoke softly. "No one killed LeAnn! Our Lord God, Jehovah, took her home to be with Him. It was her time, and the torch has now been passed onto the five of you, from her."

They all gathered around, making a circle of six, "Torch?" Madi asked.

It was quiet for a few minutes. John then spoke softly, "This secret must die with us all. No one must know about that gold. I will eliminate the gold bar in a timely fashion. I do not want some terrorists to get a hold of it." He paused and continued with his thoughts, "Otherwise, others may lose their lives over it."

He paused taking a long deep breathe, put his warm pipe in his shirt pocket, "Will you all please pledge to keep this a secret, before God and the six of us?"

It was once again silent for a long moment before Marie Ann spoke, "There seems to be only one answer." She looked at Jess, "Yes, I pledge to not speak of it again!"

Jess nodded, "I agree with you, Love." It was dark, and there was enough light from inside the house for Jess to make eye contact with each of the others. "But, I've also pledged to uphold the constitution of the United States and the Republic of Texas. Then, the most important pledge in my life is to Jesus Christ my Lord. As long as this pledge with John doesn't interfere with my other previous commitments, I will say, yes!"

"I agree with you, Uncle Jess and say, yes," Charles said.

Madi's thoughts were made clear when she sneezed, and said, "Wow!"

Jack smiled, "You should feel better. And, God bless you, too!"

Everyone echoed his comment.

Madi said, "Thank you! God has, He is and He will! Thank you!" A little girlish giggle came out, "I'm about to sneeze again! Hold on!" She raised her head back and let out a thunderous sneeze, "Excuse me, must get a handkerchief before my nose runs away with me."

Charles handed her his, "Will this do the job for now? It's clean!"

"Ah, yes! Thank you. It's a bit chilly out here, but I'll be fine." She blew her nose, stuffed the handkerchief under her belt and grabbed Charles and Jack's hands. "I also agree with Jess' commitments and statement. Yes!"

"Jack? You're next!" Jess pressed, looking at him.

Jack spoke, "I usually do not make hasty commitments. This requires you give me a few minutes to think it over. Please?"

John agreed, "That request is well taken, thank you."

"Well, I do agree wholeheartedly with Uncle Jess and Aunt Marie Ann," Charles said, "Like I said a few minutes ago... It's a yes, for me too!" His aunt and Madi squeezed his hand in theirs.

"I know I'm out numbered, but that has nothing to do with my decision." Jack said. "I'm convinced that Hitler's gold should stay buried forever. I agree, yes!"

"Jess, would you pray for us all?" John requested.

"Yes. Thank you, John." He prayed God's special wisdom to be placed in each of them in the coming days, that they would glorify Him.

Silently, they retired to their rooms for the night.

#

When everyone arrived in the kitchen for breakfast, the next morning, the gold bar was still on the table. John moved it behind the old wood-burning cook stove into the firewood box and stacked logs on top of it. Then, the ladies set the table.

After breakfast, before Jack and Charles called for an aircraft to Lajitas, Jess had everyone go out on the enclosed portion of the back porch in the early morning sun with their morning coffee. He had set up the video camera again and began recording. He leaned against the railing and tossed an old leather saddlebag over his shoulder. It was from the mine.

"I've called this special meeting to divide up the spoils from the Amarillo Mariposa Mine," he said. "According to my instruction from my Grandfather Hanes; to you two Rangers, Charles and Jack, from your Great Grandfather Hanes; to you John from your old friend; and to you Madi, as a member of our fellowship; I now empty this saddlebag of its contents, of which, Marie Ann Hanes has signed the inventory."

On the porch table, he slid out sacks full of ten-dollar gold coins and silver dollar Morgan coins into seven different piles. Each pile had two sacks of gold and two of silver. He laid the emptied saddlebag across the railing and picked up the attaché case from the Alpine bank.

"We have divided these evenly as well," Jess said. "Now, put two additional sacks on each of the six piles. Each pile should have two sacks of silver and four sacks of gold. Correct?" he asked and closed the case.

Everyone said, "Yes!" in unison.

"Now, here are seven heavy canvas bank bags for your pile of coins. We have also divided an even amount for all of Grandfather Hanes' grandchildren who are not here," he said and then added, "We will put their portion back in the Alpine bank and contact them by certified mail about their fortune. I suggest we fill these bags for the other grandchildren and hide them separately in the house until we leave."

Marie Ann held up her hand, "Jess, shouldn't we contact an attorney for proper ownership certificates on the mines?"

"Yes, even the one that collapsed and exploded. We should be able to take care of that at the bank when we get there."

"Question, Uncle Jess," Charles said.

"Yes, Sir."

"I'm not complaining, just making an observation. Why do you and Aunt Marie Ann only have one sack, together? And not two separate sacks?"

"I can answer that, Uncle Jess," Madi stated with her beautiful broad smile and raised hand.

"Thank you Madi, I'm flattered with that, 'Uncle Jess'," Jess said. "What's the answer?"

"You two always share as, 'one'!"

"Always. Madi! Always! Thanks be to God!" Jess replied, nodding his approval. Marie Ann looked up at him, still with his arm around her shoulder. Bending down, he kissed her waiting lips.

The young men hollered, "Yea!" John smiled and lit his pipe, again. Puffing away, he sounded with a loud, "Hallelujah!"

"May I make a request?" John asked, placing his pipe on the table against the sacks of coins. Then he held out his hands to the others to make a circle around the table and bowed his head.

"Almighty, Jehovah. Keep us safe with this bounty that it will never fall into the hands of evil men. I invoke Your blessing on us. Amen!"

The others echoed, "Amen!"

CHAPTER THIRTY-SEVEN

Professor Stapleton had traveled to Alpine to the University of Sul Ross in order to present a lecture on physics for upper classmen. LeAnn's funeral and burial was over, and John was trying to return to his work at the university. Charles and Jack returned to their Texas Ranger border duties.

Madi was in Austin on marshal business. Jess and Marie Ann stayed at the ranch, temporarily, to feed and take care of the horses until the ranch hands returned.

After the morning chores were finished, they sat in an old WWII jeep next to the open barn doors in the shade. They were discussing the letter Jess' Grandfather Hanes had left him about the mine information and what had happened in the cavern to LeAnn.

Marie Ann acknowledged his last remarks with a smile. They both sat quietly, lazily, with their eyes closed, listening to the stillness of the open range country.

"I need a *siesta!* A little nap would be nice during this peaceful morning," she said, yawning and turning to get out of the seat. "But, I suppose that we should go fuel your aircraft before it gets warmer. Will you be checking LeAnn's aircraft too?"

"We should," Jess said. "Let's pull them out of the barn and leave them in the shade. It will help keep the fuel from expanding so bad. Last week, I lost fuel through the overflow vent when it expanded from the heat of the sun.

They both stopped when they heard the pounding of running feet approaching from around the side of the barn. It sounded like the horses were loose.

"How did they get out of the barn?" Marie Ann questioned, as she started for the barn.

Jess was right next to her when they went around the corner of the barn. They were face-to-face with three light tan uniformed Arab soldiers who came to a dusty halt, pointing their automatic weapons at the two. They were all surprised at the sudden appearance of the others.

"Hold on here! What are you men doing?" Marie Ann hollered waving her hands in resistance.

Jess grabbed Marie Ann's arm, stepping in front of her, "State your business!"

The soldiers stood their ground, shouting at the two in Arabic. Jess recognized the men as Middle Eastern Arab troops. Neither group understood the other. A tall, giant of a man climbed up out of the ravine behind the soldiers, panting heavily from running.

The closer the man got to them, the more Jess stepped back. Moving Marie Ann behind him toward the barn, he whispered to Marie Ann, "I know that big ugly guy from Morocco. He was supposed to be dead. Move back, Love! When I tell you, get to the house and call the Rangers! I'll try to stall these guys."

She moved out of sight around the corner of the barn.

"Now!" Jess hollered, holding up his hands to halt their advance.

That big Arab looks like Alvarez in the face, but this guy is not as fat as what I remember. He should be dead! Jess thought to himself.

He had not seen Marie Ann, but the other three had. One started to pass Jess. Jess suddenly gave him a sidekick on the knee with the heel of his western boot, knocking the soldier to the ground. The soldier lost his grip on his weapon, which was flipped back against the barn. The other two men put their weapons off of 'safety' and were about to shoot Jess when Alvarez yelled at them to stop.

One of the soldiers turned to him and told him about the woman who had disappeared around the barn. Alvarez motioned him to go after her. Jess stepped in front of him.

Alvarez told his man to step away and walked up within inches of Jess' face. "Mr. Hanes, you are still alive?" His breath stunk of garlic. "I know you from photos my father's files had on you. We did not expect to see you in this part of Texas!" He still was trying to stare down Jess. "Stubborn man you are! I will kill you this time with my bare hands, and leave you here for the rats and vultures to eat."

'So this is Colonel Alvarez's son! No wonder he looks familiar'!

Alvarez stepped away from Jess and indicated to the two soldiers to take Jess. Two shotgun blasts were heard from the house. Jess turned in that direction and was hit in the back of the head with a rifle butt. They dragged him to the back porch of the ranch house and dropped him face down in the dirt, where he regained consciousness.

Alvarez hollered in Arabic for the soldier to come out of the ranch house. No answer. He drew his 9mm Beretta and started up the steps, when a shotgun blast came through the screen door hitting him full in the chest. The blast bowed him backward, knocking him off the porch. His two other bodyguards sprayed the doorway and porch wall with lead from their automatic weapons.

Jess had only heard the shotgun and felt Alvarez hit the ground next to him.

The bodyguards looked down at Alvarez, then to one another, turned and ran for the barn, leaving their weapons behind. Marie Ann ran out on the porch, firing two more rounds from the shotgun, not reaching the two departing men. They were long gone by the time she picked up one of the dropped rifles, aiming in the direction where they disappeared around the barn. She fired a burst of rounds from the rifle into the corner of the barn, just to let them know she was serious. The rifle locked open, it was empty.

Jess rolled over and started to sit up as she began to reload her double-barreled shotgun. Alvarez rolled, drew a long bladed knife from his boot and jabbed its blade through Jess' left shoulder, pinning him to the ground. His large body hovered over Jess with all of his weight on the knife handle, holding Jess pinned. They wrestled for control of the knife, but Alvarez was crazed stronger than Jess, pulling the knife out and placing it against Jess' throat. He turned Jess over, throwing his other arm around Jess' forehead holding him tightly against his chest. He then rolled Jess on top of him for a shield.

Alvarez screamed at Marie Ann, gritting his yellow teeth with foaming saliva spitting from between his ugly large lips, "Drop that weapon! I will slit him from ear-to-ear!"

Blood was flowing from the knife hole in Jess' shoulder, saturating his light green short-sleeved flight suit. It began to run down to his armpit, to his elbow and dripped onto the ground. Alvarez squeezed him tighter.

Marie Ann leaned the shotgun against the porch railing and moved toward the kitchen door. She froze when Alvarez knife began to draw blood from Jess' neck.

Alvarez had to push Jess aside in order to sit up straight, but he held a handful of hair, keeping Jess where he wanted him. Blood was seeping from the front of his shirt through the double '0' buckshot holes, where Marie Ann had shot him. He held Jess between him and Marie Ann, to the point where he could not see her. He rolled up on his knees and then stood, using Jess as a prop to get up.

Even though he was taller than Jess, squatting behind him, he could not see Marie Ann. She grabbed the shotgun and slipped into the kitchen.

Jess brought his left knee up between Alvarez's legs into his groin. The knife's handle caught in Jess' belt as the big man bent over, and it fell to the ground. His cheek was against Jess', and his foul breath stank. With all the strength Jess could muster, he swung upward with both fists entwined, hitting Alvarez solidly under the jaw. His front teeth cut through his tongue; blood flew all over the front of Jess and Alvarez. His eyes rolled up, as he staggered backward, shoving Jess away from him. Jess fell onto the porch steps. Like a drunk, Alvarez slowly turned and began trying to run toward the back of the barn. Jess lay stunned across the two bottom steps.

Marie Ann jumped out on the porch and fired both barrels at the same time from the shotgun. Then, she leaned down and helped Jess sit up. They heard the professor's dog, Snake, continue barking, straining to get loose. Finally, he broke loose from his rope restraint and had a good grip on Alvarez's leg. Alvarez was dragging Snake and trying to beat him off with his fists. The other dogs were barking, but were still penned up.

Suddenly, out of nowhere, a large mule deer with a huge rack of horns, charged head down, catching Alvarez squarely in the chest with its two main center horns. It lifted both Alvarez and Snake off the ground, snorting and rearing its head.

Alvarez let out a curdling scream that echoed off the near canyon walls. Both horns of the deer pushed out through Alvarez's back while he was lifted again from his feet. Snake would not let go. The big man grabbed the other longer horns with his hands, trying to push himself off the center horns. The deer continued battering Alvarez's body against any object it could, and then bashed him against a barn roof post. The post snapped, and the roof began to collapse. The deer dragged the limp semi-conscious Alvarez draped across its head with the man's arms around its neck.

The large buck staggered under the heavy load of Alvarez's body and reared its head as if catching its second breath. Snake let go and rolled away from the deer. He jumped up, snarled and stood his ground. The deer turned and stumbled across the graveled runway, dragging Alvarez between its front legs. They disappeared in the distance over the edge of a deep arroyo.

Jess told Marie Ann to get one of John's rifles behind the kitchen door with a scope on it and ammo. She ran out of the ranch house carrying a large caliber hunting rifle and first aid kit. She had watched the buck deer do its damage while calling the sheriff and Texas Rangers.

Jess had taken his red bandana from his pocket and stuffed it into the hole in his shoulder. He lay flat on his back to stop the bleeding, hoping he could put enough pressure on the backside where the knife blade had come out.

Marie Ann talked to Jess about all the things she had planned for them and told him he better not die on her. Tending his wounds, she rolled him on his side, stuffed a wad of compressed gauze into the hole in his back shoulder, and then taped it in place.

Sitting up, Jess grit his teeth, "I don't think he did much damage to my shoulder. I'm sure I can use my hand and extend my arm up...that won't last long!" He felt a bit light headed.

"Sure! You're not in shape to do anything!" she said. "You've lost too much blood!" She lifted his left arm, "Put your hand inside your shirt and let it carry the weight of your arm."

"Did you see that big 'mulely' lift Alvarez into the air?" Jess asked. "It was the biggest deer I've ever seen. We should track it!"

He started to get up on one knee, holding onto Marie Ann's shoulder as she knelt next to him. She helped him get to his feet.

"I don't think you're going anywhere fast. You're white as a sheet! You better sit here on the steps in the shade for a few minutes. I'll get some water!"

What was left of the screen door slammed, as she went inside for water. Jess squinted his eyes from the sun glare, starring out toward where the deer and Alvarez had disappeared. He slowly stood up and little by little, walked over to the rifle Marie Ann had laid next to him against the porch railing. He then squatted down next to the old Remington .306 rifle. He picked it up by the scope and set the barrel end of the rifle on the toe of his boot. Then, he flipped the scope's rubber covers off and balanced the rifle on his good shoulder. Taking a deep breath, he headed toward the arroyo.

Jess knew young Alvarez would be a hard man to kill, like his father in Morocco, and he wanted to find where the deer had taken him.

If Alvarez had survived, Jess was considering helping him out of his misery. "Lord Jesus, I need your strength! This merciless attitude is not good!"

The previous experience Jess had with young Alvarez's father still churned inside Jess. He had given up his hatred for the man while in Morocco, but Satan still tried to make him bitter. Jess had asked God to forgive him for his determination to kill Alvarez. The rifle would be used to kill the deer, if it was still alive, no matter if Alvarez was or not.

Marie Ann ran up next to Jess, crying, "What in the world are you doing Jess Hanes? You're bleeding too bad to be out here!"

"I want to see if the deer is dead, if not, I'll shoot it. I will not shoot Alvarez in his condition."

"Leave him to the sheriff and rangers," she pleaded, holding on to his arm that carried the rifle.

They both scanned the arroyo for the deer, "There Jess!" She pointed toward the other side.

She helped lift the rifle, putting it to his shoulder and resting the barrel on hers, "Can you get a good look like this?"

"Yes! Take a deep breath and hold it," Jess said. "I think he is still alive. But, the deer seems to be dead. Take the rifle and put the sling over my shoulder."

"What are you going to do?"

"Go get your first aide kit, water, and catch up with me." When she turned to leave, Jess held her arm, leaned toward her and kissed her lightly on the cheek. Startled, she was about to say something and he touched her lips with his finger, "And, bring your cell phone, Love! And, the portable radio out of my aircraft too!" He released her arm, smiled, turned and started down the edge of the arroyo.

Marie Ann stood there with her mouth open and put her hand over it. Tears came to her eyes as she ran back to the ranch house.

When Jess got to Alverez he was dead also. Jess sat down against the opposite sand bank of the *arroyo* in the shade rehearsing his difficulties with Alvarez and his father. He laid the rifle across his lap, pulled the slide bolt back ejecting a cartridge. He rolled it around in the palm of his hands, not really concentrating on it or the rifle. He had a habit of always looking at the caliber of a cartridge and just glanced at the end of the one in his hand…a caliber .308.

He began to wonder, 'Why does a .308 round stick in my mind?' Jess train of thought was interrupted by the Ranger's helicopter landing. He shuffled around trying to get relief from his wounds, and then remembered the holes in his aircraft were the size of .308 and the sheriff didn't find any slugs. He looked at the rifle with its scope. Swiftly as possible he shoved the cartridge back into the rifle and slid the bolt shut. He took quick aim at the sand the deer was laying in and fired the rifle. The helicopters landing covered the blast of the rifle. Then, he retrieved the spent slug from the sand and put it in his pocket along with the empty cartridge.

#

That afternoon, after the two Texas Ranger brothers and their Texas Ranger uncle made their reports, the FBI was notified in El Paso. The U.S. Marshall sent her report by fax to Washington. Sheriff Baker and his men had finished their survey of the area, took the dead deer and the two dead Arab men: Alvarez and the soldier in the kitchen.

Jess, Marie Ann, John, Jack, Snake, Charles and Madi sat in rocking chairs on the front porch of the ranch house. Jess and Marie Ann had iced tea in one hand, and with the other, she held his weak hand. John was puffing on his favorite pipe. Jack was humming some western song and scratching the top of Snakes' head, between the ears. Charles and Madi were rocking, holding hands.

"Maybe we can go metal detecting tomorrow, looking for Aztec gold!" Jess commented, trying to stir up any excitement.

No reply from anyone. Other than the low humming of Jack, the light panting of Snake, the occasional noise from a straw being sucked on, telling its user there was no more tea; the puffing of John on his pipe; the whispering of Charles and Madi; peacefulness settled around the ranch once more.

It was not long before Jess and Marie Ann stood, it was getting time to get ready for bed. He asked Jack if he was all right and shook hands with him. In the dark, no one saw the slug and empty cartridge he passed to Jack.

Jack hesitated, not knowing what Jess was trying to palm in his hand, "I'm fine Uncle Jess. You two sleep good!" He stood, kissed and hugged his aunt. He put the items Jess had passed to him in his pocket.

Jess leaned over and whispered in Jack's ear, "Ask agent Simms if that matches the slug taken out of him. I bet it does! Remember LeAnn's actions at the mine?"

Another thirty minutes and the sun would drop behind the far mountain ranges, causing multiple colored streaks to finger out through the western sky toward the dark east, cooling the temperature. It was too late in the year for bugs to be out, so the seven friends lingered until way after dark. In the distance, coyotes could be heard, yipping back and forth to each other. Then, an occasional yip would turn into a croon, causing the others to howl – all echoing off the canyon walls behind the ranch house.

It was not long until all the lights where out and an occasional snore could be heard. Then, almost in unison, the four men's snoring was in harmony with nature outside. The ladies were a long time in deep sleep, not bothered with the quartet's melody.

All was well, for now!

- THE END -